Above It All

Also by Cindy Myers

The View from Here

"Room at the Inn" in *Secret Santa*

The Mountain Between Us

A Change in Altitude

Above It All

CINDY MYERS

KENSINGTON BOOKS
www.kensingtonbooks.com

KENSINGTON BOOKS are published by

Kensington Publishing Corp.
119 West 40th Street
New York, NY 10018

All Kensington titles, imprints, and distributed lines are available at special quantity discounts for bulk purchases for sales promotion, premiums, fund-raising, educational, or institutional use.

Special book excerpts or customized printings can also be created to fit specific needs. For details, write or phone the office of the Kensington Sales Manager: Attn. Sales Department. Kensington Publishing Corp., 119 West 40th Street, New York, NY 10018. Phone: 1-800-221-2647.

Kensington and the K logo Reg. U.S. Pat. & TM Off.

eISBN-13: 978-0-7582-9487-6
eISBN-10: 0-7582-9487-5
First Kensington Electronic Edition: July 2015

ISBN-13: 978-0-7582-9486-9
ISBN-10: 0-7582-9486-7
First Kensington Trade Paperback Printing: July 2015

10 9 8 7 6 5 4 3 2 1

Printed in the United States of America

To Jim, forever and always

Chapter 1

"Happy birthday, Mommy."

"Happy birthday!"

Squeals and giggles, punctuated by applause, filled Shelly's ears as she blew out the candles on the black-and-white cake her husband, Charlie, must have ordered from the Last Dollar Café. She smiled across the table at her spouse. A burly guy with a full, ginger beard, he wasn't given to romantic gestures, but he'd come through for her this birthday. Not only had he ordered her favorite cake, he'd managed to get the day off from his job running a road grader for the county and he'd promised to take the boys fishing this afternoon, giving her a rare few hours all to herself, an unimaginable luxury.

"Happy birthday, sweetie." Charlie kissed her cheek as she cut into the cake. She served the boys, Cameron and Theo, first, then gave Charlie an extra-large slice. Finally, she sank a fork into her own serving. The combination of rich fudge cake, velvety vanilla cake, marshmallow cream filling, and chocolate frosting made her want to moan with delight.

"Good cake, Mom." Seven-year-old Cameron grinned at her, revealing the gap where a new tooth was just coming in.

"Good!" five-year-old Theo agreed, his mouth smeared with chocolate.

"The cake is wonderful. Thank you. And thank you for the presents." In addition to the cake and the promise of an afternoon's freedom, she'd received a T-shirt decorated with the boys' handprints from their sitter, Debbie Starling, a rock shaped like a heart that Cameron had found in the river, a new romance novel from Charlie's mom, and a lilac bush from Charlie.

The boys had already finished their cake and showed signs of restlessness. "Who wants to go fishing?" Charlie asked.

"I do! I do!" They jumped up and began racing around the table, more like two puppies than human boys.

Charlie grabbed one boy under each arm, growling like an angry bear. They squealed and giggled. Shelly finished her cake, the sounds of her happy family filling her with such joy that tears threatened. Her own childhood had been so different from the life she lived now. How had she ended up so lucky?

"Go on, get in the truck. Cameron, help your brother buckle up. I'll be out in a minute." Charlie sent the boys racing for his truck. He turned to Shelly. "Sure you don't want to come?"

"I'm going to spend the afternoon in a bubble bath, reading about some sexy Scottish Highlander."

"Are you now, lass?" He did a fair imitation of a Scottish brogue and nuzzled her neck. "You'll have to tell me all about it, later."

Laughing, she pushed him away. "Go. Before the boys decide they want to learn how to drive the truck."

When the door closed behind him, she sighed and sat back in her chair. She debated eating a second piece of cake, but the second helping of anything was never as wonderful as the first, so she covered the cake and carried their dishes to the sink. She'd see to them later. For now, she was going to run that bath, do a quick check of her e-mail, then forget about everything for a while.

She headed upstairs to the master bath, which Charlie had redone two years ago, with an oversize claw-foot tub she'd found in Lucille Theriot's junk shop, and slate tiles the green and gray of river stones. They'd added golden oak wainscoting and clean white plaster on the walls. As a girl, she'd dreamed of an elegant retreat like this. But the best feature of the room, one even her fertile childhood imagination couldn't have conceived, was the five-foot picture window over the tub, which afforded a view of Mount Garnet, a jagged peak capped with snow most of the year. Now, in August, a riot of wildflowers—red paintbrush, blue columbine, purple bee balm, and yellow black-eyed Susan—spilled across the meadow at the foot of the mountain like spatters of color dotting a painter's smock. Who needed bouquets from the florist, with a scene like this right outside her window?

She turned the taps to start the water running, poured in a generous glug of vanilla bubble bath, then moved into the bedroom, to the desk in the corner where her laptop sat open. Charlie had fixed up this little corner office for her, too, with twin bookcases filled with her favorite novels and her collection of Colorado history books. She logged into her e-mail and waited for it to load, scanning the headlines that filled the homepage. The usual assortment of celebrity gossip, political speculation, and crime news. Here in tiny Eureka, Colorado, all of that seemed so far away.

Then her gaze fixed on a picture in the corner of the page, of a dirt-smeared, wide-eyed toddler with a halo of white-blond curls. Her heart pounded and in an instant she felt the bone-weariness and aching hunger of that little girl, the fierce need to be held and comforted, and her fear of the reporters around her.

WHERE ARE THEY NOW? asked the headline. WE REMEMBER THE TWENTY-FIFTH ANNIVERSARY OF THE RESCUE OF BABY SHELLY.

Unable to stop herself, she clicked the link to the story.

"Those five days in August of 1990 changed our family forever," says Sandy Payton, seated in the kitchen of the home she and husband, Danny, built after the rescue of their older daughter, Shelly. Sandy was only nineteen when her child disappeared through a crack in the dry earth, into a previously unknown cavern beneath the family's ranch land in northwest Texas. Eight months pregnant with her second daughter, Mindy, Sandy could only watch helplessly and pray as rescuers from around the world descended on the ranch to try to save the little girl, whose picture dominated news reports over the next five days as volunteers worked day and night.

"We'll always be so grateful to all the people who helped, not only during rescue efforts, but for years afterward," Sandy told this reporter. "Shelly needed a lot of help to recover from her ordeal, but I'm happy to report she's doing well today."

Sandy says she and her elder daughter remain close, but she declined to reveal Shelly's location, out of respect for her privacy.

Feeling sick, Shelly shut off the computer and closed her eyes, but she couldn't shut out the flood of memories—trapped in that cavern, terrified of the dark, cold and hungry. But worse than the physical suffering had been the sense of abandonment. She wanted her mother and father even more than she wanted food or blankets. She didn't understand what had happened. One moment she'd been playing; the next, she'd been plunged into this alien landscape. She worried about monsters, or devils, but most of all, she feared she had been forgotten. Exhaustion eventually dulled her senses.

She found a puddle of water and drank from it, and curled up in a patch of sand and slept.

She'd spent five days in the cavern. The time was a blur of memory. She had had no idea that the whole world was focused on the search for her. When rescuers finally opened a passage into the cavern, she'd been pulled into blinding light—not from the sun, for it was dark when they reached her, but from the spotlights belonging to fifty television crews that filled her grandparents' ranch. Reporters shouted and jostled for a view of her, and camera flashes exploded around her. Shelly clung to her mother, crying, but instead of holding her close, Sandy held the girl out to the cameras. "Say thank you to all the wonderful people who've rescued you," she commanded.

That photo of the blond, blue-eyed toddler dangling from her mother's hands had appeared on the front pages of papers all over the world. BABY SHELLY SAFE! screamed the headlines. BABY SHELLY WILL CELEBRATE HER FIFTH BIRTHDAY ABOVE GROUND!

She should have known better than to log online today, of all days. The twenty-fifth anniversary of her rescue. Mom would be sure to find a way to exploit that. Sandy Payton had made a career out of being Baby Shelly's mom. She'd shown a natural talent for milking the public's interest in the story. Every year on the anniversary, she sent out press releases with updates on Baby Shelly. By the time Shelly was eight, she'd come to dread her birthday. By the time she was fifteen, she'd rebelled, refusing to talk to the reporters anymore, or to let herself be photographed.

The day she graduated high school, she left home, never to return. Some people probably thought she was cold and uncaring, the way she'd cut off communication with her family. But her parents, especially her mother, Sandy, didn't think of Shelly as a beloved older child, but as a meal ticket.

People from all over the world had sent money to care for poor Baby Shelly, who lived with her teenage parents in a mobile home on her grandparents' run-down ranch. Shelly had read various reports of the sums raised—most reported close to $300,000 sent to the adorable toddler who'd been lost underground for five days. Sandy and Danny Payton used the money to buy a house near the ranch. They bought into a dry cleaning franchise, which failed, and then a shoe store, which also failed. They said they had put aside money to pay for Shelly's education, but when she asked for the funds to go to college, she learned the money was gone.

"You can always get more money," her mother had told her. "Now that you're eighteen, you should write a book. People will love it."

A wave of nausea washed over Shelly. She stumbled into the bathroom, just in time to shut off the water and keep the tub from overflowing. She let a little of the water drain, then stripped off her clothes and sank into the bath. Gradually, she began to relax. Seeing the story had been a shock, though it shouldn't have been. She knew what her mother was like, and what the press was like. Of course they'd exploit the anniversary. But she was safe here in Eureka. Charlie was the only one who knew her background. Whenever other people asked about her childhood, she made some remark about how she'd grown up "very ordinary and boring." Her accent branded her as being from Texas, so she didn't deny it, but because she never talked about or visited family, most people assumed her parents were dead, and she let them think that. Her parents didn't know she'd married Charlie Frazier, or about her two boys. Maybe it wasn't fair to deprive the boys of a set of grandparents, but Shelly just couldn't risk it. If her mom ever found out where Shelly lived, the family would have no peace. Shelly wouldn't subject her boys to the constant public scrutiny that had ruined her own childhood.

When the water turned cold and her toes and fingers shriveled like walnut shells, she pulled the plug and climbed out. She'd pour a glass of wine and settle onto the sofa with her new book. Sure, it was only three in the afternoon, but she could have one glass of wine on her birthday, couldn't she?

She was searching for the corkscrew when the doorbell rang. She debated pretending she wasn't home, but most people knew her car and could see it parked in the driveway. They also knew it was her birthday and that she'd taken the day off to celebrate. Eureka was that kind of place—people kept tabs on each other.

She set aside the wine bottle and went to check the peephole. All she could see was the back of a blond head. Whoever was standing there had turned around, possibly to admire the view of the mountains from this lot on the edge of town. Was this a lost tourist in need of directions? Who else would be out here in the middle of the afternoon?

She pulled open the door. "May I help you?"

The woman turned around and for a moment Shelly had the dizzying feeling of falling. She grabbed hold of the doorframe to steady herself and stared at her mother.

Or rather, this wasn't Sandy Payton, but a stranger who looked the way Sandy had looked twenty-five years ago— teased, bleached-blond hair, a gap between her two front teeth, and an overabundance of eye makeup. "Hello, Shelly," the woman drawled. "I'll bet you thought you could hide from us forever."

"Mindy." The blonde couldn't be anyone but her little sister, born a month after Shelly's rescue. Mindy had emerged from the womb screaming and demanding attention and had never really stopped. "How did you find me?"

"It wasn't easy." Not waiting for an invitation, Mindy shoved past Shelly into the house. She stopped just inside the family room to set down an oversize blue suitcase and look around—at the trophy bull elk Charlie had shot two winters ago, at the boys' toys piled in the corner, at the worn but comfortable plaid sofa and matching love seat. "Well, isn't this . . . quaint," she said.

"Mindy, what are you doing here?" Shelly stared at the suitcase, fighting panic.

"Maybe I wanted to visit my big sister. How long has it been? Eight or nine years?"

It had been ten. On Shelly's twentieth birthday, when Sandy, fifteen-year-old Mindy in tow, had ambushed her outside her apartment with a camera crew from *20/20*. Shelly had had enough of annually reliving her tragedy for profit. She'd packed that night and moved to Colorado, and done her best to disappear. She'd legally changed her name to Green, then changed it again when she married Charlie. She never talked about her past and, on her birthday, she did her best to forget those five days underground, and all the days after that in the glare of the spotlight, had ever happened.

It was harder to ignore the flesh-and-blood woman standing in front of her. "How did you find me?" she asked again.

"I hired a private detective. A good one. It cost a lot of money, but my publisher was happy to pay up."

"Your publisher?" Shelly's blood felt like ice water.

"I'm writing a book." Mindy dropped her purse onto the sofa, then sank down beside it. She wore a pink denim miniskirt, high-heeled sandals, and a pink tank top that stretched across the well-endowed chest she'd also inherited from their mother. "They sent some ghostwriter dude to help me, but I told them I really didn't need him. I mean, how hard can it be?"

"What's the book about?" Shelly asked, though she already knew the answer. Part of her held on to the hope that she was wrong.

"What do you think?" Mindy snarled at her. "The book is about you—the blessed Baby Shelly, rescued from the bowels of the earth. As written by her sweet-but-neglected little sister."

"No." Shelly swallowed, then said the word again, louder, and with greater force. "No. I won't help you write a book. I don't want anything to do with it."

"Don't take that attitude with me." Mindy popped up from the couch and rushed at Shelly so fast Shelly took a step back. Mindy grabbed her arm. "You owe me this. Our whole life, you got everything, while I got the leftovers. Well, I'm not going to let you cheat me out of this chance. This publisher is willing to pay me a lot of money for your story, and I'm going to give it to them."

"I don't know what you're talking about—leftovers." Shelly tried not to show how shaken she was by Mindy's words. "Mom doted on you. The two of you were just alike. I was the outsider, the one who never fit in with your shopping trips and fashion shows. You were Miss Sweetwater County, for goodness' sake!"

"I only entered that pageant to try to get Mom's attention," Mindy said. "But it didn't work. August seventh rolled around and it was back to 'my darling Shelly.' Whatever money we had went to pay for your clothes and do your hair, so that you'd look good for the television cameras."

"But she wouldn't let me get my teeth fixed." Shelly ran her tongue over her newly straightened teeth, free of braces for only a few months now. "She wanted people to think we were still too poor to afford things like that, so I had to wait until I was grown, and pay for them myself."

"It was still all about you," Mindy said, refusing to be sidetracked from her rant. "Mom spent all her spare time writing letters and making phone calls to the press, to try to get attention for you."

"Attention I never wanted," Shelly protested. Honestly, had she and Mindy really grown up in the same household? Aside from the annual money grab over the anniversary of her burial and resurrection, Shelly had felt ignored by her family. She was the studious, shy, and reserved child in a family of brash and coarse rednecks. While her parents and little sister raced four-wheelers around the family ranch, Shelly stayed in her room, reading *Jane Eyre* and dreaming of living in Victorian England. As far as she was concerned, the world her parents and Mindy reveled in was a scary, dangerous place. But they could never understand that.

"I can't help it if you were too stupid to appreciate a good thing when you had it," Mindy said. "But I'm not stupid. This is my one chance to make something of myself, and I'm going to take it. With or without your help." She sat on the sofa again, arms and legs crossed, chin jutting defiantly.

Shelly sank onto the opposite end of the sofa. Fear of what lies Mindy might put into her book warred with an aching desire to find a way to mend fences with her little sister. No matter how much the woman before her might annoy her now, she had once been the tiny blond baby Shelly had carried around like a doll. In those early years, before Mindy became too aware of "the legend of Baby Shelly" as Shelly liked to call it, Mindy had worshiped her big sister. And Shelly had adored her. Mindy had been the one person in her life who didn't expect to gain anything by knowing her. Leaving her parents behind had been hard, but leaving Mindy had been even harder.

"You can stay here a few days," she said. "We'll talk."

Mindy immediately relaxed her defensive posture. "Thanks," she said. She surveyed the living room once more. "I guess this place isn't so bad, considering you're here in the back of beyond." She focused on the toys in the corner. "The detective I hired said you had kids."

Her stomach knotted at the prospect of introducing her boys to an aunt they'd never even known existed. "I have two little boys, Cameron and Theo. They don't know about the whole 'Baby Shelly' thing," she said. "So don't tell them. They don't need to know."

"What about your husband? The detective said you had one of those, too." She wrinkled her nose, as if a husband was an unfortunate acquisition, like a smelly dog, or a cat with fleas. "Does he know?"

"Charlie knows, but we don't talk about it." Confessing her true identity to Charlie had been one of the hardest things she'd ever done; she'd been sure he'd either want to capitalize on her fame, like the rest of her family, or he'd run as fast as he could away from her and the media circus that was always a threat if anyone stumbled on her real identity. When he'd done neither, she'd known he was a keeper. "I like to keep the past in the past," she said.

"Right. Well, I'm not so crazy about the past, either, but I do like to think about the future. Especially a future where I have lots of money to spend." She stood and hefted the suitcase. "Why don't you show me to my room?"

Shelly led the way to the guest room up under the eaves. "It's kind of small, isn't it?" Mindy wrinkled her nose at the quilt-covered bed and four-drawer dresser.

"If you don't like it, there's a very nice bed-and-breakfast, the Idlewilde—or you can try the motel."

"No, this'll do." Mindy plopped the suitcase on the bed. "You run on and I'll get ready to meet the rest of the family. Won't they be surprised to see me?"

Surprise wasn't the word Shelly would use to describe her own feelings, she thought as she hurried down the stairs. Shock. More than a little loathing. And a puzzling nostalgia—not for the way things had been, but the way she'd always wanted things to be. She'd always wanted a close relationship with a sister who understood and sympathized with her. Instead, she'd gotten Mindy, who, to hear her tell it, had been born with a grudge against her famous sibling.

Maybe this visit was a chance to change that dynamic. She didn't want to live the rest of her life wondering what would have happened if she'd made more of an effort to be the kind of sister Mindy needed. The kind of sister that Shelly really wanted to be.

Lucille Theriot leaned against the counter in her junk and antiques shop, Lacy's, and frowned at the letter in her hand. Printed on thick, creamy paper with the state seal at the top, the letter didn't bode well for the town. Missives from the state seldom did, a fact Lucille had learned in her six years as mayor of Eureka.

The string of cowbells hanging on the back of the shop door clattered and clanged as the door pushed open and Maggie Clark rushed in, flyaway strands of her red hair forming a halo around her head as she was backlit against the bright day. "Hi, Maggie," Lucille said. "If you're here to help with the decorations for Hard Rock Days, they haven't come in yet. I'm hoping they'll show up tomorrow."

Maggie frowned. "Was I supposed to help you today? I can't keep track of anything anymore." She adjusted the baby sling across the front of her body, then pulled the door to, shutting out the rumble of a motorcycle driving past and the voices of a group of tourists on the sidewalk. August was the busiest time of year for the town, when vacationers flocked to the cooler mountains to admire the scenery and speak wistfully of wanting to live in such an idyllic setting "someday." Most of those daydreamers, confronted with the reality of harsh winters and the remote location, sensibly stayed away, but a few let the mountains cast a spell, and remained here year round. Maggie was one of the ones who had stayed, having come to town a year ago to claim an inheritance, and never left.

"I'd say you have a good excuse." Lucille laid aside the letter and reached both arms out for the baby. She didn't make a conscious decision to hold the baby—she just couldn't help herself. Besides, Eureka's youngest citizen was her godchild. She couldn't see little Angela Clark and not hold her.

Smiling, Maggie unhooked the sling and handed over the sleeping infant. Angela stretched her little arms and legs in sleep, then curled into herself again, sucking at the pacifier between her lips. "How's my darling angel?" Lucille asked, smiling at the infant.

"She looks like an angel now, but she was a little demon at two this morning." Maggie sank into a chair with the universal weary look of a new mother. "She refused to go back to sleep. Fortunately, our rooms are pretty soundproof. So I don't think she woke any of our guests."

Maggie and her husband, Jameso, managed the Idlewilde Bed and Breakfast, but they also held part-time day jobs, Maggie as a reporter for the paper, the *Eureka Miner,* and Jameso tending bar at the Dirty Sally Saloon. "I don't believe your mama," Lucille cooed to the baby, who had opened her eyes and was staring up at her. "You would never be anything but a little angel."

"Maybe next time she wakes up howling, I'll bring her to your house." Maggie covered her mouth to hide a yawn. "Anyway, I came over here to warn you."

Lucille reluctantly looked away from the baby. "What did you come to warn me about?" she asked.

"A guy stopped by the paper looking for you. A private detective named Duke Breman." She fished a business card out of the pocket of her jeans and handed it to Lucille.

Lucille studied the card, a white square with embossed black lettering. " '*Duke Breman, Private Investigations, Austin, Texas,*' " she read. "He's a long way from home."

"He said it was urgent that he talk to you."

"What did you tell him?"

"I sent him over to the library."

Lucille smiled. "You're an evil woman, Maggie Clark."

"I thought it wouldn't hurt to have Cassie give him the once-over before he got to you." Cassie Wynock, the librarian, suspected every newcomer to town of being up to no good and didn't suffer fools gladly.

"Did he say why he's looking for me?" Lucille rocked the baby in her arms.

"No. He was pretty tight-lipped. Good-looking, though. Cassie might decide to be nice to him."

"How old a man is he?"

"Fifties? Dark hair, graying at the temples. Lines around the eyes—brown eyes. About six feet tall, nice shoulders. Like I said, good-looking." Maggie grinned. "Maybe he wants to ask you out."

"I'm sure strangers are flocking to town to date me." Lucille moved behind the counter, using the excuse to turn away from the younger woman and hide the flush of embarrassment that still warmed her cheeks whenever she thought about her last romantic relationship. Gerald Pershing had been a handsome stranger in town, also from Texas. He'd wooed her, then swindled the town out of most of its budget. When the town council had managed to trick him into giving them part of the money back, he'd returned and continued his pursuit of Lucille, while also trying to milk more money out of the town coffers. He'd left a couple of months ago and Lucille prayed she'd seen the last of him.

"You'll let me know when you find out what he's up to?" Maggie asked.

"Are you asking as a reporter or a friend?"

"Both." Maggie shoved up out of the chair and came to lean on the counter. "News is pretty slow this time of year. Until Hard Rock Days, we have to make do with the occasional tourist lost in the mountains, or a traffic jam caused by a timid RVer on the mountain passes, but that's it."

"Hard Rock Days is one of our biggest claims to fame," Lucille said. "Though that isn't saying much, I guess. Still, we get a good crowd to see the drilling and mucking competitions."

"Watching guys slam hammers down onto steel drills and haul carts full of mine waste always makes me nervous," Maggie said. "It looks so dangerous."

"It is dangerous," Lucille said. "Though not as much as it probably was for real miners. Still, the ore-cart races and drilling competitions are a good way to remember the miners who are the reason Eureka is even here."

"Don't let Cassie hear you say that. According to her, her ancestors founded the town to bring civilization to the wilderness."

"They came here looking for gold like everyone else," Lucille said. She handed over the letter with the state seal.

"Here's something for the paper. The state wants us to come up with a plan for managing noxious weeds."

"Noxious weed? Do we have a pot problem in Eureka?"

"Noxious weeds, plural. Invasive species and things like that. We're supposed to pull them, poison them, or mow them down with goats."

"Goats?"

"It's the preferred method." Lucille leaned over and pointed to a group of addresses at the bottom of the letter. "There's a list of people who rent goats to cities to control their noxious weeds."

"So is Eureka going to rent goats?"

"I'll have to take that up with the town council."

"That ought to make for a livelier-than-usual meeting." Maggie folded the letter. "Can I keep this long enough to make a copy?"

"Be my guest." Lucille turned her attention back to the baby, who'd fallen asleep again.

"I'm tempted to wake her so she'll be more likely to sleep tonight," Maggie said. "But she looks so sweet, I haven't the heart."

"I take it Jameso's working this afternoon?" Lucille said. Maggie and her handsome husband usually traded off child-care and duties at the inn.

"Yes. Now that Olivia's left the Dirty Sally, they're always short-handed. You wouldn't think in a town this size, where there aren't that many jobs, that it would be so tough to find a new bartender. But so far no one has stayed more than a few weeks."

"Being on her feet all day was getting too hard for Olivia." Lucille's daughter was five months pregnant with her second child.

"Oh, I understand," Maggie said. "And Jameso doesn't mind, not as much as I do. I'm hoping they'll find someone to fill the position soon, so we can have a few more nights home to-gether."

The door jangled open to admit Cassie Wynock, gray curls bobby-pinned close to her head, prim gray skirt swirling about her calves above her sensible oxfords. "What have you done now, Lucille?" she demanded.

"I don't know, Cassie. What have I done?"

"A private detective came to the library looking for you just now. He said his name was Duke." She wrinkled her nose. "That can't be his real name. What mother names her child Duke?"

"Maybe she was a fan of John Wayne," Lucille said, her expression perfectly sober. Cassie wasn't known for her sense of humor. Lucille wondered if she even had one.

"He said he was from Texas. You certainly seem to attract a lot of attention from men from that state." Cassie sniffed.

"Remarkable, since I've never been there," Lucille said. "What did you tell him?"

"I sent him to the Last Dollar. I wanted a chance to question you before he got here."

"Maybe he'll eat Janelle and Danielle's pie and forget all about you," Maggie said. The café, next to the Dirty Sally, had the best food in town.

"Why is a private detective looking for you?" Cassie asked.

"I don't know. I haven't done anything." Lucille didn't do a very good job of hiding her annoyance. Cassie brought out the worst in her. Well, Cassie brought out the worst in most people.

The phone rang. Lucille returned the baby to Maggie and went to answer it, grateful for the interruption. "Hello?"

"Lucille, this is Danielle."

"Oh, hello, Danielle." At the sound of the name of one of the two owners of the Last Dollar Café, the other two women leaned toward Lucille, listening.

"There's a gentleman here looking for you. He's a private detective. What should I tell him?"

"You can send him over to the shop. I can't imagine what he wants with me, but I don't mind talking to him."

"Okay, I'll do that. I tried to talk him into eating lunch first, but he seems pretty intent on finding you."

"He doesn't know what he's missing, turning down your lunch special," Lucille said.

"You're so sweet. I'll send him over, if you're sure it's okay."

"Thanks for running interference, but I don't mind talking to him, really."

She hung up the phone, then shuffled through some papers on the counter.

Cassie was the first to break. "Well? Is he coming over?"

"He is. Don't you have work to do at the library?"

"Sharon is there. I don't need to hurry back." She sat in a chair by the door, feet together, hands primly in her lap, back straight.

Lucille turned to Maggie, who held the baby against her shoulder. "I'd never hear the end of it from Rick if I left now," Maggie said. Rick Otis owned and edited the *Miner*. He would probably consider the arrival of a private detective in town as pertinent news.

Lucille shrugged and resumed opening the mail. It probably wouldn't hurt to have witnesses to whatever this Duke fellow had to say. She slit envelopes and unfolded the contents, only to transfer all of it to the recycling bin at her feet. Most of the mail was advertisements or catalogues from various galleries and auction sites she dealt with. Mingled with mail for the shop were communications for the city, but Eureka didn't even have a town hall, and few paved streets, so they weren't likely to need a new computer system or the latest in hazardous waste disposal.

The cowbells jangled and all three women turned to watch a tall, dark-haired man enter. Lucille's first thought was that Maggie had not been kidding when she'd said the guy was handsome: dark hair, craggy features, brooding brown eyes, and enough silver in his hair and lines around his eyes that she didn't feel like a perv lusting after him.

He didn't flinch at the trio of women staring at him. He nodded to each of them. "I'm looking for Mayor Lucille Theriot," he said in a deep, velvety voice.

"I'm Lucille." She resisted the urge to smooth her hair. "What can I do for you?"

"Duke Breman." He offered his hand and she shook it. It was softer than she'd expected, smooth and warm, but with a firm grip.

"What can I do for you, Mr. Breman?" she said again.

He glanced over his shoulder at Maggie and Cassie. "Is there some place we can talk privately?"

"No, there isn't," Cassie said. She stood and joined them at the counter. "If you have something to say, you might as well say it in front of God and everybody. There are no secrets in a town this small."

"You're the librarian, right?"

"Yes." Cassie stood up straighter, but at only five foot two inches, it didn't make her look any taller. With her cap of gray curls, white blouse, gray skirt, and sensible shoes, she looked like a stern Sunday school teacher.

He shifted his gaze to Maggie. "And you're the reporter."

She nodded. "My husband and I also run a bed-and-breakfast, the Idlewilde, if you're looking for a place to stay."

"I'll keep that in mind. I'm not sure how long I'll be in town." Duke returned his attention to Lucille. "I take it you already know I'm a private detective."

"Yes. And I can't imagine what you want with me." When he hesitated, she added, "You can go ahead and talk in front of these two. They're right that we don't have many secrets around here."

"I'm looking for a man named Gerald Pershing. I understand you're a friend of his."

Cassie gave an un-ladylike snort. Lucille glared at her. "I know Mr. Pershing," she said. "I wouldn't say I was his friend." What exactly did a woman call a former lover turned adversary?

Duke took a small notebook from his jacket pocket and consulted it. "But he and the town of Eureka did share interest in a gold mine in the area, the Lucky Lady?"

"That's right. Gerald sold his shares in the mine to the mine manager, Bob Prescott, and left town at the end of June."

"Do you know where he was headed when he left here?" Duke asked. "Or where he is now? Has he been in contact with you since he left?"

"No to all those questions," she said.

"Is Gerald missing?" Maggie asked.

Duke glanced at her, then turned back to Lucille. "No one has heard from him since he left Eureka. I was hoping he'd been in touch with you."

"What's the old reprobate done this time?" Cassie asked.

Duke looked pained. "I'm not at liberty to say."

"I take it you're working for a private client, not law enforcement?" Lucille asked.

"Yes." He tucked the notebook back into his pocket. "I'd like to talk to you more, but it doesn't look like now is a good time. May I call you?"

"If you like." Lucille tried to look more nonchalant than she felt. In fact, her heart was racing as if she'd run down the street. "My number is in the book."

"I'll be in touch, then." He nodded to each woman in turn. "Good afternoon, ladies."

When he was gone, Lucille sagged against the counter. "Well," she said.

"Don't go looking so starry-eyed," Cassie said. "I wouldn't trust that one as far as I could throw him."

"You never trust anyone, Cassie," Maggie said.

"At least I don't go making a fool of myself with every handsome man who comes along," the librarian said.

Cassie had been foolish about plenty of men, but Lucille didn't bother to point this out. "I'm touched that you're so concerned about my welfare, Cassie," she said.

Cassie gave another snort. "I don't give a fig about you,

but I do care about this town, and I won't see you drag its name through the mud again." She left, the cowbells jangling behind her.

"Well, I care about you," Maggie said. She walked over to Lucille and squeezed her shoulder. "Let me know if he says anything to upset you."

"And you'll do what? Sic Jameso on him?" While Maggie's husband was about Duke's size, and fifteen or twenty years younger, Lucille wasn't sure he was as tough.

Maggie smiled. "That's a thought. Mostly, I'd just offer sympathy. Though I could write nasty things about him in the paper."

"I doubt if he'll upset me. I have no idea where Gerald is now, and I don't care."

"Do you think he swindled somebody else and that's why this detective is trying to track him down?"

"Probably. I feel sorry for whoever it is, but I can't help them."

"Oh well, it's a little excitement in an otherwise dull summer. One thing you can say for Eureka—we're not much for scandal and deep, dark secrets."

Chapter 2

By the time Travis Rowell parked his 1999 Chevy pickup in front of the Last Dollar Café in Eureka, Colorado, he had the shakes from drinking coffee for the past fifteen hours and both knees ached from being behind the wheel so long. He'd driven all the way from Dallas because he couldn't afford to fly, and because he didn't like to fly. He wasn't afraid of flying, mind you; he just hated the hassle.

He unfolded himself from the driver's seat of the truck and surveyed the place where he was going to be exiled for the next few weeks or so. There was plenty of picture-postcard scenery, he'd give it that, provided you liked looking at mountains, rocks, and trees. The town itself resembled some Old West movie set, complete with dirt streets and false-fronted stores. Red geraniums and pink petunias bloomed in baskets that hung from light posts in front of almost every business, including the café where he'd parked. The Last Dollar proclaimed jaunty lettering over the door—were the prices so high it would empty your wallet to eat there, or did you have to be desperate, down to your last dollar, to attempt it?

In any case, he wasn't particularly hungry. He wanted to

get to work and get this over with. The sooner he had his story, the sooner he could head back to Dallas and his girl-friend, Trish. He'd only taken this gig because of her, any-way. The money from this job would set him up with enough cash to pay off some debts and finally tie the knot.

An old man, skinny as a scarecrow and sort of dressed like one, in canvas trousers held up by suspenders and a checked flannel shirt, sleeves rolled up to reveal knobby elbows, emerged from the café and scowled at him. Travis smiled and waved to the man, then turned his back and pulled out his phone. He punched in the number he'd memorized by now and tapped his foot while he listened to it ring. One . . . two . . . three . . .

"Hello? Where are you?" The woman's nasal twang and demanding tone made Travis's right eye twitch. "I called and left a message an hour ago," Mindy Payton said.

"Don't get in a panic," he said. "I'm here. In beautiful downtown Eureka. And I didn't get your message, probably because the service is so spotty here in the back of beyond. I have to hand it to your sister—when it comes to places to hide out, this little burg in the middle of nowhere seems just about perfect."

"Oh, it's perfect, as long as you don't want to go shop-ping, go to the movies, eat almost anywhere besides that café, or see anything besides rocks and deer."

Travis grinned. The one good thing about this gig was that Mindy, his erstwhile partner, had to suffer as much as he did. Maybe more. Marvelous Mindy, with her big hair, makeup, and high heels, would be as out of place here in Grizzly Adams country as Tinker Bell in a blizzard. And speaking of blizzards. "We'd better get busy," he said. "I want to be well shed of this place before the first snowfall. This place proba-bly turns into Siberia in winter."

"We'll both be out of here long before then."

"So she's here, right? Your famous sister? That detective wasn't lying through his teeth about that, was he?" Paying off the ex-cop who'd tracked down Shelly Payton for him had taken most of the meager advance he'd been able to wrangle from the publisher. The expenses of getting to Eureka had taken the rest. But it was all going to be worth it in the end. The public would line up to hear the true story of Baby Shelly, all grown up and turned recluse in the Colorado mountains. Especially if the author of the book was her sweet baby sister, Mindy. Travis had even wrangled a byline for himself, as well as a cut of the royalties. "With Travis Rowell" would be his ticket to even bigger and better things.

"So have you talked to Shelly?" he asked. "Was she glad to see you?"

"I'm staying at her house. She was so thrilled to see me, she moved me right into her spare bedroom."

Some of the tension went out of his shoulders. This was going to be easier than he'd thought. "Great. Why don't I come over now and introduce myself?" And maybe the sister had another spare room he could use, to save the cost of a motel room. After all, if he was going to document her life for her adoring fans, he should probably spend as much time as possible with her.

"I think we need to take it slower," Mindy said. "She and I need some time to bond, then I can bring you in."

So much for feeling optimistic. Travis had been around the block enough times to know how to read between the lines. "You haven't told her about the book yet, have you?" he said.

"I told her. I mean, I had to tell her. What kind of person do you think I am?"

Travis thought Mindy was a whiny, spoiled, manipulative leech, but he knew enough not to share that opinion with her. "What did she say? Is she going to cooperate with us?"

"She's not sure. She wants to help me, of course, but the past is so painful. . . ." Mindy's voice trailed away, as if talking about the past hurt too much. Though of course she'd spent her whole life profiting from that very past.

"Let me come over and talk to her. I'm sure I can win her over." Travis prided himself on a certain amount of charm.

"I don't know," Mindy said. "I think it's too soon to bring you into the picture."

"It's the perfect time." Travis tried to hide his impatience. "Look at it this way—she's been stuck here in the middle of nowhere for a while now. After all those years in the limelight, she's bound to be missing it. I mean, wouldn't you? I sure would. She's probably dying for a chance to be the center of attention again."

"Oh, I'm sure she is," Mindy said, sounding bitter.

"See, that's the genius of our plan," Travis said. "You show up, all young and beautiful and fresh from the city." Might as well lay it on thick. One of the reasons he was so perfect for this job was that he was good at massaging inflated egos. And Mindy's ego was almost as pumped up as her chest. "She's going to want to show you up—to compete. You're the key to our getting the story we want."

"She'll be jealous of me, you mean."

"Absolutely! I mean, look at you. You're gorgeous. You have a big book contract. You're going places. And where is Shelly going? Nowhere. She'll be dying to try to grab some of the attention away from you. It's just human nature."

"You're probably right." Mindy still sounded doubtful.

"I know I'm right." He shifted his phone to his other hand, leaned into the truck, and grabbed his notebook. "Give me directions to her place and I'll stop by and introduce myself. I'll make it a point to flatter you and let her know you're the big deal here, not her. She'll be begging to talk to me before I'm through."

"All right." She sounded more cheerful now. "She lives just out of town. Take a street called Pickax on up the hill and around, then turn on Camp Robber Way. Can you believe these street names? Anyway, it's the house at the very end, on the left."

"I'll be right there."

He found the house easily enough; how could anyone get lost in a place this small? It was typical for the area—a log cabin that looked as if it had squatted on the side of the mountain for a century or more, the metal roof streaked with rust in places, a black stovepipe jutting into the sky. Travis parked his truck and strode up a dirt path to the front door and lifted the heavy knocker.

A woman's voice called from the other side of the door. "Who is it?"

"My name's Travis Rowell. I'm a friend of Mindy's."

The door opened enough to reveal half a woman's face: one blue eye, a pale cheek, a hank of light brown hair. "Mindy, there's someone here to see you," the woman—it must be Shelly—called over her shoulder.

"Actually, it's you I came to see, Shelly."

She flinched at his use of her name. Which made no sense. He'd read the private dick's report—she went by the name Shelly still. Probably because it was easier than trying to get used to being called a completely different name. She was Shelly Frazier now, though.

"Well, open the door, silly. He won't bite!" Mindy's high, girlish voice drifted to him. The door opened wider to reveal the sisters standing side by side. The resemblance was more obvious now—they had the same narrow noses and wide, blue eyes, though Mindy had enhanced her features with copious makeup and bleached and curled her hair. Shelly was plainer, clearly older, and unsmiling.

"Come on in, Travis." Mindy grabbed his arm and dragged him forward, past her sister and into the open front room of the house, with its soaring ceiling, large black woodstove, and dead animal heads on the walls. Right out of a Ralph Lauren ad, minus the pouty models, though Shelly certainly had the pout down. "Shelly, this is the guy I was telling you about—the one who's helping me write my book," Mindy said.

The guy who was actually *writing* the book, he could have pointed out, but he knew enough to keep his mouth shut.

"It's great to meet you, Shelly," he said. "This is a gorgeous place you have here."

Shelly folded her arms across her chest and scowled at him. "I've already told Mindy, but I'll tell you, too. I'm not interested in any book about my life. I prefer that the past stay in the past."

Her attitude didn't surprise him; he'd expected as much, considering all the trouble she'd gone to to hide her identity. But his years as an investigative reporter had taught him how to sweet-talk reluctant subjects. "But this is your chance to really tell your side of the story—to show people that you're not the person who's been depicted in all the articles over the years."

Her stubborn expression never changed. "I'm not interested, Mr. Rowell."

"Call me Travis, please." He shoved his hands in the pockets of his jeans, a deliberately casual pose. "I don't want to pressure you. I'll just hang around here a few days, talking to people in town, gathering background information. I'm sure Mindy and I have enough for the book without your cooperation, but I want to assure you that I would really prefer to present your side of the story." Without her cooperation, he didn't have a story—the publisher had made that clear. He wanted an exclusive account in Shelly's own words, something that would stand out among the sea of books cribbed from news accounts and conversations with third parties that had cropped up over the years. But Travis hoped the threat of such a retelling would make Shelly feel more cooperative.

"You can do what you like, Mr. Rowell," she said. "I'm going to have to ask you to leave now."

"Shelly, wait!" Mindy clutched at her sister's arm. "All we want is for you to talk to us a little. Tell me what you've been up to for the past ten years. I mean, it's not as if anyone's going to use the information against you. People love you—they always have."

"They love the cute blond toddler who was trapped in the cave. They don't even know me."

"Then here's your chance to let them know you," Travis said. "Think of it like Facebook, and our readers are your friends."

"I have real friends," she said. "I don't need any more."

"Shelly, please!" Mindy's voice soared to a piercing whine. Travis frowned at her. She needed to shut up and let him handle this.

"I'll leave now," he said. "Just think about what I've said. You can set the parameters for our conversation. If there are things you want to keep off-limits, I'll respect that." Though he would do his best to find a way around any restrictions. After all, that was his job, and he was good at it. He took out his wallet and withdrew a card. "Here's my number. Call me anytime to discuss this further."

"Where are you staying?" Mindy asked.

"I have a room at the local motel."

"You need to leave now, before my husband gets home," Shelly said.

"Is he a jealous man?" Travis asked. "I promise you, he has nothing to worry about from me. I'm practically engaged to a wonderful woman in Dallas."

The lines between her eyes deepened and she shook her head. "Just . . . go."

He nodded, and backed toward the door. She was a tough one, but he knew he'd wear her down eventually. People liked him. They trusted him. He had that kind of charming, easygoing personality.

He was climbing into the truck when the door opened again and Mindy raced out. Surprising how fast she could run in heels. She sagged against the driver's side door, winded by her sprint in the thin air. "Don't worry, I'll work on her," she said. "She'll come around."

"Don't badger her," he said. "In fact, act as if you don't

care. That will make her curious. She'll want to talk to us to find out what we're up to."

"I have learned a few things we can use in the book, and I have some ideas."

Of course she did. Mindy had the idea that she was going to contribute something useful to this project, beyond her access to her sister. It was in his best interest to let her keep thinking that. "I'd love to hear your ideas," he said.

"There's a bar in town—maybe the only bar. Called the Dirty Sally."

"Lovely name," he said dryly.

"I think it's named after a mine. Everything up here is, I guess. Anyway, let's meet there tonight. About eight o'clock?"

"All right." He could use a drink after the day he'd had. "And don't worry about your sister. Before this is over, she'll be telling me her deepest, darkest secrets."

Charlie came home with the boys while the dust from Travis's truck was still settling in the driveway. Cameron and Theo, knees streaked with mud from the creek, hair wind-blown and cheeks sunburned, burst into the house first, both talking at once, their voices high-pitched and eager. "Mom, we caught the biggest . . ."

"Fish so big I thought it was gonna break the—"

"Fishing pole bent almost in two! Dad—"

"Had to help us reel it—"

"Into the bank and Theo almost—"

"Stuck his finger with the hook but—"

"It was just a scratch. No worries." Charlie finished up the story and kissed Shelly on the cheek. He smelled of creek water and fish bait and the cigars he only smoked when he was fishing. "Did you have a good birthday afternoon?"

Shelly thought longingly of the bubble bath she'd never gotten to enjoy, and the romance novel that still lay on the table, unread. "Something came up," she said.

"Oh?" His eyebrows rose in question.

She looked past him to the boys, and the stringer of trout they held between them. "What a gorgeous bunch of fish," she said. "We'll have to have them for supper, won't we?"

Cameron pushed his lips out in a doubtful expression. "But it's your birthday. We should have something you like."

"Aww, honey." She had to swallow past the sudden knot in her throat. "I can't think of anything better for my birthday dinner than trout you caught." She patted his shoulder and took the stringer of fish. "Now you both go upstairs and get cleaned up and Dad and I will take care of these."

"Race you!" Theo shouted, and headed for the stairs. Cam thundered after him.

Charlie took the stringer from him. "You don't even like trout," he said.

"I like it fine." She started to turn away, but he caught her arm. "What came up?" he asked. "Why do you look so upset?"

"I look upset?" She thought she'd been hiding it well.

"You get this pinched look around your eyes when you're unhappy," he said. "And your shoulders hunch."

She straightened her shoulders, then sighed. Why bother pretending? "My sister's here," she said.

"Your sister?" Deep lines formed on his forehead, as if he was trying to remember something important. Probably the fact that she had a sister; it wasn't as if she ever talked about her family.

"Mindy. Five years younger. The spitting image of my mom at twenty-five."

"So . . . she came to see you for your birthday?" He watched her closely, gauging her reaction.

"She hired a private detective to find me so that she could pick my brain for the book some publisher is paying her to write."

"Whoa, back up a minute. Your sister is a writer?"

"No, she's not a writer. She has some ghostwriter, a reporter or something, who's going to do the writing. She's just supposed to get me to go along with the idea."

"What idea is that?"

She pressed both hands to her temples, trying to squeeze out the headache forming there. "She's writing about Baby Shelly. Some tell-all tome or something. All about what I've been up to for the past ten years."

His face relaxed some. "That's going to be a short book. It's not like you've been up to anything scandalous or anything."

"She and this reporter will probably find a way to make it sound that way." She hugged her arms across her chest and hunched her shoulders. "I know how these people are. They'll do everything they can to twist things around and sensationalize—anything to make money off the legend of Baby Shelly."

"So tell her to leave." He set his jaw. "Or I'll tell her." He looked around. "Where is she?"

"She left to meet that reporter, but she'll be back later. Her things are up in the guest room."

"Then I'll talk to her when she gets back. I don't want her upsetting you."

He started toward the kitchen with the fish, but she hurried after him. "Don't say anything to her," she said. "At least, not yet."

"You want her to stay?"

"I don't know what I want." She gave him a pleading look, as if he might have an answer for all the questions bombarding her. "I was so shocked to see her, after all this time. She looks so much like our mother, but also like the little girl who was practically my best friend when we were growing up. And . . . and even though I hate why she's here, I . . . I've really missed her."

Charlie reached out his arm and she went to him and buried her face in his shoulder. "I'm a mess," she murmured.

"It's okay," he said. "You're my mess. And your sister can stay here as long as you like."

She looked up at him, into his calm brown eyes and features that looked like they'd been chiseled out of some rock. His steadiness anchored her, like the mountains that backed up to their house. "Are you sure? She can be . . . kind of hard to take."

"She can stay for a little while. Until we both agree she should go."

She nodded. "Thanks."

He patted her arm and moved away. "I'd better clean these fish. You sure you don't want me to freeze them for some other time? We could go out for dinner."

"It's okay." She smiled. "Besides, I still have plenty of cake." And two sons and a husband who added so much sweetness to her life. How could she complain about the little bit of bitterness that came with her sister's unexpected arrival?

Mindy didn't see anything special about the Dirty Sally Saloon. It looked like a typical neighborhood hangout, though maybe a little more old-fashioned, with the long, mahogany bar at one end of the room, and wooden tables and chairs scattered out front. There was a raised platform, like a stage, in one corner, but no band played on it, and in any case, there wasn't any room on the floor to dance. It was cleaner than some of the dives she'd seen in Texas, she'd give it that. But it sure wasn't anything special. She stopped in the doorway and surveyed the place, looking for an empty table, but no such luck. People probably didn't have anything to do in this town in the evenings, except drink.

She sashayed up to the bar, aware of more than one set of male eyes following her. She put a little extra wiggle into her hips for their benefit and slid onto a stool next to a grizzled old guy who was focused on draining a glass of beer. Not her first choice for companionship, but this was the only empty seat. The geezer set down the empty glass and frowned at her. "Who are you?" he demanded.

"What's it to you, old man?" she asked.

"Don't mind Bob. His bark is worse than his bite."

She looked behind the bar to the man who had addressed her. *Well hello, handsome!* Here was someone interesting, at last. She turned up the wattage of her smile for the bartender, a dark-haired, dark-eyed hottie with a neat goatee and muscular shoulders. "Hi, I'm Mindy," she cooed.

"Welcome to Eureka, Mindy. I'm Jameso. What can I get you?"

"Tanqueray and tonic, please." It was the most sophisticated cocktail she could think of at the moment.

He turned his back to mix the drink, giving her a chance to admire the rest of him. Mmmm-hmmm. Very nice. Who knew checked flannel and faded jeans could look so good? When he turned around, she made a point of brushing her hand across his as he handed her the drink. "Thank you," she said. "What did you say your name was again? James?"

"It's Jameso. Short for Jameson."

"So nice to meet you." She sipped the drink, but kept her eyes locked to his. "I'm here visiting my sister," she said. "Maybe you know her—Shelly Frazier."

"You're Shelly's sister? No kidding?"

"I know." Mindy waved her hand. "We don't look a thing alike. People used to say she was the brains and I was the beauty." People never said anything like that, but she liked the way it sounded.

"Well, I hope you enjoy your visit." He started to move down the bar, but she reclaimed his attention.

"What is there to do around here in the evenings?" she said. "You know, for fun?"

"Oh, people manage to find ways to amuse themselves."

"I'll just bet they do." She licked her lips. "Maybe you could show me around some time."

He apparently didn't hear her suggestion; something behind her had attracted his attention. His smile broadened. "Hello there, gorgeous," he said, and reached out his arms.

A redheaded woman handed a swaddled infant across the

bar, then leaned forward to kiss Jameso on the lips, a performance that sent Mindy's spirits plummeting. Still grinning, Jameso rocked the baby. "How's my two favorite girls?"

"Thrilled that the road commissioner's meeting this evening was short." The woman settled onto the stool beside Mindy that had miraculously opened up on her arrival. "I'd love a cup of tea."

"Coming right up." He started to turn away, then paused. "Maggie, this is Mindy. She's Shelly Frazier's sister, in town for a visit. Mindy, this is my wife, Maggie."

Shelly frowned at the redhead. Good hair. Decent body, but the fine lines around her eyes and the faintest sagging along her jaw proved she had to be forty if she was a day. How did she end up married to the hottest guy in town? "Nice to meet you," she mumbled.

"I had no idea Shelly had a sister," Maggie said. "Where are you from?"

"Texas. A little town you probably never heard of."

"Maggie's from Texas." Jameso returned with a steaming cup, the tag of a tea bag dangling over the side.

"Houston," Maggie said. "Thanks, sweetie."

Mindy turned away. It was either that or gag. *Sweetie.* Unfortunately, that put her facing the old geezer again. "Struck out, did you?" he said.

She started to tell him to stuff it, but the arrival of another man distracted her. "Can I get a Fat Tire?" the guy asked. He was tall and broad-shouldered, with the dark, brooding looks she went for. A little long in the tooth, judging by the gray at his temples, but still very sexy.

"Hello," she said.

He glanced at her. "Hi." He looked up to accept the beer from Jameso, who still cradled the baby in one hand. "Thanks. Cute baby."

"Meet Angela, my daughter. I'm Jameso." He offered his hand.

"Duke Breman." They shook.

"I'm Mindy." She leaned between the two. Honestly, what did it take for a girl to get noticed around here?

"Hello, Mindy," Duke said. But he said it the same way he might say "Hello, Aunt Martha." Zero interest. What was wrong with men around here?

"What brings you to town, Duke?" Jameso asked.

"I'm trying to find out some information about a guy who spent some time here," he said. "Did you know Gerald Pershing? Somebody told me he used to hang out here."

"I wouldn't say he 'hung out' here," Jameso said. "But it's the only bar in town. Everybody ends up here sooner or later."

"What do you want with that old crook?" The geezer, who was nursing another beer, spoke up.

Duke turned his back on Mindy to face the old man. "Did you know him?"

"You could say that." The old guy stuck out his hand. "Bob Prescott. I manage the Lucky Lady Mine."

"I understand Gerald owned a half interest in that mine," Duke said.

"He did, until he sold out to me and left town. Good riddance to the old son of a bitch, I say."

"Any idea where he was headed when he left Eureka?" Duke leaned an elbow on the bar. Never mind that he was crowding *her*.

"He could have gone to hell, for all I care." Bob's scowl deepened. "Why are you so interested? Did he steal from you, too?"

"I'm a private detective." He took a card case from his back pocket and handed business cards to Bob and Jameso. "A client has hired me to track him down. If you think of anything that might help me, give me a call."

"He always said he was from Dallas," Jameso said.

"He didn't go back there after he left here," Duke said.

"At least not that I can determine. He seems to have just disappeared."

"Good riddance to him," Bob said.

"Good riddance to who?" Yet another hot guy joined them. Mindy sat up straighter. Now this one had real possibilities—he was the clean-cut, lean and muscular military type—definitely closer to her age. "Hello?" she said, giving him her warmest smile.

"Hi there." He returned the smile and she felt encouraged. A quick check of his left hand showed no ring.

"I'm Mindy," he said.

"Josh Miller."

"What can I get you, Josh?" Jameso asked.

"Avalanche Pale Ale." Josh turned back to Mindy. "Are you new in town, or just visiting?"

"I'm visiting my sister, but I'm thinking about making the stay more permanent." Really, she couldn't wait to get out of the place, but she might as well let him think she was at least thinking of sticking around.

"Welcome to Eureka. I'm sure I'll see you around."

"Oh, I'm sure."

He accepted the beer from Jameso and she opened her mouth to suggest that they get together so he could show her around when a dark-haired woman hurried up to him. "Sorry I'm late," she said, her cheeks flushed. "I had to drop Alina off at a friend's house and they live farther out than I thought."

"Sharon, this is Mindy. She's new in town, visiting her sister."

"Hi, Mindy."

"What can I get you, Sis?" Jameso interrupted again.

"Diet Coke." Sharon turned back to Mindy. "Who's your sister?"

"Shelly Frazier."

"Oh, Shelly's really sweet." She took the soft drink from Jameso. "Well, I hope you enjoy your visit."

She and Josh turned away, his hand possessively on her back.

Mindy gave up on the men. She spotted an empty table and headed toward it, drink in hand. The door opened and Travis came in. Relief washed over her. Finally, a friendly face. Not that he was anything special to look at—all that frizzy hair and those wire-rimmed glasses made him look like every geek who'd populated her high school. But he was her ticket to the big payoff the publisher had promised, and she had to admire the way he hadn't let Shelly cow him. So she pasted a big smile on her face and waved to him.

"Looks like this is a pretty popular place," he said, settling into the chair across from her.

"A town this small, there's nothing else to do in the evenings but drink, I guess." She looked around at the crowd of people of all ages. "I can't believe my sister settled here. I mean, this makes our hometown look like a regular metropolis."

"A small town is perfect for our purposes," Travis said.

"How do you figure that?"

"Everybody knows everybody else's business in a small town. We'll learn loads of stuff about your sister without even talking to her."

"But the editor wants direct quotes. Saint Shelly's own precious words." Mindy made a face. "I'd just make everything up, but knowing Shelly, she'd sue."

"So you'd say she's the vindictive type? Wants to get back at her perceived enemies?"

"I know what vindictive means. And Shelly's not like that. Not exactly." She sipped her drink, trying to think how to describe her sister. "Shelly has a very clear idea—a fantasy, really—of how she wants things to be. And when real life doesn't match up with that fantasy, she gets very put out. Oh, and she has this real persecution complex. Everyone is out to get her." She rolled her eyes. "So yeah, I think she'd sue, then say I was only using her."

"Don't worry about that. I've got a plan." He raised his hand to flag down the waitress. "Can I get a Bud Light?"

"Sure thing." The waitress looked at Mindy. "You want a refill?"

"Why not?" She handed over her empty glass. "Tanqueray and tonic. Put it on his tab."

Travis frowned, but didn't object. "What did Shelly say after I left?" he asked.

"Not much. She told me again that she didn't want anything to do with our book project, and that I could stay with her as long as I didn't do anything to upset her husband and kids."

"What's he like—Mr. Frazier?"

"He's a loser just like her. Drives a road grader for the county and races snowmobiles and ATVs in his spare time. He and my dad would probably get along real well. After all the time she spent with her nose in the air, looking down on us rednecks, I can't believe she married one."

"Does he know she was Baby Shelly?"

"She says he does, but they don't talk about it. The biggest thing that happened in her life—the thing that made her famous—and she wants to pretend it never happened. I just don't get it."

Travis shrugged. "Some people don't like to be in the limelight."

"Some people are stupid."

The waitress returned with their drinks. Travis pulled out his wallet. "Do you know Shelly Frazier?" he asked.

"She works at the bank, right?"

"That's her. Her birthday's coming up and my friend and I are trying to think of the perfect gift, but we're not sure what she'd like. Does she have any hobbies or anything?"

"I don't know her that well, but I know she's involved with the historical society."

Mindy rolled her eyes. The historical society? For real?

"Are you in the historical society, too?"

The woman laughed. "No way. I'm too scared of Cassie."

"Who's Cassie?" Travis asked.

"Cassie Wynock, the librarian. Vicious old dragon. She's the president of the historical society. But I guess she and Shelly get along okay." She pocketed the bills he handed over. "Can I get you anything else?"

"Not right now. Thanks."

When she was gone, Travis pulled out a little notebook and wrote something in it. "I'll talk to this librarian tomorrow. Old women often like to gossip. We might get something good. Meanwhile, you can go to the bank and chat up her coworkers."

"How do I do that?"

"I don't know. Tell them you want to open an account. Ask where to get your hair done. You'll think of something."

"You're the reporter here. I'm supposed to concentrate on my sister and the whole family thing."

"Says who?" He tucked the notebook back in his pockets.

"Says me. After all, it was my idea to write this book. And if it wasn't for me, you wouldn't even be able to talk to my sister."

"If it wasn't for the private detective I hired, neither one of us would be talking to her." He propped his elbows on the table and studied her. "What's with that, anyway? How come Shelly hasn't spoken to her family for years? You sold the publisher on this line that the two of you used to be so close."

"We were sisters. Of course we were close." She forced herself not to fidget, a dead giveaway that she wasn't exactly telling the whole truth. She'd learned that in the acting classes she'd taken back at Sweetwater Community College. Her teacher had been real big on psychology and character motivation. Fat lot of good that did her when they put on *Oklahoma!* Mindy had been sure she could act her way to Hollywood and fame, but turned out big-chested blondes were everywhere in L.A. It was like being back home, where Mindy was nothing special.

"So what happened?" Travis asked. "How come you aren't close now?"

She traced a line of moisture down the side of her glass. "When I was little, I looked up to Shelly and followed her around like a little puppy dog," she said. When the Lord had handed out maternal instinct, Sandy must have been in the ladies' room. Shelly did most of the mothering, at least when Mindy was small. Shelly carried her little sister everywhere, until she got too big to balance on a hip, and told her stories, and secrets, and let her share her bed when Mindy was scared of thunderstorms or bad dreams.

Mindy pushed down the knot of sentimental tears that tried to clog her throat. She was getting to be as bad as Shelly, idealizing the past. "The older I got, the more I realized what a raw deal I was getting, compared to my famous, sainted big sister. No one else stood a chance in the shadow of darling Baby Shelly."

"Was there a fight? A big disagreement?" Travis hunched forward, pencil poised over his little notebook, ready to record all the sordid details. If only she had any to give him.

"She went off the rails one day and ran away. Maybe she had a nervous breakdown or something. It certainly wasn't anything we did. Everyone in my family worshipped the ground she walked on. She was my mother's whole reason for being. Her full-time job was and still is preserving the memory of and promoting the image of Baby Shelly."

"Interesting." He nodded and scribbled some notes.

"What are you writing?" she asked. He reminded her of a shrink she'd seen once—he had made notes and little comments like that, too. She got the impression he thought she was nutso, so she never went back to see him again.

"Just some notes."

"I get final approval of the manuscript, you know."

"Actually, the editor gets final approval. But don't worry. You'll get to see the manuscript when it's done."

She finished her drink and rested her chin in her hand. "We're not going to have a manuscript if Shelly won't talk to us. I tried hard to chat her up this afternoon, but she wouldn't talk at all about our family or growing up or anything."

"She's bound to soften up after a few days," Travis said. He reached into his coat and pulled out a little black box, smaller than a pack of cards. "Here. Take this."

She picked up the box. "What is it?"

"It's a voice-activated recorder. Tuck it away somewhere and use it whenever you talk to Shelly. Don't make it like you're interviewing her, just, you know, reminisce. Get her to talk about her feelings. Stuff like that will make great quotes for the book."

"Isn't it illegal to record people without their permission?" She pressed the button on the side of the recorder and heard a whirring sound.

"A technicality. After all, the government does it all the time."

She tucked the recorder into her bra. It fit snugly. "Does it show?" she asked.

"Um, no."

He was actually blushing. She grinned. At least he wasn't totally immune to her charms. Not that she was interested in him, but still, it was good to know she hadn't completely lost her touch. "How am I supposed to get her to talk about anything useful?" she asked. "Nothing I've tried has worked so far."

"You have to come at her from an angle, not with a direct attack." He sat back, legs stretched out in front on him. "For instance, maybe you say you're afraid of the dark. Ask if she's afraid of the dark. If she says yes, ask how she managed down in that dark cave, or if she thinks her fear is because of the time she spent there. If she says she's not afraid, ask how she managed in the dark cave or if she's not afraid because of what she went through down there. Tell her you remember the good times you all had as children. Ask if she remembers the Christmas when she was seven and you were two. Or the dog you had as kids, or the school play—anything like that. Once you get her talking about general memories, you can dig deeper and eventually work your way back to the cave."

She had to admit, Travis knew his stuff. "You really think it will work?"

"I know it will. You and I can arrange to meet up every day or so and I'll empty the recorder's memory and transcribe anything useful. We'll put that with whatever I get from interviewing the locals and the interviews I've already done with folks back in Texas and before you know it, we'll have our bestseller."

She tucked the recorder in a little more securely. "This might be kind of fun. Sort of like being a spy."

"Exactly." He held up his half-empty beer in a salute. "Just think of it as an undercover operation. You'll do great."

Chapter 3

The smell of cinnamon and sugar was a better stress reliever than any fancy aromatherapy oils, Shelly thought, as she pulled a tray of cinnamon rolls from the oven. She put her face close to the warm rolls and breathed deeply, eyes closed, letting the soothing aroma fill her.

"That bad, huh?"

Charlie ambled into the kitchen and poured a mug of coffee. Charlie rarely moved quickly—he was a big, deliberate man who reminded her of a bear. He made Shelly feel safe and calm. She set the tray of rolls on the stovetop and turned off the oven. "Good morning," she said.

"How long have you been up?" He kissed her cheek, and pinched a piece off of one of the rolls.

She made a show of slapping his hand. "Since about four. If you'll wait a minute, I'll frost these."

"My offer still stands. If she upsets you that much, I can be the bad guy and ask her to leave."

Of course, Charlie assumed Shelly's agitation was due to Mindy's unexpected arrival. And it was—mostly. But her anxiety had started with that online story about the twenty-fifth anniversary of her rescue. Then Mindy had showed up, and that reporter. It was like emerging from that cave into chaos all over again. She didn't know what to expect, or whom to trust. She glanced toward the stairs. The guest room was at the back of the house, but still . . .

"She won't hear us," Charlie said. "She didn't come in until almost one. She'll sleep all morning."

As a child, Mindy had been a heavy sleeper, seldom rising before noon on weekends, while Shelly could seldom stay in bed past seven, anxious to be up and active.

"Do you want me to tell her to go?" Charlie asked. He pinched off another bite of roll.

"Do you really mind having her here?" She added vanilla to the bowlful of powdered sugar, then drizzled in melted butter.

"It doesn't matter what I think. She's your sister. If she upsets you, I'll tell her she can't stay."

Having Mindy here did upset her. She reminded Shelly of too many things she wanted to forget—all those old bad feelings of only being valued for the money and attention she brought to her family, not loved for herself.

But another, accusing voice in the back of her head whispered that she ought to be over that already. She was a grown woman, with children of her own. There was something wrong with a person who couldn't even speak to her family. She ought to do her part to try to mend the rift between them. Mindy was the only sister she had. Now that they were grown, maybe they could heal the old wounds, and be close again. After all, no other woman could know her the way her sister did. "I think I want her to stay—just for a little while," she said.

"That's fine with me. What about this book idea of hers?"

Shelly beat the frosting more vigorously. "I don't want anything to do with that."

"I can understand that." He sipped his coffee and stared

out the window at the sun just beginning to break over the mountains. None of the windows had curtains or blinds; Shelly didn't want anything to block the view, and the house was set back far enough from the road and neighbors that no one could see in. "The two of you are probably going to have to talk some about what happened when you were a kid," Charlie said after a moment. "You'll have to clear the air."

She nodded. "I'll have to try to make her understand how I feel. And I guess I need to listen to what she has to say about it." She set aside the bowl of frosting and turned to face him, her back against the kitchen counter. "I know she feels like I got all the attention and she got nothing, but I would have given anything for things to be the other way around."

"If you tell her that often enough, maybe it will sink in." He turned to pour more coffee. "Wrap one of those up for me to take with me," he said. "I've got to go in early, work on one of the graders that started acting up yesterday."

She smeared frosting on the rolls, then cut off one and placed it on a napkin. He pulled her close and gave her a long kiss good-bye that tasted of coffee and sugar. He held her tightly for a moment longer than usual, the hug comforting her more than words.

The boys came downstairs a few minutes after their father left, dressed in jeans and T-shirts, though still barefoot, hair uncombed. "Cinnamon rolls!" Cameron exclaimed, and slid into his chair at the table.

Theo, the quieter of the two, said nothing as he slumped into his chair. Shelly squeezed his shoulder and set a glass of milk in front of him. "Wake up, sleepyhead," she said.

"I'm awake." He stifled a yawn and reached for a roll from the plate she set in the center of the table.

"Drew Sommersby fell asleep in Sunday school last week," Cameron said.

"Don't talk with your mouth full," Shelly corrected him.

The boy took a drink of milk. "The teacher woke him up and told him he should go to bed earlier. He told me he'd stayed up late the night before, watching a movie. It was that film about the robots, and this guy who wants to take over the world. . . ."

She listened to his rambling story while she made the boys' lunches—peanut butter and strawberry jelly for Theo, turkey and cheese for Cameron. Apple slices and homemade cookies and a frozen box of juice that would thaw by lunchtime. She glanced at the clock over the window. "It's seven-thirty, boys. Time to run upstairs and brush your teeth, comb your hair, and put on your shoes. We don't want to be late." Their babysitter, Debbie, lived the opposite direction from the bank, so on the mornings Charlie couldn't drop them off Shelly had to allow extra time.

Cameron raced up the stairs, Theo shuffling after him. "Good morning, Aunt Mindy!" Cameron called.

Mindy, wearing boxer shorts and an oversize T-shirt, descended the stairs a moment later. Hair uncombed and makeup smeared, she was a far cry from the former beauty queen. "What smells so good?" she asked.

"Homemade cinnamon rolls. Do you want coffee?"

"Please."

Shelly poured her sister a cup of coffee and set a plate in front of her, then busied herself with loading the dishwasher while Mindy drank coffee and ate a cinnamon roll. The boys thundered down the stairs. "We'll wait in the car, Mom!" Cameron called. "Bye, Aunt Mindy!" Then the door slammed and they were off down the steps.

"Your boys are certainly, um, active," Mindy said, staring after them.

"They're just boys."

"I've never spent much time around little kids. Funny, since half the girls I went to high school with are already married." She pinched off a piece of roll. "How old were you when you married Charlie?"

"Twenty-one." Though she'd felt at least a decade older. While Mindy, at twenty-five, seemed much younger.

Mindy shook her head. "I can't imagine tying myself down so young. And only having sex with one guy for the rest of your life?" She shuddered.

Shelly smiled, imagining how shocked her sister would be if Shelly told her that Charlie was the only man she'd ever had sex with—and that was fine with her. "What did you do last night?" she asked.

"I wanted to see a little of the town, so I went to that bar—the Dirty Sally." She made a face. "Sounds like it ought to be a place with strippers."

"It's named after one of the mines in the area."

"You mean, like gold mines? Do they really still do that here? Mine gold, I mean."

"They do. The Dirty Sally Mine shut down during the Depression, but there are a lot of others still around. The town owns a half interest in the Lucky Lady Mine, which re-opened a couple of months ago. And there are a few others, mostly smaller one- or two-man operations."

"That's wild." Mindy shook her head and pulled off another bite of roll.

"Did you have a good time last night?" Shelly asked.

"Not really. I mean, it was just a bunch of people sitting around talking and drinking. No dancing or anything. And there's no movie theater or mall—what do people do around here for fun?"

"Most people around here are into outdoor activities—hiking or Jeeping in the summer, skiing or snowshoeing or snowmobiling in the winter."

"That's fine for the daytime, but what do they do at night?"

"I guess they're worn out from all the daytime activities. Or they stay home and watch TV or you know, read."

Mindy rolled her eyes. "It's a wonder you don't all die of boredom."

Shelly laughed. "I guess we are pretty boring, but it suits me."

Mindy pinched off a piece of a second roll. "These are good. Where did you get them?"

"I made them."

"You mean, like, from a mix or something?"

"I mean, like, from scratch."

"Where did you learn to cook?"

"I taught myself. I like to cook." Their mother had believed in spending as little time in the kitchen as possible—if it didn't come from a can, the freezer, or a takeout menu, they didn't eat it. Shelly hadn't realized how good food could taste until she started cooking for herself.

"Of course you did." Mindy's expression turned sour. "You probably made that quilt on my bed, too, and knit your own socks."

Shelly had indeed made the quilt on the guest bed, and while she didn't knit socks, she had been known to knit a scarf or two. Clearly, Mindy didn't want to hear that. "What do you like to do for fun?" she asked her sister.

"I like to dance, and listen to music. I like going out to clubs and stuff. And shopping—I love shopping."

"We don't have many places to shop around here. And no clubs." Mindy looked so disappointed at this news that Shelly almost felt sorry for her. But at least this meant the young woman wasn't likely to stay around that long.

But Mindy rallied. "Maybe you can show me around town today."

"I'm sorry, but I can't. I have to work."

"You work at the bank, right?"

"Yes. How did you know?" Had the private detective who

had found her filled in that little detail, too? The thought of some stranger spying on her made her skin crawl.

Mindy shrugged. "Last night, people wanted to know how I ended up in Eureka. I told them I was your sister. Someone mentioned you work at the bank. What do you do there?"

"I'm a teller. Nothing exciting, I promise you. What kind of work do you do?"

"Oh, different stuff. My last job, I worked as a hostess in a restaurant. That was before I decided to become a writer."

Shelly stiffened. But she told herself she should have a more open mind. "What kind of things have you written?"

"Oh, different things." Mindy waved her hand dismissively. "This book will be my first big project. The publisher thinks it will sell really well."

"I can't imagine why anyone would be interested in something that happened twenty-five years ago."

"It's all your doing," Mindy said, her languid attitude vanished. "If you didn't pull your Greta Garbo act and disappear, people would have probably gotten tired of the whole thing by now. But now you're a big mystery—people want to know what happened." She glared at her sister. "Why did you bug out?"

"I don't owe anyone an explanation for my behavior," Shelly said.

"I think you owe me one. You owe Mom and Dad one. We're your family and you just stopped talking to us. You didn't even let us know where you were living or what your name was. You could have been dead, for all we knew. Didn't you think we'd worry? That we'd feel awful that we never knew where you were or how you were doing? How do you think Mom's going to feel when I tell she's got two grandsons she's never seen?"

Shelly had spent a lot of years convincing herself she had nothing to feel guilty about. She opened her mouth to deny that her mother would care about her or her children, but she couldn't. Now that she was a mother herself, she couldn't really believe that in some small part of her heart, her mother didn't love her. Shelly didn't agree with the way Sandy had chosen to express that love, but maybe she did, in fact, care. And how much was she hurting the boys, not allowing them to know their grandmother?

But then the image of a tabloid photo of her boys and the headline BABY SHELLY'S BABIES flashed into her head, effectively trampling the brief sentimentality. She couldn't believe that, if she did introduce her children to Sandy, the woman wouldn't be on the phone to the media at the first opportunity. "I don't have time to talk about this right now," she said. "I have to take the boys to the sitter and get ready for work." A glance at the clock told her she was already late.

"Don't you even care how much you hurt us?" Mindy asked. "How much you hurt Mom?"

"Mom hasn't thought of me as her little girl in a long time," Shelly said. "She can't look at me now without seeing dollar signs."

"Oh sure, you're all happy and settled in your big house with your good job. You've forgotten what it's like to not have money. Why should you hold a grudge against her for trying to provide for us the best way she could?"

Shelly heard her mother's voice in those words; Mindy was parroting something she'd heard so often it was burned into her brain. "Mom and Dad had plenty of money after I was rescued from that cave," she said. "It's not my fault they wasted it all."

"They wasted it all on you—on new dresses and shoes and trips to the beauty parlor. I had to wear your hand-me-downs."

"I would have gladly traded places with you."

"It's easy for you to say that, because you know you never would have had to."

Shelly sighed. This was an old argument she thought she'd

put behind her. "Neither one of us can go back and change what happened in the past," she said. "I'm sorry you were hurt."

"You think we took advantage of you and what happened to you, just because we were greedy," Mindy said. "But you turned your back on us a long time ago. Maybe Mama spent so much time focused on what happened to you because it was the only way she knew to get your attention." Mindy shoved back her chair and stormed out of the room. Shelly listened to her feet pounding on the stairs, then the door of the guest room slammed.

She grabbed her keys and purse and headed toward the door, but memories of her mother crowded out every other conscious thought. Sandy had been only a year older than Shelly was now, holding court for a group of reporters at Shelly's twelfth birthday party. "We're so proud of Shelly," she'd said. "She's come so far, overcoming the trauma she experienced. She's so smart and sweet. We know one day she's going to make us all proud."

They were the kind of words any mother would say. Words Shelly herself might say about her boys. But at the time, Shelly had been sure her mother was faking it, saying the words like lines in a play, to try to impress the reporters. Sandy had concocted this fantasy of the perfect, loving family that she liked to present to the rest of the world. Shelly, a withdrawn and mistrustful preteen, hadn't believed the words were true.

But what if they had been true? What if Sandy really had been proud of her daughter? What if at least part of her desire to show off for the press had grown from that pride, however twisted or misplaced?

What if Sandy really did love her daughter for more than the money she brought in—and Shelly was the one in the wrong, for turning her back on her family when they needed her most?

*   *   *

Maggie stared at the blinking cursor on the screen and tried to concentrate, when all she really wanted to do was put her head down on her desk and take a nap. Angela had refused to go to sleep last night, transforming from gurgling, happy infant who wanted to play, to angry, wailing baby. Maggie and Jameso had taken turns walking up and down the hallway with her, cooing and bouncing and pleading with her, until the three of them had finally collapsed in exhaustion on their king-sized bed sometime in the early morning hours.

Maggie yawned and tried to remember what it was she was supposed to be writing about.

"What's wrong with you?" Her boss, Rick Otis, emerged from his office, a coffee mug from Eureka Bank in his hand. Maggie had two identical mugs in her kitchen at the B and B. One she'd received when she opened her account at the bank. The other she'd inherited from her father, Jacob Murphy. She'd never known the man while he was alive, but his death had brought her to Eureka, and a completely new life.

"Earth to Maggie," Rick said. "I asked you a question."

"Nothing's wrong. I'm just tired." Exhausted. But she'd be fine—in eighteen years or so.

"Have a cup of this coffee." He held up the mug. "It'll wake you up."

"Caffeine isn't good for the baby." She was still nursing, and pumping breast milk to fill bottles for when she was away. She checked the time on the computer—almost ten. Maybe she'd run home to feed the baby—and grab a nap. The thought of the bed, with its fluffy down comforter and many pillows, almost made her moan with longing.

"Nobody told my mother that," Rick said. "She drank coffee all day long, and smoked like a chimney, and I turned out all right."

That contention might be debatable, considering Rick's curmudgeonly, loner ways. But Maggie wasn't about to argue the point. "Did you need me for something, Rick?" she asked.

"What do you know about this detective who's in town?" he asked.

So much for hoping she could sneak back to the B and B. Rick obviously wanted to gossip. He defended his interest as "having a nose for news" but he was more of a busybody than any woman in town. "Do you mean Duke?" she asked.

"How many other private investigators are running around Eureka this week?"

"There might be dozens, for all I know," she said.

He scowled at her—though really, Rick's normal expression was a scowl, so only someone who knew him well could sense the change—a slight deepening of the lines on his forehead and a squinching up of his crooked nose. "I thought new mothers were supposed to be all sweet and happy," he said. He was dressed in his summer uniform: baggy khaki shorts, an aloha shirt—this one featured dogs on surfboards—and black Converse high-tops.

Maggie's laugh was this side of hysterical. "Who told you that lie?" Of course, she was thrilled and crazy in love with Angela, maybe even more so than the average new mom, since at forty, she had thought her opportunity to be a parent was behind her. She'd let her first husband talk her into not having children. By the time he'd left her, she figured it was too late for the children she'd always wanted.

Then her father had died, she moved to Eureka, met Jameso . . . and here she was.

"What are you smiling about?" Rick asked.

"Oh, nothing." Everything. It was just so amazing how life turned out sometimes.

"So what do you know about Duke?" he asked.

"Almost nothing. He says he's looking for Gerald Pershing." The supposed financial manager from Dallas had swindled the town out of most of its funds, only to be swindled in turn when the city fathers and mothers sold him a half interest in a bogus gold mine—that turned out to be loaded with gold ore after all. After being trapped in a mine collapse for five days in late spring, he'd sold out his interest in the Lucky Lady Mine and left town—everyone in Eureka hoped for good.

"Who hired Duke to look for Pershing?" Rick asked.

"I have no idea."

"Well, we need to find out," Rick said. "He's staying at your B and B, isn't he?"

Technically, the Idlewilde Inn belonged to Maggie's best friend, Barb Stanowski, who lived in Houston. Maggie and Jameso managed the property for her. And yes, Duke had checked into the inn late last night, following Maggie home from the Dirty Sally to unload his bags and claim the smallest back bedroom, the only one available now that summer tourist season was in full swing. "How do you know where Duke is staying?" she asked.

"I already called the motel and he's not there. Unless he's got a private rental, that leaves the Idlewilde. Plus, you're a terrible liar. He's there, isn't he?"

She nodded.

"Great. You can chat him up, find out who's paying for him to come all the way here from Texas."

"Who Duke is working for isn't any of my business," she said. "Or yours."

"It might be news." Rick sipped his coffee. "What if Pershing drove off a cliff after he left here? He was certainly in a hurry to get away."

"Anything is possible, Rick." Maggie tried to focus on the computer screen once more. She was working on a story about last night's road commissioner meeting. How could she make the purchase of ten tons of road base and the repair of one of the county road graders into interesting reading? Clearly, the subject wasn't doing anything to help her stay awake.

"Chat him up," Rick said. "See if you can find out anything. Maybe there's a story there."

"You talk to him," she said. "You're the one who's so interested." Though Rick did his share of reporting for the weekly paper, he tried to put as much work as possible off on Maggie.

"He's a man. He'll respond better to you."

"Right. Because over-forty new moms are so sexy."

Rick made a face, then brightened, "Speaking of sexy, have you seen Shelly Frazier's sister?"

"Mindy?" It was Maggie's turn to make a sour face. "We've met." The young woman had been practically drooling over Jameso last night in the Dirty Sally. Not that Jameso had reciprocated, of course.

Not for the first time, Maggie reminded herself that she needed to get used to the fact that other women would look twice at her handsome, younger husband. But Jameso loved her. He had turned his back on his player ways to marry her. Last Christmas, he had skied over a mountain pass in a blizzard to bring her the engagement ring he'd had specially made for her—if that wasn't true love, she didn't know what was.

Except, now he was married, and to a forty-year-old new mom who felt anything but sexy. Arrgh. She gave up and rested her head on the desk. Even jealousy couldn't beat out exhaustion.

"I didn't even know Shelly had a sister." Like a dog with a bone, Rick continued to worry the subject. "She never talks about her family."

"Lots of people don't talk about their families," Maggie said, her voice muffled by the fact that her mouth was pressed against the blotter. "You don't talk about your family."

"I'm not a woman. Women always talk about their families."

"I never did." What had there been to talk about? She was an only child, raised by a woman whose husband deserted her when Maggie was three days old. Her mother had died of cancer a few years before, and her dad had succumbed to a heart attack eighteen months ago. End of story.

"I never said you were normal," Rick said. He set the coffee mug on the edge of her desk and turned to stare out the front window. His eyebrows rose. "And speaking of women who aren't normal . . ."

The door opened and Cassie Wynock charged inside. "I have the press release about this year's Founders' Pageant," she said, waving a sheet of paper over her head.

"So you're doing that again?" Rick asked. "Once wasn't enough?"

Cassie's cheeks, already flushed from her walk over from the library, grew redder. "Of course we are. This play is the most important part of the Hard Rock Days celebration."

"I thought the competition for the Hard Rock trophy was the most important part," Rick said. "We always run a picture of the winner on the front page."

"Watching half-naked men pull heavy ore carts and wield hammers appeals to a certain lowest common denominator," Cassie said. "The Founders' Pageant is a much more elevating tradition."

"Last year was the first year the play was done," Rick said. "That doesn't make it a tradition. And for people who don't want to watch the Hard Rock competition, we've got the craft fair and the street dance."

"Well, the pageant should be a tradition," Cassie said. "We should honor the founders of the town."

Meaning, they should honor Cassie's great-grandfather and great-grandmother, who featured prominently in the play, which Cassie had written and in which she played a starring role. "Who's in the play this year?" Maggie asked.

"I'm repeating my turn as Emmaline Wynock, and Doug Raybourn will reprise his role as my great-grandfather, Festus. Lucas Theriot will play the boy who spreads the news of the gold find. Then we have some new roles. I'm thinking of adding a schoolteacher. I decided we needed more representation of women."

"Is Bob reprising his role as the town drunk, Jake?" Rick asked.

Maggie shot him a scolding look. Cassie had it in for Maggie's father, and had written the part of the drunk as a dig at him. Never mind that Jake Murphy had already been dead six months by that time. For Cassie, the past was as vital as the present, and apparently it was never too late to exact revenge.

Cassie's face grew even redder. "I'm not letting Bob Prescott near the production," she huffed. Last year, Bob had not only stolen the show with his onstage antics, he'd almost burned down the opera house where the play was staged with his fireworks finale.

Cassie shoved the paper at Rick. "Run this to let people know we need help with sets and costumes."

"I thought the members of the historical society and the drama society took care of all that." Rick took the paper and handed it to Maggie.

"It never hurts to get the community involved," Cassie said.

Maggie couldn't imagine too many people would be lining up to volunteer to work with Cassie.

The librarian finally looked at Maggie. "I'll let you know when we hold the dress rehearsal so you can come take pictures," she said. Not waiting for an answer, she turned and left.

"What if I don't want to take pictures?" Maggie asked the closed door.

"You'll take pictures," Rick said. "People will want to see it. Besides, it's always a good idea to keep tabs on what Cassie is up to."

"You make her sound as devious as Gerald Pershing." As far as Maggie was concerned, Cassie wasn't devious, just mean.

"She might be worse," Rick said. "After all, librarians know things. And they know how to find out things."

Maggie wanted to laugh, but Rick's expression was too serious. He really did look, well, almost afraid of Cassie. "What kind of things?" she asked.

"Secrets? Lies?"

"Then it's a good thing I don't have secrets," she said.

His eyes met hers, dark and troubled. "Everyone has secrets, Maggie. You just have to know the right questions to ask."

On this note, he drifted back into his office. Maggie stared after him, a chill running up her spine. What the heck was Rick talking about? What secrets was he hiding—especially from Cassie, of all people?

Chapter 4

Travis couldn't remember the last time he'd been in a library. High school? College, maybe, though his college days were a blur of too much beer and not enough sleep. But he had a degree, so studying must have taken place somewhere in there.

The Eureka library occupied what once must have been a house, white pillars flanking an ornate wooden door into which had been inserted a brass book-return slot. When Travis pushed open the door, a buzzer sounded, apparently to alert the librarian that she had a customer.

The woman who emerged from the back rooms of the building was not his idea of the small-town librarian. A fall of dark hair framed a heart-shaped face and big Bambi eyes. She reminded him of his favorite Dallas Cowboys cheerleader, or a waitress he'd known at Hooters. . . .

"Hello. May I help you?"

He snapped out of his fantasy and offered his most charming smile. "I was trying to remember the last time I was in a library. Back in college, I think."

"So, a while ago, huh?"

So much for charming this one. He'd almost forgotten one

lesson he'd definitely learned in college: the best-looking women were almost always stuck up. "Who really needs a library when you have the Internet?" he said.

She shook her head disapprovingly. "Don't let Cassie hear you say that."

"Cassie Wynock, the librarian? I came here hoping to talk to her." He leaned across the counter. "I was hoping you were her."

The young woman took a step back. "Why do you want to talk to Cassie?"

"I'm a reporter with the *Dallas Morning News*. I'm working on a story and I was told Cassie might be a good source of information." No one ever checked with the paper, and he did still have his old press pass if a particularly suspicious person gave him any flack.

He waited for the woman to ask what his story was about, or who had suggested he talk to Cassie. People in small towns were always up in each other's business, right?

But she merely shook her head and took another step back. "Cassie should be here in a few minutes. There are chairs in the magazine section where you can wait." She nodded toward a grouping of chairs around a scarred mahogany table. She started to turn away, but Travis had learned to never give up on a potential source.

"What's your name?" he asked.

She frowned, as if debating answering this simplest of questions. Did she dislike him so much, or was she this standoffish with everyone? "Sharon," she said at last. No surname, but right now that didn't really matter.

"I'm Travis. Travis Rowell." He offered his hand, but she'd already turned away.

"I have work to do, Mr. Rowell," she said. "You're welcome to make yourself comfortable while you wait for Cassie."

"I don't suppose you have any coffee?" he called after her retreating figure.

"We're a library, not a café. But the Last Dollar has very good coffee, if you want to buy some."

"See, that's why libraries are going the way of eight-track tape players and slide rules," he said. "They don't pay enough attention to what customers really want."

"Young man, did you come here to read, or to harass my assistant?" The strident voice echoed in the quiet room, bouncing off bookshelves and display cases, seeming to come from everywhere at once. Travis looked around and finally spotted a short, squat woman in gray marching down an aisle toward him. A halo of gray curls framed a round face with a circle of pink rouge carefully applied to each cheek. She wore a gray knit dress and flat gray shoes. From the shoes up, she looked like someone's sainted grandmother. But the sour set of her mouth and the arctic scorn in her eyes cancelled out the grandmotherly image.

Unless, of course, your grandmother hated you.

"Ms. Wynock?" He had to work a little harder to keep his smile in place, but he was a pro. "I'm Travis Rowell, from the *Dallas Morning News*."

"It's *Miss* Wynock." She marched past him and took her place behind the front desk. "If you're going to put that in the paper, you want to get it right."

Her directness caught him off guard. "Oh, of course."

She clasped her hands together and continued to glare at him, as if expecting more. "Um, I . . ." he stammered.

"Aren't you going to write that down?" she asked.

"Right." He pulled out his notebook and scribbled *Miss Wynock*. He was tempted to add *scary old bat* but was afraid she was the type who could read even his poor handwriting upside down.

"Are you ready?" she asked.

Ready for what? "Yes," he stood with pen poised over his notebook. "Of course."

"Then I'll tell you everything you need to know."

So it was true what he'd heard about small towns and gossip. Someone had already informed the librarian that he was on the hunt for inside information about Shelly Frazier, and she couldn't wait to give him all the dirt.

He slipped a small digital recorder—twin to the one he'd given Mindy—from his pocket. "Maybe I'd better record this," he said. "I don't want to miss a word."

Cassie nodded in approval and waited while he turned on the device and set it between them. Conscious of her watching, he spoke into the recorder. "Interview with Miss Cassie Wynock, head librarian of the Eureka County Library and president of the historical society." He leaned back. "Proceed whenever you wish."

She cleared her throat, folded her hands in front of her, and began speaking. "My great-grandfather, Festus Wynock, came to this area in 1889. In 1890, he founded the town of Eureka. Along with my great-grandmother, Emmaline, he began a tradition of instilling a rich culture and respect for our heritage that persists to today. As the sole remaining heir to the Wynock heritage, I felt it was my duty—"

"Whoa. Wait a minute, Cassie." Travis held up a hand to silence her. "While I'm sure your family history is a fascinating story, I'm not sure it's pertinent to the matter at hand."

She stared at him, owl-eyed behind steel-framed spectacles. "Not pertinent? Of course it's pertinent. Without my great-grandparents, there would be no Eureka today. The Founders' Pageant is all about them."

"Founders' Pageant?" What did this have to do with Shelly?

"This was all in the press release I sent. Didn't you read it?"

"I never saw a press release."

"I faxed it over last Thursday. All about how this year's show is going to be bigger and better than ever."

"You sent a press release about a local pageant to the *Dallas Morning News*?"

"We get a great many visitors from Texas, so I thought it would be of interest. When you said you were from the paper, I naturally assumed that's why you were here."

He nodded. Clearly, the woman was a little nuts, but that didn't mean she couldn't be a good source of information. "The press release must have arrived while I was already on my way to speak with you about another matter," he said.

The V between her eyes deepened. "This isn't more about Gerald Pershing, is it?" she asked. "Because I really don't want to talk about him. I hardly knew the man."

"Who the hell is Gerald Pershing?"

Cassie pruned up her lips. "There's no need for profanity."

He took a deep breath. Time to calm down. "I don't care about this Pershing guy, whoever he is. I wanted to ask you about Shelly Frazier."

"Shelly Frazier?" Now Cassie looked as confused as he had been.

"I understand she's a member of the historical society."

"Yes, she's currently our secretary, but I can't imagine that little mouse has done anything to warrant mention in the paper."

"It's not anything she's done lately that interests our readers." He leaned forward, glad to be back in control of the conversation. "They care about Shelly because of something that happened when she was a child. Do you remember a story twenty-five years ago, about a child trapped in an underground cavern in North Texas? Everyone called her Baby Shelly."

"You think our Shelly is Baby Shelly?" Cassie eyed him skeptically. "I'm sure she's much too old."

"She's thirty. And I know she was Baby Shelly. I confirmed the information with her yesterday."

"Thirty? I was sure she was at least forty. Sharon!"

The assistant popped out from between the stacks, like a prairie dog shooting out of a burrow. "Yes, Cassie?"

"How old is Shelly Frazier?"

"I'm not sure. Maybe early thirties?"

"I thought she was older."

"No, I don't think so."

"I don't really think—" Travis began.

"Did you know that Shelly Frazier was Baby Shelly?" Cassie ignored him and directed the question at her pretty assistant.

"Well, I, um, I guess I assumed she was a baby once," Sharon said. "I mean, we all were."

"Oh, you're too young." Cassie waved her away and turned her attention back to Travis. "What does any of this have to do with me?"

"I'm looking for the people in town who know Shelly best." He lowered his voice, his tone confiding. "Since the two of you work together closely in the historical society, and since you are a longtime resident with a clearly observant nature, I'm sure you could provide the kind of detail that really enriches a story like this."

"You think I have all the dirt on Shelly and I'll give it to you."

He grinned. "I wouldn't put it quite that way, but yes. I want you to tell me everything you know about Shelly today, so that I can provide a complete picture for my readers."

She crossed her arms over her chest. Oh, she was a shrewd one, all right. A woman who was used to getting what she wanted. If he wanted her to talk, he'd have to sweeten the deal. "I'd be sure to include a mention of the Founders' Pageant with your comments," he said.

"I can't help." She pressed her lips tightly together, a sealed vault.

So she wanted to play hard to get. Never mind. He knew how to handle difficult people like her. "I'm sure whatever information you can provide will be very helpful," he said.

"I can't give you any dirt on Shelly because there isn't any to give," she said. "The woman does her job and keeps quiet. She's devoted to her family and she never makes waves."

"Seriously? Nobody's that perfect."

"You're wasting your time and mine. Move along." She actually made a shooing motion with one hand, as if he was a five-year-old walking too near her flower beds. Her steely gaze made it clear he wasn't going to get anything more out of her. The assistant, Sharon, had disappeared back among the stacks. Travis switched off the recorder and pocketed it.

"Thank you for your time, *Ms.* Wynock," he said, and left the building.

Outside, standing on the sidewalk, bright sun almost blinding him, he debated his next move. If all the people in town were like Cassie, thinking Shelly was a saint, he wasn't going to get anywhere. What he needed to find was someone who didn't like Shelly Frazier. The woman her husband had dumped in order to marry her, or the clerk she'd beaten out for the job at the bank. Where was the cranky neighbor or jealous rival? Those were the kinds of people who would give him the juicy quotes readers wanted. He couldn't make Shelly look too bad—after all, people still had a soft spot for sweet Baby Shelly. But as much as they'd loved the innocent toddler, they'd take delight in knowing she'd had at least a little more tragedy in her life, and that she'd made mistakes, just as they had. He couldn't even think of what he was doing as digging up dirt, really. He was only gathering material to make Shelly more sympathetic. More human.

He checked his phone. Only ten-thirty. Too early to talk to the patrons of the Dirty Sally. Later, if he could buy a few drinks for the right person, no telling what he could find out. But not now. For now, he'd stop by the local newspaper. In a town this small, a fellow journalist might have just the information he needed.

On Monday, Mindy made herself wait until noon before she headed into town. She'd spent Sunday trying to get Shelly to open up about her past, but her sister had refused to talk about anything juicy at all. Shelly had passed the day cook-

ing and sewing and reading; Mindy had been ready to run
screaming from the house, she was so bored. She'd telephoned
Travis to complain, but he'd been no help. He was spending
the afternoon in his motel room, watching a ball game and
drinking beer. "Every assignment has some down time," he
said. "You have to learn to suck it up."

Easy for him to say; he wasn't staying with a sister who
didn't even have cable. She took a deep breath and straightened her shoulders. Never mind. She could finally get to
work and be on her way to getting back to the city, where she
belonged. Ten minutes ago, she'd watched Shelly head out on
her lunch break. Now was Mindy's chance to interview her
coworkers.

The Eureka Bank occupied a gray stone pile crouched in a
grove of blue spruce, each tree protected by a chicken-wire
cage. Trees in bondage. A good name for a rock band. She
laughed at her own joke. She'd have to try it out on a local—
if she ever met anyone who might actually get it.

A white banner with red and blue letters stretched over the
bank's wide front door advertised something called Hard
Rock Days. Mindy paused to read the dates. Was this little
town really hip enough to have a rock festival? Maybe she
wouldn't die of boredom after all.

The inside of the bank featured two desks, two smaller
glassed-in offices, two tellers' windows behind a brown granite counter, and a few green plants Mindy would bet were
fake. One of the tellers, a stocky blonde wearing an unbe-
coming shade of yellow, leaned out over the counter and
beamed at Mindy. "May I help you?"

Mindy glanced at the woman's nameplate. Tamarin. "Hi,
Tamarin. I'm Mindy Payton—Shelly's sister."

Confusion clouded the blonde's baby blues. "Shelly?"

"Shelly Frazier. I'm her younger sister."

"Shelly's sister!" Tamarin's voice rose to a squeal. "I had
no idea. Does Shelly know you're here?"

"I'm staying at her house. You know, catching up on old

times." Mindy laughed, keeping the tone light, not the mule bray that sounded so much like their mom. "I popped in to surprise her, hoping we could have lunch."

"Oh, hon, you just missed her. But she usually goes home for lunch. You want me to call and see if she's there?" She already had the phone in her hand.

"Oh no, don't bother her." The last thing Mindy wanted was for Shelly to know she was here, snooping around. "I'll meet up with her later anyway. I just thought it would be fun to see where she works." She tried to keep an expression of avid interest as she looked around the bank. A middle-aged man in one of the offices was talking on the phone, a serious expression on his face. Was he turning down a loan applicant? Calling about a late payment? More likely, he was building a fantasy football team or planning a fishing trip. No other employees—or customers—were in sight. Travis had suggested she pump Shelly's coworkers for information, but what, exactly, was she supposed to find out?

"There's not much to the place." Tamarin waved her hand to take in the small area.

That was definitely an understatement. Mindy could imagine few things more mind-numbing than to be stuck here all day, having to smile and be nice to everyone who came through the door. "Have you worked with Shelly long?" she asked.

"Oh gosh, forever. Or, at least ever since I came to Eureka." Tamarin wrinkled her nose in thought. "It's been five years now, I guess. I met her first at the historical society. She was pregnant with her youngest, and I'd just had my Tommy, so we had a lot in common. Then my husband, Tom, was killed in a mining accident and I had to go to work. Shelly told me about the job here and we've been working side by side ever since."

"So you two are pretty good friends?" Mindy leaned forward, her tone confiding.

"Oh, the best." Tamarin's smile faltered a little. "But she

never mentioned a sister. Come to think of it, she doesn't talk about her family at all. I kind of thought she didn't even have one."

Tamarin was giving Mindy the hairy eyeball now. Maybe she thought Mindy was a bank robber, trying to case the joint. Any second now, she'd push the button under the counter for a silent alarm and cops would surround the place. She'd better think fast.

"After the scandal, I think she was too ashamed to show her face," Mindy said. "But the rest of us never felt that way. Like I told her last night, we were always ready to welcome her back with open arms."

Tamarin's eyes widened until she resembled a Kewpie doll. "What scandal?"

"Oh, it was nothing, really." Mindy looked around again. "If she'd given the money back and apologized, she never would have had to leave town at all. But that's all water under the bridge. She has nothing to be ashamed of."

Tamarin's mouth hung open. Coupled with the goggle eyes, she resembled a cartoon frog. Mindy brightened her own smile. "I'll try to catch up with her at home. It was nice meeting you." As she pushed through the door onto the sidewalk, she glanced over her shoulder and saw Tamarin still gaping at her. She laughed. If she couldn't find out any good gossip about Shelly, she might as well make some up. See how Perfect Big Sister deals with that!

Monday afternoon, Maggie stared at her computer screen, mesmerized by the blinking cursor. She tried to focus on her article about the dangers of invasive weeds, but all she could think about was how much she wanted to sleep. Once upon a time, she had fantasized about hunky men and hot sex, but since the arrival of Angela her daydreams revolved around soft mattresses, crisp cotton sheets, and blissful slumber.

The cowbell attached to the paper's front door clanged and a lanky man with a fuzz of auburn hair around his head stepped in and looked around. He spotted her and reached her desk in three strides. "Travis Rowell, *Dallas Morning News*," he said, and offered his hand.

"Maggie Clark, *Eureka Miner*." She shook hands. "Can I help you?"

"You sure can." He grabbed the rolling chair that was usually occupied by Ellie Harrington, the ad sales rep/circulation manager/administrative assistant and general dogsbody, and rolled it over to face Maggie. "I stopped by Saturday afternoon, but your office was closed. In fact, pretty much everything in town seems to shut down over the weekend."

"We only put out the paper once a week," Maggie said. "So, unless something big is happening, we close at noon on Saturdays. What can I help you with?"

"I'm working on a story," he said. "A really big story. I'm hoping you can help me with some background info."

She rolled her chair back a little, unsure of the eagerness in his expression. She couldn't imagine anything in Eureka to get this excited about. "What kind of story?"

"What can you tell me about Shelly Frazier?"

She blinked, trying to put a face to the name. "Shelly from the bank?" Of all the people she might have guessed would be involved in something newsworthy, Shelly was not one of them.

"Right. What do you know about her?"

"Nothing, really. I mean, she's very nice."

"No one is nice all the time."

"Some people are." Though she wasn't so sure about him. He was starting to make her uncomfortable. "Why do you want to know about Shelly?"

He looked around, as if to verify they were alone, then leaned toward her, his voice low. "Can you keep a secret?"

"It depends on the secret." She was, after all, a reporter. And if this story was really so big . . .

"Shelly Frazier is Baby Shelly."

"Who?"

"Baby Shelly. The cute little girl who was trapped in the underground cavern in North Texas twenty-five years ago."

Maggie remembered now. She'd been fifteen at the time. She and her mother—and everyone else she knew—had been glued to the television as the dramatic search for the curly-haired tot unfolded. When rescuers had finally pulled the little girl, dirty and bruised, from beneath the ground, Maggie and her mom had hugged each other and cried happy tears. But she had a hard time connecting that child with the sweet but reserved mom and wife who cashed her checks at the Eureka Bank. "Are you sure?" she asked.

"Absolutely. She confirmed it to me herself yesterday."

"That's interesting, but since that all happened so long ago, I don't see how it's big news."

"How long have you been a reporter?"

Maggie stiffened. She'd taken the job with the *Miner* the year before, when she'd first arrived in Eureka. She had no journalism degree, but she could compose a grammatical sentence and was willing to work for the poverty wages the paper provided. "I don't see what that has to do with anything," she said.

"If you'd been around very long at all, you'd realize that the twenty-fifth anniversary of almost anything is news, especially if the person involved has been hiding from the press for the past decade."

He made it sound as if Shelly had been living as a recluse or something. "Shelly has been working at the bank and taking care of her family," she said. "She's not a fugitive from justice."

"She moved, changed her name, and she refuses to talk to the press."

"She has the right to her privacy." Though Maggie didn't know Shelly very well, she liked her, and she felt the need to defend her from this abrasive man.

"People all over the world feel invested in her story," he said. "It's my job to give that to them."

"So talk to Shelly. I don't see how I could help you, anyway."

"I'm looking for background on her life here in Eureka. What she's like, things she's done . . ."

"I can't help you."

"Then point me toward someone who can." He pulled a reporter's notebook and the stub of a pencil from the back pocket of his jeans—a quaint touch in this day of smartphones and tablet computers. "Who's the biggest gossip in town?"

"Eureka isn't like that!"

"Of course it is. All small towns are."

"You'd better leave now."

He stuffed the notebook back into his pocket. "As soon as I do, you're going to call Shelly, aren't you?"

That was exactly what Maggie intended to do, but she'd never admit it to him. "Go," she said.

He stood, his expression still smug, and flipped a card onto the desk in front of her. "If you learn anything interesting, give me a call," he said. "And don't try to scoop me on this. My paper can afford a lot of lawyers and they're not afraid to use them."

Chapter 5

Maggie resisted the urge to make a rude gesture to Travis Rowell's back as he left her office. She waited until she was sure he was out of sight before she picked up the phone and punched in the number for the bank.

On the second ring, the door from the street burst open and Cassie rushed in, face flushed and out of breath. "I thought I saw that reporter fellow come in here," she gasped.

"What reporter fellow?" Maggie was curious to hear Cassie's take on Travis Rowell.

"He says he's from the *Dallas Morning News,* but I bet he's really working for one of those scandal sheets—the *Inquisitor,* or whatever it's called."

"The *Enquirer?*"

"I might have known you were familiar with it." Cassie dropped into the chair Travis had vacated.

"How do you know him?" Maggie asked.

"He came by the library Saturday morning. What did he want from you?"

"You first," Maggie said. "Why did he come to the library?"

Cassie narrowed her eyes, apparently debating whether to hold her ground, but curiosity—or maybe impatience—won out over stubbornness. "He wanted me to tell him everything I know about Shelly Frazier. He said something about her being Baby Shelly—the toddler who was trapped in that cavern in Texas years and years ago."

"That's what he told me, too," Maggie said. "I wonder why he came to you first."

Cassie sat up straighter. "Libraries are always a source of information."

"And maybe someone told him you work with Shelly on the historical society." And that she might very well be one of the biggest gossips in a town full of them.

"Yes, but I certainly didn't know this about her. I'm still not sure I believe him. If it's true, why has Shelly kept it a secret?"

"She's a private person. Or maybe she's trying to avoid being hassled by people like Travis Rowell. Guys like him give journalists a bad name."

Cassie made her sour lemon face again. "He made me believe he was here to write a story about the Founders' Pageant."

"For the *Dallas Morning News*?"

"Well, certainly not for the *Enquirer*."

"Why would people in Dallas be interested in anything going on in Eureka, Colorado?" Maggie asked.

Cassie sat forward on her chair, back rigid. "What happened here in Eureka is historically significant, not only for Colorado but for the country. Towns don't just spring up unassisted, you know. My ancestors made a vital contribution and . . ."

Maggie closed her eyes. Cassie was off and running now. She should have known better than to stir her up. "I get it, Cassie," she interrupted. "But setting that aside for a moment, how are we going to keep this Rowell character from hassling Shelly?"

"I really don't see that as our responsibility. If she couldn't even trust us enough to confide in us, I don't think we owe her any special consideration."

"She's a friend. And friends look out for each other."
Though Maggie wasn't sure Cassie had any real friends. But if
she made more of an effort to help others, that could change.

"Maybe she should give him what he wants. Talk to him
and he'll leave her alone. Besides, it could be a good thing for
the town, to have it known that Baby Shelly is living here."

Maggie stared at her, trying to choose her words carefully.
She didn't want to send the librarian off on another rant but
honestly, was Cassie crazy? "How do you figure that?" she
asked.

"Tourists would come to see her. We could even find a way
to incorporate her story into the Founders' Pageant. Make it
a draw."

"You're serious, aren't you? You'd take advantage of that
poor woman to make a buck."

She bowed up again, indignant. "I despise a mercenary
mentality, but no one is more loyal to Eureka than I am. I
have accepted that a certain amount of pandering to out-
siders is necessary to keep the community coffers full. And
since Shelly already lives here . . ."

"It's a horrible idea, Cassie. Don't do it."

The librarian rose. "Don't try to tell me what to do."

"Shelly won't cooperate with you."

"We'll see about that." She turned and left, the heels of her
sensible shoes striking the wood floor with an almost military cadence.

Now Maggie absolutely had to talk to Shelly, and warn
her not only about Travis, but about Cassie as well. She
picked up the phone again, but she hadn't punched in the
first number before the door opened again and private detective Duke Breman stepped in. "Hello, Maggie," he said.

"Hello, Mr. Breman." She laid the phone on the desk and
busied herself straightening the papers in her in-box. His direct gaze—not to mention his movie-star good looks—un-
nerved her.

"I wanted to look through your archives," he said. "I'm interested in any articles you might have written about Gerald Pershing."

"We never did a feature on him, if that's what you're wondering," she said.

"I want to see anything that mentions him."

"His name probably comes up in some of the articles about town council meetings," she said. "When he proposed the town invest with his company, and later, when he was half-owner of the Lucky Lady Mine. And of course, there were plenty of articles when he was trapped in the mine after the explosion."

"I want to see all of them."

Maggie checked the clock. It was almost five. "I have to leave in a few minutes. You can come back tomorrow, or you can go to the library. They keep the last year or so of papers in their stacks, and they're open until six."

He made a face. "I'll come back here tomorrow. I'd rather not have to deal with that librarian."

She laughed, amused that a big, tough guy like Duke could be cowed by the town curmudgeon. "Cassie's bark is a lot worse than her bite."

"I'll check back with you in the morning."

He started to leave when an idea struck her. "Have you met a man here in town, Travis Rowell?" she asked. "He showed up about the same time you did, says he's a reporter for the *Dallas Morning News*."

Duke shook his head. "I haven't met him. Why? Is he asking about Gerald Pershing also?"

"No. He wants to know about Shelly Frazier, the bank teller."

Duke's expression remained blank. "I only want to know about Pershing."

"I just thought you might have met up with him, seeing as how you're both from Texas."

"It's a big state."

Well, it had probably been a crazy idea, anyway, thinking the two strangers were linked. "If you do find out where Gerald went, punch him once for me," she said.

"I'll add you to the list." He turned away again, but paused with his hand on the doorknob. "What can you tell me about Lucille Theriot?" he asked.

Maggie bit back a groan. What was it with these nosy strangers, asking about her friends? "Lucille is very nice. She's smart and funny and a good friend. If you want gossip about her, you won't get it from me."

He nodded. "I wasn't looking for gossip. I'm having dinner with her tonight and I wanted to know what to expect."

"I guess you'll have to show up and find out."

By the time he had left and Maggie finally made her phone call to the bank, it was after five and they were closed. She debated trying to find Shelly's home number, but decided it would be better to wait until the next day and talk to her in person. Besides, she needed to get home and start supper. She and Jameso had a rare night home together, and she didn't want to miss it.

She shut down her computer and was gathering her purse to leave when the door opened once more and Jameso entered, Angela in his arms.

Maggie's heart beat a little faster and she caught her breath at the sight of father and daughter—her family. She still wanted to pinch herself sometimes, knowing her life had taken an exceptionally lucky turn when she'd come to Eureka. She'd arrived in town, a broke, unemployed new divorcée and ended up married to the handsomest guy in town, with the baby she'd always wanted but thought she'd never have.

"Hello there." She moved out from behind the desk and kissed first Jameso, then Angela. "What a nice surprise. Did you come to walk me home?" Tonight was his night off from the Dirty Sally, a night when they could eat dinner as a family and go to bed at the same time, something she always looked forward to. "If you're very good, I'll let you carry my books."

"And kiss you behind the lilac bushes?" He shook his head. "Sorry, but I'll have to pass. I promised D. J. and Josh I'd help them with something."

"Help them with what?"

"It's a surprise." He deposited Angela's diaper bag on her desk. "I shouldn't be too late."

"What about dinner?" she asked, dismay and confusion warring.

"We're just going to grab something."

"I meant what about dinner for us? This is one of the few nights a week we have together and I was really looking forward to it."

"Sorry. I promised the guys."

What about me? she wanted to whine, but he'd already left.

She cradled the baby to her shoulder and watched him leave, a tall, long-legged figure striding down the street away from her. While she'd been looking forward to an evening surrounded by family, he apparently couldn't wait for an excuse to get away. After only three months, were marriage and fatherhood wearing on him?

When they'd met, Jameso had been a restless figure on a fast motorcycle, a man with a reputation as a fighter and a womanizer and a rogue, a younger version of her father, Jameso's best friend. She'd immediately pegged him as not relationship material, but hormones—and maybe fate—had pushed them together. She had dared to hope love had changed him, but really, wasn't that the stuff of fairy tales and romance novels?

Jameso was Jameso, and she ought to love him in spite of, or even because of, his flaws and foibles. But if it was true that people didn't really change their basic natures, for love or any other reason, then Jameso would always be the irresponsible playboy he'd been when they met, and she'd always be the fatherless divorcée who had trouble trusting men. It didn't seem the best pairing in the world, or one designed to foster the happily ever after she'd spent years longing for.

Chapter 6

This is not a date. Lucille sipped from her water glass, then set it precisely in the middle of the coaster on the table in front of her in the booth in the Last Dollar Café. She avoided staring toward the door, aware that the handful of locals in the restaurant—and maybe even some of the tourists—were watching her. Monday evenings were not the busiest time in the restaurant, but why had she told Duke Breman she'd meet him here? She'd put him off as long as she could, but the man was nothing if not persistent. She should have insisted they talk at the shop, during regular business hours. Dinner together was too much like a date.

Even though it wasn't.

The door opened and she jerked her head up in time to see the private detective enter the restaurant. He nodded to the owner, Danielle, then indicated that he'd be joining Lucille, though he hadn't looked directly at her yet. Had he scoped out her location from the sidewalk? She pressed her palms flat on the table to keep from fidgeting as he made his way to the booth.

"Hello, Lucille." His voice was a deep rumble that vibrated through her. So much for thinking she could treat this as a normal business meeting. Every nerve in her body was fluttering, reminding her she was a woman and this was the sexiest man to hit town in a good while. He slid into the booth across from her. "Sorry I kept you waiting."

"I'm one of those people who shows up everywhere early," she said. At least she sounded calm.

"That shows you're very responsible and conscientious. Good qualities in a mayor."

She supposed she ought to be reassured he was thinking of her as merely a politician, but the disappointment left a bitter taste in her mouth. She took another drink of water. "Did you have some questions for me? Though I'm not sure I'll be much help to you."

"Let's order dinner first. Then we can talk."

As if she'd been waiting for her cue, Janelle, the other owner of the café, glided forward. Tall and lithe, she wore a pink bandana twisted in her short blond hair, and a T-shirt that depicted a trio of kittens. "What can I get for you two?" she asked, her German accent making even these words sound exotic. "Today's special is pork chops and mashed potatoes. We also have a very good vegetable lasagna."

"I'll have the pork." Duke handed over his menu. "And iced tea."

"The lasagna, and a side salad with ranch. No onions."

"No onions." Janelle winked. "Will do."

Lucille bit back a groan. Janelle wasn't known as a gossip, but all it would take would be the wrong person overhearing her order to decide that the mayor had plans for a hot and intimate evening with the newest handsome stranger in town. After all, she had a history . . .

"Everyone tells me if I want to know about Gerald Pershing, I should talk to you," Duke said. "That you knew him best."

"Everyone says that, do they?"

"Word is you had an affair with him."

Well, it wasn't as if that was a big secret considering how she'd made such a fool of herself over him. She took another sip of water, wondering if she should excuse herself to go to the ladies' room and gather her composure. But no, she was almost used to talking about the sordid events now. "I'm not sure 'affair' is the right word. We went out a couple of times and slept together one night. When I woke the next morning, he was gone, and most of the town's money with him. I was seduced and swindled. The first time he met me, he must have seen 'sucker' written in large letters on my forehead."

"Or perhaps he saw an attractive, interesting woman whose company he could enjoy, while still achieving his goal of getting money from the town."

Oh, he was a smooth talker. But she was too old for such flattery. "That still makes me a sucker."

"Yet he came back to Eureka, a few months after he left."

She nodded. "Yes, he did. He said he wanted to make things up to me, but I'm sure he was merely looking for another easy target."

"You sold him shares in the Lucky Lady Mine."

"The town had taken the mine in lieu of back taxes. We sold him shares we thought were worthless. But they turned out not to be."

Danielle delivered his tea and he stirred sugar into it. "Good thing for the town's economy."

"Good and bad. Now we were partners with a man we all despised."

He instantly became more alert, like a dog on point. "All of you? Or you most of all?"

"I think it's safe to say there was no love lost between Gerald Pershing and anyone in this town. As half-owner of the mine, he had a say in its operations, and he took every opportunity to make things difficult. No one was sorry to see him go."

"Why did he go?"

"He didn't confide in any of us that I know of. He just left. Maybe after being trapped five days in a collapsed mine tunnel, he'd had enough."

"That would be the kind of experience that could make a man question his actions in life," Duke said. "But the timing seems odd. He didn't even stay around long enough to recover from that ordeal."

"He wanted to be away from us, I guess."

"Yet he did transfer his interest in the mine to the manager, Bob Prescott."

"They were trapped together all that time. Maybe he felt he owed Bob. I don't know."

"I tried to set up a meeting with Prescott, but he's put me off. Maybe you could put in a good word for me."

She laughed. "Bob doesn't take advice from anyone. If you want to talk to him, buy him a few beers at the Dirty Sally. When he's lubricated enough, he might change his mind about you."

"I'll keep that in mind. Anyone else I should talk to while I'm here? Someone he might have confided in?"

"I thought I'd made it clear Gerald didn't make friends while he was here."

He shrugged. "My job is to keep asking questions. Sometimes I get answers that lead to solutions."

"I've tried to answer your questions—now I have a few of my own." All this talk about Gerald's nefarious deeds had definitely made her less nervous around the detective. "Why are you so interested in finding Gerald?"

"My client is paying me well to do so. And apart from the money, my reputation depends on me doing a good job."

"Who's your client?"

He shook his head. "That information is confidential."

"Then tell me why your client is so interested in tracking him down? Did he swindle someone else?"

"I can't tell you that, either, but if I did, I promise the answer would surprise you."

Danielle delivered their plates, steam rising from the lasagna in fragrant waves. Duke picked up his fork and eyed his pork chops approvingly. "I've eaten almost every meal here since I got to town, and every one has been excellent."

"We're lucky to have Janelle and Danielle. They could probably make a lot more money in a big city, but they like it here."

"Did Gerald eat here often?"

"I'm sure he did, but I doubt if he revealed where he was headed when he left here in between bites of a morning omelet and fried potatoes."

"You never know. Are you sure he didn't drop any hints to you? People get careless during pillow talk."

"We weren't talking that night." She felt her face heat. Say what she would about the man, he'd been very, um, thorough in bed. She hadn't had the breath—or any interest—in conversation.

He sliced off a piece of pork and chewed thoughtfully. She concentrated on her lasagna, but was aware of his eyes on her. What did he see? Was he wondering what Gerald had seen in a fiftysomething longtime divorcée who was tall and lanky and plain—not anyone's idea of a femme fatale?

"Let me run another idea by you," he said after a moment. "What if Pershing never left town?"

She blinked, and hastily swallowed a bite of pasta. "You mean, what if he's hiding out in the hills or something? I suppose anything is possible, but Eureka is a small place, and I doubt he'd be able to keep that kind of thing secret for long."

"I'm not talking hiding. What if someone did away with him before he left town?"

"Murder!" The word came out as a yelp, and half a dozen heads turned in their direction. She lowered her voice and leaned toward him. "That's crazy."

"You said everyone in town hated him."

"That doesn't mean they'd murder him. And why would they? He signed over his shares in the mine and said he wanted to leave. Why bother trying to stop him?"

"He left and came back once before. Maybe someone wanted a more permanent solution."

She laid down her fork, suddenly sick to her stomach. "I can't believe anyone I know would do such a thing."

"You might be surprised at what people will do. Maybe the murderer even did it to protect you."

"Me?" She stared, unable to breathe.

"Most of the people I've talked to have a fairly high opinion of you. They all talk about how Pershing embarrassed you. One of them might have decided to solve the problem by doing away with him altogether."

The idea was horrifying. Yet fascinating, too. "If someone killed him, what did they do with the body?"

"Stuffed it down an abandoned mine shaft. Tossed it over a cliff. I imagine there are a million places you could lose a body around here."

"In that case, you might never find him."

"All I need to find is evidence that points in that direction. If I can't find his body, I might find his car, or his belongings. Those things are harder to get rid of."

She shook her head. "This is crazy. I won't believe it."

"If something does turn up, I'll take what I find back to my client, and to the police. It will be up to them to decide what to do next."

"I hope for everyone's sake this isn't true. I'd rather that Gerald is lying on some Caribbean beach somewhere, living off his ill-gotten gains."

"If I do find evidence that suggests he was murdered, you know you'll be the primary suspect, don't you?"

"Me!" Again, she drew stares from the others in the café. She swallowed. "I did not murder anyone. Why would you think that?"

He buttered a slice of bread and tore off a bite. "You have the most to gain from Gerald Pershing's death."

"I don't see how you can say that."

She had to wait for him to finish chewing before she got an answer. He took a drink of tea, then looked her in the eye, his gaze searching, and surprisingly tender. "I probably shouldn't tell you this, but maybe you have a right to know," he said.

"Know what?" She resisted the urge to grab him by the collar and shake him.

"Pershing left a will. If he is dead or declared dead, half of his assets will go to you."

Wednesday was Maggie's next day to work. She fully expected to come to work that morning and find Rick demanding that she write a story about the discovery of Baby Shelly right here in Eureka. If Cassie already knew about it, not to mention Mindy and no telling who else, it was only a matter of time before word got back to Rick.

But he remained mute on the subject, instead telling her to write an article about this year's Hard Rock Miner competition.

"All right," she agreed. "Do we have a list of this year's entrants?"

"I've got it here somewhere." He dug around on his cluttered desktop and extracted a sheet torn from a yellow legal pad, one side covered with his precise, narrow handwriting. "Here you go."

She squinted at the paper. "Badger, Dangerous Dave, the Human Dynamo, the Dark Knight . . . Is this some kind of joke?"

"It's a tradition for entrants to use assumed names," Rick said. "That way, no one knows who is really competing until the last day. Or at least, they can pretend not to know. It's part of the fun."

"How am I supposed to write about these guys when I don't even know who they are?" she asked.

"Use your imagination. Have fun with it."

She shook her head, but resigned herself to the task and moved back toward her desk.

"Maggie?"

"Yes, Rick?"

"Don't you want to know what your dad's nickname was?"

"I'm afraid to ask." Her famously volatile father had won the Hard Rock Miner competition three years running; she had all of his trophies.

"He competed as the Mad Irishman. Fitting, don't you think?"

She might have pointed out that she couldn't judge the suitability of his nickname, since she had never known her father while he was alive. But she'd learned plenty about Jake since moving to Eureka. He was the kind of larger-than-life character who lingered in people's memories, maybe especially in a small town like this.

Rick was still chuckling to himself a few minutes later when he left the office. "I'm going to get a haircut," he said. "Hold down the fort while I'm gone."

"Sure." She glanced at the chair where Ellie usually sat; the older woman had Wednesdays off, because she kept her two grandchildren for her daughter, who worked a double shift that day at the hospital in Grand Junction. Now, when Maggie had the office to herself, would be the perfect time to knock out the Hard Rock Miner article, but it also might be her best chance to talk to Shelly. She should have tried to reach her yesterday, but she and Jameso had the day off together and—perhaps because he felt guilty about ditching her Monday night—he'd suggested a picnic in the mountains. They'd ended up waiting out an afternoon thunderstorm in the cabin her father had left her, making love in the bedroom while Angela slept, rain drumming on the tin roof, lightning splitting the sky with brilliant bolts.

Needless to say, Maggie hadn't thought of Shelly until this morning, when she'd awakened late, filled with a sense of dread.

She'd already put off the task as long as possible, but she really couldn't wait any longer. No telling who Travis Rowell would blab to next. She called the bank first, and Tamarin Sherman answered the phone. "This is Shelly's Wednesday afternoon off," she said.

"Thanks. I'll call her at home. Good-bye."

"Wait!"

"What is it?" Maggie asked.

Tamarin lowered her voice. "Have you heard anything about some . . . some scandal Shelly was involved in?"

Maggie stiffened. "A scandal?"

"Something to do with money? Maybe she stole it or something?"

"Shelly? That doesn't sound like her at all." And it certainly didn't have anything to do with Baby Shelly.

"I know, right? But her sister said something the other day that made me think . . . oh, never mind."

"Have you asked Shelly about this?" Maggie asked. "What does she say?"

"I haven't said anything to her yet. I don't know what to think."

"I haven't heard anything like that. Maybe you misunderstood her sister."

"That must be it. I should just call Shelly and ask her. If you talk to her before I do, don't say anything, okay?"

"I won't. I promise."

She ended the call with Tamarin, then looked up Shelly's home number in the local phone book—which actually included numbers for everyone in three counties, since the listings for Eureka alone would have made up only a phone pamphlet—and punched it in.

Shelly answered on the third ring. "Hello?"

"Hey, Shelly, it's Maggie Clark."

"Oh, hi, Maggie, what's up?"

"I'm sorry to bother you on your afternoon off, but something happened the other afternoon that I have to ask you about."

"Oh?" Apprehension weighted the single syllable.

"That reporter from Dallas, Travis Rowell, stopped by the office Monday afternoon."

"What did he want?"

Maggie's stomach knotted, but she took a deep breath and pushed on. After all, her job was to ask hard questions, wasn't it? "He told me you were Baby Shelly—the toddler they pulled out of that cave in Texas twenty-five years ago. Is that true?"

"Maggie, I don't want to talk about this." Shelly didn't sound angry, merely weary.

"I just wanted to find out if it's true, or if he's spreading a false rumor."

"It happened a long time ago. I don't know why anyone wants to bring it up."

"People still remember," Maggie said. "I remember. You were, well, you were a part of our lives. I think people still care and would like to know what happened to you."

"Maggie, please don't write about this for the paper. If you do, other papers will pick it up and it will be reprinted all over the country and the next thing I know I'll have people camping out on my front porch, wanting interviews."

"If Travis writes about you for the *Dallas Morning News* it's going to be out there anyway," Maggie said. "At least I'll tell the truth, not some sensationalized version designed to grab headlines."

"According to Mindy, he doesn't work for the *Dallas Morning News*. I mean, he apparently did at one time, but now he's strictly freelance, and as far as I can tell, he hasn't sold my story because I won't talk to him. And I'm sorry, but I don't want to talk to you, either."

"I'll admit I'm disappointed, but I'll respect your privacy."

"No one understands," Shelly said. "But haven't you ever had something in your life you didn't want to relive in the papers?"

Maggie recalled the days following her husband's announcement that he was leaving her for an older, richer woman. As Maggie was a Junior Leaguer and best friend to prominent socialite Barbara Stanowski, her impending divorce had caught the attention of a Houston gossip columnist. She still remembered the sick feeling that had engulfed her when she read the two-line item in that writer's weekly column in the *Houston Chronicle*. Her private shame was there in black and white for everyone to see. She'd called Barb, practically hysterical, demanding to know what she could do to stop this. Barb had gently urged her to calm down and accept that she could do nothing but wait for this to pass.

But what if the scandal had been so big and compelling that it hadn't faded from the public's memory overnight? How much worse to know that whenever anyone looked at you, they were thinking not of you, but of something that had happened to you? Something that hadn't even been your fault?

"I'm sorry," Maggie said. "I hadn't thought about how traumatic being trapped like that must have been for you. Of course you wouldn't want to relive it."

"Being trapped in that cavern wasn't nearly as traumatic as everything that happened afterward," Shelly said. "All the attention and publicity made it impossible for me to have a normal childhood. I've worked hard to build a quiet, ordinary life for myself and my family. The last thing I want is to expose myself and my children to the circus that was everyday life growing up."

"I understand and I respect that," Maggie said. "And don't worry—I'll respect your confidence. I may be a reporter, but I'm your friend first."

"Thanks. I wish everyone else was as understanding, but I figure as long as I don't talk to them, they won't have much to write about—though I'm not sure that's enough to stop Travis."

"Is he a friend of your sister's? I've seen them together around town."

"I don't think they're friends, exactly. I think he's latched on to her to try to get to me." She sighed. "I've got to go now. I've got brownies in the oven."

"Good-bye. And don't worry about me."

"Thanks, Maggie. I really appreciate it."

Maggie hung up the phone and stared at the page in her notebook, on which she'd written *Shelly Frazier = Baby Shelly?* She tore out the page and crumpled it into a ball. The conversation with Shelly had left her feeling sad and out of sorts, as if she'd spent the day wearing clothes that were too tight. Here was this perfectly nice woman, living a quiet, happy life with her family, and then a reporter and her long-lost sister had shown up in town, spreading rumors and causing trouble.

Really, why couldn't people mind their own business and leave well enough alone? Why did something always have to interfere with people's happiness?

Chapter 7

"If Travis thinks he can hide from me in a town this small, he's got another think coming," Mindy muttered as she drove through what passed for downtown Eureka. Gravel popped beneath her tires as she slowed to make the turn onto Main. Honestly, what kind of town didn't even bother to pave the streets?

She passed under another big banner for Hard Rock Days. It snapped in the afternoon breeze, the liveliest thing on the otherwise still street. Mindy craned her neck, trying to see into the businesses, then slammed on her brakes when she caught a glimpse of curly hair in front of the hardware store, but it was only a tall woman. Where was Travis? She'd texted him twice and called and left a message, but he hadn't bothered to answer. Maybe his phone had flaked out on him. It wasn't like he could write this book without her, after all.

She sped up and swung onto Main. She'd check out the motel again. If nothing else, she could sit in the parking lot and wait for him. Anything was better than going back to Shelly's place, with those loud, wild boys and that husband of hers, who hardly said two words. In the evenings they did dumb stuff like play board games and read. If Mindy had to spend too many more nights with that bunch, she'd go crazy.

She sped up, anxious to get to the hotel, but she'd scarcely gone two blocks before the whoop of a siren attracted her attention. She swore when she looked in the mirror and saw the heart-stopping strobe of red and blue lights. Still swearing, she flipped on her blinker and pulled to the side of the road.

She watched in the rearview mirror as the cop, in a khaki-colored uniform and tan Stetson, stepped out of the patrol car and walked toward her. At least he was young. And good-looking, too. She smiled as he drew near enough for her to recognize him. Oh yeah. This could be very interesting.

"Hello, officer." She greeted him with a smile when he stopped by her window.

"Good afternoon, ma'am. Did you realize you were speeding?"

"Was I?" She put a hand to her chest in her best imitation of a flustered Southern belle. "I'm new in town and I'm not familiar with all the streets. I was trying to find my way and I wasn't paying enough attention to the signs, I'm afraid."

"May I see your driver's license and registration?"

"Certainly." She squinted at his name tag. "Officer Miller." She handed over the documents. "Didn't I see you in the Dirty Sally the other night?" He hadn't been in uniform, but she'd recognize those eyes anywhere.

He made a noncommittal noise and wrote something on his clipboard. "Wait here and I'll be right back," he said.

"Oh, I wouldn't dream of leaving," she purred. "Not when we were just getting to know each other."

While he returned to his patrol car to run her license or whatever it was they did, she refreshed her lipstick and fluffed out her hair. She'd read somewhere that men in these mountain towns outnumbered women. Even a guy as good-looking as Officer Miller would probably welcome the chance to get to know a beautiful newcomer, especially considering the decided lack of glamour among the local girls. Even though Mindy had no intention of staying in town long, she could at least make her visit more entertaining.

He returned and handed back her paperwork. "You were doing forty in a twenty-five-mile-per-hour zone," he said.

"Really?" She laughed. "I had no idea. I'm not normally a reckless driver or anything. I guess I was just so enthralled by the view, I forgot myself." She indicated the distant mountains, visible from any part of town.

"I thought you were trying to find your way." He continued writing, not looking at her.

"Well, that, too. I've only been in town five days. I'm visiting my sister, Shelly Frazier." Might as well let him know she wasn't an ordinary tourist, but practically a local herself.

The mention of Saint Shelly worked wonders. He looked up at her, his smile making him doubly handsome. "You're Shelly's sister?" he asked. "She is such a sweet woman."

"I'm her younger sister. From Dallas."

"Your license says Joshua."

"That's just a suburb. But I'm really a city girl."

"Guess you're feeling a little out of place in Eureka," he said.

"I am." She laughed again. "Of course, it's beautiful, but I could use some help learning my way around. Maybe you'd like to help a girl out and give me a tour sometime when you're not on duty."

"I'm sure Shelly would do a better job of showing you around. I've only been here a few months, myself."

"Was that your girlfriend I saw you with the other night? The pretty, dark-haired woman?"

"Not exactly." He turned the clipboard toward her. "I'm letting you off with a warning this time, but take it easy. Pretty much all the streets, until you get out to the highway, have a speed limit of twenty-five. Sign at the bottom, please."

She leaned forward to sign the clipboard, placing her hand

over his as she did so. "If she isn't your girlfriend, I definitely think the two of us should get together," she said.

He took the clipboard—and his hand—away. "Thanks, but I'm not interested." He touched the brim of his hat. "Have a nice evening. And tell Shelly I said hello."

He walked back to his patrol car, not even giving her a second glance. She rolled up her window and glared at her reflection in the rearview mirror. What was wrong with the men in this town? She was pretty, and fun to be with, and a lot sexier than anyone she'd seen around here. Honestly, most of them never seemed to wear anything but jeans and hiking boots. And they apparently didn't know what a flatiron or lip gloss was.

The officer tapped his horn and motioned for her to move out ahead of him. She put the car in gear and proceeded at a snail's pace, back onto the highway. As she neared the highway, she spotted a familiar pickup in the other lane, headed in to town. Travis!

Normally, she would have whipped around in a U-turn right then in order to follow him, but a check behind her showed the patrol car still on her bumper, so she put on her left blinker and turned into the motel parking lot. As the officer cruised past, she gave him the finger, but kept her hand in her lap. After all, she wasn't stupid.

Back in town, she had to do the same slow cruise up and down the streets, until she spotted Travis's rattletrap truck parked down from the Dirty Sally. She should have known he'd end up there. She parked beside him and headed inside.

The same hot guy was behind the bar again, no baby or wife in sight. Travis had staked out a table off to the side. Mindy stalked up to him and pulled out a chair. "I've been looking for you for the last hour," she said. "Why didn't you answer my texts or return my call?"

"I was busy." He sipped a dark beer.

Mindy spun around in her chair and signaled the waitress. "I'd like a strawberry daiquiri," she said.

"No blender drinks," the waitress said.

"What kind of a bar is this, if you can't get a daiquiri?"

"We have beer, shots, and mixed drinks."

Mindy wrinkled her nose. "I'll have a Tanqueray and tonic, then. And put it on his tab." She pointed to Travis.

"You ought to be paying for these drinks," he said. "You got a bigger percentage of the advance."

"I have my own expenses." She fluffed out her hair. "Looking this good doesn't come cheap."

He started to say something, then shook his head. "Never mind. What have you got for me so far? Has Shelly opened up any?"

"You first. What have you learned?"

"I've learned that everyone thinks your sister is perfect."

"Same song, thirteenth verse."

The waitress delivered the drink and Mindy took a long sip, then looked around. "Do they have any peanuts or anything? I'm starving."

"Focus." Travis leaned toward her. "I've been trying to find Shelly's enemies and there aren't any. Maybe you can help me out with some names."

"Why focus on her enemies?"

"Because they're the ones who will spill the dirt."

"I haven't found anybody who doesn't like her, either." She cracked a piece of ice between her teeth and Travis winced. "I went to the bank, like you suggested. The teller there claims to be her best friend, and she didn't even know she had a sister."

Travis nodded. "That might lead to some hard feelings. Did you tell this teller that her friend was Baby Shelly?"

"No. But I did let drop that she'd cut off contact with her family because of a scandal." She grinned. "A scandal involving money."

"Is that true?" He was already reaching into his pocket for his notebook.

"Not exactly." She sipped her drink, watching him over

the rim of the glass. Too bad he wasn't better looking, or rich. He was so easy to play.

"Was it, or wasn't it?"

"Well, when she left, she took the gravy train with her. Mama had a lot harder time getting cash out of the media without Shelly there to dangle in front of them. So that makes it at least partly about money."

He sat back, clearly disappointed. "Why did she break it off with you all?" he asked.

She shrugged. "I don't know."

"You know. You just don't want to say."

Where did he come off, being so smug? "I mean it, I really don't know. Everything was going along just fine, the way it always had. All the attention was on Shelly. She was the star. I was just the extra in her big show. The next thing I knew, she'd left."

He had the notebook out now, scribbling away. What did it matter? If this did ever get published, at least the world would know the truth about her sister.

"That must have been upsetting," he said.

"Are you kidding? I was glad she was gone. Now maybe I'd get some of the attention I deserved. But it didn't work out that way. My parents were devastated. If anything, they made her into even more of a saint. Every day my mom talks about how wonderful Shelly was and how much she misses her, and on the anniversary of her rescue—Shelly's birthday—she's a basket case for a week."

"Have you told Shelly any of this?"

She drained her glass and set it aside, ready for another. "Why should I give her the satisfaction of knowing how much she hurt us?"

"I don't think she's like that. I mean, I haven't spent a lot of time around her, but I've talked to a lot of people who know her, and I think if you told her, she'd feel guilty. Maybe even guilty enough to help us out."

"Shelly doesn't want to help us. She doesn't think about anybody but herself."

"Still, what have you got to lose if you talk to her?"

Her dignity. Pride. The knowledge that she still had something on her sister, something she might use against her one day, when the time was right. But Travis was a man. He wasn't going to understand any of that. Men always saw the world in black and white. They didn't understand all the shades of gray in a relationship between sisters.

"Where is that waitress?" She turned, searching for the hippie girl, but instead, saw Shelly walking in the door.

"Uh-oh," Travis said. "She doesn't look too happy."

Mindy's first instinct was to head for the ladies' room or look for a back door. But she didn't react fast enough. Shelly had already spotted them and was headed their way. So Mindy went to plan B. "Hey, Sis." She waved. "Come to have a drink with us?"

Shelly stopped beside their table, face red, eyes wild, practically vibrating with anger. It was nice to know Miss Cool and Collected did get rattled sometimes. "I need to talk to you two, now," she said, her voice tight.

"So have a seat." Mindy motioned to the chair beside her. "Talk."

Shelly glanced around, then dropped into the chair. "Tamarin called and told me you were at the bank Monday afternoon, while I was at lunch."

"Sorry I missed you. But your friend Tamarin and I had a nice chat."

"How could you lie like that about me?" She grabbed Mindy's wrist, hard. "Tamarin called, wanting to know what big scandal I'd been involved in in Texas, and what was this about money? And by the way, why didn't I tell her I had a sister?"

"Why didn't you tell her about me?" Mindy pulled out of Shelly's grasp. "Are you ashamed of me? Of your family?"

The truth was there in Shelly's eyes, even if she wouldn't admit it out loud. "I didn't want people to know about my past," she said softly. "I didn't want the hassle."

"Well, excuse me for not being ashamed of my relationship to you," Mindy said. "For admitting that I am your sister."

"But you lied about me. You said I stole money."

"I never said any such thing. She jumped to conclusions."

"Tamarin doesn't jump to conclusions. And I know you. Since the time you could talk, you've been a master at making up elaborate stories."

"Are you calling me a liar?"

"No, but you know how to exaggerate."

"Says the woman who never even told her best friend she has a sister. How do you think that made me feel?"

Shelly smoothed her hand across the tabletop, and took a deep breath. "This isn't a joke, Mindy. I work at a bank. Banks take these kinds of rumors very seriously. I'm afraid they're going to want to open an investigation."

"So let them investigate. They won't find anything. You'll still be Saint Shelly."

Travis's chair scraped back and he stood. "I'll let you ladies talk privately." He started to slip past, but Shelly caught hold of his sleeve.

"Don't you run away," she said. "Tamarin isn't the only one who called me this evening. Maggie Clark said you stopped by her office and told her I was Baby Shelly."

He crossed his arms over his chest. "What if I did? It's not a secret or a lie. It's a fact."

"But it was my secret to tell or not tell."

He shook his head. "I don't see it that way at all. And neither should you. You're just upset because your friends are hurt and angry that you couldn't be honest with them."

She pressed her hands to either side of her head, as if sheltering from a blow. "It's already started," she moaned. "All the attention I don't want."

Mindy glared at her. "Don't pull that pitiful act," she said. "No one is going to feel sorry for you. If you didn't want all the attention, why did you ever go down in that cave?"

Shelly dropped her hands into her lap and stared. "I was four years old. I didn't go down there on purpose."

Mindy shrugged. "You may have only been four, but you were smart. And you knew you weren't going to be the baby anymore. I was coming along, and I was going to be littler and cuter than you. You had to do something desperate to keep from losing the spotlight."

"I can't believe you're even saying that. I was a child. And I was terrified down there in that cave."

Travis had taken out his notebook and was writing again, no doubt taking down every word the sisters said, documenting Shelly's feelings about the long-ago incident.

"I'm just saying that along with the attention and the money and everything else that ordeal brought you, you ought to be happy to accept the few drawbacks," Mindy said. "And think about how much worse I have it, being your sister."

Shelly's chair scraped back and she stood. "There's obviously no reasoning with you. But you're right. You are my sister. And I'm sorry I didn't warn my friends about you. I won't kick you out, but you had better learn to keep your mouth shut. No more lies."

Mindy looked away. She wasn't going to promise Shelly anything.

"And you." Shelly had turned on Travis. "You can leave now. I don't have any intention of telling you anything. If you write a book about me, it won't be with my cooperation."

"It's a free country." Travis stuffed the notebook back into his pocket. "I'll hang around a few more days, talk to people."

"I'll keep talking, too," Mindy said. "You can't stop me."

Shelly's face crumpled. Mindy knew that look. Any minute now, her sister would either burst into tears, or start begging. *"Please don't do this. My life is so hard. . . ."* Mindy gritted her teeth. She wasn't going to fall for that pitiful act any-more. Shelly had everything—a job where she literally had bankers' hours, a husband who worshipped the ground she walked on, two kids who really weren't so bad—why should she begrudge Mindy anything?

But apparently, Shelly still had some surprises left for her sister. "No one will tell you anything you can use in your book," she said. "My life is boring and ordinary. There's nothing to talk about."

Mindy would never in a million years admit that Shelly was probably right. Her sister was painfully boring. And since she'd kept mum about her past, what could people in town say about her? *She was always such a quiet person. I had no idea. . . .* Mindy stood and gathered up her purse. "I think a big part of your problem is that there are too many things you haven't talked about. Too many secrets. I'm done with all that." She walked across the room, in the model's strut she'd learned in acting class, aware of the eyes of everyone on her. Mindy would never let herself be as boring as her sister. No one was watching Shelly now, and that was just the way Mindy liked it.

"I call this meeting of the Eureka Town Council to order." Lucille tapped the gavel on the table in the library meeting room Wednesday evening and surveyed the attendees. In addition to council members Katya Paxton, Junior Dominick, and Paul Percival, town attorney Reggie Paxton, and reporter Maggie Clark, Bob Prescott was present to give a report on the Lucky Lady Mine, and Cassie Wynock was here for . . . Lucille didn't know why Cassie was here, but she showed up more often than not to express her opinion and to push some private agenda. Most of the time the council ignored her, but that never discouraged the librarian.

A few townspeople were also in attendance, the usual political junkies and folks Lucille suspected had nowhere better to go. As entertainment, council meetings didn't rate very high, but the optimists always hoped to be present on the night someone—usually Cassie or Bob—stirred up trouble.

"Has everyone read the minutes from the last meeting?" she asked.

"No one reads the minutes," Katya, the council secretary and wife to Reggie, said, opening her notebook.

"We were all here last time," Junior said. "We don't need to read the minutes."

"I guess if I ever have trouble with insomnia, I could read them," Paul said.

"Would someone please make a motion so we can move on?" Lucille said.

Junior motioned to approve the minutes, Paul seconded, and the motion passed. Lucille consulted her copy of the agenda. "Bob, give us your report on the Lucky Lady."

Bob, dressed as usual in many-pocketed canvas pants and a plaid wool shirt held up by red suspenders, shuffled to his feet. Lanky and bent, with a tonsure of white hair and a bushy white moustache, he might have been sixty or eighty. He had the weathered, solid appearance of stone that was made to endure for centuries. "Everything's fine at the mine. We passed our safety inspection and we're making progress on that new drift on level three. The smelter we're using in B.C. reports good quality on the first haul of concentrate we sent to them."

"You should all have copies of the report the smelter sent in your folders," Katya said.

Everyone shuffled papers and found the report. Lucille had read it earlier. "We can go over the line items if anyone wants," she said. "But what's the bottom line, Bob?"

"They reckon we can pull gold out of there for at least eight more years at the rate of about nine million dollars' worth a year, after taxes."

"After taxes?" Paul let out a low whistle. "That kind of money could do some real good for our treasury."

"Except that half that money goes to Bob," Junior said. "What are you going to do with that kind of money?"

Bob tucked his thumbs under his suspenders. "I might buy me a new truck."

"Maybe you could start by buying a new pair of pants," Reggie said, and the room erupted in laughter.

Lucille waited for the noise to quiet down. "Anything else?" she asked.

"Do we really have to haul the stuff all the way to British Columbia for processing?" Junior asked.

"Unless we want to build a smelter of our own, yes," Bob said. "And you don't even want to get into the regulations involved in one of those. We're better off paying the freight to Canada."

"Thank you, Bob," Lucille said. "Moving right along, item number two is preparations for the Hard Rock Days festival. Junior, do you have a report?"

Junior, a large man who owned a trucking company, hefted himself to his feet. "Everything's going along on schedule," he said. "We got all the new banners hung and they look real nice, and we've contracted with a printer in Montrose to do the posters. Participants for the Hard Rock Miner competition have until next week to register, and we've signed up a good number of businesses and organizations to have craft or food booths in the park."

"I hope we get somebody in to make it a real competition this year," Bob said. "Since Jake Murphy died there hasn't been anybody to get excited about."

"We've been advertising at competitions out of state," Junior said. "We're hoping we'll pull in some national talent, as well as the locals."

"It's not as if driving steel drills with hammers is a common skill," Lucille noted.

"Well it ought to be," Bob said. "When the apocalypse comes and we don't have all this fancy electricity and such, people will have to rely on those old-fashioned skills."

Lucille made a mark on her paper, avoiding looking at Bob. At least they could always count on him to add a colorful opinion. "Moving on. Item number three—we need to address the invasive weeds mandate from the state."

"Those legislatures must be smoking weed, to think something like this is worth wasting time and money on," Bob grumbled.

Lucille ignored him. "We put out bids for mitigation to several concerns that specialize in this sort of thing," she said. "We asked for as nontoxic an approach as possible, and of course, we don't have a lot of extra funds in the budget for this sort of thing, so that may have put off some people."

"How many bids did we get?" Katya asked.

"One." Lucille fished the somewhat wrinkled and barely legible application from a file folder. "Daisy Mott. She has a herd of weed-eating goats over in the San Luis Valley and is willing to bring them here for a month or so and have them eat all the invasive weeds. Her fee is well within our budget and all we have to agree to is to erect temporary fencing to keep the goats contained while they work, and provide a place for her to park her camper."

"Goats? Are you serious?" Bob asked.

"I've checked with a couple of other places who have used Ms. Mott's services and they say it's about the best thing going, short of strafing everything with toxic chemicals. The animals eat the plants down to the roots and most of them don't come back. After a couple of years of grazing, the problem is gone."

"Sounds like a scam to me," Bob said. "After all, this place is overrun with deer, and they're not that different from goats. If they're not eating the weeds, why should a goat?"

"Does anyone who's actually on the council have an opinion on the matter?" Lucille asked.

"Is she just going to turn the goats loose to wander through town, or what?" Junior asked.

"The plan is for her to start in the town park, then clean up along that stretch of riverfront we own, and out at the town landfill. They'd work in fenced areas, and Ms. Mott and her dog would stay with them most of the time. I under-stand she has a trained Australian shepherd."

"Ernestine Wynock Park is filled with valuable flowers," Cassie said. "You can't let goats in there. They'll destroy the place."

"Ms. Mott says we can fence off the flowers," Lucille said. "They won't want most of them, anyway. You know yourself, Cassie, that the garden club planted mostly deer-resistant vari-eties. My guess is, that makes them goat-resistant, too."

Cassie's sour expression remained unchanged. "I still think it's a bad idea."

"I can't believe I'm agreeing with Cassie, but I am," Bob said. "Next thing you know, someone will convince you pigs control mosquitoes and we'll have them wandering through town."

"Whether we like it or not, the state is requiring us to do something to address the problem of invasive weeds," Lucille said. "Ms. Mott's services are within our budget, they aren't toxic to the environment, and they stand a good chance of working."

"I motion that we accept Ms. Mott's bid and hire her and her goats to take care of our weeds," Katya said.

"I guess we don't really have any choice," Paul said.

"We could ask for volunteers to pull weeds by hand," Lucille said. "But doing that could take weeks and I doubt anyone is enough of a glutton for punishment that they'd agree to work that long."

"I second the motion, then," Paul said.

Junior raised his hand to indicate his agreement, and Lucille pounded the gavel before anyone could object. Maggie stuck up her hand. "Could I get a copy of Ms. Mott's application?"

"Talk to me after the meeting." Lucille checked the agenda. "Next item."

"I have the next item of business." Cassie rose, an open note-book clutched to her chest.

"It says Founders' Days," Junior said. "What's that?"

"I'm proposing we change the name of the Hard Rock Days celebration to Founders' Days," Cassie said.

"No way," Junior said. "It's been Hard Rock Days for the past sixty-four years."

"Sixty-five years," Bob said.

"People hear the name 'Hard Rock' and they think it's a music festival." Cassie wrinkled her nose. "Every year I get at least half a dozen people in the library who want to know where they can find a list of bands playing. Founders' Days would avoid that kind of confusion."

"Hard Rock Days is all about our mining heritage," Paul said. "People come from all over to see the single-jack and double-jack competitions, the sledge races and all that."

"We could still have that, though I don't think it should be the centerpiece of the festivities," Cassie said. "I think the focus should be on honoring the original settlers in the area, and on the Founders' Pageant."

Junior groaned. "Give it a rest, Cassie," he said. "You're the only one who cares about that boring play."

"I beg your pardon." She drew herself up to her full five feet, two inches. "I heard many people rave about last year's production. They told me they were glad to see some attention finally being paid to the real history of the area, and that the weekend had become about more than a bunch of big, sweaty men hitting things with hammers."

Lucille suspected most of these admirers were in Cassie's clearly fertile imagination. The Founders' Pageant had been an afterthought last year, tacked onto the end of the celebration. The only thing most people probably remembered about Cassie's play was the explosion at the end, precipitated when Bob had attempted to set off fireworks backstage.

"Cassie, we cannot make Hard Rock Days into Founders' Days," she said.

"Why not?"

Many answers filled Lucille's head: because you're the only one who cares about that play. Because a bunch of sweaty men hitting things with hammers draws in more tourists than a play with amateur actors standing around in period costumes ever would. But the last thing she wanted was to set Cassie off on another rant, or truly, to hurt her feelings. Most people might dismiss her play, but Cassie really cared about her family history, and she'd put a great deal of effort into producing the play, which was, after all, a harmless addition to a weekend already packed with activities.

Instead, Lucille said, "The posters for this year are already printed, and the publicity campaign is already under way."

"I think you need to reprint the posters," Cassie said. From the notebook she'd been holding to her chest, she produced a poster and unfolded it. A bold graphic in the middle proclaimed HARD ROCK DAYS! EUREKA, COLORADO, HOW THE ROCKY MOUNTAIN WEST WAS WON, with the dates at the end of August. All around this were pictures of the various activities, including the single-jacking and double-jacking competitions, where men (and women) competed to see which individual or, in the case of double-jacking, which team, could drive a steel drill into solid rock with a sledge hammer. The thrilling, tension-filled, and fast-paced competition was the centerpiece of the celebration, and the person who won the most events— which also included races hauling sledges filled with rocks, and a competition to see who could shovel the most rock in five minutes, won the title of Hard Rock Miner, and a trophy. One of the photos on the poster featured Maggie's late father, Jake Murphy, holding one of his trophies aloft. A three-time champion before he'd retired from competition, Jake was still a local legend for his strength and prowess. He was also someone the town librarian particularly hated, and Lucille had no doubt that seeing his picture so prominent on the poster had set Cassie off.

"There isn't even any mention of the Founders' Pageant on this poster," Cassie said.

"Yes, there is," Maggie said. She turned in her chair to face the librarian. "Look in the bottom right-hand corner."

Cassie scowled at the small font in that section of the poster. "Food booths, craft fair, street dance, and pageant," she read.

"We don't have room to list every event on the poster," Lucille said, hoping she didn't sound too defensive. "But everything is in the official program, I promise."

"The Founders' Pageant deserves more attention," Cassie said.

"Does anyone else want to address this issue?" Lucille looked to the council members. They stared back at her, mouths firmly closed. They were, as usual, leaving her to deal with Cassie by herself. "I don't know what to tell you," she said to the librarian. "We operate with limited resources, and we do the best we can."

"I thought the town was rich now," Cassie said. "After all, the gold mine is producing all those millions."

"We don't have the money yet," Lucille said. "And we won't for a while. It's a long process."

"If you won't help me, I'll do the work myself," Cassie said. "I'll make sure everyone knows about the pageant, and that it becomes the highlight of the celebration—the kind of thing that will bring people in from all over the country."

Lucille blinked. Something in Cassie's voice made her bombastic words sound like a real threat. "What are you planning?" she asked.

"Why should I tell you? You might steal my ideas." She folded the poster, and then the notebook. "You don't want to give me help, so I'll help myself. It's what I should have done in the first place."

Having said her piece, Cassie stalked out of the room. Lucille watched her go and felt a little sick to her stomach. Whatever Cassie was up to, it probably wasn't going to be good. But she couldn't do anything to stop her, at least not yet. She checked the agenda once more and breathed a sigh of relief. "That's all we have tonight," she said.

Reggie's hand shot up. "One more item, Madam Mayor."

So much for relaxing. As town attorney, Reggie usually didn't say much at these meetings, unless they specifically directed a question to him. If he was bringing up something now, it probably wasn't good. "What is it, Reggie?" she asked.

"It's about this private detective, Duke Breman."

Lucille went cold. She had told no one about her meeting with Duke and, although word had no doubt gotten around that she'd had dinner with him, no one had acted particularly interested in that. She had felt safe that they'd raised no suspicions, and that no one had overheard the content of their conversation. "What about him?" she choked out.

"He's been asking a lot of questions about Gerald Pershing," Reggie said. "I want to remind everyone that you are under no legal obligation to talk to him."

"Why do you think we shouldn't talk to him?" Maggie asked the question Lucille had been about to pose.

"I'm not saying you shouldn't talk to him, but be careful." Reggie adjusted his wire-rimmed glasses. With his silver ponytail and leather vest, he looked more like a member of a motorcycle club than an attorney. "Some of the things he said to me made me think he, or whoever hired him, believes Gerald may have been the victim of foul play. You don't want him twisting your words to make you seem guilty of something you didn't do."

Lucille sucked in her breath, remembering Duke's warning that she would be the prime suspect if Gerald was dead, both because she'd made it clear she despised him, and because he'd left her half his money.

"If anyone thinks Gerald did anything but leave town under normal circumstances, why aren't the police asking questions?" Maggie asked.

"Maybe suspicions are all they have at this point, and the family or some other interested party hired Duke to come up with evidence," Reggie said. "I don't know. But it never hurts to be careful. And that includes not putting anything I've said tonight in the paper."

"Despite what some people think, the *Miner* doesn't print rumors," Maggie said crisply.

"Good riddance to bad rubbish if he is dead," Bob said.

"I wouldn't go around saying that if I were you," Reggie said.

"I don't give a tinker's dam if he hears me say that or worse," Bob said. "It's not a secret there wasn't any love lost between any of us in town and Pershing."

"You were the last person to talk to him," Junior said. "Maybe this Duke character thinks you offed him."

"If I'd wanted to kill Pershing, I had plenty of opportunity in the mine before you all hauled us out of there," Bob said. "I could have bashed his head in with a rock and told everybody he was killed in the explosion. I could have even hid his body in an old tunnel and told everyone he wasn't in there."

"I don't like that you've given this so much thought," Lucille said.

"My guess is the old crook skipped the country and changed his name," Bob said. "We weren't the first bunch he'd swindled and he probably had a lot of that money tucked away in some offshore account. While Duke and whoever are wasting their time and money looking for him, he's living large on some island somewhere."

"Do you really think he had a lot of money?" Lucille tried to keep her expression casual and disinterested, even though her heart hammered. Duke had refused to say how much she might inherit, but she'd be a liar if she pretended she wasn't interested.

"He always had plenty of cash to wave around when he wanted to," Bob said.

"It doesn't matter to any of us, anyway," Paul said. "I think the best thing is for all of us to refuse to talk to this Duke character and pretty soon he'll give up and go away."

The others nodded in unison. Lucille looked down, focused on straightening the papers in front of her. They might not care what happened to Gerald Pershing and his money, but if Duke was telling the truth, she suddenly had a very personal interest in the matter. She still hadn't quite wrapped her head around the news the detective had given her. A man she despised, whose confessions of love for her she'd always believed were manipulative lies, had remembered her in his will. Was the gesture made out of guilt, or a determination to prove her wrong?

Or, had Gerald Pershing really had true, tender feelings for her? Had she been so wrong about him all along?

Chapter 8

"Where are you going?" Thursday evening, Shelly was filling a tote bag with her notebook, pens, and copies of meeting minutes when Mindy strolled into the living room. Dressed in a baby doll minidress and pink cowboy boots, her blond hair in a Pre-Raphaelite tumble around her face, she looked as if she'd stepped out of an Anthropologie ad, a city beauty weekending in the country.

Shelly turned her attention back to stuffing the tote bag. "I have a meeting of the historical society at the library."

"I'll come with you."

Shelly checked to see if Mindy was joking, but she looked serious. "I didn't know you were interested in history," she said.

"I'm not, but there's nothing else to do around here in the evening."

"You could always go back home." After six days of flitting in and out of the house at all hours, not offering to lift a finger to help with the boys or even clean up after herself, Mindy had worn out her welcome.

"You're still mad about me going to the bank, aren't you?" Mindy picked up the notebook from the table and began flipping through it. "But it was no big deal. I mean, I don't see any bank investigators over here grilling you or anything."

"I told my bosses it was a misunderstanding and they believed me," Shelly said. "But it was still embarrassing." And Tamarin was still giving her the cold shoulder, after telling Shelly she was hurt her friend had kept so much from her.

"I should have remembered how much you cared about what other people think of you." Mindy set aside the notebook. "I'm sorry if I made trouble for you. I was just having a little fun. So can I come with you tonight?"

"I don't know why you'd be interested."

"Maybe I just want to hang out with my sister."

"You mean spy on me."

"Oh, please!" Mindy rolled her eyes.

"Don't think I haven't seen you playing with that recorder." Shelly stuffed the notebook into the tote. "Everything I say, you run to relay it to that reporter."

Mindy scowled at her. "You have a real problem, you know that?" she said.

"I don't think I'm the one with the problem here." Shelly turned away, so her sister wouldn't see the tears that threatened. For a few brief minutes when Mindy had shown up on her doorstep out of the blue, a bright hope had blossomed that the two of them could be close once more. They'd be a team, looking out for each other and keeping each other's secrets, the way they'd been when Mindy was very small. But Mindy's revelation about her book deal and her real purpose for visiting had snuffed out all thoughts of reforging a familial bond. Mindy didn't care about Shelly; she only cared about the money and fame that Shelly could bring her.

"You know, you aren't as smart as you think you are," Mindy said. "You think you have me all figured out, but you haven't."

Shelly shouldered the tote bag. "Come to the meeting if you want, but you'll probably just be bored."

"I'm already bored, so it can't get worse." She turned and flounced ahead of Shelly to the car.

"Maybe your meeting won't be as boring as you think," Charlie said as the front door slammed. He looked up from the newspaper he'd been reading, in his chair in the corner. "It might be fun to see Cassie and Mindy together."

"You might have a point." She smiled and kissed him. "Tell the kids I'll come say good night when I get home."

Mindy was waiting in the car, fluffing her bangs in the passenger-side visor mirror. "So, who all is in this historical society?" she asked as Shelly slid into the driver's seat. "Any cute guys?"

"I guess Doug Raybourn is pretty good-looking," Shelly said. "But he's happily married and has four kids. The only other man who's a member is Bob Prescott."

Mindy wrinkled her nose. "The old miner, right? Definitely not cute."

"Looks aren't everything."

"Maybe not to you, but to me, they count for a lot." She returned her attention to the visor mirror.

"I guess I should warn you about someone else who will definitely be at the meeting tonight," Shelly said as she fit the key in the ignition. "The president of the historical society, Cassie Wynock. She's also the librarian and she can be a bit of a dragon."

"Grouchy old ladies don't scare me." Mindy flipped up the visor and turned toward Shelly. "But if she's so awful, why do you even bother going?"

"I like history, and we do interesting stuff. Right now, we're putting together a play about the town's founding, for the Hard Rock Days Festival at the end of the month."

"I saw a poster about that," Mindy said. "At first I thought it was talking about a rock concert. Though I couldn't imagine what band would want to perform all the way out here in the sticks."

"It's all about remembering the mining that's the reason

most of this area was settled in the first place. They have demonstrations and contests to determine the winner of the Hard Rock Miner trophy."

"Is that what all those pictures of hunky guys swinging big hammers and stuff is about?"

"Yes. It's really pretty interesting."

"To you, maybe. But you always did like that boring history stuff better than I did. I remember how you'd get all swoony over lords and ladies and castles and knights. I didn't know you cared anything about American history."

"All history is interesting," Shelly said. "I like learning how people lived in the past."

Mindy twirled her finger in a long golden curl. "Don't you think it's ironic that someone who's so interested in other people's pasts won't talk about her own?"

Shelly gripped the steering wheel so tightly her knuckles ached. So much for thinking she could have an easy-going, normal conversation with her sister. "I lived my past. I don't have to talk about it."

"No, you just pretend it never happened. That your family never happened."

Shelly winced. Maybe she deserved that. Mindy had acted as if she was really hurt to learn that none of Shelly's friends knew about her. But Mindy always had been a good actress, and considering all the other ways she'd made Shelly's life miserable, maybe her hurt feelings were an act, too. "Instead of worrying so much about my life, why don't you get on with your own?" she asked.

"Because your story is the one everyone is interested in. I'm just the little sister, the sidekick. I figured out pretty quick that if I was going to get anywhere, it was going to be by riding your coattails."

Shelly swallowed a knot of angry tears. "Then you admit you're only using me to get what you want."

"You haven't really left me any choice."

"Don't make this my fault. There are always choices."

"You chose to run away, and I don't see that it's made you any happier."

"I was very happy before you came here and brought back all the things I'd successfully put behind me."

"Right." Mindy laughed. "If you were so successful at that, you wouldn't be upset now."

When Shelly didn't answer right away, Mindy leaned toward her. "You know I'm right, don't you? I think if you talk about stuff, get it out in the open, you'll feel better, and people will quit bothering you about it, too."

"I used to believe that," Shelly said. "Every year, on the anniversary of my rescue, Mama would tell me that this was the last year I had to do the interviews and pose for pictures—that as I got older, people wouldn't be interested anymore. But the next year, she'd be back again, fanning the flames and basking in the reflected glory. The reporters never stopped calling, and I felt like I was always on display. I guess the only blessing was that they didn't have reality TV shows back then, or she would have made sure we were in one. How would that make you feel?"

"Are you kidding? I'd love it. At least with a show like that, I'd have a chance of being noticed. When we were growing up, everyone was focused on you; they completely ignored me."

"That's not true," Shelly said. "You were always involved in something—cheerleading, then pageants and plays." She had loved seeing Mindy command her parents' attention for a change. Unlike Shelly, Mindy loved being the center of attention.

Mindy shook her head. "It didn't matter how many beauty contests I won or plays I was in, I couldn't hold anyone's attention more than a few days," she said. "They always zeroed back in on Baby Shelly. I finally gave up. At least by writing this book, I'll get a big paycheck, and a chance to tell my side of the story."

"You don't need me for that."

"You know that's not true. No one wants to hear about me unless they get to hear about you first."

"I'm sorry about that, then, but I can't help you. I finally escaped that circus and I get to live a normal life. I won't destroy that just so you can fatten your bank account."

"Right. Just like always, it's all about you."

They had reached the library, so Shelly parked in the side lot, next to Tamarin's Kia. There was no sense arguing with Mindy; she'd never see things differently. Then again, she'd been raised to see Shelly as the family meal ticket. Mindy had been a little kid, a baby even, while their mother was building up the Baby Shelly legend. Though the adult Mindy had been a willing player in what Shelly saw as the selling out of her sister, could Shelly really blame her for doing what she'd been led from birth to believe was right?

Mindy opened the car door to get out and Shelly put a hand on her arm. "Listen, I'm sorry this hasn't been a better visit for you," she said. "Even though I can't help you with this book project, I want us to be friends again. I'm sorry I stayed away from you and I'll try to be . . . more welcoming."

Mindy looked wary. "Okay."

"Can we start fresh?" Shelly asked.

Mindy shrugged. "Yeah. Sure."

Not exactly an enthusiastic endorsement, but Shelly would take what she could get. "We'd better go in," she said. "Cassie gets snippy when the meeting starts late."

As it was, Shelly and Mindy were the last ones to arrive at the meeting, everyone else already in place around the conference table. Shelly braced herself for a dressing down from Cassie, but instead, the librarian greeted her with a big smile. "Shelly! It's so good to see you," she exclaimed. "I have some wonderful news to share with you."

"Uh, sorry we're late." Shelly settled her tote bag on the table. "Everyone, this is my sister, Mindy. She's in town visiting for a few days."

"How nice." Cassie's eyes flickered to Mindy, then settled back on Shelly, like a bird fixed on a juicy bug, ready to pounce. Shelly suppressed a shudder. Cassie acting all chummy like this was even scarier than when she was on the warpath. At least when she was upset with you, you knew what to expect. Cassie tapped her little gavel on the table. "Everyone, take your seats and we'll get started."

Mindy sat in a chair along the wall, while Shelly settled into her customary position at Cassie's right. Cassie stood at the head of the table, still beaming. The librarian smiled so seldom that seeing her with that expression now was unsettling. What was going on?

They dispensed with the minutes and the treasurer's report in short order, then moved to new business. "Of course, the main topic for tonight's meeting is the Founders' Pageant," Cassie said. "I've decided that this year we need to make the production even bigger and better. In light of that, you'll see I've made some adjustments to the casting."

Cassie handed around stacks of papers, which turned out to be new scripts, topped by a sheet marked Cast List.

"Cassie, we've already been rehearsing the old version for two weeks," said Doug Raybourn, who had the starring male role as Cassie's great-grandfather Festus. "You can't just change things in midstream like this."

"The changes don't substantially affect your role," Cassie said. "As for the others, I have confidence the cast will rise to the occasion."

Shelly stared at her own name, just under Cassie's on the list. *Schoolteacher, suffragette and pioneer Hattie Sanford, played by Shelly Frazier.* She flipped through the pages of the script. As far as she could tell, this Hattie character was in every scene. "Cassie, what is this?" she asked.

"Who is Hattie Sanford?" Doug asked. "I never heard of her."

"There wasn't a real Hattie Sanford," Cassie said. "Consider her a composite. She's representative of the type of women who made this town great."

Mindy snorted, but quickly composed her expression when Cassie looked her way.

"I appreciate the compliment, but I really don't want such a prominent role," Shelly said. "Maybe someone from the drama society could take it."

"But I wrote the part especially for you," Cassie said. "And I've already ordered the posters and playbills printed, with you listed as costar."

"You're giving up top billing?" Doug asked. He waggled his eyebrows at Shelly. "What have you got on Cassie?"

"I really don't want to do this." Shelly pushed the script away. She'd only agreed to take the small role she had—as one of the townswomen—because it wasn't a speaking part. It only required her to stand on stage, wearing a period costume, and cheer when Festus Wynock gave his speech about founding a new town.

"It's too late to back out now," Cassie said. "If you do, you'll be letting down the whole town."

Shelly tried to think of a way to point out that she couldn't very well be backing out of something she had never agreed to in the first place, but Cassie was already plowing ahead. "I've scheduled the next rehearsal for this Friday at seven. We'll meet every Monday, Wednesday, and Friday evening until the premiere Saturday during the festival. The initial costume fittings are next Friday."

"Cassie, no!" Shelly stood, her chair scraping back. "I can't do this. I'm not an actress. It's too big a commitment." The last thing she wanted was everyone staring at her while she stumbled through her lines.

"Oh, go ahead and do it," Mindy said, leafing through the script. "You're in pretty much every scene, and you've got some great lines. Listen to this: 'Eureka should set an example of equal suffrage. A vote for women is a vote for peace and prosperity.' "

Cassie applauded. "Excellent. You can help your sister prepare for the role."

Mindy beamed. "She hasn't had any training, the way I have, but I could probably teach her a few tricks."

"Why are you so determined for me to have a part in this play?" Shelly asked. "Why now?"

"We want to draw attention to the Founders' Pageant," Cassie said. "We want people to realize that what's most important about the festival isn't brutes pounding hammers at metal drills, but about the men and women who brought a civilizing influence to the region. What better way to do that, than to feature a woman who has survived tragedy and come back stronger?"

"What the heck are you talking about?" Doug asked. He looked at Shelly. "What tragedy?"

"Yeah, what tragedy?" Tamarin's expression was a mixture of hurt and accusation.

"Cassie's talking about Baby Shelly," Mindy said. She waved away the horrified look Shelly directed at her. "There's no sense keeping it a secret anymore. My sister is the golden-haired toddler who was trapped underground for five days, twenty-five years ago. The whole world went gaga over her, but she's been hiding out for the last ten years, so everyone's crazy to know what happened to her."

"When word gets out, I'm sure we'll have an influx of visitors to town," Cassie said. "The timing couldn't be better to garner attention for the pageant."

They were talking about Shelly as if she wasn't standing right there; she might have been back in Texas, listening to her parents debate the best way to slant her story this year. Should they play up her bravery in overcoming the handicap that lingered from her time underground, or emphasize how the transformative experience of her rebirth at such a tender age had made her kinder and more mature than the average teen? "But I don't have a handicap," Shelly had protested, but her mother told her to shut up. She didn't have to actually show a scar to reporters in order for them to believe she'd been somehow permanently marked.

"No," she said, loudly enough that they all stopped talking and turned to stare at her. "I won't do it. You can't force me." Then she turned and fled, before her tears fell and made her look more foolish. All her worst fears were already coming true. People no longer looked at her and saw Shelly Frazier, wife, mom, and friend. Instead, they saw Baby Shelly, someone they could manipulate and use for their own gain.

She'd hoped Eureka would be different, a place where she could live an ordinary, normal life. But there wasn't anything normal or ordinary about what was happening now. People wanted to relive the glory of her rescue, but couldn't they see that every time they did that, they were putting her back underground again?

As places went, goat herder Daisy Mott sized up Eureka as a pretty fair town. Touristy, but what place in the mountains wasn't these days? When scenery was the only thing you had to sell, you had to accept that survival depended on catering to visitors, who enjoyed the view then moved on.

When she'd called Thursday morning, the mayor, Lucille, had been as honest and straightforward as Daisy herself, admitting up front that Daisy won the bid because she was the only person who could stomach their low rates. The mayor had offered her a shady spot at the back of the town park, and permission to plug into power at the storage shed. Daisy had agreed to arrive Friday and sure enough, a crew of two young men had been waiting when she pulled up. Right now they were setting up the plastic posts and electric wire that would keep her twenty-five brown, black, and white goats from eating the lilac bushes or wandering into the street.

"How does that look, ma'am?" The younger of the two workers hefted the mallet he'd been using to pound in the stakes onto his broad shoulder and looked back at her.

"It'll be fine," she said. "Alice does most of the work of keeping them out of where they don't belong."

At the sound of her name, the blue-eyed Australian shepherd pricked up her ears and wafted her plumed tail back and forth. Her gaze stayed fixed on Daisy as she moved to the rear of the trailer where the goats kicked and bleated impatiently.

"Do you want us to move those picnic tables out of the way?" the young man asked.

"No. The girls will eat around them." And they'd enjoy climbing on the tables, though she thought it best not to mention this. She lifted the latch on the trailer door. "You might want to stand back now. They're anxious to see their new home."

The man eyed the trailer apprehensively and took three steps back. Daisy swung the gate open and the first of the herd trotted down the ramps she'd set up earlier, into Ernestine Wynock Park—or so the sign at the entrance identified the place, although the mayor and everybody else she'd talked to just called it "the town park."

Sophia led the way, her long snout extended to catch the whiff of green grass and flowers, followed by Belle and Sassy and Kate and all the other does in the herd, some with kids gamboling at their sides. Alice ran back and forth alongside and around the herd, barking and sometimes snapping to keep a wayward goat in line. Sophia stopped about halfway into the area, put her head down, and began to eat. The others followed suit.

"Well I'll be damned." The young worker removed his cap and scratched his head. "They go right to work, don't they?"

"When they've had enough to eat, they lie down and chew their cud," Daisy said. "Then they get up and eat some more. In three days, there won't be a weed left in this park."

"Anything that saves me from chopping and digging the things is good news," the young man said. "If you need anything, just call the mayor and she'll get somebody over to help you."

"Thanks, but I doubt I'll have to bother her. Alice and I have been doing this a while now, and we seldom have any trouble."

The young man and his older helper left in a rusting green pickup with TOWN OF EUREKA stenciled in fading black letters on the driver's door. Daisy unhooked a broom from the side of the trailer and stepped in to sweep out the scattered hay and droppings the girls had distributed on the drive over from the San Luis Valley.

Alice's bark warned her that someone was approaching in time for her to look up and see an older man in canvas trousers, high black boots, and a buffalo plaid shirt picking his way among the herd, moving toward her. She paused in her sweeping and shaded her eyes with her hands. "I'd be careful, moving through the herd like that, mister," she called. "Some of the girls don't like strangers too close to their kids."

"The day I'm afraid of a bunch of cud-chewing grass-eaters is the day they'd better take me out back and shoot me." He glared at Kate, who'd sidled up beside him and was tugging at the pocket of his pants. Kate only tugged harder, until the old man swatted at her with his ball cap. "What's she trying to do? Eat me?"

"They like the taste of detergent," she said. "Though from the looks of those trousers, they haven't had a close acquaintance with soap."

"That's rich, coming from a woman who's up to her ankles in goat shit." He moved closer. "What are you doing, stinking up the park with that?"

"Who wants to know?"

"I'm Bob Prescott."

"Daisy Mott." She looked him up and down, while he did the same to her. He was a little older than her, she guessed, something he'd figure out quickly enough, given the lines on her face and the white of her cropped curls. She'd never held with going out of her way to disguise the years she'd earned, though she liked a feminine touch here and there. She wore silver hoops in her ears and her western-cut plaid shirt was a soft shade of lavender, and sported ruffles on the yoke. "I'd say it was a pleasure to meet you, Bob, but I haven't made up my mind about that yet." She went back to her sweeping. "As for what I'm doing with this manure, it's all part of my service, providing free fertilizer for the flowers."

He stopped at the back of the trailer and turned to survey the goats, who had resumed mowing down weeds. "How long you been running this little scam of yours?"

"I've been renting out the herd for weed control for three years," she said. "And as you can plainly see, they do eat weeds."

"Hell of a way to make a living." He spat into the dirt between his boots.

"As opposed to your job, which is apparently to hassle people who *are* working."

"I manage the Lucky Lady gold mine."

"Then shouldn't you be off managing?" She swept the last of the manure so that it landed almost—but not quite—on top of him.

"I came to see what the city's wasting my tax dollars on now."

"Well, you've seen and you've made your opinion clear, so now you can leave."

"What did you do before you got into the goat-wrangling business?"

She didn't have to answer that question. Her personal story was none of his business. But, though she'd never admit it to him, she kind of enjoyed sparring with the old coot. A good argument kept the wits sharp. "My husband and I managed a ranch. But after he died, I decided I wanted to travel, see some new country. This allows me to do that."

"What do you do in the winter?"

"I chop firewood and read novels."

He stepped back and craned his neck to take in her truck and camper. "Nice rig you got there."

"It suits me."

"Maybe I'll stop by later and you can cook me dinner."

"Do that, and I'll try to beat some sense into you with my frying pan."

He grinned. "I like a feisty woman."

"I despise men who call women feisty."

"What if I buy you dinner instead?"

She set aside the broom and looked down on him. "First, you accuse me of being some kind of con artist, then you ask me out?"

"Do you want to go or not? The special tonight at the Last Dollar is chicken and dressing and it's my favorite."

It was her favorite, too. "What the heck. I won't pass up a free meal. I'll meet you there at six o'clock."

"Make it six-thirty."

"You just have to get in the last word, don't you?"

"I figured I'd go home first and change pants. These have been gnawed on by goats." He touched the brim of his hat in salute and sauntered away through the goats, whistling tunelessly.

Alice barked and raced up to greet Daisy as she jumped down from the trailer. "I don't know what to think of him either, girl," Daisy said as she watched Bob Prescott's retreating figure. "But I think our stay in Eureka just got a little more interesting."

Chapter 9

"Oh my goodness, look how big you've gotten!" Danielle scooped Angela out of Maggie's arms almost as soon as mother and daughter stepped into the doorway of the Last Dollar late Friday afternoon. "Aren't you just the sweetest thing? I could eat you all up." She buried her face against the child's neck, making snorting noises.

Angela gurgled and grinned and reached up for the gold hoops Danielle wore in her ears. "Watch out." Maggie grabbed her daughter's chubby fist. "She's fascinated by jewelry these days."

"Hey, Maggie." Danielle straightened, as if noticing her friend for the first time. Maggie was used to it. Angela was at that particularly adorable age where even strangers were drawn to her. As Mom, Maggie was merely the vehicle for toting the little princess from admirer to admirer. "How are you?" Danielle asked.

"Good." She scanned the dining room. "I'm meeting Jameso for dinner. Is he here yet?"

"Right behind you." Two warm hands rested on either side of her waist and warm breath stirred her hair as he planted a kiss on the top of her head. Already smiling, Maggie turned to greet her husband. The appreciative look in his brown eyes always made her heart beat a little faster. She'd decided—for now, at least—to forgive him for leaving her home alone Monday night, especially since he'd offered to buy her dinner tonight.

"Hey there, gorgeous." Jameso directed these words not to Maggie, but to the little girl in Danielle's arms, who was already reaching for him. Angela cuddled to his chest while he kissed her, much as he had Maggie. Maggie laughed.

"What's so funny?" he asked.

She shook her head. "I was just thinking about the first time I saw you, up at my dad's cabin. You looked like some motorcycle bandit, all black leather and scowls."

"She tried to hit me with a stick of firewood," Jameso told Danielle. "Can you believe it?"

"You probably deserved it." She motioned for them to follow. "I've got a table for you over here. The high chair's already set up."

Diaper bag and purse in tow, Maggie followed her little family across the restaurant. The Last Dollar was, as usual, busy, with a healthy mix of locals and tourists. "Is that Bob Prescott over there with a woman?" Jameso asked as he settled Angela into her high chair.

Danielle leaned forward, her voice low. "Her name's Daisy Mott. She's in charge of the goat herd the town hired to clear weeds from the park."

"Bob hated the idea of having goats in the park," Maggie said. "He made a big fuss at the meeting where the town council voted on it."

"Well, apparently, he doesn't hate the woman in charge of the goats." Danielle glanced toward the booth where Bob and Daisy appeared to be in heated conversation. "You should hear the two of them, bickering like an old married couple. I think they like it."

"Fighting as foreplay?" Jameso cocked an eyebrow.

"Oh please." Maggie covered her eyes. "Now I need to wash my mind with lye soap."

"You don't think we'll still be doing it when I'm Bob's age?" he asked.

"Considering I'll be positively ancient by then, I can't imagine," Maggie said. She was eight years older than Jameso, something she didn't like to be reminded of.

"I'll get your drinks and Janelle will be over in a sec to get your order," Danielle said. "Iced tea and Diet Coke, right?"

Maggie nodded. She loved living in a place where the locals knew her well enough to anticipate her drink order. As Danielle left them, she spread her napkin in her lap and let out a long sigh.

"Tough day?" Jameso asked.

She shrugged. "The usual. A tourist rolled an ATV up on Corabelle Pass. Nobody seriously hurt, thank goodness. Cassie is pushing for more coverage of the Founders' Pageant."

"I'm sure Rick loves that." Rick Otis, the editor and publisher of the paper, loved to needle the grouchy librarian.

"He told her to buy an ad, which of course set her off on another rant. And you're right, Rick loves it. I just wish they'd have their sparring matches somewhere I don't have to listen." Danielle delivered their drinks. Maggie gave her a grateful smile and stripped the paper off a straw. "How are things at the B and B?"

"Calm for the moment. All the rooms full. That private detective asked to extend his stay for another week."

"What did you tell him?"

"We had the room available, so I figure, why not?"

She took a long sip of the soft drink, the sweet, fizzy soda reviving her further. "He gives me the creeps, poking around in everybody's business that way."

"Maggie, half the people in town specialize in poking around in other people's business."

"Yes, but they live here. He doesn't. And I don't think

staying another week is going to help him find out what happened to Gerald."

"I wonder what Gerald's up to now?" Jameso asked.

"No good, I'm sure."

"Maybe Bob did off him." He slid his gaze toward the booth where Bob and Daisy had stopped talking for the moment, both focused on their dinners.

"If Bob wanted him dead, he could have killed him in the mine and made it look like an accident. At least, that's what he said at the council meeting the other night."

"If your dad was still alive, I'd suspect he was the one who got rid of Gerald," Jameso said.

"Seriously? You think Jake would have killed him?" She shivered. Jameso had known her father much better than she had, and Jake Murphy had a reputation as having a bad temper and a dark side, but still, she didn't like to think of him as a killer. Sure, he'd killed people in the war, but cold-blooded murder was a different story.

"He didn't like troublemakers," Jameso said.

"Then how did he ever make friends with you?"

"Ha ha."

"Well, we know Jake didn't have anything to do with Gerald's disappearance. I think the man doesn't want to be found, and he's smart enough to keep his whereabouts a secret. No one's going to find him until he comes out of hiding."

"Maybe you're right. But it's another week's rent on the room, so it's all good. And before I forget to tell you, that fancy espresso machine Barb ordered for the kitchen arrived, but I haven't unpacked it. I told her I didn't want it, but you know her."

"She won't take no for an answer." Her best friend, Barb, had decided to put her party planning and decorating skills to use by opening a bed-and-breakfast, but, not wanting to live in Eureka full time, she'd handed over management duties to Jameso. The job came with a plush apartment on the top floor of the restored Victorian mansion, complete with a nursery outfitted with every toy and baby gadget "Auntie Barb" could buy.

"Maybe I'll take a look at it when I get home," Maggie said. "Then at least we can tell her it's set up in the kitchen, even if we never use it."

Jameso grunted and studied the menu, while Maggie studied him. His thick, black hair showed not a hint of gray, though glints of silver showed in his goatee, and fine lines fanned out from the corners of his eyes when he smiled. A lifetime of working and playing outdoors—skiing, hiking, rock climbing—had weathered his skin to a year-round tan, and his hands bore the scars and calluses of hard use. Yet he could touch her so tenderly. . . .

"Do you know what you want to order?"

Jameso's question woke Maggie to the fact that Janelle, Danielle's partner in the café and in life, was standing by their table, pencil poised over her order pad. Dressed in a short denim skirt and a blue-and-white baseball jersey, the Nordic blonde looked ready to hit the softball field. "I'll have the special," Maggie said.

"Two specials coming up." Janelle leaned down to let Angela wrap her chubby fist around one beringed finger. "Anything for the little angel?"

"She likes those teething biscuits Danielle baked for her," Maggie said.

"One biscuit for the baby, coming up."

Janelle hurried away and Jameso leaned back in the chair and yawned. "I should have ordered coffee," he said. "It's going to be a long night."

"You're working too hard," Maggie said. "You can't keep up this pace, working all day at the B and B and half the night at the Dirty Sally." Not to mention other nights helping friends. She pressed her lips together, determined not to go down that road.

He looked away, smile vanished, eyes half closed. "Don't start, Maggie."

He hated it when she nagged, and she hated being a nag. But not saying anything didn't accomplish anything, either. "With what I make at the paper, and the salary Barb pays you, you don't have to keep working at the Dirty Sally," she said.

"We can always use extra money," he said. "That Jeep of your dad's isn't going to last forever, and we should probably think about setting up a college fund for Angela. And retirement accounts . . ." His voice trailed away, his expression bleak.

Maggie could almost read his thoughts. Jameso Clark, carefree bachelor and perpetual Peter Pan, reduced to contemplating retirement funds and college accounts, like a tied-down, responsible adult.

"We'll do fine without those things," Maggie said. Tentatively, she reached out and stroked his hand. "If you don't want to quit, at least cut back. Instead of four nights a week, do two."

He pulled his hand away; he might as well have slapped her. She sat back in her chair, and fussed with rearranging the silverware, struggling for composure.

"This isn't about you, Maggie," he said after a moment. "Not everything is about you. Sometimes it's about me. About what I need to do to feel like I'm still in control of my life."

"I'm not trying to control you."

"I know. But a lot of changes have happened really fast."

If she hadn't been so sad, she might have laughed at that understatement. In less than a year she'd showed up in town, had a whirlwind affair, gotten pregnant, gotten married, and moved into the B and B. Everything she'd thought she knew about her future had changed in the blink of an eye. How much worse was it for Jameso, a man who'd successfully avoided thinking about the future, much less planning for it, for thirty-two years?

"Good changes." He looked at Angela, who was busy playing with the colored plastic beads strung along the front of the high chair.

Maggie took a big swallow of the soft drink, hoping to force down the knot of tears that threatened. "A lot of changes," she said, when she thought it was safe to talk.

"I like the job at the Dirty Sally," he said. "Most of the time. And we're doing okay, me handling the B and B during the day and working at the bar a few nights a week."

Except that I don't see enough of you, she thought. But she didn't say it. The last thing she wanted was to come off like some clinging, needy wife who didn't want to let her husband out of her sight.

"I don't want to keep you from something you enjoy," she said stiffly.

Janelle delivered their dinners—two plates piled with roast chicken, homemade cornbread dressing and gravy and seasoned green beans, along with a teething biscuit made from some recipe Danielle had found online and made especially for Angela. The food looked and smelled delicious, and probably was, but Maggie hardly tasted it as she ate mechanically, fretting and seething about what she couldn't help seeing as Jameso's need to run away from her four nights a week.

"Hey there, handsome." No woman would have missed the flirtatious tone in the greeting. Maggie looked up from her meal in time to see Mindy Payton crossing the room toward them. Her white-blond curls spilled from a topknot tied with purple ribbons and she wore her purple T-shirt pulled up and knotted in back to reveal a glittering stud in her navel. Painted-on low-slung jeans completed the outfit, which guaranteed the eyes of every man in the room—from Bob to Jameso—were fixed on her.

"I'll see you later tonight, won't I?" Mindy put her hand on Jameso's shoulder and stood with her boobs practically in his face.

He grinned up at her. "You bet. It's karaoke night. Are you planning to sing?"

"I just might." She tilted her head coyly. "Some people tell me I sound just like Beyoncé."

Maggie wanted to slap the smiles off both their faces. "Hello, Mindy," she said, as much to remind Jameso she was still here as to warn off the younger woman.

"You remember my wife, Maggie," Jameso said. "Maggie, this is Shelly Frazier's sister, Mindy."

"We've met," Maggie said. "At the bar." How was it Jameso didn't even remember? "How is your sister?"

"Shelly's fine."

"You two don't seem to spend much time together."

"Neither do you and your husband." She trailed her hand along Jameso's shoulder. "See you later, tiger."

Tiger? Maggie's vision clouded with a red haze.

"Don't do it, Maggie."

She jerked her gaze away from Mindy's departing figure to look at Jameso. "Don't do what?"

"Whatever you were contemplating doing to Mindy. You'd never win. She looks like the type who's been in more than one girl fight."

"Then she needs to keep her hands off of you," she said. "And you need to tell her to back off."

"She just likes to flirt. It doesn't mean anything. She knows I'm married."

Maggie would have felt better if he'd said "happily married." "I don't trust her," she said. "It's hard to believe she's Shelly's sister. They're nothing alike."

"You don't have to trust her. You can trust me. Isn't that what being married is all about?"

She nodded, and focused her eyes on her plate. She wanted to trust Jameso, but doing so was harder than she'd have thought. Her first husband had left her for another woman after twenty years of what she'd thought was a good marriage. Her father had abandoned her mother when Maggie was only three days old. The lesson was clear: People you were supposed to be able to count on let you down. Jameso hadn't fared much better. His father had been an abuser who had driven the boy away as soon as he could make it on his own. As much as they both tried to put their pasts behind them, they couldn't escape the grip of events in their pasts.

She stabbed at a bite of chicken and chewed without tasting it. People talked about living in the moment, but now was such a slippery, elusive context. She'd read books about envisioning your future to make your dreams come true, and she'd spent a lot of time trying to conjure up an image of a perfect life that was yet to be.

In the end, the past was the only thing solid enough to hold on to. She'd been there, lived that, and knew what it felt like. Even the bad things were hard to let go of. They were familiar. And no matter how counterproductive or crippling, people always insisted on dragging the past with them into that uncertain future, an anchor that could ground them and hold them in place, or a weight that would pull them under for good.

Saturday afternoon, Lucille had just completed the sale of a large folk art painting of a rooster to a couple visiting from Wisconsin when she looked up and found Duke Breman standing in front of her counter, those brooding eyes of his boring into her. She suspected him of purposely trying to fluster her, the way he must try to unnerve those suspected of crime. And it annoyed her that he was, mostly, succeeding. "Did you need something, Mr. Breman?" she asked.

"The sign on your door says you close at five." His eyes remained fixed on her.

"What if it does?" She busied herself straightening the postcard rack that sat at the farthest end of the counter. When he didn't respond—or even move, for that matter— after several seconds, she snapped, "Didn't your mother ever tell you it's rude to stare?"

"Was I staring?"

She gave up on the postcards, which she suspected she was

only making more of a mess, and faced him. "What do you want from me, Mr. Breman?"

"I want you to call me Duke. And I want you to go for a ride with me. Now."

Every part of her that was proud of being independent and a feminist and a woman who stood up for herself resented the way he ordered her around. Which made the small part of her that melted at his air of command that much more difficult to bear. "I'm sorry to disappoint you, but I have work to do," she said.

He looked around the empty shop, but said nothing. She opened the cash register and stood with both hands over the drawer. "You need to leave so I can lock up now," she said.

He looked at the floor, then shifted his weight to one hip, then the other. She half-expected him to scuff the toe of one boot on the old wooden floor. "I'd really like it if you'd go for a ride with me," he said, still addressing the floor. "You could show me your town. I wouldn't have to go back to the Idlewilde so early and spend the rest of the evening alone. And I'd like to get to know you better."

He was either a very good actor, or his previous abruptness was a front for a certain amount of apprehension about approaching people—or maybe just women, or maybe— maybe—her in particular. She glanced out the store's front window. The sun bathed the street in a golden glow, and the mountains beyond rose green and blue and white, almost too beautiful to believe. Suddenly she wanted nothing more than to be out enjoying that beauty, not stuck in here counting cash or tallying receipts. She closed the drawer. "All right," she said. "Let me get my purse and lock up."

He waited while she took care of these chores, then she flipped the sign on the door to CLOSED, pulled the door shut and made sure it was locked, and followed him to the late-model black pickup she'd seen parked in front of the Idlewilde Bed and Breakfast. He opened the passenger door and she managed to haul herself up into the cab without help from him. She resisted the impulse to make a snide comment about Texas men and their trucks; in truth, a good share of men—and women—in the mountains favored these oversize, rugged vehicles.

He slid into the driver's seat, clicked his seat belt, and started the engine. "Where to?" he asked.

"What do you want to see?"

"The mountains."

"You're in the mountains. You drove over them and around them to get here. You see them every day wherever you are in town."

"But I haven't explored them. I haven't seen them through the eyes of a local."

"Why do you want to see them through the eyes of a local? Do you think that will help you in your investigation? Gerald wasn't a local."

He almost—but not quite—smiled. "I thought I was supposed to be the suspicious one."

"I just don't understand what you want from me." She twisted her hands in her lap, sure he could sense her agitation, and helpless to hide it.

He looked out the windshield, his big hands resting loosely atop the steering wheel. "Maybe I just want to spend some time with you, in a way I thought would be more relaxing—less threatening, maybe—than asking you on a date. Away from prying eyes or agendas." He looked at her at last, some of the haughtiness gone out of his eyes. "Just two friends, going for a drive to enjoy the beautiful day and the scenery."

His words should have relaxed her, but she felt as if every nerve was knotted too tightly for mere reassuring words to undo. "Head up County Road Three," she said. "It's the right turn just before you get to the Idlewilde."

He shifted into gear and began the slow drive through town. "Did you ever think of paving these streets?" he asked, as he steered around a pothole.

"Some people think the dirt streets add to our quaint, rural charm," she said.

"Probably not anyone who has to drive them on a regular basis."

"People are surprisingly resistant to change. Even if we had the money in our budget—which we don't—I'm not sure we could convince a majority of the voters that we need to pave the streets."

"I hear the Lucky Lady Mine is earning the town money."

"Not as much as you'd think. We have a lot of capital costs up front."

"You could always make a donation to the town coffers if Gerald Pershing turns out to be dead and you inherit his money."

She hugged her arms across her chest to ward off a sudden chill. "I don't see why Gerald would have left me his money. I can't believe that's even true."

"I saw a copy of the will. Your name was there, along with your address here in Eureka."

"You're not making me feel any better." Strangers thousands of miles away apparently knew about a relationship she only wanted to forget.

"Seems to me that kind of money could make a big difference in your life," he said.

"I already have everything I need."

"Not many people can say that."

But it was true. She'd never been a woman who coveted clothes or collected shoes or jewelry. Her house was old, but she had made it her own, and she was comfortable there. She didn't need a new car or cosmetic surgery or anything else money could buy. She didn't even have a desire to travel. "I guess that's one advantage of living where the nearest mall is two hours away and television reception is spotty, at best," she said.

"I'm not sure I could live like that." He flexed his fingers on the steering wheel and flipped on his blinker to make the right turn onto County Road Three.

"I wouldn't want to live any other way," she said. "Everything I love is here in Eureka."

"I don't think pizza delivery, paved roads, and decent Internet service would ruin your little rural idyll," he said.

"Maybe not. And in time I'm sure we'll have all those things. But my point is that money isn't going to make me any happier than I already am. Take the next right."

He did as she directed and they bumped onto a much rougher, narrower road. "Where, exactly, are we going?" he asked as he wrestled the big truck around a boulder in the road.

"A place that belongs to a friend of mine. It has beautiful views, and it will tell you a lot about the people who are drawn to this area."

"Hmmmph." He said nothing more as they drove five slow miles farther up the mountain. Lucille gripped the armrest to steady herself, and noted how much rougher the road up here had become with disuse. Not that it had ever been a busy thoroughfare, but the neglect was one more example of the changes coming to the area, whether the old-timers like her approved or not.

She leaned forward to better get her bearings. "Take the drive on the left up here. Just past that little blue spruce."

He slowed the truck to a crawl, then swung into the rocky drive that headed almost straight up the slope. "You're just trying to get me up here and scare me," he said.

"I would hope it takes more than a steep mountain road to scare you."

He made no answer as they followed the drive around a curve and a cabin came into view. Lucille smiled: This, at least, hadn't changed. Someone, probably Jameso, had trimmed the weeds back from the cabin's foundation, and a fresh load of kindling filled the old washtub by the door, ready for the next visitor to make a fire.

Duke parked the truck on the only level spot in sight and shut off the engine. He studied the cabin, with its rusting metal roof and assortment of windows, no two the same size. A porch extended across the front of the structure, and beneath it steel braces secured the whole building to the mountain. "Who lives here?" he asked.

"It belonged to a man named Jake Murphy." She opened the door and climbed out. "Come up on the porch and I'll tell you about him."

He followed her up the rock-lined walkway to the porch. She felt along the top of the door for the key, then used it to unlock the door. "Even if you use a key, it's breaking and entering," Duke said.

"The cabin belongs to Maggie Clark." Lucille shoved on the door to open it. "She won't care that we're here, though if it makes you feel any better, I will tell her about this visit the next time I see her."

He followed her into the front room. Though he was behind her and she couldn't see his face, she knew the moment he registered the view. She heard the sharp intake of his breath and felt him go still. A wall of large windows along one side of the room revealed a vast expanse of blue sky, puffy clouds floating by close enough to touch, like cotton batting ripped from an old quilt by a playful kitten. The effect was of being suspended in space, or looking out from the world's tallest tree house.

After a long moment in which the only sound was of their breathing, Duke said, "Waking up to that view every morning could make a man question his sanity," he said. He moved into the room to stand beside her, one hand on the back of a love seat upholstered in green suede. "Who was this Jake Murphy?"

"Jake was Maggie's father, but before that he was an important part of the community, which is strange, really, considering he was sort of a recluse. He lived up here, with no running water and no electricity, year-round, for more than fifteen years."

"So what was he, some kind of rural wise man? A guru or something?"

She laughed. "Jake was definitely not a guru. He was a drinker and a fighter. He had a mean streak, and he liked to thwart convention and authority. But he could also be incredibly generous. He defended the underdog. When some bigot burned down Janelle and Danielle's chicken house, Jake built them a new one. And he let it be known that anyone who tried that kind of thing again would have him to answer to. If anyone needed help, they could count on Jake to provide it. He made the town his family."

"But you said Maggie was his family," Duke said.

"That's right. And that's one of the ugly things in his life. It shocked some of us, really, when we found out Jake had walked out on Maggie and her mom when Maggie was only three days old. He hadn't had any contact with her since."

"But he left her the cabin."

"Not just the cabin, but the French Mistress Mine and everything else he owned. It wasn't a lot, but it was enough to get her established here."

He moved past her into the cabin, and examined the stack of books on a table by the love seat, and a collection of colored bottles arranged on a shelf by the wood stove. "Why did you bring me up here? Do you really want me to think that this hermit alcoholic with a split personality is a typical resident of Eureka?"

"There is no typical Eureka resident," Lucille said. "But Jake represents a certain type of person who finds a home here. He was running from a past he didn't like or didn't want to face. He was hiding—not necessarily from a crime, but from himself. He wanted to be a part of a family, but only on his own terms. He valued independence over community, and was willing to suffer a certain amount of deprivation in order to keep his distance from others."

His eyes met hers, probing again. "Are you trying to tell me you're like Jake?"

"We had things in common." She shifted her gaze to the windows, and the vertigo-inducing expanse of sky. "I've learned not to rely on others. I like being independent, even if it means I miss out on some things."

"You can be in a relationship with someone else and still be independent," he said.

"Can you?" She regarded him coolly. "Maybe men can. I'm not sure women, or at least women of my generation, can. I don't know if it's some nurturing gene hardwired into our brains, or some animal instinct that bows to a man's superior physical strength that compels us to put our own needs behind our partner's, or to rush to compromise if he raises objections. Some of us are better than others at holding on to our sense of self."

"So you'd rather be alone than let anyone close?" He closed the distance between them in four strides, standing so near to her that a deep breath would have made the tips of her breasts brush against his chest.

She fought the urge to step back, and lifted her chin to look into his eyes. "I've been single a long time and I always did better on my own," she said. "Maybe men need women more than women need men."

"Don't you want love?" he asked.

The weight of that word rested like a stone in her belly. "I do, but it seems that relationships always come with conditions—having to compromise part of yourself to be with someone else."

"Men compromise, too," he said. "Maybe that makes you a better person."

"And maybe it doesn't."

"You don't have to worry about me." He rested his hand on her shoulder, the fingers open, not grasping. Still, the weight of that touch—emotional, if not physical—threatened to buckle her knees. "I like strong, independent women," he said. "I like you."

"I don't know how I feel about you." It surprised her how easy the words were to say, now that she'd started to let them flow. It was as if honesty had a momentum and drive all its own. "There's physical attraction," she said. "But I don't think I'm the kind of person who can be with someone just for the sex. And after Gerald . . ." She shrugged, lifting his hand, but it remained on her, a steadying buttress like the supports under this house.

"He was just one man," Duke said.

"I know that. But the two of you feel as if you're cut from the same mold."

His fingers squeezed a little then. "Are you saying I'm a swindler and a cheat?"

"No, but you have that same macho confidence. You know you're attractive and you're comfortable with women's attention. I don't know that I can compete with that kind of confidence."

"I'm not asking you to compete. I'm not asking you for anything. Just your company. However much of it you want to give." He bent, as if to kiss her, but she turned her head away.

"You can't push everyone away," he whispered, his lips against her ear.

"I only need to hold them at arm's length," she said.

"Your arms are going to get tired one day."

"Maybe they will. Or maybe I'll get stronger. Or I'll learn how to be myself and be with someone else at the same time." She turned and left the cabin, and left him standing, staring after her. She felt his gaze on her, a physical touch as light as the brush of a feather, and as heavy as the granite that made up this mountain.

Chapter 10

Shelly tiptoed into the library, looking around her warily. Midmorning on a Tuesday, the building was silent except for the whisper of turning pages from an older man who'd settled into one of the armchairs to read a magazine. Unlike the modern glass-and-stone structures in the city, the Eureka library reminded Shelly of the book-lined refuges of her childhood, with the same tantalizing aroma of floor polish and old papers.

She would lose herself weekdays after school and Saturday afternoons, making a nest on the floor between the stacks, safe behind a wall of books. For the span of those stolen hours, she was safe from the outside world, cut off from the people who demanded details she couldn't remember about her exile underground, or those who looked upon her as a living, breathing miracle. They called her Baby Shelly even when she was a teenager, and wanted to touch her or to have their picture taken with her, or to get her autograph. They asked her for money or they begged her to pray for them. And if she said no or tried to turn away from them, they called her greedy or ungrateful or worse. Only behind the pages of books could she shut out their demands and name-calling. The library had been the first place she felt truly safe.

"Hello, Shelly."

She let out a whoop and jumped six inches off the floor, almost dropping the folder she carried.

Sharon stared at her. "I didn't mean to startle you," she said.

"No, it's all right." Shelly held her hand to her chest, as if that would still her furiously pounding heart. "I was looking for Cassie. She's not here, is she?"

"She left half an hour ago for her appointment at the beauty shop."

Shelly nodded. Every Tuesday at ten, Cassie had a shampoo, trim, and set at Maxi's Cuts. While she was under the dryer was probably the safest time of any to venture into the library. "I needed to use the copy machine for the historical society minutes," Shelly said. "Then I thought I could just leave them for her."

"Good idea." Sharon led the way to the copy machine at the back of the office. "If she sees you, she'll go on another rant about the Founders' Pageant. She's decided it isn't enough to draw in the local crowd; she wants to be world famous."

Shelly winced. If only Cassie knew that world fame wasn't all adulation and roses. Strangers you'd never even met wanted to know the intimate details of your life, and were quick to scrutinize, criticize, and gossip. For every person who had sent a nice card or letter or check to Shelly and her family, there had been two more who felt the need to write or call to catalogue their faults or condemn them to hell. Sandy and Danny had been able to shrug off those people as crackpots, but Shelly couldn't help feeling bullied by their words.

"I guess she told you she wants me to take a bigger part in the play," she said as Sharon switched on the copy machine.

Sharon gave her a sympathetic look. "I take it you weren't so crazy about the idea?"

"The last thing I want is a bunch of people flooding into town to gawk at Baby Shelly, all grown up."

"I guess the public can be pretty cruel," Sharon said. "I read the headlines on those tabloids at the checkout counter and I always feel sorry for the celebrities. I'd hate someone digging into my life like that."

Shelly could have hugged her; Sharon was the first person who'd expressed an inkling of understanding. "It's not just the public scrutiny," she said. "Once the word gets out, my family is going to know where I am. I mean, Mindy already found me. And it's not that I don't love my sister—I do. But my parents . . ." She didn't know how to finish that sentence. How to explain about Sandy and Danny? She wanted to believe that somewhere down inside they loved her, simply because she was their child. But all the evidence pointed to them loving her image, and the attention and money she could bring them, not Shelly herself.

"I haven't spoken to my mother or father in ten years," Sharon said. "Jameso's been estranged from them longer than that. Not all parents are good parents."

Shelly stared at her. "I had no idea."

Sharon shrugged. "My dad didn't believe in sparing the rod, and my mom never said a word against him. I married a guy when I was fifteen, just to get away from my dad. Joe turned out to be just as controlling, in his own way, though he never raised a hand against me. So I'm one person, at least, who doesn't judge a person who decides she's better off without the family who raised her."

"Wow. I . . . I appreciate your telling me." She slid the first page of the minutes onto the glass of the copier, trying to control the trembling in her fingers. Her parents had never physically harmed her. They never even spoke harshly to her. They just never listened to her, never considered what she wanted or felt or hoped for. She felt like a puppet or a doll that they dressed up and fawned over, but never thought of as anything more than a possession or tool.

"We didn't have a TV when I was a kid," Sharon said. "My parents were fundamentalist types who thought television and movies were tools of the devil. So I don't know much about the whole Baby Shelly thing, except it must have been pretty frightening for a kid that little to be trapped underground that way. So I can see why you wouldn't want to relive that over and over for other people's entertainment."

Shelly pressed the buttons to make six copies of the minutes—one for each member of the Historical Society Board. Funny how, though it was the event that had led to all the other strife in her life and the break with her family, she never thought much about the ordeal that had made her famous. Over the years, coached by her mom, she'd developed a pat story to deliver to the press, a story that felt like lines from a play, and not anything that had really happened to her.

Even that aspect of the whole Baby Shelly legend had angered her—that no one cared how she really felt. They only wanted to hear the story that played on their emotions. The story of a terrified little girl who soldiered on bravely, holding on to the faith that someone would save her. "The weird thing was, after the first day, I wasn't that scared," she said. "It was like . . . I don't know how to describe it, but this calm settled over me. I wandered around down there a little, and found a puddle to drink out of, then I just lay down and slept. When they pulled me out and all those people and lights and cameras were trained on me—that was a lot more frightening than being underground. It sounds crazy, but I felt more trapped by all of them than I did in that cavern."

"I can imagine," Sharon said. "I get freaked out in crowds, and I really don't like people staring at me. Cassie asked me to be in her play and I told her no way."

"She won't take no for an answer from me. You know how she is."

"I know." Sharon laid a hand on Shelly's arm. "Don't let her bully you. Do what I do—nod and smile and keep saying no. After all, she can't force you to put on that costume and recite your lines."

Shelly smiled at the picture that formed in her mind of the little librarian trying to do just that. "You're right. I'll just have to stand my ground with her. Thanks for the advice. And thanks for understanding, too."

"Remember, you have a lot of friends on your side."

"Thanks. That means a lot." She'd been strong enough to leave the spotlight in the first place; she could resist the pull of it now. All she wanted was her old life back, with her husband and kids and friends—the people who really mattered to her. The ones who loved her for who she was, not because she'd been hapless enough as a kid to fall into a hole in the ground.

Cassie exited the salon and checked her watch. Eleven-fifteen. Maxi had taken longer than usual this morning to do her hair—too much time on the phone with other clients. Next time Cassie saw her, she'd suggest she hire a reception-ist or a shampoo girl to take those calls. The stylist ought to be focused on her customer.

She started down the sidewalk toward the library, then did an about-face and strode toward the park instead. Apparently, Lucille and the rest of the town council had gone through with their ridiculous plan to graze goats in the park. Goats might very well eat weeds, but they'd be just as likely to mow down the flowering perennials Ernestine Wynock and the members of the Eureka Women's Club had planted and tended in the park for years. People in town didn't have enough respect for the work and care that those women had put into beautifying the town. They needed to realize that beautiful surroundings didn't just show up by themselves. If it weren't for Cassie, people might forget about their heritage altogether.

She heard the goats before she saw them, a steady chorus of "baaah" and "maaah" growing louder as she neared the entrance to the park. She stopped beneath the iron archway to admire the sign. ERNESTINE WYNOCK PARK proclaimed the vinyl banner tied to the arch. Cassie had hung that banner herself earlier this year, with help from two young people. It was holding up nicely; just as well, since the town was too cheap to purchase a suitable permanent sign. After the Founders' Pageant was over, she would have to go to work on getting that done.

The goats were gathered around a short, sturdy woman with snow-white hair, who was handing out something from a bucket. As Cassie walked closer, the woman's words carried to her. "Now Stella, don't be a pig. Share with Kate. Sophia, there's plenty for everyone. Here you go, Belle. And some for you, Sassy. That's my good girls."

The bucket empty, the woman upended it. "That's all, girls. Back to work with you." She made shooing motions and after a moment the goats quieted and moved away, to resume grazing.

The woman looked up and spotted Cassie. "Hello," she said. "You just missed treat time."

"Why are you feeding them anything?" Cassie made her way to the woman, stepping carefully to avoid scattered piles of goat pellets. "I thought their job is to eat weeds."

"Yes, and they eat plenty of them. But I give them nuggets once a day as a treat. Plus it keeps them tame and easy to manage." She looped the bucket over one arm and extended the other. "Daisy Mott."

"I'm Cassie Wynock."

"Any relation to Ernestine Wynock?"

Cassie was pleased the woman had made the association. "Yes. She was my grandmother. And she's responsible for many of the plantings in this park."

"And you came to check to make sure the goats weren't

destroying her handiwork." Daisy nodded. "Well, you don't need to worry. The flowers are fenced off, and in any case, Alice knows to keep the girls away from the ornamentals."

Cassie followed Daisy's gaze to the black-and-white dog who was patrolling the herd, her gaze intent for any who might stray from the boundary she'd set. Then she looked at the flower beds. The lilacs, daisies, and columbine appeared untouched behind a strand of electric wire. "You seem to have everything under control," she said.

"Alice and I manage just fine, though I probably don't have to tell you, there are plenty of people who don't think a woman—especially one my age—is capable of much of anything."

"Yes, I know exactly what you mean." Didn't people—especially men—underestimate Cassie constantly? She'd had to take matters into her own hands to get the park renamed after her grandmother, and there wouldn't even be a Founders' Pageant if she hadn't taken it upon herself to write, direct, and star in the production. Just think of all she might accomplish if she ever got any real support!

She looked around and spotted the truck with the camper on its back. "Is that where you live?"

"When I'm out with the goats, yes. Winters, I have a little cabin in the San Luis Valley. It suits me."

"I've always wanted to travel," Cassie said, struggling to keep the wistfulness from her voice. "But of course, as head librarian, and president of the historical society, I have so many responsibilities here."

"You never know. One day you may decide to pull up stakes and set out, like I did. The older you get, the easier it is to do what you want, I say."

"I admire your spirit," Cassie said. She stood a little straighter. Obviously, Daisy Mott was a woman of good character and discernment. One might almost say she and Cassie were cut from the same cloth. "If you would like to use our library during your stay in Eureka, I'd be happy to extend you temporary borrowing privileges. And we have computers for public use, as well."

"I might just take you up on that," Daisy said. "Thanks." She shifted the bucket to her other hand. "It's been a pleasure talking with you, but I'd better make sure the girls have fresh water. Those nuggets are kind of salty."

"By all means. I have to return to my work as well." They nodded good-bye, and Cassie made her way back across the park to the entrance. She paused to look back over her shoulder and saw Daisy filling her bucket at the spigot. Too bad she was only visiting in town. It would be good to have someone her own age who identified with her struggles. As a strong, independent woman, she'd always had trouble making friends, but maybe, as Daisy had said, it was never too late.

With a new burst of confidence, she returned to the library, in time to see Shelly descending the steps. What better sign that fate was on her side, helping to bring her latest great idea to fruition? "Shelly!" she called, hurrying to catch up with the younger woman. "You're just the person I've been wanting to see."

Shelly clutched a folder to her chest and took a step back, but Cassie had reached her before she could retreat. "We really didn't have a chance to talk about my ideas for your role in the play the other night," Cassie said. "I think you may have misunderstood my intentions."

"I understood, Cassie," Shelly said. "You want me to take a bigger role in the play so that you can advertise that Baby Shelly is in your production, so that people will come from all over to gawk at me."

"They won't be gawking," Cassie said. "They'll be watching the Founders' Pageant, and learning about Eureka's history. It would be a great thing for the town, to have so many new visitors. I'm afraid that's the harsh reality, when the treasury depends so much on tourist money."

Shelly folded her arms in front of her chest. "I don't want to do it," she said. "I don't want to be in the spotlight."

"I don't know why not," Cassie said. "Why wouldn't you want to be famous?" How could someone who had reached those lofty heights ever turn her back on such public acknowledgment?

"Fame is never about you," Shelly said. "Not really. It's about something that happened to you or who your family is. Sometimes it's about something you did. But it's never really about who you are, inside."

"I think you're wrong about that. People want to get to know you. To know more about you—and about the place where you live."

"It's not like that at all. People aren't interested in that. They act like they like you, but they really don't."

No one pretended they liked Cassie, though she preferred to think she had at least earned people's respect. But in addition to respect, she craved admiration. How wonderful it would be to have the things that were important to her become important to other people also. She'd never feel invisible in a crowd of people again. Never have to fight for even a scrap of attention. "You only say that because you don't know what it's like to be truly anonymous," she said. "As Baby Shelly, you have the opportunity to share your opinion. To influence others."

"But I don't want those things. I just want to be left alone."

Really, the girl was merely whining now. "And I'll be happy to leave you alone, after the Founders' Pageant," Cassie said.

Shelly shook her head. "I can't do it, Cassie. You'll have to find someone else." She stepped around the librarian and started down the steps again.

"There comes a time when you need to stop thinking about yourself and think of others," Cassie said. "Think of the town that has sheltered you and given you a home. How could you begrudge doing this one thing to give back to them?"

Shelly's shoulders hunched, as if she were being pelted with rotten fruit, not words. Cassie wanted to run after her and shake her. She'd spent her whole life giving back to this town that was her home and her family's legacy. Here this young woman had a chance to pay her—and all the women and men who had come before her—back for that legacy, and she was ignoring the offer. All Cassie wanted was to use Shelly's name to garner a little bit of attention for the pageant and yes, for Cassie herself. That wasn't really so much to ask for, was it?

"Your problem, Travis, is that you want to have everything without sacrificing anything."

Travis winced at the strident tone in his girlfriend Trish's voice. She hadn't been too keen on his leaving to take this job, and clearly absence had not made her heart grow fonder. He knew he should apologize and placate her, but a man had to defend himself, right? "There's nothing wrong with wanting a good life," he said.

"Then maybe your definition of a good life and mine are different. You want to run all over the country, writing about all this exciting stuff, but you can't make any money at it and you still live like a nineteen-year-old frat boy. I want marriage and a home and to be able to send my kids to college one day."

Verse one hundred and twenty-two of a familiar argument, he thought. Why couldn't she see that he was working hard to make her middle-class American dream come true? All he needed was a little more time. If she had a little more faith in him it wouldn't hurt, either. "This book is really going to pay off," he said. "You'll see."

"Have you even talked to Shelly yet? Has she agreed to cooperate and help with the book?"

"I haven't persuaded her yet, but I will."

"Why should she? She hasn't agreed to any of the other

deals publishers have waved at her over the years, and I hate to break it to you, Travis, but you're not that charming."

He flinched; she might as well have slapped him. "Trish, you wound me."

"I'm sorry." He wished he could see her face, to decipher if she was really contrite, or merely going through the motions. "I'm tired of being apart and never being able to plan for the future."

"Things will get better, I promise." How many times had he said that before? But he meant it this time. He was taking a big risk with this book project, but that's how the high rollers got ahead, wasn't it? By risking everything on a dream they believed in?

"They could be better right now if you'd come back to Dallas and work for my dad," Trish said. "He's offering you a really sweet job managing publicity and communications for his firm."

"I'm just not cut out to work in an office."

"The newspaper was an office. And this would still be writing, only for a heck of a lot more money than you made before. And you could still write other things in your spare time." Her voice softened, sweet and cajoling. "Isn't it worth it so we can be together?"

This was the Trish he missed—the girl who smiled at him across the breakfast table, and rubbed his shoulders when he'd spent long hours at the computer. Why couldn't things be that good between them all the time?

"Travis?"

He knew he had waited too long to answer the question. "Trish, honey, I just need—" he began.

"I have to go now," she said, cutting him off. "Call me when you've got some good news."

He stared at his phone and debated calling her back and apologizing, but he could tell she wasn't in the mood to be so easily soothed. Until his situation changed for the better, this was an argument he couldn't win. Better to let her cool off, while he focused on getting this job over with as quickly as possible.

He pocketed the phone and walked into the Dirty Sally, where he'd been headed when Trish's call came in. The familiar beer-and-burgers aroma of the saloon surrounded him, and he felt some of the tension go out of his shoulders. He'd spent so many evenings in bars like this, when he worked for the paper, then traveling on freelance assignments. He could walk into any city in the world and feel at home in a place like this, surrounded by conversation and warmth, yet not compelled to take part. People in bars were easy to talk to, to confide in. Maybe the alcohol lowered their inhibitions, or maybe it was only the knowledge that everyone was on even footing here, each person trying to relax and let go of the cares of the day.

He found a seat at the bar. "Jack Daniel's, straight up," he ordered.

Jameso raised an eyebrow. "I saw you on the phone outside. You just get bad news?"

"Something like that." He shifted, trying to get more comfortable on the barstool. "My girlfriend is upset I'm staying away so long."

Jameso nodded and poured the whiskey.

"She wants me to come home and take a job working for her dad," Travis said. "Settle down and grow up."

Jameso winced. "Be a responsible adult."

Travis nodded. "You've heard the speech?"

"Oh yeah. Many times. From several different women."

Travis slugged back a good jolt of whiskey, making a face as it burned down his throat. He set the glass down and wiped his mouth with the back of his hand. "But hey, you're doing okay—smart, pretty wife, cute baby, nice place. You own that fancy B and B, don't you?" He'd checked out the place when he first came to town, but the rates to stay in the restored Victorian were too steep for his budget.

"I don't own it," Jameso said. "I manage it. One of Maggie's friends owns it. But yeah, I'm doing okay." He posed, one fist clenched to his chest. "I may not be a responsible adult, but I play one on TV."

Travis chuckled and took another sip of the whiskey. It went down more smoothly this time. "You mind my asking, you been married long?"

"Two months."

Travis did the math. "So that means . . ."

Jameso nodded. "Yeah, we got married the day the baby was born. Maggie didn't want to rush into anything."

"That's a new twist. My girlfriend would get married tomorrow if I'd agree."

"So why don't you agree?"

"Oh, you know. I want to be able to give her something besides my old truck and my collection of vintage concert T-shirts. She wants a house, and that takes money. That's why I'm so intent on making this book project work. It's why I agreed to work with Mindy."

Both men turned to look toward the small stage in the corner of the bar, where Mindy was overemoting to a version of Beyoncé's "Diva." Her voice wasn't bad, but she was throwing herself around on the stage and twisting up her face like someone in the throes of some kind of seizure.

Jameso turned away and began wiping down the bar. "I didn't have a pot to piss in when Maggie and I married," he said. "Still don't, but she says she doesn't care and I guess she means it."

"So you're saying I should marry Trish and not worry about the rest."

"I'm only the bartender. I listen, but I don't give advice." He pulled two beers from the tap and slid them across to the waitress.

"But I'm asking." Travis leaned toward him. "If you were in my shoes, what would you do?"

"I think you should think about what you really want. Marriage is hard. I mean, your wife, and kids if you have them, are always there. A part of you, even when you're not with them. And they're depending on you, even if nobody ever says that. You can't escape it."

"That's heavy, huh?" Even the words were a weight that pressed on his chest.

"It is," Jameso said. "And it's not. Sometimes it's kind of . . . I don't know. Comforting. I mean, being single and carefree is fun, but sometimes it's lonely, too."

"Do you think women feel that, too? One thing that Shelly said when I talked to her was that she just wanted to be a wife and mom and not deal with anything else. Like that was better than being famous or having a lot of money or anything."

"Maybe it is. I've never had money or been famous, but I can't imagine they'd be better than seeing my little girl smile at me or snuggling up next to Maggie on a cold night. You want another whiskey?"

"No. I guess I've got some thinking to do and I need a clear head." He took out his wallet. "Let me pay you."

"Don't worry about it. This one's on me."

"Thanks." He walked outside, and stood in the empty street in front of the building, head tilted back to look up at the stars. Here away from the city, the sky looked like some kid had gotten a little heavy-handed with the glitter. It didn't even look like the same sky he saw over Dallas.

What did he really want? He wanted Trish and he wanted money and his name on a book and respect and a house and . . . everything. The trick was to figure out how to get all that and not lose himself in the process.

Three steps from the top of the stairs that led to her apartment, Sharon saw the man's shadow. She froze, holding her breath, and studied the looming, dark figure. Her heart pounded, even as she told herself to calm down and take it easy. Her ex, Joe, was still in prison in upstate New York. The police would have told her if he'd been released or gotten out somehow. Josh Miller would have told her. Even if he was free, Joe had no reason to come all this way to harm her. Surely he didn't. But maybe one of his buddies, the men who had joined him in his radical survivalist encampment, had decided to pay her a visit. Men like that couldn't be said to be completely sane. . . .

"Mrs. Franklin?" A man emerged from the shadows, a tall, broad-shouldered man in a western-cut jacket, with silver-streaked hair. "It's Duke Breman. We met at the library."

All the breath rushed out of her and she gripped the stair railing and pulled herself up the last three steps. "Of course, Mr. Breman, I remember you."

"Call me Duke." He nodded toward her apartment door. "I understand Gerald Pershing used to live here?"

"Yes. I rented the place after he left." She moved toward the door, keys in her hand.

"I understand he left a lot of his things behind. I was wondering if you'd mind if I took a look at them."

Before she could answer him, footsteps pounded up the stairs. Her daughter, Alina, fourteen and beginning to lose some of her childhood lankiness, leapt onto the landing, her high-tops making soft thumps on the carpet. She drew up short when she saw Duke, her cheeks reddening. "I didn't know you had company, Mom."

"This is Mr. Breman," she said. "You can go on in and start your homework while I talk to him out here."

"I was gonna ask if I could go over to Lucas's? We can study together, then I can have dinner with him. We're working on a project for social studies."

"If it's okay with Olivia and D. J., it's okay with me. Is your brother still at basketball practice?"

She shrugged. "I guess so. You know they usually run to

six-thirty or seven, then he's working at the Last Dollar until nine."

"He probably told me that and I forgot. All right. You can go to Lucas's. Call me when you're ready to come home. I don't want you riding your bike out that late."

"D. J. might give me a ride."

"Call me anyway when you're on your way, so I won't worry."

"You always worry." Alina hugged Sharon and kissed her cheek. "See you later. Nice meeting you, Mr. Breman."

"She seems like a good kid," Duke said, as Alina thundered back down the stairs.

"She is."

"Is Lucas her boyfriend?"

She shook her head. "Just a friend." Lucas was the first classmate who'd befriended Alina, and the two had been close ever since. Maybe when they were older it would grow into more, but Sharon wasn't ready for that yet.

"You have a son, too?"

"Aiden. He's sixteen." When Sharon and Joe had divorced last year, Alina had come to Eureka with Sharon, while Aiden chose to remain in Vermont with Joe. But when Joe's beliefs became even more radical and isolationist, the boy had left, hitchhiking all the way across the country to get to his mom. Since then, the three of them had formed a tight little family. Life in Eureka suited them, and she'd gotten close to Jameso again. She hadn't realized how much she'd missed her brother until she had a chance to get to know him again.

"Could I come in and see Pershing's things?" Duke asked.

"There's really nothing to see," she said. "Just some furniture and a few books and things like that. Nothing personal."

"I might see something that would provide a clue to where he might have headed when he left Eureka."

"Sharon? Is everything all right?"

She didn't realize how tense she'd been until she heard Josh's voice and relief flooded her, like a sedative injected into her veins. He stepped from the stairway, imposing in his tan Eureka County Sheriff's Department uniform, pistol at his side. Usually when he saw her, he smiled, the corners of his blue eyes crinkling, his face lighting with a warmth that always made her feel a little unsteady.

But he wasn't smiling now. He fixed Duke with a quelling frown, the kind of look he must give lawbreakers when he made an arrest. "Mr. Breman, can I help you with something?"

Duke hooked his thumb in the pockets of his jeans and rocked back on the heels of his eel-skin boots. "I was telling Mrs. Franklin that the items Gerald Pershing left behind in her apartment might give me a clue as to where he was headed when he left Eureka."

"And I believe I heard her tell you she didn't want you in her apartment," Josh said.

"No, Josh, it's okay." She put a hand on his arm. Now that he was here, she didn't mind the detective looking at her and Gerald's things. "It's okay if Mr. Breman wants to take a quick look."

"You're welcome to come with us, if you like," Duke said.

"Oh, I'm coming with you," Josh said. He took Sharon's keys from her and opened the door, then led the way inside.

The apartment was one of four units added above the hardware store. It was modern and bright, with blond oak floors and large windows that afforded a view of the surrounding mountains. It only had two bedrooms, but Sharon had turned a small study into her room and given the master bedroom to Aiden and the second bedroom to Alina. "The furniture was all his, except the beds," she said, indicating the leather sofa and club chair and dark wood tables in the living area.

"Did he leave the TV, too?" Duke asked, walking over to the large flat screen on a console across from the sofa.

"Yes." The children had been particularly happy with that acquisition, since they'd never had television before, though she didn't have cable or a satellite dish. They used it to watch movies, though.

"He must have been in a hurry to leave, or determined to travel light," Duke said.

"My understanding was that he already had a home in Dallas," Josh said. "Maybe he didn't see any point in moving a bunch of heavy furniture he didn't need."

Duke nodded, and stopped in front of a three-shelf bookcase in the corner. "You said he left behind some books. Any of these?"

Sharon joined him, aware of Josh close behind her. She studied the books, then pulled out a travel guide to Mexico, a book about gold mining, and another on conversational Spanish. "That bottom shelf is mostly his, too," she said. "The paperback thrillers and the other travel books. I kept them because Aiden likes to read those."

"Did you get rid of anything?"

"He left behind a few clothes. Not much—a jacket with a rip in the sleeve and some socks with holes in them. I threw them out, though there was a pair of shoes and some slacks I donated to the local thrift store."

"Did he leave anything more personal—photos, letters, or financial paperwork?"

She shook her head. "Nothing like that."

He flipped through the guide to Mexico. "Looks like he's underlined some things in here. Do you mind if I take this with me? Maybe he was headed to Mexico."

"Maybe you'd better take the guide to Italy and the one to Greece, too," Josh said. "They're on the bottom shelf."

Sharon couldn't tell if the look Duke sent Josh was one of

annoyance or embarrassment at being caught out, but there was no missing the animosity between the two men. It radiated in the air like a noxious cloud. "Take anything you like," she said. "As long as they're not my personal books, I don't care."

"So when you moved in to this apartment, you didn't find anything that might indicate where Gerald Pershing was headed next?" Duke asked. "No credit card receipts or scribbled notes—things you might have tossed in the trash because you thought they weren't significant?"

"I didn't find anything like that," she said. "The only things I threw out were those old clothes and some leftover Chinese takeout and some lunch meat from the refrigerator."

Duke balanced the three guidebooks on his palm. "I'll return these if I decide I don't need them."

"Wherever Pershing ended up, I don't think you're going to find anything here in Eureka," Josh said, all but herding the detective toward the door. "He packed up and left and we haven't heard from him since."

"No one's heard from him since he was here," Duke said. "That's not his usual pattern of behavior. He hasn't used his credit cards or his phone, and no one has seen his car, since the day he was pulled out of that mine. That strikes me as suspicious."

"Maybe he'd planned to disappear," Josh said. "He made another identity for himself. It happens."

"Or maybe one of the people here in town who had a grudge against him decided to make sure he never came back to bother them again." Duke's grim tone and expression sent another chill through Sharon.

"Who did you say you work for, again?" Josh said.

Duke's smile was fleeting and didn't reach his eyes. "I didn't say."

"If Gerald's family or business associates suspect foul play, they should contact the police," Josh said. "So far, you're the only one raising these suspicions."

"I guess I'm just the suspicious type." He paused in the doorway and addressed Sharon. "If you think of anything—anything you remember from when you moved in that might be significant, let me know." He handed her his business card, then nodded to Josh and left.

When he was gone, Sharon sank onto the sofa. "That man makes me nervous."

Josh settled onto the sofa beside her. "It's an interviewing technique. Make people nervous and they tend to talk more."

"Is that one of those things they teach you in cop school?" she asked.

"Something like that."

"Do you think he was ever a cop?"

"Maybe. A lot of private investigators are. It helps to have an in with a department."

"Well, I hope he got what he wanted from me. I'd just as soon not talk to him again."

"I saw Alina on my way up. She said she was on her way over to Lucas's house."

"Yes. She's going to have dinner with him. Aiden is working at the Last Dollar after he gets out of basketball practice."

"Why don't you come over to my place for dinner? I'll make pasta or something simple."

He'd made several of his simple—but delicious—dinners for her over the past few weeks. "This is getting to be a habit."

He covered her hand with his. "I hope you think it's a good habit."

"It's growing on me." She turned her palm up to twine her fingers with his. "Thanks for being patient with me." Josh had stood by her and helped her in the aftermath of her divorce, and those weeks when Aiden was missing. She knew he wanted more than the platonic friendship she'd allowed so far, but after years at the beck and call of controlling men— first her father, then Joe—she was savoring the opportunity to learn how to stand on her own feet. But the more time she spent with Josh, the less attractive a life alone seemed to be.

"I understand why you don't want to rush into anything." He traced one finger along her jaw, sending a warm shiver of awareness up her spine. "Just remember, I'm a very patient man. And a stubborn one."

She smiled, then stood and tugged him to his feet. Arm in arm, they walked across the hall to his apartment. She wasn't sure if she was ready to take the next step with him yet, but she was definitely getting closer.

Chapter 11

"So, tell me what Art in the Park is all about." Maggie switched on her pocket recorder and began her interview for the next edition of the *Eureka Miner*. Olivia Gruber, all blond and pink elfin delicacy, five months pregnant, yet still glowing and stylish in a way Maggie was sure she had never been, stared at the device as if it were a wild animal, one that might bite at any moment.

"Pretend the recorder isn't here," Maggie coaxed. "You're just talking to me, as a friend."

"All right." Olivia tucked her straight blond hair behind one ear, revealing two tiny diamond studs and a silver ear cuff. "Art in the Park is a new program offered by the Eureka Recreational League, to provide free art classes for kids. Anybody between the ages of four and fourteen can participate, and older kids can come help out if they want."

"What kind of art will you be doing?" Maggie asked.

Olivia glanced toward the row of easels set up near the park entrance. "Today we're painting with watercolors. Next week we're going to do nature collages. We're going to do sun prints on T-shirts one week, and maybe play around with sculpture." She relaxed a little, getting into her subject. "This is the first year, so we're only doing four weeks, on Wednesday afternoons, but I hope next year we can do more—maybe separate the kids into different age groups. It's a good time for it—school has just started, but everyone's calendar isn't too crowded, and the weather is good."

Maggie nodded encouragingly. "Tell everybody where they can find your artwork."

"Oh, everybody knows that already," she said.

"Some of the people who read the paper are visitors here, and they might want to know."

Olivia flushed. "Oh. Okay. Well, my mom's shop, Lacy's, sells my T-shirts and jewelry, and there are some at Nona's Gifts. And I have a few paintings hanging in the Last Dollar and they're for sale."

"You also did the mural that's on the back wall of the café, didn't you?"

"Maggie, you know I did."

"So tell me something interesting about the mural that I can put in my article."

"Like what?"

"Like anything I can quote. I have to fill eight inches with this piece, so help me out here."

"Well . . . it was my first big art project. And it made me think maybe I really could be an artist."

"How many children are signed up for Art in the Park?" Maggie asked.

Olivia looked again at the easels. "Ten, so far, but anybody can walk up and join, so we'll probably get more." She glanced toward the back of the park, where Daisy Mott's herd grazed, Alice the dog watching from the shade of a lilac bush. "I hope they aren't too distracted by the animals. If they are, I can always ask them to paint them."

Maggie switched off the recorder. "That ought to be enough. I can always fill in with information about the rec league." She dropped the gadget into her purse. "Now, tell me how you're doing. You look great."

"I feel good. The worst of the morning sickness is over and I have a little more energy. The doctor says everything is going according to schedule."

"I know this is a nosy question, but I'm going to ask anyway. Do you know if you're having a boy or girl?"

"A girl." Olivia's smile brightened her face. "D. J. is thrilled and Lucas is excited, too. She's probably going to be the most spoiled little girl ever."

"A playmate for Angela. They'll only be a few months apart."

"Where is that little angel today?"

"With her dad at the B and B."

"Jameso sure has settled down. When I first went to work at the Dirty Sally, I heard so many stories about his wild escapades that I never would have believed he could be domesticated, but you did it."

Maggie couldn't keep back a frown. "How domesticated is open to debate," she said. "He still spends four nights a week tending bar. I can't get him to give that up. And lately he's been spending another night with D. J. and Josh Miller. And he won't tell me what he's up to." She couldn't decide which aspect of this bothered her most—that Jameso was taking one more night away from their precious time together, or that he wouldn't reveal what he was doing that was so important.

Olivia shook her head. "D. J. won't tell me what they're up to, either. But I'm wondering if it has something to do with Hard Rock Days. Maybe they're planning to compete."

"Jameso told me he did that once, with my dad, but that he has no desire to do it again."

"D. J. didn't act all that interested when the guys at the County Barn were trying to put together teams," Olivia said. "Maybe they're planning some kind of practical joke or something. That would be more their style."

"Jameso and D. J. maybe, but Josh doesn't strike me as the joking type."

"I guess we'll just have to wait and see. But D. J. has promised me they won't be meeting like this much longer."

"I wish I could say the same about Jameso's job at the Dirty Sally."

"The Dirty Sally wouldn't be the same without Jameso there."

"Somehow, I like to think the drinkers in town would find a way to carry on without him." She straightened, trying for a calm expression. "I'm trying to be Zen about it and let him work it out on his own. But I worry he feels trapped. Marriage and fatherhood all happened pretty suddenly."

"Ha! He was thirty-two. About time he grew up." She patted Maggie's hand. "He'll be fine."

Maggie opened her mouth to say that Jameso would be fine if women like Mindy Payton stopped throwing themselves at him, when Mindy herself pulled up to the entrance in her faded blue Corolla and climbed out. She was dressed almost conservatively today, in short shorts, platform espadrilles, and a loose, floaty tank top, her impossibly blond mop of curls tamed by a pink headband. Shelly's two boys, Cameron and Theo, climbed out of the car's backseat and ran past her through the entrance arch.

"I guess this is the right place for the art classes?" she asked as she walked toward them, doing her runway strut, hips jutted out, stepping along an invisible tightrope.

"That's right." Olivia smiled at Cameron and Theo. "Hey, boys. We're going to get started in about twenty minutes or so, but you're welcome to pick out an easel and do some drawings with colored chalk if you want."

"I guess you're babysitting today?" Maggie forced herself to smile and sound pleasant as she addressed Mindy.

"I told Shelly I'd bring the boys here and she can pick them up when she gets off at the bank." Her gaze shifted toward the goats at the other end of the park. "What kind of place keeps livestock in the city park?" She laughed. "And I thought I was originally from the sticks."

"And here I thought you were a sophisticated city girl," Maggie said. She caught Olivia's eye and had to bite the inside of her cheek to keep from laughing.

"Oh, I haven't lived in the country for years." Mindy fluffed her hair. "I moved to Dallas when I was still a teenager to pursue my modeling and acting career."

"I see." Maggie congratulated herself on not saying the half dozen snide remarks that came to mind. "Well, I'm sure you're anxious to get back to it. It must be very boring for you here."

"Oh, I'm managing to find a few ways to amuse myself. The right company can make even a boring place exciting." Her sly smile sent a shiver up Maggie's spine.

"Are you gonna fill all those easels up by yourself, Olivia?"

The women turned to see Bob Prescott striding toward them. "Hello, Bob," Olivia greeted the old man, a regular at the Dirty Sally, where she'd waited tables and tended bar when she first came to Eureka.

"When are you going to come back to work?" Bob brushed a kiss on her cheek and nodded to Maggie. "Nothing against that husband of yours, but he don't put a proper head on the draft like this little gal."

"My bartending days are over," Olivia said. "I'm teaching art to kids." She nodded to the easels.

"That was some performance you put on last night," Bob told Mindy. "I don't think Eureka has ever seen anything quite like that."

"Why, thank you." She fluttered her eyelashes. "I was happy to be able to share my talent."

"What talent is that?" Maggie tried to keep the edge from her voice.

"The Dirty Sally's got a karaoke machine now," Bob said. "Mindy did quite a few numbers. She was very enthusiastic." He winked.

"I tried to talk Jameso into doing a duet with me, but he was too busy behind the bar," Mindy said.

"Jameso doesn't sing," Maggie said.

"Oh, but he does!" Her eyes widened. "By the end of the evening, we talked him into singing a Bob Seger song. He did a great job."

Maggie looked to Bob, who nodded. "He did. I wouldn't have believed it, but he has a pretty good voice."

Maggie wished she were a better actress, or that she knew how to keep her face from betraying her dismay. How did she not know that her husband could sing? What other secrets about himself was he sharing with others but not her? She looked at Mindy, which was a mistake; Maggie had to curl her hands into fists to keep from slapping the smirk off the younger woman's face.

"What are you doing here, Bob?" Olivia asked, filling in the awkward silence. "I thought this time of morning you were usually at the mine."

"Daisy's moving the goats today and I volunteered to help her." He nodded toward the herd, and the white-haired woman who'd emerged from her camper and was making her way toward them.

"Anxious to have the goats out of town?" Maggie asked.

"Well, they aren't going far," Bob said. "Brice Alcott, just north of town, hired her to do weed mitigation on his place. He saw what a good job the girls did here, so he wanted to try it out."

So now the goats were "the girls." Maggie fought to hide her amusement. "I thought you weren't a fan of the goats," she said. "You swore they were a scam."

"I never said that." He looked offended.

She was sure he had, but Daisy was within earshot now, so

Maggie kept quiet. "Hello Maggie, Olivia," Daisy said. "I don't think I know your friend."

"This is Mindy," Olivia said. "She's visiting from Dallas."

Daisy nodded, then turned to Bob. She looked less pleased to see him. "You're early. I'm not supposed to be at the ranch until this afternoon."

He shoved his hands in his pockets and looked almost sheepish. "I needed to get away from the mine for a while, so I figured I'd come hang out with you."

"I've got work to do. I don't have time to entertain you."

"You don't have to entertain me. I can take it easy in your trailer until you need me."

Daisy's eyes narrowed. "What are you up to, old man? Don't you have work to do at the mine?"

"Why do people keep asking me that?"

"I think maybe Bob is trying to avoid the mine right now," Maggie guessed. "Maybe he doesn't want to run into a certain private detective who's made it clear he wants to interview the last man to see Gerald Pershing alive."

"You mean that good-looking, tall drink of water I've seen around?" Daisy asked. "I heard he was an investigator from Texas."

"I know who you're talking about," Mindy said. "He is good looking, though a little old for me."

The others ignored her. "What have you done now, Bob?" Daisy asked.

"I haven't done a blasted thing," Bob said. "But I don't care to waste my time with a man who's spent entirely too much time nosing into business that don't concern him."

Mindy yawned. "I guess I'm not needed here anymore," she said. "Maybe I'll do a little shopping. Is there someplace in town where I can get my nails done?"

"You might ask at Maxi's salon," Olivia said. "It's over on Third Street. Behind the post office."

"Thanks. I'll do that. I think a good manicure is so important to a woman's appearance." She frowned at Maggie's unpainted nails. "See you all around." She fluttered her fingers and sashayed back to her car.

"She's certainly, um, interesting," Daisy said when Mindy had driven away.

"She put on a show last night," Bob said. "Throwing herself around on the stage like she was having some kind of fit. After a few beers, it was pretty entertaining."

Maggie didn't want to talk about Mindy, or about last night, anymore. "Bob, do you know anything about Gerald Pershing's disappearance?" she asked.

"If I did, would I tell you, Ms. Reporter?"

"Who is Gerald Pershing and why is everybody so interested in him?" Daisy asked.

"He was a lying, thieving, good-for-nothing swindler who tried to steal all the town's money," Bob said. "I don't have any idea where he is now, though hell wouldn't be a bad location for the likes of him."

Daisy turned to Maggie. "Care to translate that into plain English?"

"Gerald worked an investment scam that took most of the town's treasury," Maggie said. "The town got some of the money back by selling him shares in a fake mine, which turned out to have gold after all."

"Then he tried to steal the money back by ordering all these safety improvements for the mine," Bob said. "But instead of seeing to it that the improvements were made, he siphoned off the money."

"Which came back to bite him when there was an explosion and part of the mine caved in and there was no way out," Olivia continued the story. "Bob was trapped down there with him for five days. By the time they were finally rescued, Gerald had agreed to sell his mine shares to Bob. He left town and no one has seen him since."

"Good riddance," Bob said.

"So why not just tell this Duke character that you didn't have anything to do with Gerald's disappearance and you don't know where he is, and be done with it?" Maggie asked.

Bob studied her. "If you'd known your father better, you'd know the answer to that question," he said.

Maggie stiffened. "What does Jake have to do with this?" She'd heard plenty of stories about her father since she'd come to Eureka. He hadn't had the guts to contact her during her lifetime, but he'd left everything he owned to her, and she'd met plenty of people who would attest to both his kindness and generosity, and his toughness and at times, downright meanness. She'd formed a picture of a complex, angry, hurting man she'd probably never figure out. "I thought the two of you were enemies."

"Oh, we didn't see eye to eye on most things, that's for sure. But one thing Jake knew is that it never hurt for people to think you're capable of killing a man—even if you never have, and have no intention of doing so. You'd be surprised the trouble you can avoid with a reputation like that."

Except that Jake had killed people, Maggie thought. In the war, at least. That was one of the demons that drove him.

"Come on, killer." Daisy took his arm. "I'll let you hide out in my camper, but you'll have to pay me back later."

Bob looked wary. "How will I do that?"

"Oh, I'll think of something. Don't worry."

Olivia waited until they were gone before she spoke. "What do you think? Did Bob 'help' Gerald disappear?"

Maggie pulled out her car keys. "I think there are some questions I don't want to know the answers to." Maybe that included not knowing why she still felt left out of so much of her husband's life. She'd always thought love should bring people closer but sometimes, it seemed, it put up barriers that she didn't know how to get around.

*　*　*

The darkness in the cavern was unlike any darkness Shelly had ever known. It was the darkness of outer space. The darkness of the womb. The blackness swallowed up all sense of time and place, creating a dizzying disorientation that forced her to sit flat on the ground, frozen in place.

She shut her eyes, rather than stare into that blackness, and breathed deeply of the damp, musty smell of the place, an ancient aroma that hinted at dry bones and dripping limestone. Fine gravel covered the ground beneath her palms. In the quiet, she could hear her heartbeat, and the blood rushing in her veins.

After a while, her initial panic gave way to calm, an enveloping peace, sheltered from all conflict and danger, cocooned here in the darkness and silence.

But just as she settled into this tranquility, she heard a distant uproar. The noises grew louder, until she could hear people shouting her name, begging her to come out. She moved onto her knees, crouched on all fours, staring at a crack of light overhead, which gradually widened to a blinding beam aimed directly at her. Rough hands clutched at her, pulling her out of her sanctuary. She fought against her captors, trying to back away from them, but she stumbled into a spider web, the sticky strands catching in her hair, twining around her arms. . . .

"Shelly! Shelly, wake up!" Charlie's hand on her shoulder, warm and solid, and his voice in her ear, familiar and caring, pulled her from her struggle against the sticky spider's webbing and strangers' reaching hands. She blinked up at him, heart pounding, too frightened still to speak.

"You were having a nightmare. You're all tangled up in the sheet." He carefully unwound the linen from around her and patted her shoulder. "Are you okay?"

She nodded. "Yes. Now I am. Thanks."

Though Charlie was six years older than Shelly, his face

was younger than his years, apple-cheeked and unlined. A baby face, people said, which had led him to grow a full beard when he was still in his twenties. Now the beard was flecked with silver, but the face above it remained smooth and young. Worry lines etched his forehead as he studied her now. "You want to talk about it?"

Did she? Could she? "I dreamed I was back in that cavern—the one I fell into when I was four."

"No wonder you were struggling. That must have been terrifying." He lay down beside her and pulled her close.

She rested her head against the pillow of his shoulder. Charlie was a big guy, well muscled and well padded. She liked the combination of softness and hardness—he made her feel comfortable and safe. "In the dream, it really wasn't," she said. "It was very dark and very quiet—peaceful. I wanted to stay there."

"Then why were you struggling?"

"I was just beginning to enjoy myself when all these people showed up, shouting and shining bright lights, reaching for me to pull me out. I was trying to get away from them."

His hand on her shoulder tightened its grip. "Is that how it was when you were little? Did the people who tried to rescue you frighten you that way?"

"My memory of that time is all mixed up," she said. "It was so long ago, and I think I've made myself forget part of it—the worst of it. I don't remember being cold and hungry and thirsty and scared, but I must have been. I remember I cried, and that I missed my mom and dad. I believe I was happy to see the first rescuer. He was a man in workman's coveralls and a hard hat, and when he lifted me out he held me as gently as you'd hold a baby." She hadn't thought of that man in years. He was a cowboy who worked at one of the local ranches, who had volunteered to help with the rescue efforts. She wondered where he was now, and if he ever thought of her, and wondered what had happened to her. Would he buy a copy of Travis and Mindy's book to read about her? Or was it enough for him to know he'd helped save a little girl who had moved on with her life?

"Your parents must have been sick with worry," Charlie said. "I can't even imagine what I'd do if something like that happened to the boys."

"They must have been," she said. "I think if something like that happened to Cameron or Theo, I'd want to hold them so tightly and never let them go, but Mama wasn't like that. When the man who'd pulled me out handed me to her, she held me out for everyone to see. Suddenly, there were all these bright lights and flashbulbs going off, people pushing and shoving to get closer to me, people shouting questions and shoving big microphones at me. I was terrified, trying to get away, but Mama just held me out there, an arm's length from her. 'Say thank you to all the nice people who have been praying for you,' she said. But I couldn't say anything. All I could do was cry."

"That's a crazy thing for a little kid to go through." He kissed the top of her head. "But you're okay now. You made it through all of that."

"Yeah, I'm okay now." Most of the time, anyway. She hadn't even thought of her time in the cavern in years, until Mindy showed up, and brought it all back. Now here she was, reliving it for the second time in two days. It was as if talking about that time with Sharon had broken down some barrier, and sent the memories flooding in.

"What has you so upset now?" He idly stroked her hair. "Is it that reporter, giving you a hard time? Or your sister?"

"No, it's actually been good seeing Mindy again, though I worry about her. And Travis is annoying, but I can handle him." She rolled to face him. "I think it's Cassie and this business with her play."

"I know you're shy about taking a bigger role in the play, but you had fun doing it last year. I think you'd be good. She wants you to play a schoolteacher, right?"

"She wants to put Baby Shelly up on stage so a crowd of people will come to stare at me."

"Awww, honey, I don't think it will be like that. I mean, it's an amateur historical pageant. It's not like she's reenacting your rescue or something like that."

"It's on the posters she had made up—Shelly 'Baby Shelly' Frazier."

"So a few people might drop in out of curiosity. It's not like they'll drag you offstage or anything. They'll see you and they'll go on their way."

"I don't want to be Baby Shelly. Ever again. For any reason." She flopped onto her back and crossed her arms over her chest. She'd hoped Charlie, of all people, would understand.

"I don't get why you're so upset." He sat up, so that he was looking down at her. "Nobody's asking you to relive your past, and you don't have to talk about it if you don't want to. But you *were* Baby Shelly. It's part of who you are, the way brown hair and blue eyes and a Texas accent are part of you. Why do you care if people know it?"

"How would you like it if the only reason people were interested in you was because you won the snowmobile races last winter?" she asked.

"I wouldn't care. Because that kind of fame doesn't last. People lose interest. They forget and move on."

"I was pulled out of that cavern twenty-five years ago and people are still interested."

"Only because your mother kept fanning the flames. But you don't have to do that. If you just admit that yeah, you're that girl and you don't think it was that big a deal, the furor will die down. People will move on to the next big thing."

"But what if it doesn't die down? What if people won't shut up about it? You don't know what it's like, Charlie. I couldn't go to the grocery store when I was little without some old woman wanting to come up and give me a hug, or some kid wanting to pose for a picture with me. And there was my mom, giving some sob story about medical bills from all the trauma, or what a hard time the family had had getting back on our feet, until my 'fans' had coughed up a few bucks for her to tuck away. I never saw any of that money again, and every time she went into her begging act I wanted to crawl right back into that cavern and never come out."

"There are a lot of reasons I don't think any of that will happen." He held up one hand and began to count off on his fingers. "One, you won't be asking anybody for money. Two, this isn't Texas. Three, a lot of people don't even remember who Baby Shelly is. Four, if some old woman does want to hug you or take your picture, would that really be so bad? Give her her moment and move on."

"So you think because of what happened to me, I don't have a right to privacy?"

"We live in a small town, honey. How much privacy do you really have? And it's not like Eureka is exactly close to anything. Anybody who comes here to see you is going to have to go to some trouble, and most people won't do it."

"Cassie seems to think they will. She's sure if she gets me up on that stage, the Founders' Pageant will have its biggest audience ever."

"Would that be such a bad thing? If you think about it, all that tourist money benefits the town, and the town pays my salary. Or don't you remember last winter, when Lucille was scraping the bottom of the barrel just to pay city employees? Even with the Lucky Lady paying off, there's no guarantee those hard times won't show up again."

"So it's all right for me to use what happened to me to make money, as long as the money benefits us?" She sat up and glared at him. "Can't you see how that makes you just like my mother?"

"No, it doesn't make me like your mother. And I don't

care about the money. But I do care about you getting over this phobia you have about anyone knowing what happened to you when you were a kid. Can't you see how much that's hurting you? How that's hurting our family? Instead of hiding or running away, maybe you should accept your past and move on with it. Maybe standing up on that stage and letting people see you as you are today—happy and healthy and part of a community—would help you get over it and really move on, instead of just pretending to."

She gaped at him, anger and hurt choking off any reply she might have made. He slid out of bed and reached for his shirt. "I have to go to work," he said. "Don't bother coming downstairs. I'll grab coffee at the shop."

He left the room and she slid back down in bed and rolled over, her back to the door, hot tears wetting the pillow beneath her head. She couldn't believe that Charlie—the man who had always loved her and protected her and stood by her—was acting this way, as if she was the one in the wrong, instead of people like Travis and Mindy and Cassie, who wanted to use her and what had happened to her. Why would he say she needed to expose herself to the scrutiny and exploitation she'd lived with all her life? Yes, it had happened a long time ago, but as long as people like Travis and Mindy and Cassie were around, it could definitely happen again. And this time she didn't have only herself to think about, but the children. Why hadn't she mentioned the boys to Charlie? Surely he didn't want them exposed to the same kind of spotlight she'd had to endure.

And it wasn't just the press and gawking strangers she'd have to deal with. Once word got out she was living in Eureka, she had no doubt her mom and dad would rush to be with her. They might even move here, so that Sandy could be close to the Baby Shelly franchise, back in her element churning out press releases and updated photographs. This place that Shelly loved, her peaceful little sanctuary, would become another nightmare. Charlie didn't want that, she was sure.

He hadn't lived through what she'd lived through. He didn't realize how wrong even the most well-intentioned acknowledgments of her time as a media darling could be. He didn't understand it wasn't her own peace she was trying to protect, but his and the boys'. She couldn't afford to let the past intrude on the peaceful world they'd built together. She'd never forget what happened to her, but that didn't mean she had to live with it as part of her future.

Chapter 12

Bob's pickup truck bucked and shimmied up the rough road that led to the Lucky Lady's main adit. He gripped the steering wheel with both hands and gunned the engine, pushing hard up the last steep incline. Red-tinged dust and white exhaust fumes mingled in a cloud behind him, marking his path up the side of the mountain.

Headlights shone through the cloud, proving he hadn't left behind the black pickup that had been following him since he'd turned off the main road just south of town. Bob cursed under his breath and kept going, around a pile of rock that had trickled down from the cliff above, and into the gravel lot that marked the entrance to the Lucky Lady Mine. Half a dozen trucks and SUVs already occupied the lot, belonging to the men who were following the rich vein of gold ore Bob had accidentally discovered down here in the spring.

The pickup truck pulled into an empty space across from Bob, and Duke Breman got out. His previously shiny black four by four was coated in a thick shroud of dust, and a fresh starburst showed in his windshield. "Maybe you should spend some of the money you're making from this mine to grade the road," he said.

"The road keeps gawkers and tourists away." Bob headed toward the mine entrance. The crunch of gravel told him Duke was following.

"I need to talk to you a minute, Mr. Prescott," Duke said. "I've been trying to get hold of you for the better part of a week now."

"Then you ought to be smart enough to realize I'm avoiding you on purpose," Bob said, never slowing his stride. "I don't want to talk to you."

"You were the last person to see Gerald Pershing alive. You spent the five days before he left town trapped underground with him." The detective sped up, and moved to block Bob's path. "If anyone has a clue about what he did or where he went when he got out, it's you."

"I don't give a damn about what Gerald Pershing did or where he went." Bob started to move past him, but Duke stepped to one side to block his progress once more.

Bob glared at him. "I don't want to have to make you move, but I will if I have to," he said. "Don't think because I'm old that I can't do it. I've beat younger men than you in a fight." He balled his hands into fists. Years of working in mines had made him strong and wiry, and he'd learned the dirty fighting of barroom brawls and back-street beatdowns. Duke might get in a few good blows before he went down, but Bob would win in the end. He always did.

"I don't want to fight you," Duke said, his voice and his expression perfectly calm. "I just want to talk to you. I'm not a cop or a lawyer or anyone who's looking to get you into trouble. I'm just a guy trying to do a job. Talk to me and I won't bother you again."

Bob looked him up and down. The big Texan had a take-no-bull manner, but he didn't seem to be putting out any crap, either. "All right," he said. "You want to know about that piss-ant, Pershing, I'll tell you what I know. But you have to come down in the mine with me. I'm not going to waste my time standing here in the hot sun."

The day wasn't all that hot; if anything, the breeze funneling between the mountains carried the first crisp hints of autumn. But the sun shone down from a cloudless turquoise sky, and the thin atmosphere made it feel warmer than it was. And anyway, he wanted Duke on his territory when they spoke. Rule number one when you sparred with anyone—grab the home-field advantage.

"Fine. I'll come into the mine with you."

Bob led the way into the adit. They stopped in an anteroom and Bob handed Duke a hard hat. "Wear this. And try not to slip in those fancy cowboy boots of yours. It's wet in places in the tunnels."

They passed through a set of double doors into the main tunnel. Solid rock surrounded them, and water dripped from the ceiling and gathered in puddles at their feet. Utility lines hung from hooks at the top of the right-hand wall, and caged bulbs suspended overhead provided the only illumination. The low hum of ventilation fans softened the echo of their splashing footsteps.

"Where are we going?" Duke asked after they'd walked several hundred yards uphill. He sounded out of breath, and he was probably cold and pretty wet, since, unlike Bob, he wasn't wearing a coat.

"We're going into the mine."

He waited for Duke to ask where in the mine, but the detective kept his mouth shut.

As they moved farther into the mine, the percussive scream of the drills filled the air. Bob fished a pair of earplugs out of his jacket pocket and handed them to Duke. "Put these in," he said, raising his voice.

He took out a second pair and pushed them into his own ears, muffling the din a little, then led the way down a curving side tunnel—the drift that had been carved out to follow the seam of ore. The drift widened and the noise became almost deafening. Two men took turns operating the big jack-leg drill, feet planted wide, muscles in their bare arms bunched as they wrestled against the machine's vibrations.

"What are they doing?" Duke asked.

"They're drilling a series of holes in the rock," Bob shouted. "They'll fill the holes with dynamite, light the fuses, and the explosion will break up the rock. Then a mucking machine will come in and haul the rock away." That was simplifying the process considerably, but it was good enough for a tourist like Duke. "They're cutting out a seam of ore that may run as much as a half mile back into these mountains."

Duke nodded.

"Wait here." Bob put out a hand to stop him, then moved forward alone and talked to the man who was waiting for his turn at the drill, an Aussie with a string of degrees longer than Bob's arm, but a hard worker all the same. He gave a report on the morning's work—everything was going as expected.

"Kelly Merton worked for a big opal mine in Coober Pedy before he came here," Bob explained to Duke when he returned to the detective's side. "He's a third-generation miner, knows his stuff."

They stood for a while, watching the slow but steady progress of the crew.

"Is this where you and Gerald were trapped?" Duke asked.

Bob nodded. "The chamber was a lot smaller then. A bunch of rock collapsed, revealing that vein." He pointed to the lighter vein of rock along the wall.

Duke looked skeptical. "It doesn't look like gold to me."

"It is. When you've been in this game as long as I have, you recognize it when you see it."

"As half-owner of the mine, wasn't Gerald excited about the find?"

Bob shook his head.

"Why not?"

He sighed. They were either going to have to stand here

shouting at each other, or move somewhere quieter. He chose option B. Turning, he led the way back down the drift, then farther along the main tunnel to another set of doors, into an older, currently unused section of the mine. He stopped to collect a battery-powered LED lantern from a niche in the wall and lighted their way into a slightly larger chamber, fitted out with a camp bed and a couple of chairs. Makeshift plywood-and-canvas walls and a ceiling kept out most of the damp, though a thin trickle of water ran along a ditch next to the wall.

"Does someone live down here?" Duke asked.

Bob sank into one of the chairs and set the lantern on a folding table beside him. "I bunk down here sometimes."

Duke sat in the other chair. "I thought you had a house in Eureka."

"I do, but I like it down here. I've spent at least half my life underground in one mine or another. Most people don't feel that comfortable underground."

Duke glanced up at the low ceiling. "Maybe because it reminds them too much of being buried."

"Nobody bothers me down here," Bob said.

Duke nodded, though he didn't look that comfortable himself, sitting there, back straight as a ramrod, hands clasping his knees.

"You said you had questions," Bob prompted. "So ask."

"Why didn't Gerald Pershing stick around to collect his half of the proceeds from the new gold find?" Duke asked. "Doing so would have made him a rich man."

"He didn't want anything to do with this place, after he almost died down here."

"The news report I read said the two of you suffered no serious injuries, and that you had food and water that sustained you until your rescuers arrived."

"When the ceiling collapsed, he was buried under a pile of rubble. I dug him out, and gave him food and water out of my supplies." Not that he hadn't made the old reprobate beg first. Just a little.

"So you saved his life," Duke said.

"I guess you could call it that. Mainly, I didn't want to be stuck down here with a dead man. Before very long, a body fouls up the air."

Duke's eyes widened. "You sound like you're speaking from experience."

"This wasn't my first mine cave-in."

Duke blinked, then resumed his all-business expression once more. "So, are you saying that he was so grateful to you for saving him that he gave you his shares in the mine? That doesn't fit with the picture of Gerald Pershing I've been getting from other people who knew him."

"No, he was not particularly grateful that I'd saved him. But he was smart enough to know he was tempting fate by spending any more time in this mine."

Duke frowned. "How is that?"

"I told him, the Tommyknockers don't take kindly to cheats and liars. They'd make him pay for his past scams. He'd been lucky enough to have me nearby this time, but next time he might be alone, and he might get more than just a knock on the head and some dust in his lungs."

"The Tommyknockers?"

"The spirits that inhabit the mines. They guard them. They play tricks on people they don't like, and warn those they do like if something is about to go wrong."

Duke smirked. "Let me guess—the Tommyknockers love you."

"No. They're not too fond of anyone invading their territory, but we respect each other. Gerald didn't respect anyone and they recognized that all right." The detective could think him an old fool if he liked, but Bob hadn't survived underground for so many years without learning a thing or two about the differences between this world and the one up above. Not everything could be explained by book learning and logic.

Duke leaned forward, elbows on his knees. "Are you telling me these crazy stories of spirits in the mine frightened Gerald into giving up his interest in the project and rushing out of town?"

"A man with a guilty conscience will go out of his way to avoid being made to pay for his sins, whether by malicious spirits or a court of law."

"What's that supposed to mean?"

Bob shrugged. "You're the detective. You figure it out."

"So what happened? When did he decide to give you the mine shares?"

"After a couple of days down here, I guess. You kind of lose track of time after a while."

"Just like that—'Hey, Bob, I want to give you my shares in the mine.'"

"If that's the way you want to picture it, go right ahead."

"I don't want to picture it any particular way. I want to know what really happened."

"The exchange was legal and voluntary," Bob said. "If it hadn't been, he could have taken me to court or filed a protest or something. But he didn't."

"Maybe because he couldn't," Duke said.

Bob knew the detective wanted him to ask what he meant, but he kept his mouth shut, waiting. If you kept quiet long enough, the other person would eventually talk. Most people hated silence.

For a long moment, the only sound was a faint hum from the lantern and the distant creak of settling rock.

"What was that?" Duke asked, looking up at the ceiling.

"The mine is like a living thing. It breathes and settles."

Duke looked like he was trying to decide if Bob was serious or crazy. Or maybe seriously crazy. The old man grinned.

"The rescuers pulled you both out of the mine and Gerald took off," Duke said after a moment. "He wouldn't even let the EMS crew check him out. He went back to his apartment, packed most of his things, and left. Or at least, his things were all gone when someone stopped to check on him that afternoon."

"Who checked on him?" Bob asked. This was a part of the story he hadn't heard.

"Rick Otis, editor of the *Eureka Miner*. I guess he wanted to interview Gerald for the paper."

Bob nodded. "Rick was probably disappointed not to get the scoop, but most of the rest of us were glad to be finally shed of Pershing."

"The two of you must have spent a lot of time talking while you were trapped," Duke said. "Did he mention what his plans were after he left Eureka?"

"He did not. He said he was going to leave, but he never said where he was going."

"Did he talk about any favorite place, a country he'd like to see, or a favorite vacation spot?"

"He might have talked about any of that stuff, or none of it," Bob said. "He was one of those people who's in love with the sound of his own voice, and most of the time, I wasn't listening."

"So he didn't, for instance, say he'd like to go to Mexico?"

"He could have said he was going to Mars and I wouldn't have paid attention. I would have thought by now you'd be clear on the concept that I didn't like the guy. Nobody I knew did."

"Because he supposedly swindled the town out of money it couldn't afford to lose? Or because he was fighting you on how to best manage the mine? Or all of the above?"

"He treated us like we were all a bunch of rubes. Like we couldn't see through his lies."

"The town did give him money to invest. He didn't force you to hand over the funds."

"So you say."

"What do you mean by that?"

Bob crossed one ankle over his knee and narrowed his eyes at the detective. "Maybe I've said too much already."

"Are you saying Gerald *forced* the town to hand over the money to him? Did he blackmail someone? The mayor?"

"There you go, making up crazy theories. He wasn't blackmailing the mayor, or anybody else, though I wouldn't have put that past the old reprobate."

"Then what are you talking about?"

Bob sighed. He might as well tell the man, before he made up even wilder theories of his own. "Nobody from the town council will come right out and say so in public, so don't bother asking them, but I heard that Gerald arranged to transfer twice as much money into his investment account as the town had authorized. Of course, the bank swore that everything had been on the up and up and perfectly legal, but they would say that, wouldn't they?"

"So the general dislike for Gerald has to do with the money?"

"No, it is not just about the money! Are you always this dense, or is this your technique—worming information out of people by annoying them to death?"

Duke ignored the jibe. "Or is your animosity more personal?" he asked. "Did you dislike him because he made your mayor look like a fool? Because he seduced her and then ran out on her?"

So he knew about that, did he? "Lucille's a big girl," Bob said. "She can look after herself."

"Still, they say hell hath no fury like a woman scorned. Maybe she was waiting to confront Gerald when he got to his apartment and they had words. She killed him, then tossed the body down a mine shaft somewhere."

"So Lucille's your top suspect?" Bob laughed. "Boy, you watch too much television. I'd like to know how the person almost everybody in town knows—the mayor—could do all that and no one would notice? And are you forgetting a sheriff's deputy lives right across the hall from Pershing's apartment?"

"I was only laying out one possible scenario." Duke stretched his legs out in front of him and settled back in the chair, hands folded on his flat stomach. "Actually, the mayor isn't my number one suspect—you are."

Well, that was no surprise, was it? The man hadn't been exactly subtle when he talked to other people in town. Sit at the bar in the Dirty Sally long enough and you'd know everything everybody said to everyone else in town, and Bob spent more time propping up that bar than almost anyone, so he'd heard pretty much every word Duke had to say about him, from one source or another. He shook his head. "If I didn't kill Pershing after five days underground, listening to his whining, then I clearly don't have it in me. Besides, while he was packing up and quitting town, I was celebrating over at the Dirty Sally."

"So you really have no idea where he went or what happened to him?"

"I've already answered that question every way I know how."

"And you can't think of anyone else Gerald might have confided in?"

"I told you that, too. He didn't have any friends around here."

"Someone's got to know something," Duke said. "People don't just disappear."

"They do it all the time," Bob said. "Don't tell me you find everybody you're paid to hunt down."

"I find most of them. If I didn't, I wouldn't stay in business."

"I guess Gerald Pershing's going to ruin your record, then." Bob picked up the lantern. "Time to go," he said.

Duke checked his watch. "You quit at four?"

"Right now, the mine runs three shifts, around the clock.

We have to get as much done as we can before snow closes the roads."

"Why not just plow the road and keeping working in the winter?"

"We could do that, but the cost of keeping the road clear and the water running and the electricity pumping would take a big chunk of the profit. For all man's technology and might, he can't beat Mother Nature. Better to shut down for a few months and start up again in the spring. It's not like the gold is going anywhere in the meantime." He moved past the younger man, holding the lantern high.

"If the mine operates around the clock, why are you leaving at four?" Duke asked.

Bob turned to look at him. "I own half the mine. I don't have to work myself into a lather running it. And four o'clock is when the Dirty Sally opens. Now are you coming with me or not? Because I'd be happy to leave you here sitting in the dark to come up with more wild theories about whatever happened to Gerald Pershing."

Duke popped out of his chair. "I'm coming." He moved up behind Bob, almost stepping on his heels. "But I still think you know something you're not telling me."

"I'm almost seventy years old. I know lots of things. But no law says I have to share them with you."

"You know more about Gerald Pershing than you're saying."

"Or maybe I just like pulling your chain, did you think of that?" Bob laughed at the nonplussed expression that distorted Duke's face. Then he hurried down the tunnel, forcing Duke to trot after him to keep up.

Shelly hesitated outside the guest bedroom door, listening to Mindy, who was singing a credible rendition of "Born This Way." She had a sudden memory of her sister at twelve years old, a hairbrush held to her face like a microphone, singing along with Michael Jackson and dancing around her bedroom in pink fuzzy house shoes and baby-doll pajamas, while Shelly laughed and applauded.

Somehow, they'd lost that closeness over the years. They were such different people now, Shelly wasn't sure they could ever get it back.

She knocked and the singing stopped. "Who is it?"

"It's me."

"The door's open."

She pushed open the door and found her sister seated cross-legged on the bed, a manicure set open beside her. "What do you think of this color?" Mindy asked. "It's called Tahitian Blue." She held out one hand for inspection.

"It's pretty." Shelly moved farther into the room and shut the door behind her. "It matches your eyes."

"You think so?" She fanned her fingers alongside her face. "Maybe that's why blue is my favorite color."

"I thought purple was your favorite color." She felt foolish as soon as the words were out of her mouth. After all this time apart, how would she know what her sister liked and didn't like?

But Mindy didn't take offense. "Sometimes purple is my favorite, too."

Shelly sat on the edge of the bed. "Uh-oh," Mindy said.

"What do you mean, uh-oh?"

"You're wearing that look people get when they're about to say something they don't really want to say." She brushed a final coat of the bright blue enamel onto her pinkie, then capped the bottle and looked at Shelly. She'd outlined her eyes in heavy black liner, so that they looked like doll's eyes, huge in her pale face. "Are you going to kick me out?"

"No!"

Mindy leaned toward her, fingers spread wide. "Look, if this is about what happened at the Dirty Sally last night, I swear I did not know that guy was married and anyway, that woman threatened me first. I told her if she didn't get off my case I'd let her have it and I guess she didn't believe I meant it. So the whole thing was her fault, really."

Shelly shook her head slowly, trying to keep up with the flow of words. "Are you saying you got into a fight at the Dirty Sally last night?" she asked.

Mindy grinned. "It wasn't much of a fight. After I slapped her down to the ground that cute bartender, Jameso, pulled me off of her, and her husband got her out of there in a hurry. She didn't lay a finger on me."

Shelly opened her mouth to lecture Mindy on the dangers of public brawls. She could have ended up hurt, or in jail, or sued . . . but she pressed her lips together and decided not to waste her breath. Lecturing Mindy had never worked before. And her sister was a grown woman now. It wasn't Shelly's place to tell her what to do. "I'm glad you weren't hurt," she said. But she couldn't resist adding, "But maybe you should be more careful about the men you hang out with."

"Hey, I figure if a man is married, it's up to him to keep his vows. Besides, Jameso is still the best-looking dude in the place, so I spend most of my time talking to him."

"Jameso is married."

"I know. To that redhead, Maggie." She laughed. "You should see how green she turns whenever I'm around and I mention her husband. I would tell her she doesn't have anything to worry about—Jameso and I are just friends. But it's more fun to see her squirm."

"Mindy, that's cruel."

"Hey, it's not my problem if she doesn't trust her husband. And the man works at a bar. It's not like women aren't ever going to hit on him. She needs to get over it."

"You might feel differently one day, when you're married."

She laughed. "When I get married, my man is going to be so crazy about me that he won't even look at another woman. I'll make sure of that." She selected a bottle of clear polish from the collection on her bedside table and twisted off the lid.

"Do you have a boyfriend back in Dallas?" Shelly asked. "Anyone you're serious about?" Why hadn't she asked this question before? She was ashamed she hadn't even bothered to find out about her sister's life. She'd been too focused on not revealing anything about her own.

"No way! I'm too young to settle down like that." She began brushing polish on her left hand. "Of course, I'm not saying if the right rich, hot guy came along I couldn't be persuaded, but I've got lots of time before I have to limit myself to just one guy. It's more fun to play the field, you know?"

"I guess I don't know," Shelly said. "I didn't date a whole lot before I met Charlie."

"It's because you're so quiet. I mean, you're pretty enough. You could stand to wear more makeup and fix your hair and stuff, but some guys go for that natural look. But believe it or not, most guys have trouble approaching a woman they don't know. You make it easier for them if you're friendly and you chat them up. If you're too quiet, they think you're stuck-up and assume you're going to shoot them down, so why bother?"

"How did you learn so much about men?" Shelly asked.

"Reading *Cosmo* and going out to bars." She started to work on her right hand. "How did you and Charlie meet?"

"He came into the bank where I was working to deposit a check." She smiled, remembering. "I thought he was really nice and after a couple of months he asked me out. He said he liked my smile."

"A couple of months? Well, you can't say he's a fast worker."

"Fast enough. We'd been dating six months when we decided to get married."

"Six months? So it was practically love at first sight. I thought that only happened in books."

"It just felt . . . right." She'd been on her own for a while by then and she'd been pretty lonely. Being with Charlie felt comfortable and safe. Maybe not the most exciting reason to fall in love with someone, but it had worked for them.

"And you lived happily ever after in boring little Eureka, Colorado. How sweet."

"I hope you meet a great guy and fall in love someday," Shelly said. "You deserve that kind of happiness."

"I never thought of love as something you deserve or don't deserve," Mindy said, not looking at her.

"That's not what I meant. I just want you to be happy."

Mindy laughed. "I was just pulling your chain. You're so easy to get a rise out of." She replaced the cap on the polish and began fanning her fingers. "So, what is it you want to tell me? The bad news?"

"No bad news." She spread her hands flat on her thighs, studying her own short, unpolished nails. "I wanted to know if you'd help me practice for the Founders' Pageant. I know you've taken acting classes and I thought . . ."

"So you decided to do it—to play the schoolteacher, or whatever it is crazy Cassie wants you to do in her little pageant?"

"Charlie thinks I should, and I know if I don't I'll never hear the end of it from Cassie. And . . . and maybe it won't be so bad."

"The play, or finally admitting to everyone that you really are Baby Shelly?"

"I *was* Baby Shelly. A long time ago. I can't imagine that many people care about it now." She sighed, though it came out more like a groan. "But the only way I'll find out is to just do it. Instead of always being afraid of what will happen, I'll finally know."

"I hope you're wrong about people not being interested, or no one's going to buy our book," Mindy said.

"This doesn't mean I'm going to help you and Travis with your book." She put up a hand to stop Mindy's protests.

"You're free to write whatever you want about your life, and I can't stop you from talking about our childhood together," she said. "But what I do now—and what my husband and children do—is my business and mine only. I won't share that with strangers."

Mindy's pout now wasn't that different from her pout when she was thirteen and didn't get her way. Shelly braced herself for a full-blown tantrum. Such histrionics hadn't persuaded her back when they were teenagers, but she still hadn't liked the messy fallout from such scenes.

But maybe Mindy had matured. She relaxed and moved the manicure set and polish to the bedside table. "Okay, I'll help you with the play. But you do know that a week isn't that much time to prepare."

"I know. But I'm good at memorizing things, and I figure if you give me some acting tips . . ."

"Yeah, memorizing the lines is the easy part. And I can coach you well enough for an amateur performance like this, I guess. Do you have a script?"

"I do. It's downstairs."

Mindy stood and straightened her denim capris and sleeveless blue shirt, knotted at her waist to show off her belly-button bling. "Then let's go," she said. "Let's see how embarrassing Cassie is going to make this for you."

Shelly followed Mindy downstairs. "Where are the boys?" Mindy asked.

"They're at that free Art in the Park thing that Olivia Gruber is teaching on Wednesday afternoons," she said. "They had a great time last week."

"I thought you had to work Wednesdays at the bank."

"Only every other Wednesday afternoon. The weeks I work Saturday, I get Wednesday off early."

"I guess that's not so bad, though I'd be bored to tears if I had to stand behind that teller's cage all day."

"What kind of work do you want to do?" Shelly asked.

"Oh you know, acting, singing. And writing, of course.

I'm really into the writing now. I'm thinking after I finish this book with Travis, I'll write one on my own. Maybe a romance novel. Something really sexy."

"What were you doing in Dallas, before you came here?"

"Oh, different stuff. I had a job dancing for a while. Made really good money, but the guy who ran the place was kind of a sleaze, and I really wanted to get into more acting—really making use of my talents. Then this book deal came along, so I figured I needed to give that all of my attention. I mean, I've got plenty of time for all that other stuff, right?"

Do not ask what kind of dancing, the voice in Shelly's head that possibly belonged to her sense of self-preservation sounded loud and clear. If Mindy had been stripping for a living, Shelly did not need to know.

"Here's the script." She handed Mindy the blue three-prong folder with her copy of the Founders' Pageant—the new and improved version.

" 'Eureka Dawning,' " Mindy read. She made a face. "I guess she chose that because *Birth of a Nation* was already taken."

Shelly laughed. She'd forgotten how funny her sister could be.

Mindy grinned. "Okay, the first thing we need to do is go through and highlight all your lines. That makes it easier to make sure you don't miss any. Then we'll do a simple read-through and talk about staging and the emotions you want to convey. How does that sound?"

"It sounds great." Mindy made what had seemed to Shelly to be a huge, unmanageable task sound doable. "I'm really impressed."

"Okay, so find a highlighter and let's get started. And something to drink would help. Do you have any Cokes? Reading all this stuff makes your mouth dry."

An hour later, when Charlie and the boys came home, they found the sisters collapsed on the sofa in a fit of giggles, empty Diet Coke cans and a half-empty bowl of popcorn on the coffee table in front of them.

"You two look like you've been having a good time," Charlie said, surveying the scene.

"What's so funny, Mom?" Cameron asked.

"It's this play," Mindy said. "Some of these lines Cassie has written are so cheesy. Listen to this: *The future of education in the Rocky Mountains begins here, today, in Eureka.*"

"No, this one is better," Shelly said. She struck a dramatic pose. *"In future years, when people speak of the great centers of learning, they will add the name Eureka, Colorado, to that of Athens, Rome, and London."*

Cameron made a face as if he'd eaten something sour. "Are you really going to say that onstage, Mom?"

"Not exactly like that, honey. Your aunt Mindy's helping me rewrite some of the lines to sound better."

"She is?" Shelly supposed she couldn't blame Charlie for sounding so surprised. She hadn't said too many nice things about her sister since Mindy had arrived here.

"She really has a knack for this," she said. "She's being a big help."

"Nice to know I'm good for something, huh?" Mindy winked at Charlie, who actually blushed. Shelly had to cover her mouth with both hands to hide her laughter.

"The trick will be to convince Cassie that our changes are for the better," Mindy continued. "But I've got some ideas for handling her. I've dealt with my share of prima donna directors."

"Are you an actress, Aunt Mindy?" Theo stared at her, clearly awed.

"I've done some regional theater and some commercial work," Mindy said.

"Wow! Wait 'til I tell the guys at school I have an aunt who's a real actress."

"Come on, boys, let's wash up and let the girls finish their rehearsing." Charlie shooed the children toward the stairs.

"Cute kids," Mindy said when she and Shelly were alone again.

"Yeah, they are. I wasn't sure I was cut out to be a mom, but they're turning out really well, in spite of the things I might have done wrong."

"Mom wasn't exactly big on, what do you call them, 'teachable moments,' was she?" Mindy said. "Most of the time we just figured stuff out on our own. Though I guess I had a little bit of an advantage—I had you."

"You did your share of helping me out, too," Shelly said. "I'm sure Mom and Dad felt like it was us against them sometimes." The girls had done their share of plotting against their parents, a united force to circumvent rules and punishments.

Mindy's face lit up. "Do you remember the time Mom had scheduled an interview with that reporter from the *Ladies' Home Journal* or something, and you didn't want to do it?" she asked. "So I did it for you?"

"Oh my gosh, I hadn't thought of that in years." Shelly looked at Mindy in wonder, remembering. "You made me pay you five dollars."

"And you had to let me play all your cassette tapes for a month." Mindy grinned in triumph.

"I'll never forget the look on Mom's face when she found out what we had done," Shelly said.

"I remember. You hid and she went to find you, and left the reporter in the living room. Then I walked in and introduced myself as you. By the time Mom came back—she hadn't been able to find you—the interview was half over. Mom looked like she couldn't decide whether to strangle me or hug me."

"You gave a lot better an interview than I would have," Shelly said. Mindy had been sweet and charming and happy to tell her story—Shelly's story—about falling into the hole in the ground and eventually being rescued by an adoring public. After all, by that time ten years had passed and the legend of Baby Shelly permeated their lives. Any member of the family could have recited the details by heart.

"I don't think the magazine ever realized what we'd done," Mindy said. "Though I remember a few people commented that the pictures made you look a lot younger than fifteen."

"Yes, but you always looked older than your age, and we had the same hair." She glanced at Mindy's platinum curls. "Back then, anyway."

They collapsed in noisy giggles again, holding each other.

"Dad, why are Mom and Aunt Mindy laughing so much?" Cameron asked.

"It's just something sisters do," Charlie said.

"I've really missed you, Mindy," Shelly said softly. "I've missed having a sister."

"I'll always be your sister," Mindy said. "No take-backs."

"Yeah. No take-backs." Some things she'd gladly give back but maybe the people in her life—her sister for sure—shouldn't be one of them.

Chapter 13

Maggie was surprised to find Jameso preparing to leave when she arrived at the B and B after work on Monday. "Where are you going?" she asked. "I thought it was your night off."

"It is, but something came up." He shoved his wallet into his pocket and grabbed his keys. "We've got a new couple in Room Four, from Arizona, here for four nights. The wife is gluten-free and they took the last of the extra pillows. The retirees from Alaska said they'd be in late, but they have a key. We're out of light bulbs for the chandelier in the public dining room, but the hardware store said they'll have some more tomorrow."

"What came up?"

"Just something I need to take care of. Don't worry." He kissed her cheek. "I won't be too late. I left dinner in the refrigerator—chef's salad. And there's some of that honey-mustard dressing you like."

Then he was gone, out the door and down the stairs. A moment later, his motorcycle roared to life and he was off, taking all the relief and pleasure of coming home at the end of a long day with him.

Maggie shed her purse and tote bag in the living room,

where Angela cooed at her from her playpen. "What's your daddy up to?" she asked. She went to the kitchen and poured a glass of tea from the pitcher in the refrigerator, then sat at the table, angry and out of sorts. He'd left before she could even start an argument with him; right now yelling at him would at least have relieved some of her frustration, but he hadn't even given her that satisfaction.

Desperate to talk to someone, she took out her phone and scrolled to Barb's number. By the fourth ring she was ready to hang up, but Barb's voice greeted her, sounding out of breath. "Darling, what are you doing calling at this hour? Is something wrong?"

It was the kind of question people always ask when a call is unexpected, but the concern in her best friend's voice made Maggie tear up. "I'm sorry. I wasn't thinking about the time difference between Colorado and Paris. What time is it?"

"It's after two in the morning, but no worries. I'm still awake. We just got back from the opera. A really wonderful performance of *The Magic Flute.*"

Maggie smiled, picturing tall, slender, blond Barb in a beaded evening gown, Mozart's music still echoing in her head. They lived such different lives, but the differences didn't matter when it came to their friendship. "It sounds like you're having a good time in Paris," Maggie said.

"I am, but I'm ready to come home. You can't get a decent margarita here, and the waiter looked aghast when I asked for iced tea. But enough about me. What's going on with you? You sound upset."

"I am upset—with Jameso. Since he isn't here to yell at, I thought I'd call you."

"What has that handsome rogue done now?" Barb asked.

Maggie had almost forgotten that Barb was head of the Jameso Clark fan club. She'd decided he was perfect for Maggie the first day they met, long before Maggie herself was willing to admit the attraction. "I'm not sure," she said. "You know he's still working at the Dirty Sally four nights a week. Which means four nights a week we don't see each other. If you add in the nights I have to cover meetings, that's even less time we have together. But lately he's been disappearing other nights. The other night he said he'd promised to help D. J. Gruber and Josh Miller with something. Tonight when I got home, he was on his way out to take care of some mysterious 'business,' which he wouldn't elaborate on. He left before I could ask any questions."

"Business? He used that word?"

"Yes. But what kind of business could he possibly have at six in the evening?" She hugged herself, trying to squeeze out the ache around her heart. "And why won't he tell me what it is?"

"Maybe it's another surprise, like your ring."

Maggie stared at the diamond-and-turquoise ring that glittered on the third finger of her left hand. Shortly before Christmas, Jameso had suddenly left Eureka on a mysterious errand. He'd refused to tell her what, and a blizzard had almost kept him from returning in time for them to celebrate the holiday together. But he had made it home, and brought with him this ring, which he'd commissioned from a jeweler in Montana, especially for her. "I wish I could believe it was something as wonderful as this ring," she said. "But I don't think it's anything like that. And I hate that he's staying away from home so much. What if he's just avoiding me—and the baby?"

"Jameso adores you and Angela," Barb said. "I'm sure of it. But he hasn't exactly lived a settled life before now. It's understandable that domestic routine is going to wear on him sometimes. I don't think you can begrudge him a night out with the boys once in a while, as long as he doesn't come home drunk or end up in jail."

"If he really is out with the boys." She pressed her lips together, but it was too late. She'd said her worst fear out loud.

"What do you mean?" Barb's voice was wary.

"I don't know what I mean," Maggie said. "It's just . . .

when I go into the Dirty Sally there are always women hanging around him. Younger, beautiful women."

"But none of those women are you," Barb said. "Jameso loves you."

"He flirts with them."

"I flirt with men, but that doesn't mean I'm going to leave Jimmy. It's fun to flirt, and if you're a bartender like Jameso, it's practically part of the job."

"I know! And I feel awful for even thinking it, but what if he *is* cheating on me? I was too dumb to recognize the signs with Carter."

"Jameso is not Carter."

"That's what worries me. From everything I've heard, Jameso was a real player before I met him. And we married so quickly, and then the baby and this job . . . maybe he feels trapped."

"Maybe he does. So he keeps the job at the Dirty Sally to assert his independence, and he goes out with his friends once in a while to blow off steam. There's nothing wrong with that."

"You're right." She sighed. "I just wish I could be sure."

"Then ask him."

"Ask him?"

"Ask him if he's cheating on you. But be prepared for the answer. And you have to trust him enough to believe him when he says no."

"What if he says yes?" She had to force the words out; saying them left her breathless.

"He won't. As my grandmother always said, 'Don't borrow trouble.' "

"You're right," Maggie said. "And I hate being like this."

"Being like what?" Barb asked.

"Suspicious. Jealous. I want to trust him, but . . ."

"I know." Barb stifled a yawn. "Don't be too hard on yourself. You're a newlywed, too. And probably still hormonal from the baby to boot. Give yourself some time."

Barb was right. The best approach was probably to wait this out. Give Jameso a chance to come to her, though she could think of few things more difficult. Because what if he decided never to confide in her? What if this rift between them became wider and wider? She shook her head. No sense playing that game. "I'll let you go and get some sleep," Maggie said. "Thanks for listening."

"It will be all right, Maggie. Keep telling yourself that until you believe it."

She ended the call. Talking with Barb had made her feel a little better. And Barb was right. Everything would be all right. Jameso loved her. He wouldn't cheat on her. Never mind that every other man she'd ever loved—from her father to her first husband—had ended up betraying her. Jameso was different. And she was different now, too. She had to remember that.

"They told me I'd find you here."

Bob looked up in time to see Daisy slide onto the barstool next to him. He looked a little worse for wear, in need of a shave, his shirttail half out, his eyes bloodshot. She'd hoped for better from him, somehow, and didn't try to hide her annoyance. "How long have you been drinking?" she asked. The last thing she wanted was to deal with a drunk.

"Most of my life." He drained the last of the pint glass in front of him and let out a satisfied sigh. "I hope you're not here to lecture me on the evils of demon alcohol."

Not drunk, she decided. Not yet, anyway. "I never had much use for a man who drank," she said.

"You strike me as the type who doesn't have much use for men in general." He signaled the bartender. "So it's about the same difference, I guess."

The bartender, a good-looking younger man with dark brown hair and a goatee, came over to them. "What can I get you?" he asked Daisy.

"A Coke, please. Lots of ice."

"Do you know what those sodas will do to your stomach?" Bob asked. "Not to mention your bones."

"I suppose you think beer is good for you," she said.

"It must be. I've never been sick a day in my life. That's because alcohol kills germs."

"You must be responsible for the death of a lot of germs," the bartender said, as he set a glass of Coke in front of Daisy and slid another pint glass to Bob.

"Do you ever actually work at the mine?" she asked. "Or is 'manager' just an honorary title?"

"When you're efficient, you don't have to spend all day working." He held his glass up in salute. "I'm a man who has my priorities straight."

From what she'd learned asking around in town, holding up the bar at the Dirty Sally was one of those priorities. Daisy sipped her drink and thought about what she should do next. She needed help, and Bob had seemed the most likely person to come to her aid, but maybe this wasn't such a good idea.

"You're still here, so I guess I haven't offended you too much," he said. He swiveled toward her. "What did you want to see me about?"

She set down the glass, trying to control the trembling in her hand. Dammit, she thought she'd pulled herself together better before she came in here.

His hand closed over hers so quickly she didn't have time to pull away. He had big hands, with scarred knuckles and grease tattooed into the lines crisscrossing the fingers. Workingman hands, strong and capable. He leaned close, his grizzled face filling her field of vision. "What's got you so upset?" he asked, his voice just above a whisper.

She looked away. "It's foolish."

His fingers squeezed hers, warm and reassuring. "You never struck me as the foolish type."

She nodded and gently pulled her hand away to lace the fingers together with the other hand in her lap. "A bear stole one of my kids today. It came right out of the woods while I was standing there, snatched it up, and carried it away. Alice tried to go after it and the bear swatted her off her feet. I had to hold her back; I was so afraid she'd be hurt, too."

"This up at Brice Alcott's ranch? That back pasture you're working in?"

She nodded. "The doe has been crying for her baby something awful. But there was nothing I could do. The bear just snatched it up and . . ." She closed her eyes, wishing she could shut out the memory of the bear tearing at the little kid while the mother bawled and Alice barked.

"I'm sorry you had to see that," Bob said.

She'd been sure he'd make fun of her—tell her to buck up, that eat or be eaten was the way of the world. She hadn't been prepared for his kindness, which somehow moved her closer to tears.

She took a steadying breath. "I know I should be tougher. That when you have livestock, you're going to clash with wildlife. But I guess I've been lucky, so far. I haven't had to deal with anything like this."

"You don't have a gun?" he asked.

"I have a twenty-two for killing snakes and scaring off coyotes," she said. "I'm afraid if I shoot a bear with something like that, it will just make her mad."

"So you think it was a sow?"

She nodded. "I know it was. She had two cubs with her. Which is another reason I don't want to kill her. But I need to protect my goats. It was so easy for her to rush in and get that kid that I'm afraid the next time she's hungry she'll be back for more. The girls are all upset and Alice is frantic, trying to herd them up and watch the woods for the bear. I hated to even leave them to come here, but I felt I had to."

"I've got a rifle that will take care of your problem, no question."

"I told you, I don't want to kill her. The cubs will starve to death." She glared at him, then realized he'd only made the statement to get a rise out of her—and maybe to distract her from her grief and worry.

She swallowed her anger. "What am I going to do?" she asked.

"First, we call the wildlife officer. You're entitled to reimbursement for the loss of the kid, so you might as well claim it. And he'll give us some rubber bullets."

"What will those do?"

"They'll hurt like hell when Mama comes back for another serving of goat. They'll make her think twice about trying again."

"I don't know if I'm a good enough shot to hit her."

"Maybe not, but I am."

"So you'll help me?"

He swiveled to face the bar once more and picked up his glass. "As soon as I finish this beer. A little alcohol steadies my aim."

She couldn't decide if he was serious, or merely trying to get a rise out of her. She suspected the latter, so she played along. "I still don't approve of drinking," she said crisply. "But when a man is already so flawed, what is one more vice?"

"You women are never happy unless you're righting some wrong or working on some reform," he said. "The way I see it, I'm enough of a project to make the right woman downright delirious."

She clapped her hand over her mouth, but not quite in time to cover a particularly unladylike snort. He winked at her. "At least you aren't watering up on me anymore."

Her mother had always told her to appreciate a man who could make her laugh. But her mother had probably never met anyone like Bob Prescott.

"Do you want to make cookies?'

It was Wednesday afternoon and Mindy had been almost-napping on the sofa. For a moment, she wondered if she was dreaming. So many childhood afternoons had begun with this question from Shelly. If they were bored or lonely or upset about anything, their therapy of choice was baking cookies. It was a wonder they weren't both three feet wide, they'd found such solace in butter and sugar.

"I'm going to make some oatmeal cookies for the boys' lunches," Shelly said. "Do you want to help?"

"Sure." Still shaking off the lethargy of sleep, she followed Shelly into the kitchen. Unlike the strictly utilitarian kitchen of their youth, used primarily for brewing morning coffee and microwaving quick meals, this was clearly a room Shelly spent a lot of time in. In addition to open shelves of pottery and appliances, a large rack filled with every spice imaginable, and a cupboard devoted entirely to boxes of different kinds of teas, Shelly's kitchen contained a big wooden table with comfortable chairs, and a bookcase filled with books—cookbooks and picture books and paperback novels. A framed cross-stitched sampler by the door read HOME IS WHERE THE HEART IS.

"Should we do oatmeal with raisins or oatmeal with dried cranberries?" Shelly asked. She moved to stand behind a gleaming mixer at the kitchen's granite-topped island.

"Oatmeal with chocolate chips." Mindy took her place opposite and surveyed the ingredients Shelly had assembled. "Where's the butter?"

"I'm using coconut oil. Trust me, it tastes amazing with the oatmeal." She took a bag of semisweet chips from the cabinet. "The chocolate is a good idea."

"Of course." Mindy grinned.

Though they hadn't made cookies together in a dozen years or more, they fell easily into their roles: Mindy measured and handed over ingredients for Shelly to add to the mixing bowl. When the batter was ready, they took turns scooping out spoonfuls and arranging them on the cookie sheets. Shelly's sheet was filled with uniform rounds of dough, arranged in straight lines; Mindy's cookies meandered across her baking sheet like stepping-stones of various sizes and shapes. But Shelly didn't comment on this. She merely slid both sheets into the preheated oven, then began gathering ingredients to put away.

Mindy began to help, then her phone rang, the strains of "Bad Romance" overly loud in the Wednesday afternoon stillness. She jerked the phone from the front pocket of her jeans and frowned at the screen. Travis. She silenced the cell and slid the phone away once more.

"Take your call; I don't mind," Shelly said as she wiped crumbs from the island.

"It wasn't anyone I wanted to talk to." Travis's attitude that he was the one in charge of this book project annoyed her. After all, her name would be on the cover of the book, in nice big type. The agent she had hired had made sure of that. Travis was only "with Travis Rowell," in a much smaller font. His job was to help her with the writing, not to boss her around.

The phone rang again, harsh and insistent. "Sounds like whoever it is won't take no for an answer," Shelly said.

"It's Travis," Mindy admitted. "I guess I'd better answer it."

"He does strike me as the persistent type." She opened the oven to check the cookies, humming a little under her breath.

Honestly, she was the perfect picture of a domestic Madonna. She could do commercials for Betty Crocker or something. "Are you always so calm about everything?" Mindy asked.

"You know that's not true. I wasn't exactly calm the other night in the saloon."

Mindy grimaced, fighting the pinch of guilt at the back of her throat. She'd been annoyed with Shelly when she'd visited the bank that day, annoyed that her sister was ignoring her and shutting her out. Here in this kitchen, with the smell of freshly baked cookies filling her with sweet memories of their childhood closeness, her anger felt out of place. Even wrong.

"I'm calm because I'm happy," Shelly said. "I'm exactly where I want to be, doing exactly what I want to do."

How could someone who was only thirty years old be so settled in life? The idea struck Mindy as absurd—and a little frightening. Might as well dig a grave and lie down in it if you abandoned all ambition at such a young age. But no denying, her sister seemed happy and content.

"You'd better call Travis," Shelly said. "He'll keep bothering you if you don't."

Mindy went into the living room. Charlie had taken the boys to the art classes in the park. Her two nephews were turning out to be quite the little artists. Mindy had never spent much time around kids, but Cam and Theo were actually a lot of fun. They, at least, didn't question her motives or look at her with disapproval. And she got a kick out of them calling her Aunt Mindy.

The phone went off again as she stepped into the empty room. "Hello?" she said, silencing the driving beat of the Lady Gaga hit.

"About time." Travis's nasal drawl filled her ear. "Where have you been? I haven't heard a word out of you for days."

"I've been doing what you said I should do. I've been spending time with my sister."

"Good. What have you got for me? Lotsa juicy quotes, I hope."

She glanced over her shoulder, toward the kitchen. Shelly was taking a sheet of cookies out of the oven.

"Well? Do you have anything good?"

"Maybe."

"I get it. You can't talk now. The wrong person might hear. Meet me at my hotel room. We'll have privacy there."

There he went, ordering her around again, like he was in charge. "I can't meet you right now," she said. "I'm busy."

"Doing what?"

She started to tell him it was none of his business, but instead she said, "We're baking cookies."

"Baking cookies?" He laughed so loud she had to hold the phone away from her ear. "For real?"

"Yes, for real. Why is that so funny?"

"You don't strike me as the cookie-baking type."

She probably wouldn't have described herself as the cookie-baking type either, but coming from him the words sounded like an insult. "There are a lot of things you don't know about me," she said.

"And I'm grateful for that, believe me. All I care about is your sister's story. So meet me at my room in half an hour and let's get on with it." He sounded annoyed now, even more impatient than usual.

"What's wrong with you?" she asked. "Why are you in such a bad mood?"

"The sooner I get the material I need to put together a rough draft of this manuscript, the sooner we can both leave this town," he said.

"I'm writing this book, not you," she reminded him.

"Whatever. I'm in Room 216, at the Eureka Motel, in case you've forgotten. See you."

He hung up before she could protest further. She slipped the phone back into her pocket and returned to the kitchen.

"Everything okay?" Shelly looked up from transferring a batch of cookies to the cooling rack.

"Travis wants to meet." She didn't say "to talk about the book." No sense upsetting the tenuous truce the sisters had forged.

"You don't have to go if you don't want to," Shelly said.

The words, and the concerned tone in which they were delivered, thrust Mindy back to a summer afternoon when she was twelve, and Shelly was seventeen. They'd been baking cookies then, too, and Mindy had confided that she'd been invited to the birthday party of a girl she didn't like.

Shelly's sympathy that afternoon had given Mindy the courage to tell her mother she didn't want to go to the party, but Sandy made her go anyway. The birthday girl was the daughter of the man who owned the bank in their small town, and it wouldn't do to risk insulting the family.

Mindy opened her mouth to remind Shelly of these long-ago events when the back door burst open and Cameron rushed in, waving a piece of paper like a flag, the colors on the page glinting purple and green and yellow in the overhead fluorescent light. "Mom, look what we made!" he shouted.

"We each did one." Theo ran in after his brother and stood, bouncing up and down with excitement. With his brown curls and round, ruddy cheeks, he most resembled his mountain-man father, while Cameron had his mother's blue eyes and more angular features. "They're nature colleges."

"Collages," Cameron said. "With leaves and flowers and stuff."

"They're beautiful," Shelly said, admiring each boy's work.

"Hmmm, what smells so good?" Charlie kissed his wife's cheek and nodded to Mindy. He was friendly to her, but he kept his distance, as if he wasn't quite sure what to make of her. Mindy wondered what Shelly had told her husband about her.

"Cookies!" Theo announced, and stood on tiptoe to admire the cooling sweets.

"Wash your hands first, then you can tell me all about your afternoon," Shelly said.

"I'll take these and put them on the bulletin board." Charlie took the pictures from his sons, then reached over and swiped a cookie from the rack. Laughing, he dodged Shelly's swatting hand and headed for the large corkboard in the den where they displayed a rotating selection of the boys' artwork and school papers.

"Come on now." Shelly ushered the boys toward the downstairs bathroom. "Where did collect the items for your collages?"

Mindy stood in the middle of the empty kitchen for a moment, feeling hollowed out with longing for something she couldn't even name. The things Shelly had—husband, children, home—weren't things she'd even wanted before, but standing here now in her sister's kitchen, surrounded by such tender treasures, the ache for them threatened to overwhelm her.

She had to get away—from this feeling, and from the memories that made it hard to think straight. She fled out the front door, to her car, pausing only to grab her purse and keys from the living room chair where she'd dropped them earlier.

Chapter 14

Ten minutes after leaving Shelly's house, Mindy knocked on the door of Travis's hotel room. He answered with a beer in one hand, a slice of pizza in the other. "You're just in time for dinner," he said. "Help yourself." He motioned to the pizza box and six-pack on the table by the window.

It wasn't homemade cookies and Shelly's elk stew, but maybe he was right. Maybe she'd always been more of a cheap-beer-and-takeout-pizza kind of girl.

"So, you've been spending a lot of time with your sister." He sat on the side of the bed and motioned for her to take the only chair. "That's good. Is she talking to you?"

"Some."

"You've been recording these conversations, I hope."

"Some." She twisted the cap off the beer and took a long drink, delaying telling him more. She'd had the recorder running while they baked, and before that when Shelly had come to her room and asked for help with the play.

"Then let's hear it." He held out one hand and snapped his fingers, a gesture she'd grown to loathe during a brief stint as a cocktail waitress at a Dallas steakhouse that catered to high rollers. Men with money, not manners, the woman who trained Mindy had told her her first day on the job. Nothing Mindy had seen had proved the woman wrong.

"Are you sure this is legal—recording someone secretly like this?" she asked.

"The government does it all the time," he said.

"I mean it, Travis. I don't want to end up getting sued."

"You won't get sued. The publisher has rooms full of lawyers to make sure that doesn't happen. Besides, all we're going to do is say that Shelly said these things to you—her sister. The recordings are just backup. Proof, if anyone—including Shelly—says otherwise. So, what did you get?"

"She talked about how she met her husband."

His expression brightened. "That's great. Readers will love that."

"But she thought she was just talking to me," Mindy said. "Not a bunch of readers."

"And like I told you already, the book is about you and your relationship to your sister, so those kinds of conversations are fair game. Think of it this way. Suppose you had a conversation with your sister, then you went upstairs and wrote down everything you remembered in your diary. Then, when you sit down to write your book, you consult your diary to refresh your memory. This is just like this."

Except it wasn't like that—not really. But Travis wasn't going to listen to any argument she made about the rightness or wrongness of recording Shelly without her knowledge. And this wasn't really about legalities anyway, not really. "I'm not ready for you to hear it," she said. "Not yet." She hugged her arms across her chest and stared at her knees.

"Is it because there's something embarrassing in your conversation?" He set aside the crust of pizza and raised his right hand, like a man swearing in court. "I promise to keep everything confidential. Think of me like a priest, or a doctor."

"I'm having second thoughts about doing things this way,"

she blurted. "Shelly already thinks I'm just interested in using her. If she finds out I'm taping her that will only prove she's right."

"Whoa! Am I hearing you right? Since when are you so concerned about what Shelly thinks of you?"

Since Shelly had reminded her of how close they'd once been. When she was small, and right up until Shelly had gone away to college, really, her older sister had been the one person Mindy knew deep down that she could count on. While her mother and father were too focused on who they could impress or how much attention they could attract to Shelly, Shelly herself had been the one to worry about Mindy—what she was doing, how she was feeling.

It had been a long time since Mindy had allowed herself to think about how big a hole Shelly had left in her life when she broke off contact with the family, but these past few days, living in Shelly's house, being drawn in as a part of her family, Mindy had realized how much she'd missed the bond they had once had.

"Didn't you tell me you didn't owe your sister anything, since she'd turned her back on you years ago?" Travis asked. "Everybody knows her story; this is your chance to tell your side of things. To show people that Baby Shelly isn't the saint they all think she is."

She winced. She'd said all those things. And she'd meant them at the time. But now she wasn't so sure. "I think the book would be a lot better if we convinced Shelly to cooperate with us," she said. "I'm sure I can persuade her. I just need a little more time."

"In case you've forgotten, we have this thing called a deadline," he said. "If we don't turn in a manuscript by then, the publisher could make us return the advance—which I'm willing to bet you already spent."

Her cheeks felt hot. "I had to pay my way here, and then I had other expenses." She'd been behind on all her bills and had run up some pretty steep credit card charges in the months before the book deal came through. By the time her half of the advance money arrived, less her agent's fifteen percent, she'd needed most of the money to get her out of hock to her creditors. There hadn't really been much left over.

"Believe me, sweet cheeks, I know," Travis said. "You and I are in the same leaking financial boat, which is why we have to take whatever we can get and run with it."

She glanced toward her purse, where she'd stashed the recorder. "Maybe I should listen to it on my own, and pick out the parts we should use."

"Better if you leave that to a professional," he said. "Trust me, I know what the public is interested in." He leaned forward and picked up her purse. "Is the recorder in here?"

"Travis, give that back!"

But he'd already pulled out the little recorder. He clicked a button. "Three hours. You've been busy. There ought to be a lot in here we can use." He pulled out his notebook and switched on the machine. Mindy's voice, higher and twangier than she imagined herself sounding, said, "What do you think of this color?"

She pulled her knees to her chest, her heels hooked on the edge of the chair, arms wrapped around her shins, and listened, half sick to her stomach, as Travis replayed the sisters' conversation, fast-forwarding past long silences or inconsequential chitchat.

"This is great," he said, scribbling furiously in his notebook. "All this stuff about her feelings toward her family is priceless. And that bit where you did the interview for her when you were kids? That's the kind of inside information readers will love."

She rested her chin on her knees and said nothing. Would Shelly ever forgive her for this? Not to mention how pissed off their mother would be when she found out. Sandy wouldn't like the world to know how much her older daughter resented her.

At last, Travis switched off the recorder. "You did a great

job," he said. He held the little device out to her. "Take this back and see if you can get her to tell you what she did after she left home, but before she got married. Oh, and ask her if she does anything to commemorate her rescue each year. You know—private rituals or anything. Readers would eat that up."

She folded her arms across her chest, refusing to take the recorder from him. "If it's private, maybe we shouldn't tell everyone," she said.

"Listen to you." He opened her purse and dropped in the recorder. "You're the one who wanted to write this book, remember?"

She nodded.

"And why did you want to do that?"

"I needed the money."

"And?"

"What?" She lifted her head and looked him in the eye. "You don't think money is a good enough reason?"

"Money is a good reason, but it's never just about money. There's always an 'and.' "

He thought he was so smart. As if a journalism degree made him an expert on human psychology. "I wanted people to know that what happened to Shelly wasn't just about her," she said. "That it affected me, too. That I lived my whole life in the shadow of something that happened before I was even born."

Travis snatched up his notebook from the bed beside him and began writing. "This is terrific stuff. We'll definitely put this in the book."

She sat up straighter and put her feet on the floor. "So you don't think I'm being greedy?"

"Not at all. You've suffered, too, and people need to hear your side of things. Plus, the money you'll make from this book will give you the freedom to do whatever you want."

"Yeah." He was right. This book was really her big chance. Maybe her only chance.

He leaned forward and put a hand on her arm. He wasn't

being fresh or anything—it was more of a brotherly gesture. "The secret to life, Mindy, is to decide what you really want, and go after it with everything you've got. You're doing that, and I admire you for it."

"I guess I am." She took a deep breath and nodded. "Shelly always said she wanted the best for me. So she'll understand about the book. Maybe not right away, but eventually."

"Of course she will. It's clear from these recordings how much she cares about you."

"Yeah." Shelly did love her. That realization surprised Mindy. She hadn't expected to find out that Shelly still cared, after so much time apart. Even more surprising was how much she loved Shelly. Once she'd scraped away all the layers of anger and resentment, what remained was that little glow of love, like an ember from an old campfire that refused to go out.

"I don't like this one bit." Daisy dropped into a lawn chair next to Bob, who cradled a rifle across his chest and squinted over the pasture, toward the goats clipping weeds at the edge of the woods.

"A lesser man might take that comment personally," he said. He plucked a travel mug from the cup holder on the arm of the chair and sipped. He'd sworn to Daisy that the cup contained only coffee, but she wouldn't have put it past him to add a shot of something stronger.

"I'm grateful for all the help you've given me," she said, trying for a softer tone. After all, he'd helped her negotiate the paperwork to file her claim with the Department of Wildlife, and he'd collected the rubber bullets the wildlife officer had said "should" scare away the bear. No more goats had gone missing in the two days since the first attack, but Bob had shown her signs that the bears had been in the area—big clumps of droppings, and black fur caught in the barbed-wire fencing.

"Then what's your problem?" He looked at her, his blue eyes holding a sharpness that sent a warm shiver down her spine in spite of herself. She didn't want to be attracted to Bob Prescott. He wasn't the kind of man she liked—he was too old-fashioned, too chauvinistic, and ornery as an old billy goat. She felt betrayed by her own body—that the lure of all that testosterone and he-man machismo overcame her better sensibilities.

"I don't like using my girls as bait." She motioned toward the goats, munching contentedly through a patch of thistle and leafy spurge that was threatening to take over this pasture. "It feels wrong, sending them out there defenseless, waiting for them to be attacked." Bob had convinced her to lock Alice in the trailer, where she wouldn't chase off the bear.

"You know where the term 'scapegoat' comes from, don't you?" he asked.

"Not really."

"It's from the Bible. A goat was driven into the desert or sacrificed to atone for sin. The goat took the fall so that everyone else would be okay."

"I'm not sacrificing any of my girls for anything," she said. "That's barbaric, and we are not barbarians."

"Speak for yourself, honey. We're all a lot closer than you think. Besides, none of your goats are going to be sacrificed. I'm going to pepper the bear's hide before she gets hold of one."

"That part bothers me, too," Daisy said. "After all, she's a mother, trying to provide for her children. That shouldn't get her shot."

He gave her that raking gaze again, not a dismissive look, but more like he was trying to see deeper into her, to her core. "Woman, are you even listening to yourself?" he asked. "You don't want your goats eaten, but you don't want the sow punished for trying to feed her young'uns. The world don't work that way and you know it."

"I know it." She sat back in her chair, weary from the argument she'd been having as much with herself as with him. "But I'm entitled to my opinions, no matter how contradictory they are."

"Hmmph." He returned to contemplating the goat herd and the woods beyond. "If there's one thing women are never short of, it's opinions."

Just when she was beginning to think there was more to him than the old codger act, he had to come up with a chauvinistic remark like that. "Since when are you an expert on women?" she asked. "Have you ever been married?"

"Three times. Enough to make me know I'm not walking down the aisle again."

She gaped at him. He grinned. "You didn't think I could have found three women who'd put up with me long enough to get hitched, did you?"

She looked away, unwilling to admit she'd been thinking exactly that. "What about you?" he asked. "Was your late husband the first one?"

"And the only one," she said.

He didn't have an answer for that. He took another swig of his coffee. The aroma rose to her, rich and dark. "Do you really think the bear will show up today?" she asked.

"No way of knowing. All we can do is wait." He settled back into his chair. He looked content to sit there for the next week, but she was restless, unable to stay still.

"Tell me about your wives," she said.

He shifted the rifle, cradling it almost like a child, the barrel pointed over his left shoulder. "Nosy, aren't you?"

"Yes." She lifted her chin. "I don't mind telling you about my husband."

"Except I don't care to hear about him. I'm sure he was a fine man and all—better than me in every way."

"Roger was a fine man, but he certainly wasn't without his faults."

"I'm glad to hear it. Otherwise, I'd have suspected you of lying."

She didn't know what to say to this, so she fell silent once more. Roger Mott had spoiled and indulged her; she'd only realized how much after he was gone. He'd let her have her way, even when she didn't make the best decisions, something that had gotten her into trouble at times after he was gone. His common sense had always reined in her flightier tendencies.

But there had been freedom in succeeding or failing on her own, as well. Roger would never have approved of the goat rental idea, and would have found a way to talk her out of the business, or he would have nudged her toward a different, safer, and maybe even more profitable approach. But she wasn't trying to get rich from natural weed control. She simply liked living like a gypsy six months of the year, with her girls and Alice for company.

"I think it's the differences between men and women that make marriage so difficult," she said. "And at the same time more rewarding. When the relationship is good, it's because you've both managed to overlook or overcome your differences in the interest of realizing something better."

"And I thought men and women generally stayed together for sex."

She turned to glare at him, then recognized the glint in his eye. "You take great joy in goading me, don't you?"

"Only because you're so easy to get a rise out of."

It was true. Though she was tough in many ways, she wore her emotions close to the surface. She felt things so deeply, from the beauty of a sunrise to the wound of harsh words. "One thing age has taught me is to not be afraid of showing my feelings," she said. "I've always thought—"

"Shhh." He held up a hand, cutting her off in midsentence. She froze. "What is it?"

"Shhh! Hear that?"

She leaned forward, straining her ears. Then it came to her—a shuffling, snuffling sound. Her heart pounded, as if she'd been running hard. "Is that her?"

"Think so." He shifted the rifle, barrel pointed toward the ground.

The goats must have heard the noises, too; they raised

their heads and looked around, ears twitching, shifting from hoof to hoof. Stella, the oldest doe and the herd's leader, made a worried sound, an anxious whine deep in her throat.

All at once, the bear exploded from the edge of the woods, her great, lumbering body quickly closing the distance between her and the goats. The girls raised high-pitched cries of panic; inside the trailer, Alice barked and scratched at the door. "Oh no!" Daisy rose, hand over her mouth to muffle a scream.

In one fluid motion, Bob stood, raised the rifle to his shoulder, and fired. The reverberation momentarily deafened Daisy. Her ears rang and the scent of gunpowder stung her nose. The bear gave a cry of rage and turned to flee, limping, the two cubs whirling about and racing after her.

"You've hurt her!" Daisy cried.

"She's stung, but she'll be okay," he said. "And she'll think twice about coming back here."

"How can you be sure?" Daisy asked.

He gave her a withering look that made her feel about three feet tall, but she fortified herself with a deep breath and stood up straighter. "I think we should go after her," she said. "To make sure she's all right."

"Now I know you're certifiable." He fiddled with some adjustment on the rifle.

"I don't think it's crazy to want to check on her," she said.

"You want to go chasing off into the woods after a wounded bear—a bear who might just as soon turn and attack you?"

She swallowed hard against the metallic taste of fear that bloomed in the back of her throat. "I didn't say we needed to get close to her—only that I want to make sure she's okay."

He sank into the lawn chair once more. "Help yourself. But I'm not fool enough to go with you."

"Fine." She grabbed her sweater from the back of the lawn chair and tugged it on. "I certainly don't need your help. Good-bye."

She marched toward the woods with as much dignity as she could muster, aware of his gaze boring into her back, as straight and unforgiving as the bullets he'd fired. By the time she reached the edge of the woods, she was beginning to feel a little foolish. After all, what was she going to do when she did see the bear? It wasn't as if she could give it a physical examination. It was either hurt—in which case she couldn't do anything to help it and would have to live with the knowledge—or it was fine, in which case she hoped it would never come anywhere near her or her goats again.

Then there was the problem of how to track the bear. When she reached the edge of the woods, she could no longer hear the animal crashing about. She studied the dried leaf litter at her feet, trying to picture in her mind which way the animal had lunged.

Two minutes deeper into the woods, a crashing and thrashing behind her made her look around for a tree to climb. Bears couldn't climb trees, right? Or was that mountain lions? She turned toward the noise, a scream frozen in her throat.

"Don't go getting hysterical, it's just me." Bob shoved a pinion branch out of his way.

"What are you doing here?" she demanded, trying to hide her relief behind feigned indignation.

"Call it self-preservation. If something happened to you, I'd end up feeling guilty." He moved past her and surveyed the area. "Any sign of the bruin?"

"No. I mean, I'm not sure what to look for."

"I think you're on the right track." He pointed ahead. "Looks like she went that way."

She followed him along a faint path between the trees. Some kind of animal trail, she guessed. It made sense the sow would follow this easier route. Another two hundred yards and the trees began to thin. They broke out into a clearing, atop a bluff. "Do you recognize where we are?" he asked.

"Nothing looks familiar." She squinted in the harsh afternoon sunlight. "Is that a road over there?"

"County Road Ten." He indicated the faint, gravel track on the opposite bluff. "It cuts over to the highway another five miles or so farther on. It's kind of a shortcut from town, though not many people use it. The road's kind of rough, and slick as snot when it rains."

She looked around them, at the countryside as silent and empty as a church midweek. "I don't see any sign of the bear," she said.

"She might have gone on down into the ravine." He walked to the edge of the bluff. "There's a creek down there. A good place to find more food and to lick her wounds."

She followed him and looked down into the gully. Heavy underbrush and shadows obscured the bottom. "I don't think I want to go after her badly enough to climb down in there," she said.

"Climbing down might not be so bad, but climbing out would be a bitch," Bob said. "Not to mention you could turn an ankle or fall and break a leg and have to wait for Search and Rescue to fish you out. Then you could tell them how you came to be down there in the first place—trying to track a bear you'd just gone out of your way to chase off."

"All right, all right." She held up her hands in a gesture of surrender. "I'll admit this was not my best idea. I'll just have to take your word for it that she's okay, and that she won't come after my goats again. I guess we'd better go back now." She started to turn away, but he caught at her sleeve.

"Wait a minute," he said.

"What?" She didn't turn back. She was tired and she had a headache and she didn't like the way her emotions were always in turmoil around him.

"There's something down there," he said. "Something that's not right."

She angled toward him and found him bent at the waist, staring into the ravine. She followed his gaze and caught her breath. "Do you mean that glint of metal, or something shiny? Could it just be the light reflecting on the creek water?"

"I think it's a car." He pointed. "See that broken tree? The car must have went off the road, crashed through that tree, then landed on the bottom of the ravine."

A shiver raced up her spine as she stared at the brown top of the broken fir. "That damage doesn't look recent," she said softly.

"No, I'd say this happened a while ago." He started down into the ravine.

"What are you doing?" she asked.

"I'm going to check it out. You stay up here. Do you have your phone with you?"

"Yes." She put a hand on the pocket where the cell phone rested.

"I'll call you when I know more."

"Be careful," she said, the words out of her mouth before she could stop them.

He grunted, and kicked his way down the steep slope. "More careful than whoever is in that car, anyway."

Chapter 15

"I'm calling a staff meeting."

Maggie had scarcely slipped her purse off her shoulder on a hot late-August Thursday afternoon when her boss, Rick Otis, swooped out of his office at the *Eureka Miner*. A slight man, he radiated a feverish energy that made it impossible to tell if he was forty or sixty. He favored wildly printed aloha shirts to hide his slight paunch, and cargo shorts or hiking pants, depending on the season.

"Since when do we have staff meetings?" She sat and flipped the switch to boot up her computer. "Ellie and I are the only staff you have, and you don't have to call a meeting to communicate with us."

"You and I need to brainstorm ideas for stories." He sat on the edge of her desk. This, unfortunately, meant that if she turned toward him, his crotch was almost at eye level. She resolutely kept her body angled away. The first time she'd met Rick, he'd been stark naked—and for that matter, so had she. But they'd both been in the main pool of the local clothing-optional hot springs, and at least then they'd had steam, and a crowd of other people to help her pretend they were more formally attired.

"It's not as if so much is happening in Eureka that we have to pick and choose what to report," she said. "If it happens and it's news, we report it." She also wrote her share of stories that might not be considered news in other papers, but that people in Eureka loved, such as the piece she'd done last month on Dennis Kinkaid's record for growing the largest zucchini in the county for three years in a row, or their photo feature on old outhouses in the area, which had actually won a state press award.

"I've been thinking we need to expand our coverage," Rick said. "Draw in some new readers."

"Where are these readers going to come from?" she asked. "Almost everybody in the county, not to mention a fair number of people who used to live here and moved away, already subscribe. And then you get newsstand sales from tourists."

"I was reading an article the other day about a weekly paper in Alaska—or maybe it was Arkansas." He scratched his chin, the sandpapery sound of his afternoon beard making her teeth hurt. "Anyway, some small-town paper that has over five thousand subscribers, from all over the world. They all want to read the news this guy prints."

"What kind of news?"

"Apparently, he's big on reporting Bigfoot sightings and UFO abductions."

"I'm pretty sure we're fresh out of Sasquatches and UFOs." She nudged his knee with her elbow. "Could you move? I have to write an article about the competitors for Hard Rock Days." Though what she was going to say about anonymous men with pseudonyms like "Badger" and "Dark Knight" was anybody's guess. The fake bios the competitors had submitted to go with their fake names were as suspect as their aliases. For instance, "Badger" declared that his interests were "firearms, fearlessness, and females." Come to think of it, those words might describe half the men in Eureka County.

"We've run two hundred stories on Hard Rock Days," Rick said. "We have to come up with something new. Something compelling enough that people won't be able to wait to get the next issue."

She sighed and looked up at him. "You really aren't going to let this alone, are you?"

"If we're going to survive in today's competitive market, we've got to come up with the kinds of stories people can't wait to read."

"Such as?"

"Such as—what really happened to Gerald Pershing? Why did he disappear when he left here?"

"Maybe he was abducted by aliens."

"Exactly!" He hopped off the desk and began to pace. "Or—what if he was murdered? Who would want to kill him, and why? Was it a local with a grudge? A jilted lover? A jealous husband?"

"Rick!" She stared at him, alarmed. Rick was known for his crazy ideas and occasional rants. She'd quickly learned the fevers that hit him didn't last, but this felt different, more serious. "That isn't news," she said. "It's gossip."

"And people love to read gossip."

"But you can't print it and call it news."

"Then the key is to find the news angle," he said. "What if you interview this detective fellow—Duke? Find out why he's here and what he knows."

"Why should he tell me anything?"

"Persuade him that by printing his story in the paper, he'll reach potential witnesses who could give him more information. It's like those cold-case stories the Denver paper runs all the time."

"Except that, in those cases, an actual crime has been committed," she said. "Gerald Pershing just left town."

"Duke Breman apparently doesn't think so."

"And he's pissing off a lot of people in this town, with his accusations and insinuations."

"Pissed-off people buy papers," Rick said. "If nothing else, they want to know what we're saying about them."

"Rick—let it go. You can't run an inflammatory story with no basis in fact and call it news."

"Television does it every day of the week."

"We're better than television."

"Right. Which maybe is why print journalism is dying. We need to give the people what they want."

"The people in Eureka don't want any more of Gerald Pershing," she said. "Most of them were sick to death of the man before he ever left, and Duke's snooping hasn't made them feel any differently."

"I don't agree, but we'll table that discussion for now. There's an even bigger story we should be looking into—one I guarantee will pull in readers, not just locally, but nationally. Maybe even internationally."

She didn't like the sound of this. "What story is that?"

He snatched up a press release from the stack on her desk—the latest missive from Cassie, about the Founders' Pageant. Ellie had placed it there with the rest of yesterday's mail, but Maggie hadn't been desperate enough for something to do to read it yet. Now her eyes locked on the headline, in a bold, all-caps font across the top of the page that read BABY SHELLY TO STAR IN EUREKA FOUNDERS' PAGEANT.

"Baby Shelly!" Rick thumped the paper. "That's our big story. She disappeared from the public eye ten years ago, and suddenly we find out she's been living here for most of that time. All those legions of Baby Shelly fans who've been waiting all this time to find out what happened to her will go crazy for a story like that."

"Rick, no! If Shelly had wanted everyone to know about her past, she would have told someone before now." She remembered the young woman's anguish when Maggie had questioned her about Travis Rowell's accusations.

"Obviously, she told Cassie Wynock. Or someone else told Cassie." Someone like Travis, but Maggie didn't want to bring him into the picture. The idea that another reporter had scooped him would send Rick into a frenzy, even if that reporter might or might not work for a paper in another state.

"Maybe her sister said something," Maggie said. "It's definitely not something Shelly ever talks about."

"And why doesn't she talk about it? What has she been hiding from? That's something you need to find out when you interview her."

"Me?"

"Yes, you. You're the reporter, remember? Besides, she'll probably feel more comfortable talking to another woman. You're good at getting people to open up about themselves."

Normally, Maggie would have savored this rare praise from her boss, but she wasn't going to let herself get sidetracked by his flattery now. "Rick, Shelly is my friend. And I think she's entitled to her privacy." Not to mention, she'd already promised Shelly she wouldn't write about her past. And no matter what Rick said, she had to keep her promise.

"Would you say the same thing if your friend was accused of murder, or if she was a witness to a crime? Wouldn't you be rushing to her doorstep to interview her then?"

"This is completely different and you know it. Shelly hasn't done anything wrong."

"But she's done something newsworthy."

"I don't know if I agree with that."

"It's not your decision to make," he said. "Finding out that Baby Shelly is living right here in Eureka is big news, and we're not going to miss out on the chance to scoop the national press with the story."

Maggie tried to keep her voice from shaking as she spoke. "If you want the story so badly, you talk to her," she said. "I won't."

Rick stopped and gave her an assessing look. "I thought when I hired you, you had more gumption than this."

"I've got plenty of gumption," she said. "Gumption enough to respect Shelly's wishes for privacy."

"How do you know what her wishes are if you haven't

even talked to her about this? You're assuming she doesn't want to talk to the press because she's avoided doing so for ten years. But now that her story is out, did it ever occur to you that she might prefer talking to a friend, instead of the hordes of nameless reporters who are probably going to descend on this town once word spreads?"

"Do you really think national news will make that big a deal out of something that happened twenty-five years ago?" she asked.

"Maybe not, if she hadn't hidden from the spotlight for the last decade. The very fact that she'd been so reclusive makes her mysterious and desirable. If you think otherwise, you've underestimated the public's appetite for celebrity."

Maggie shook her head. "But it happened so long ago . . ."

"Some stories never die. Look at D. B. Cooper. He jumped out of that plane over Oregon almost fifty years ago, but if he suddenly showed up today he'd be the headline in every paper and on every television news story in the country. If Jimmy Hoffa—or his corpse—turned up, you'd be reading about it for days."

Maggie suppressed a shudder. "I hardly think Shelly is in the same category as those two."

"No, she's better. Because her story isn't of some lawbreaker or suspected lawbreaker. The Baby Shelly story is all about a cute little toddler rescued from the grave. Reading about it makes people smile all over again. In the midst of all the bad news, a story like this reaffirms people's belief in the goodness of their fellow man and that miracles do happen. Think about that and maybe you'll get over your squeamishness—you're not invading a friend's privacy, you're giving people a reason to feel hopeful and happy in the midst of all the tragedy in the world."

"You should have been a car salesman, Rick." He almost—*almost*—had her believing he was right.

"I'm not a car salesman, I'm a journalist. And if you want to be one, too, you'll call Shelly and schedule an interview.

Tell her what I just told you—that she has a better chance of telling her story the way she wants it if she talks to you. And if she gives you an exclusive, we'll help her fend off the rest of the press."

She wanted to put her hands over her ears and close her eyes to shut him out. Because he was starting to make sense, and she knew she was going to have to at least approach Shelly about this story—or give up on a job that, most of the time, she loved. "I'll talk to Shelly," she said. "But if she says no, I won't pressure her."

"If she says no, come back to me and I'll help you build an argument to persuade her to open up to you."

"Then why don't you talk to her in the first place?" she asked, her voice rising dangerously close to a wail.

"Because that wouldn't make you a better reporter." He looked smug. "Let me know what she says. Meeting adjourned." He strode back into his office and shut the door behind him.

She glared at the closed door, wishing she could think of some scathing comeback that would leave her pride intact. But she'd never been good with quick retorts. And then there was the fact that Rick was right. She had a degree in English, not journalism. She could write, but Rick had had to teach her how to construct a compelling news story. She should probably be more grateful to him, but, then again, there weren't exactly any other candidates standing in line for a job with such low pay and lousy hours. So she figured they both benefited about equally from her taking this position.

The front door opened and Ellie entered, a large coffee in one hand, a stack of mail in the other. A large woman with a mass of black, curly hair and a penchant for brightly colored loose shirts and lots of jangly silver jewelry, she was a recent—and welcome—addition to the *Miner*'s staff. "Hey, Maggie," she said, setting the coffee on the edge of her desk and flipping through the mail. "Two obituaries for you today."

Considering Eureka's already small population, two deaths in one week was noteworthy. "Who died?" Maggie asked.

"Old Rolly Peterson—Mack Peterson's dad? Out at the Lazy J?"

Maggie shook her head. Though she'd been in town over a year now and knew most people, at least by reputation, this one didn't ring a bell. "I don't guess I knew him."

"Well, he doesn't make it to town much. Rolly was, let's see . . ." She scanned the printout in her hand. "Ninety-eight. Died at home in his sleep. What a way to go."

Maggie took the sheet of paper. One of her jobs was to rewrite the obituaries into an interesting profile of the deceased, with a picture if she could find one in the files or obtain one from the family. "Who's the other one?"

"Mavis Gilroy. She moved away last year. She was eighty-six. She owned the house Olivia and D. J. Gruber live in now."

Maggie collected this printout as well. Though she'd never met Mrs. Gilroy, she knew the house well. That was the thing she liked about small towns—the connections. Everything and everyone was related in some way, woven together by threads of friendship or genetics or location, into a tapestry that could be either comforting or smothering, depending on your point of view.

Yet, even with this closeness, people still kept secrets. Had anyone—even her best friends—known that Shelly was the toddler who'd held the attention of practically the whole world for five days a quarter century ago?

She picked up her purse and draped it over the shoulder. "I'm going for coffee," she said. "I'll be back in half an hour or so."

"Sure." Ellie settled behind her desk. "If Rick asks, I'll tell him you're working on a story."

"Thanks."

Maggie walked the block and a half toward the Last Dollar, past Lucille's junk and antique store, Lacy's, where a sign on the door informed her that the mayor was attending an auction in Telluride and would be back at noon. Outside the hardware store, she nodded to Josh Miller, who was emerging from his apartment upstairs. She wondered how his romance with Jameso's sister, Sharon, was progressing. Marriage to a controlling husband had left Sharon wary of rushing into a new relationship, but Josh appeared patient enough to wait for her. Maybe he wouldn't have to wait much longer; the last few times Maggie had seen the two together, they'd looked pretty cozy.

She waved to other people as she passed, acquaintances and friends, threads in the tapestry she was weaving around herself here in Eureka. Coming from the big city and a small family, she'd found it surprisingly easy to fit into the weft and warp of the community. People accepted her—as longtime Eureka fixture Jake Murphy's daughter, as Jameso's girlfriend, then wife, and as herself, Maggie Stevens, another orphan seeking shelter who'd found her place in a community that was more than a little off the beaten path.

Danielle was on the front porch of the Last Dollar, watering the troughs of red and white geraniums under the windows. She swept a lock of dark hair out of her eyes and smiled up at Maggie. "Hey there," she said. "Are you here for an early lunch or a late breakfast?"

"Coffee," Maggie said.

Danielle followed her into the restaurant, which was empty except for one table of tourists, who were finishing breakfast. She collected a thick white mug and the coffeepot and led Maggie to a booth by the window. "Do you want anything to go with your coffee?" she asked. "Pie, or a piece of cake? I think we've got a couple of slices of buttermilk pecan coffee cake left."

"It sounds delicious, but I'd better not. But . . . do you have time to have coffee with me?"

Danielle glanced around the almost empty room. "Sure. Just a sec."

She returned a moment later with a second steaming mug and a small pitcher of cream. "You want this, right?" she said, and slid the pitcher toward Maggie, then took a seat across from her. "How are you doing?"

Danielle was one of those people who asked this question not as a polite greeting, but because she really cared. She looked into Maggie's eyes, as if searching for a clue as to her friend's mood and health. But Maggie didn't know how to answer the question this morning—not honestly.

She poured cream into the mug and stared at the swirls of white in the dark liquid. "Do you think it's human nature to never be satisfied with what we have?" she asked. "Is it a way of keeping us striving to do better, or is it just a big flaw in our character?"

"What are you unhappy about?" Danielle sipped her coffee and studied Maggie over the rim of the cup.

Buying time to think of a good answer, Maggie glanced around the café. The tourists were gathering their belongings and preparing to leave.

"Don't worry," Danielle said. "I can keep a secret. Well, except from Janelle, but she doesn't tell anyone anything."

"I've just been feeling a little . . . unsettled lately," Maggie said. "I mean, I must be about the luckiest woman in the world. I came to town with pretty much nothing and now I have a wonderful husband and a perfect baby girl, a beautiful place to live and a job I enjoy—yet, apparently, that isn't enough."

"No one can be deliriously happy all the time," Danielle said. "The perfect baby is cutting a tooth or suddenly decides she hates strained carrots; the wonderful husband wakes up grumpy; you have a boring or frustrating day on the job." She shrugged. "All those little things get to you, like sand in your shoes."

"You never look like you're out of sorts or having a bad day. You're always so serene."

Danielle laughed. "I have my days—ask Janelle. But I try not to take my moods out on my customers. It's bad for business."

"This is more than just a bad day." Maggie sipped her coffee, trying to find the words to describe the turmoil in her head. "I pick fights with Jameso, about stupid stuff. I hate that he spends so much time at the Dirty Sally, yet I know he enjoys the work. And why should I ask him to give up something he loves, when he never says a word when I have to work late covering a town council meeting, or spend Saturdays taking pictures at some festival?"

"You're newlyweds. I think part of the process in the early days of a relationship is seeing how far you can push each other. Does he really love me enough to put up with this? How about this?"

Maggie blinked. The intuitive logic of those words hit her low in the gut. "You really think that's it?"

Another shrug. "Hey, I'm just an amateur. I'm guessing, but it makes sense to me. When Janelle and I first moved in together, I went through a phase where I was a huge slob. I knew she was a neat freak and it was like I couldn't wait to push all her buttons, leaving clothes and shoes all over the place, not cleaning up the kitchen after I cooked." She made a face. "I was awful."

"What did she do?"

"She cleaned up after me for a while, then one day she sat me down and we had 'the talk.'"

"The talk?"

She nodded. "She told me I wasn't going to scare her away with all my messes, but that she wasn't my personal maid, either, so I had better shape up, or we would be seeing a counselor—and wouldn't I be embarrassed to have to tell a professional we were fighting over how many pairs of shoes I left in the living room and whether or not I left the lid off the flour bin?"

"Smart woman."

"Yep. I always tell her she's the brains and I'm the beauty." She made a show of patting her hair.

Maggie laughed. "Maybe that does explain why I've been out of sorts with Jameso lately, but I've been annoyed with Rick, too."

Danielle pursed her lips. "Well . . . you probably aren't the first person Rick has annoyed. He can be a little, um, forceful, until you get to know him and realize his bark is worse than his bite."

"I've gotten really good at ignoring his tantrums, but this is more than that. We've been butting heads on what makes a good news story and what doesn't. One of the things I've liked about working for the *Miner* is that I get to know most of everything that goes on in town. I've met a lot of people and I've been on the front line for everything from births to funerals—and everything in between. But I've always felt we were working together. Some of the stories Rick wants me to do lately put me in the position of adversary."

"Any particular story?" Danielle asked.

"He wanted to do a write-up about Gerald Pershing's disappearance." She gripped the mug of coffee more tightly, knuckles whitening. "There's no way to do that without implying that someone in town did away with the man. And it's all speculation, anyway. That's not good reporting—I don't have to have a journalism degree to know that."

"And Rick knows it, too," Danielle said. "That feels like an idea he'll get over soon enough."

"Maybe. But that's not the story that has me really upset. He wants me to interview Shelly Frazier."

"About the fact that she's Baby Shelly."

"You knew?" Had she been wrong about Shelly's desire to keep her past a secret? Maybe to most people in town it was old news. Only Maggie had been in the dark.

"Cassie brought one of her new posters by this morning," Danielle said. She nodded toward the front window and the sign pasted there, which advertised the Founders' Pageant, "Starring Shelly Frazier, beloved 'Baby Shelly,' celebrating the twenty-fifth anniversary of her rescue from a Texas cave."

"I wonder what Shelly thinks of that poster?" Maggie asked. "Have you seen her?"

Danielle shook her head. "I took our deposit to the bank this morning and they said she'd taken a personal day. They had one of the posters in their window, too, so everyone was talking about it."

"I feel terrible for her. It must be awful to have everyone talking about you that way."

"It's so amazing to think she's been living here all this time and we never knew." Danielle rested her chin in her hand, her expression dreamy. "She and I are the same age. I remember watching the coverage of her rescue when I was five. I didn't really understand what was going on, but I remember my mother kept hugging me and crying. We bought a card to send to the family. Of course, they must have received thousands of cards and letters—too many to read. But it was important to my mother to send it. She felt such a connection to Shelly's mother, because she had a little girl the same age."

"I think pretty much every mother felt that connection," Maggie said. She thought of her own daughter, at home now with Jameso. With all the abandoned mines in the area, it wasn't far-fetched to imagine that Angela could fall into one. Last year, during the Founders' Pageant, Olivia Gruber's son, Lucas, had fallen down one of the shafts in the French Mistress Mine, the old gold mine Jake had left to Maggie. Lucas had only spent a few hours down there, but afterward, Maggie had paid a man to build a better gate to safely close off the mine opening.

"I'm guessing her sister has something to do with the story coming out now," Danielle said. "Her and that reporter fellow she hangs out with."

"He was pretty cagey when I asked why he was in town," Maggie said. "I guess he didn't want anyone to scoop him."

She sighed. "Which is exactly what Rick wants now. He thinks Shelly will be more open to talking to a friend at the local paper than she has been to the national press. But I hate to intrude on her privacy. It feels wrong."

"I see Rick's point," Danielle said. "And I see yours, too. What are you going to do?"

"I don't know. First, I'm going to put Rick off as long as I can and think about it some more. Then maybe I will talk to Shelly. But as a friend, first. Not a reporter."

The door from the kitchen burst open and Janelle rushed in, her face flushed, short blond hair windblown. "Dani!" she cried.

Danielle rose. "What is it?" she asked, her voice rising in alarm. "What's wrong?"

"I went to the grocery to get some more breading for tonight's Wiener schnitzel and I heard the most awful news." She covered her cheeks with both hands.

"What news?" Maggie asked, as Danielle put her arm around her partner to comfort her.

"They've found Gerald Pershing. Or rather, they have found what's left of him."

Chapter 16

Lucille stood on the side of County Road Ten, hot sun burning the back of her neck while a shiver raced through her. Gravel rolled beneath the soles of her favorite blue sandals as she rocked back and forth, her gaze fixed on the wrecker and the steel cable extending from its winch to the ravine below. "You're absolutely sure it's Gerald Pershing?" she asked Bob, who stood beside her, a rifle incongruously cradled in one arm.

He nodded. "I recognized the car."

"But he wasn't the only person who ever drove a car like that," she said. "This could have been a tourist, driving too fast on a rainy night. . . ."

"It was Gerald. I'm sure." He looked grim.

"But how could you be sure? I mean, he'd been down there a while. . . ." She swallowed down a sudden surge of nausea.

"He still had that silver hair. And he had this ring, remember?" He rubbed below the knuckle of his own ring finger.

She remembered the ring—big and yellow gold, inset with a fat diamond that had to be at least two carats. "The ring was pretty unique," she admitted. "Still . . ."

"I spent five days in close quarters with the man," Bob said. "I remember the ring."

She nodded. As much as she'd grown to dislike Gerald, she didn't want to think of him dying this way, marooned in a remote ravine, injured and trapped. Maybe he'd gotten lucky and been killed instantly.

"I can't remember the last time I was out this way," Bob said. He looked around the usually deserted road. They stood where the gravel two-lane made a sharp curve to avoid a rock outcropping that jutted from the crumbling slope of a hill.

"I can," Lucille said.

He looked at her expectantly. She squinted down the road, the gravel shoulders lined with vehicles driven by rescue workers and the curious. Tall yellow sunflowers jutted up between and around the cars, their heads nodding like a crowd of bonneted spectators surveying the action. "Gerald and I drove out here one afternoon, when we were first getting to know each other," she said. "I showed him this shortcut to the highway."

"Well, hell, Lucille." Bob shifted the rifle to his other arm. "You're not going to feel guilty about him going off the road, are you?"

She shook her head. Well, probably she would feel a little guilty, but she wasn't going to beat herself up about it.

"Here it comes," someone said, and they turned in time to see the nose of the car rise up out of the gully. The driver's side front quarter panel was accordioned, the windshield mostly missing, jagged fingers of spidered glass jutting into the front cavity.

Even damaged this way, Lucille recognized the vehicle—a red Cadillac convertible. Gerald had left the top up, though when they'd been dating he'd put it down as much as possible. They'd raced along back country roads like teenagers, and once they'd made out in the front seat, as if they were thirty years younger.

"You're not going to get all hysterical, are you?" Bob asked. He watched her as if she were a live hand grenade.

"I'm not the hysterical type."

"No, you aren't." He took a step back, looking relieved.

"Bob, I understand you're the one who called this in." Josh Miller strode toward them along the shoulder of the road.

"I'm the one who found him," Bob said. "Daisy Mott called it in."

"So Ms. Mott was with you?" Josh took a notebook from his pocket and began writing. "I'll need to talk to her, too."

"Daisy was up on the other side of the ravine. We were tracking a bear that's been after her goats. We saw something shiny down in there. I thought it might be a car, so I went down to take a look. She waited up top."

"Any luck with the bear?" Josh asked.

He patted the stock of the rifle in his arms. "I hit her with some rubber bullets the wildlife officer gave me. Hopefully she'll remember and stay away from Daisy's herd."

"What did you do when you saw the car?" Josh asked.

"I thought I recognized it, but I went close enough to make sure I was right. I looked through the busted windshield and saw Gerald there inside."

"You recognized him?" Josh asked.

Bob made a face. "Have you seen the body?"

Josh shook his head.

"Let's just say, Gerald doesn't look much like himself these days. But I recognized the silver hair, and that big gold-and-diamond ring he always wore. And it was his car, so . . ." He shrugged.

"Did you touch anything?"

"No. I called Daisy and she called y'all. I hiked up here to meet the rescue folks." He looked past Josh, scowling. "What are you doing here?"

Lucille followed his gaze and saw Duke Breman moving toward them, long strides covering ground quickly. "I went into the Last Dollar for lunch and everyone in the place was talking about this." He turned to Lucille. "Have they really found Gerald Pershing?"

"I don't know," she said. "I haven't looked." She nodded toward the wrecker. The driver was winching the convertible onto the flatbed. "That looks like his car."

"It was Gerald," Bob said.

"What was he doing out here?" Duke asked.

"I don't know," Bob said. "Maybe you can ask him."

"This road is a shortcut from Eureka to the highway," Lucille said. "A back way."

"Did he usually take this route to the highway?" Duke asked.

"I don't know," she said. "Maybe he didn't want anyone to see him leaving town."

"Or maybe he was in a hurry to get away," Bob said.

Duke looked at Josh. "Do they know what happened? Why he crashed?"

Josh shook his head. "The accident investigators will take a look, but with a scene this old, they might not find much. Weather and other traffic will have wiped out any skid marks. Maybe he was traveling too fast and missed the curve. Or maybe a deer or something ran out in front of him and he swerved to avoid it. We may never know."

"At least now you can report back to whoever hired you that the man is dead," Bob said. "Quit trying to make people think something shady was going on and leave us be."

Duke ignored him and addressed Josh again. "Were there any signs of foul play?"

"Again, sir, I don't know the answer to that. There will be an investigation. But at this point, it appears to be an unfortunate traffic accident. We see more than our share on these mountain roads."

"What happens now?" Lucille asked.

"They'll transport the body to the coroner's office in Montrose," Josh said. "He'll rule on the cause of death. Our accident investigation team will report on our findings. We'll want to notify his next of kin. Would you happen to know who that might be?"

"He mentioned a son, but I don't know how to get in touch with him," she said. "Or even his name."

"I can give you that information," Duke said.

Lucille sent him a sharp look. Did that mean he had been hired by the family? Did they know the terms of Gerald's will? What did they think of his surprise bequest? What did they think of her?

"That's all I need from you folks right now." Josh closed the notebook and tucked it back into the front pocket of his uniform shirt. "Mr. Breman, I'll call later for the information on Mr. Pershing's next of kin, once we're certain it's him."

"I tell you, it's him," Bob said.

"If I have any more questions for you, I'll be in touch," Josh said.

"Can you give me a ride back to Daisy's place?" Bob asked. "I left my truck there."

"Sure. I'll drop you off."

"Is Daisy his girlfriend?" Duke asked when Bob and Josh were gone.

"I have no idea," Lucille said. "I try not to speculate too much on people's relationships."

"A good policy," he said.

He looked pensive. She found most men difficult to read, but he was more opaque than most. "Are you disappointed?" she asked.

"Why would I be disappointed?"

"I got the impression you were hoping to uncover a murder plot."

"No. I was hired to find out what happened to Gerald and I have."

"So I'll ask you the same question I asked Josh: What happens now?"

"I go back home and file my report. Once a death certificate is issued, the executor of the estate will contact you."

The words sent a chill through her. She hadn't exactly forgotten that Gerald had supposedly remembered her in his will, but she'd tried hard to put it out of her mind. Such a bequest didn't make any sense. "What if I don't want whatever he left me?" she asked.

"It's a lot of money. You should take it."

"How much money?"

"Close to a million dollars, give or take a few thousand."

She'd never been punched in the gut before, but she imagined it felt like this—aching and breathless and swaying on her feet. Duke put a steadying hand on her shoulder. "Are you okay?"

She nodded, and found her voice. "It seems wrong to accept money from a man I avoided for the last months of his life."

He kept his hand where it was, big and warm and undeniably masculine. She had to resist the urge to lean into him. "He wanted you to have it," he said. "You could think of it as payback for the way he treated you. Guilt money."

"That's even worse."

He took his hand away and shoved it into the front pocket of his jeans. "Don't overthink this," he said. "Invest some, spend some, give some away, but don't agonize over it."

"I have a new grandchild on the way. I could open a college fund for her and for her brother."

"Do something for yourself, too. You should travel."

"Where would I go?" She'd lived several different places in her life, but she'd never taken a real vacation anywhere. She lived in a place where other people vacationed. The idea of leaving seemed exotic and alluring.

"How about Austin?"

A nervous tremor shimmied through her stomach, but she managed to keep her expression neutral. "Why would I want to do that?"

"You could always come see me." He flashed a grin that threatened to buckle her knees. "I'd show you a good time."

The words brought her back to her senses. "That's a line I've heard before."

"The good ones are worth repeating." He held out his hand. "Seriously, I want to keep in touch."

"You have my number." She slipped her hand in his.

"Not the most enthusiastic invitation I ever received," he said.

"I think you'll agree I have good reason for being cautious." She glanced toward the wrecked convertible.

"Fair enough." He leaned over and planted a kiss beside her temple. "Just know that I'm a man who likes a challenge."

He turned and walked away, leaving her a little lightheaded, with a smile she didn't want to let go.

"You'll let me know when you hear from the family? Let them know we'd like to publish the obituary, since so many people in town knew him. Thank you." Maggie hung up the phone and stared at the page of notes in front of her. Rick was going to get his story on Gerald Pershing after all, though not the scandalous murder mystery he'd expected. Gerald's death had been much more mundane, though just as tragic.

Jameso came up the stairs, Angela in his arms. The baby was wearing a new sunsuit Barb had sent from Paris, where she and her husband, Jimmy, were spending three weeks. The letter accompanying the gift had made Maggie laugh: *I wish I was in Eureka with you and the darling child. Too much chocolate, cheese, wine, and bread. I'm going to get fat.*

"Who was that on the phone?" Jameso asked.

"The funeral home in Montrose. I was checking to see if any arrangements had been made for Gerald Pershing." She stood and took the baby and held her, studying that sweet, innocent face. Life was going to bang her up in ways Maggie couldn't even imagine; the knowledge made her shudder.

"Heck of a thing," Jameso said. "Him dying that way and no one even knowing he was down there."

"It could have been years before anyone found him, if Bob hadn't been tracking that bear," Maggie said. She pressed a kiss to Angela's soft cheek and closed her eyes, breathing deeply of that sweet, baby scent, fighting the sadness that dragged at her.

Jameso squeezed her shoulder. "Hey, don't let it get to you. He's not worth getting upset over."

She looked up, surprised, and more than a little touched that he'd noticed. "I was just thinking about how quickly life can go wrong. One minute you're cruising along in a red convertible, the next you're dead, alone and at the bottom of a ravine."

"Maybe Gerald got what he deserved," Jameso said. "Maybe his life of swindling and cheating caught up with him."

"You mean, like karma? I didn't know you believed in things like that."

"I'm not sure what I believe. But I like the idea that people who do bad things have to pay for their deeds in this life, even if I can think of too many examples where that doesn't happen."

"I don't know. I'm not sure I'd want every mistake I ever made in the past to come back to haunt my future," she said. "If that was true, no one could ever really start over. I mean, I'd always be looking over my shoulder, waiting for the past to catch up with me."

"Come on. You never did anything bad."

"Not terrible, no. But we all make mistakes. I'd really prefer to think we can put our pasts behind us, and be better people in the future."

"Maybe you're right," he said. "God knows, I've made enough mistakes in my own past. I try not to dwell on them." He tugged a ruffle into place around Angela's chubby leg. "I think that was Jake's problem, you know?" he said.

"Fighting his past?"

"He couldn't forgive himself for mistakes he'd made a

long time ago. That's why he drank. Why he was so angry. I almost fell into that trap myself. You pulled me out."

She studied him. "Do you really think so?" She'd always seen him as a man who didn't need help from anyone.

"I know so. That night we met—when I went up to Jake's cabin and found you there?"

"Yes." It had been her first night in Eureka. She was sad and disoriented and more than a little scared. Jameso had roared up on his motorcycle, handsome and dangerous in black leather. She'd been afraid of him and fascinated and even a little offended by him. But she'd also been attracted, and though she'd fought the attraction at first, afraid of making another mistake, she'd given in at last, and she'd never be sorry about opening herself up to love that way.

"I didn't really go up there just to check on his house," he said. "I planned to get roaring drunk, to try to forget about my messed-up life for a while. Meeting you made me want something different, instead of the same mistakes and anger and hurt over and over again." He pulled her close, his arms encircling her and the baby. "I want to focus on the future, and the good things in my life now."

"I want to do that, too. And then something happens to pull me back. It's like fighting a riptide, pulling at my ankles. It's exhausting."

"Then hold on to me. I'll get us safely to shore. Maybe that's one of the things marriage is about—rescuing each other, riding out the bad times to get to the better times."

She had a picture of them, old and graying, still clinging to each other on choppy seas. She closed her eyes and leaned her head on his shoulder. If they could see a future like that with each other, then surely they could get there together. They just had to believe, and not let go.

"Can you believe they found him, after all this time?"

"I heard the air bag trapped him and he must have lingered for days."

"I heard he hit his head in the crash and died instantly."

"You have to wonder about karma, you know? Still, what a horrible way to go."

Cassie wanted to cover her ears to block out the conversations swirling around her in the library's conference room. Even here, where they'd gathered to rehearse the Founders' Pageant—people couldn't stop talking about Gerald Pershing. Leave it to that old blowhard to grab the spotlight even when he was dead. Cassie cleared her throat. "We'd better get started."

"At least now they know he wasn't murdered."

"They don't know anything. Maybe someone shot him and that's why he went off the road. Did you ever think of that?"

"It's time to start," Cassie said, louder.

"I wonder where they'll send the body? Do you think he had family?"

"What about Bob? He and Gerald never got along, and yet he ended up with those mine shares. Do you think he knew the body was down there all along?"

Cassie slid out a chair and climbed onto it. "Everyone! Listen to me!"

All conversation died as everyone turned to stare. "That's better." She forced a smile to her lips. No one had to know how nervous she was about this. Last year, the debut of the pageant had been big, but this year was going to be so much better. She would have the attention of the world on her.

"Now, if everyone is ready, we'll get started. Shelly"—she turned to the young woman, who was seated in a corner, head bowed over her script—"I thought it might be appropriate if you addressed the audience before the play begins."

"No."

Oh really, was the girl going to be difficult about everything? "Think of this as your chance to say whatever is on your mind." And if she could say in the press that Baby Shelly was going to speak, it might draw even bigger crowds.

"No, Cassie." Shelly's smile was tight, no teeth showing.

"I think the focus should be on the play—on the founders and . . . and your script. Anything else wouldn't really be in keeping with the spirit of the day."

"Because we all know crowds of people will be coming to learn about the history of Eureka," Doug Raybourn said. Doug was the best actor in the company and he knew it; when Cassie glared at him, he merely smirked.

She'd have to deal with Shelly later. Maybe the girl was right and they should keep the focus on the play. Or maybe Cassie herself could say something to introduce both Shelly and the play. Something about rebirth and new beginnings— that sounded suitably poetic. Yes, that might be the best solution. And really, it was probably most appropriate that she speak first. "All right, let's get on with rehearsal." She opened her script and cleared her throat.

"Sorry we're late." Mindy Payton, along with Travis Rowell, pushed through the clot of actors around the door to the conference room. "We were over at the Dirty Sally and lost track of time."

Cassie could have guessed the young woman's where- abouts from her flushed cheeks and bright eyes. Disgraceful, these young people and their loose ways. "I don't know why you're here," Cassie said. "This meeting is a rehearsal for the play. Only actors should be here."

"I'm helping Shelly, remember?" She moved over to join her sister. "You're the one who suggested it."

Cassie frowned. "I meant you should work with her at home, in between our rehearsals."

"Well, I'm here now, so I might as well stay," Mindy said.

The young woman clearly wasn't going to leave without a fuss that Cassie didn't have time for. "Fine, but *he* doesn't need to be here." She nodded to Travis.

"I'm here in my capacity as a reporter." Travis followed Mindy into the room, notebook in hand. He grinned at Cassie. "Is that all right, Miss Wynock?"

"Oh, well." She smoothed her hair. "If the paper is interested, I suppose that's all right." Maggie had confirmed Cassie's suspicions that Travis wasn't really a reporter for the *Dallas Morning News*, but maybe she was just jealous. It wouldn't hurt to let him sit in on the rehearsal, on the off chance that he would write about it for *some* newspaper.

"He's not—" Mindy began, but Travis stumbled into her, apparently stepping on her foot. She cried out, and he steadied her with his hand on her arm.

"Sorry," he apologized. "That was clumsy of me. Are you all right, Mindy?"

"Uh, sure." She moved closer to Shelly.

"All right, then." Cassie returned her attention to the script. "Let's get started. Shelly, I believe you have the first lines."

Shelly cleared her throat and held up her script. *"What a desolate place this is, Emmaline,"* she said. *"And yet, there is such wild beauty in these mountains, too. I'm glad you and Festus invited me to make the trip west with you."*

"This wild land needs the gentling touch of women like us," Cassie said. *"We are the ones who carry the keys to civilization in our breasts."*

"Yes, I long to see culture and the maturing influence of education brought to these far reaches of humanity," Shelly read.

"Wait a minute! Hold on a second." Mindy stepped between the two women.

"What is it?" Cassie asked. "Why are you interrupting?"

"Because you two haven't been speaking five minutes and you're already boring the audience to death."

Someone behind Cassie giggled. "I thought boring people was the point," Doug said.

"No, no, no," Mindy said. "Instead of you two standing and declaiming at each other, you need some action. Something interesting."

"The action comes later," Cassie said. "When gold is discovered and Festus founds the town."

"But can't the women be doing something besides talking?" Mindy asked. "Maybe they could be panning for gold or something."

"Women didn't pan for gold," Cassie said. "At least, I'm sure my great-grandmother didn't."

"But they probably did laundry in the river, right?" Mindy said. "Maybe they find some gold then."

"The women aren't focused on gold," Cassie said. "They're focused on the wealth to be found in education and civilization."

"Like I said, boring." Mindy rolled her eyes.

"This is not a shoot-'em-up melodrama," Cassie said stiffly. "This is an educational, historically accurate dramatic presentation."

"She's got a point, Cassie," Doug said. "The opening could stand to be spiced up a bit." He turned to Mindy. "Do you have any ideas?"

She took Shelly's script and flipped through it. "Instead of starting with a boring speech, why don't you begin with them running from the Indians?" she said. "Over on page ten."

"The point of that scene is that the Indians, the local Utes, turned out to be friendly," Cassie said.

"Exactly," Mindy said. "It's a great twist that the audience won't necessarily be expecting."

Cassie resisted the urge to gloat. After all, she was responsible for that bit of brilliance. But she had to keep her mind on her job here. "I don't think it's wise to start out with the pioneers looking so foolish," she said. "I wanted to introduce the characters as good, intelligent people before I showed their mistakes."

"Haven't you heard that people like flawed characters?" Mindy asked. "Start with them fleeing the Indians—that's how they find this pretty little valley, right? It's exciting, it's action-oriented, and then after they've made friends with the Indians and decide to stay, the women can decide to build their school while the men go off to dig for gold."

"I like it," Doug said. Others around him murmured agreement.

"What do you think, Shelly?" Cassie asked.

"Um, I think maybe we should try it." Shelly looked from her sister to Cassie.

Cassie pressed her lips tightly together. She wouldn't let any of them see how their criticism hurt. She'd worked hard to write a sophisticated presentation, but Mindy's ideas were probably more in line with the mentality of the tourists who would likely make up the majority of the audience. People who wasted their time with reality television and game shows probably weren't up to the kind of edifying drama she'd been aiming for.

"Fine," she said. "We'll give it a try. Everyone, turn to page ten. Festus, I believe you start."

Doug posed, one hand on his hip, the other shielding his eyes, as he gazed across an invisible valley. Cassie moved to his side. *"What is it, dear?"* she asked, brow furrowed, eyes wide, doing her best to convey anxiety.

"Indians," he said. *"This could mean trouble."*

From there, they progressed through the scene, with Festus leading his little band of pioneers into a valley, where they end up trapped by the Indians, who turn out to be welcoming, not hostile. In the end, the Utes agree to let the pioneers live on the land and Festus and the chief shake hands while the rest of the cast looks on.

"It's a pretty good scene," Doug said when they were done.

"Yes, but it hardly showcases the characters of Hattie and Emmaline," Cassie said. "They're supposed to be the stars."

"The audience will be looking forward to them all the more for the delay," Mindy said.

"Do you really think so?" Cassie asked.

"Trust me, I have professional experience." Mindy directed her dazzling smile to the company in general.

Cassie turned to Travis. "Be sure you emphasize in your

article that Shelly and I are the stars of the production," she said. "That the focus is as much on the female pioneers as the men."

"Right. I'll, uh, put that in my article." He bent his head and scribbled in his notebook.

"All right, then." Cassie turned back to the beginning of the script. "We'll put the conversation between Hattie and Emmaline here. And I suppose they could be picking flowers or something suitably genteel while they talk. That would certainly emphasize the beauty of the area."

Doug snorted. "You don't think your ancestor did her own wash?"

Cassie ignored him. "Now, Shelly, if you could speak up a little. We want to be sure the audience hears you."

"Lift your chin up and look out at the audience, that will help," Mindy said. "And don't worry about seeing them—the stage lights will be bright enough for that not to be a problem."

Cassie nodded. "That's right." Say what you would about the young woman's flighty personality, she appeared to know what she was talking about. She lifted her own chin. "Let's begin that scene again."

An hour later, they'd run through most of the scenes once. Mindy, backed up by Doug and some of the other actors, had persuaded Cassie to shorten a couple of scenes. She hated to lose the beautiful dialogue she'd written, but of course, she always had the option of adding back in her own speeches during the actual performance.

"I think we've done enough for tonight," she said, at five minutes past nine o'clock. She closed her script. "Thank you for your help, Mindy."

"You should be in the play," Doug said.

"Well, I am a professional," Mindy said. "But this is really for local amateurs, right? I'm just happy to help."

"I'm sure you've been a big help to your sister." Cassie smiled at Shelly.

"Oh yeah. A big help." Shelly fussed with her tote bag, her hair falling forward to cover her face.

"I want you to do well in your big debut," Mindy said.

"I'm sure you do," Shelly said. "After all, the more attention on me, the better for you." She raised her head, eyes dark with more emotion than Cassie had ever seen her display. Was Shelly angry about something?

"Oh really, Shelly. Everything is not always about you," Mindy said.

"How I wish that wasn't true." She slipped the tote bag's straps over her shoulder and moved past her sister, out the door.

Doug was the first to break the silence that followed. "What was that about?" he asked.

"I don't know." Mindy shook her head. "She's the one who asked me to help her with the play."

"She probably didn't think you were going to be so good at it," Travis said.

"Do you think she's jealous?" Doug asked.

"Shelly, jealous of me?" Mindy laughed. "Trust me, that's never going to happen."

"You might be surprised." Travis stuffed his notebook into his messenger bag, his expression thoughtful. "Your showing up in town has changed a lot of things for Shelly. Maybe it's even changed her opinion of you."

Chapter 17

Late Friday afternoon, Shelly fussed with setting the old oak farm table she'd bought at an estate sale the first year she and Charlie were married. She folded starched cloth napkins this way, then that, moved the water glasses half an inch to the right, then stepped back to admire the effect. Some people turned to yoga or long-distance running for stress relief, but she preferred simple domestic tasks. Setting the table or folding laundry or making beds became a moving meditation, centering her on home and family, and the things that really mattered in her life.

"You don't have to go to all this trouble for me," Mindy said from the doorway. She sauntered into the dining room, country chic in a hot pink tank top and tight jeans ripped just so at the knees. Shelly had not seen her sister since she'd run out of the rehearsal last night. She'd heard Mindy come home late, stumbling a little on the stairs and cursing under her breath as she made her way up to the guest room under the eaves. When Shelly left for work this morning, Mindy was still asleep.

"It's not for you." Shelly set a vase of flowers in the center of the table—three blossoms cut at different heights, as elegant as anything out of a magazine. "I do this every night." But of course, Mindy hadn't noticed.

"Oh please." Mindy rolled her eyes. "Why bother? I doubt if Charlie or your boys care. And you're eating macaroni and cheese, for Pete's sake. Who are you trying to impress?"

"I like my family to sit down to a nice table."

"You always did have to be Miss Perfect."

The acid tone in her voice made Shelly flinch. "There's nothing wrong with setting a nice table for my family."

"There's nothing wrong with letting people use paper napkins either, or letting them eat in front of the TV, for that matter. We did it all the time when we were kids, and it didn't stunt our growth or anything."

Pain, like a hand squeezing at the base of her skull, made Shelly's head pound. She opened her mouth to argue, then closed it, shook her head, and turned away. Mindy wouldn't understand, so why get into it?

"What?" Mindy followed her into the kitchen.

"Nothing." She bent to open the oven door. The aroma of hot, melting cheese made her mouth water.

"You were going to say you wanted something better for your kids, weren't you?"

Heat suffused her face, and not from the oven. "Is that so wrong?" she asked softly. All those evenings of thrown-together dinners in front of the television, she'd longed for her family to sit down together at the table and talk about their days. She wanted them to focus on each other instead of characters in a television show.

"That's the trouble with you, Shelly," Mindy said, her voice rising. "You always thought you were too good for the rest of us. You let all that attention from the newspapers and magazines and television go to your head. You wouldn't share any of your good fortune with the rest of us. You couldn't even share your stupid little historical-society play with me last night without getting all bent out of shape. No wonder

Mama worked so hard to keep the fever over Baby Shelly alive—that was all we ever had of you."

Her voice shook on the last words. Shelly whirled and was stunned to see her sister pale, her eyes glossy with unshed tears.

"Mindy, I never—"

"Just shut up." Mindy clamped her mouth shut, swallowed hard, and turned and fled from the room, her feet pounding hard on the steps all the way up to the little guest room under the eaves.

Shelly turned off the oven, tossed aside the quilted mitt she'd donned, and followed her sister. She hesitated at the bottom of the stairs. What if Mindy locked her out? Maybe that was part of their problem—they'd been locking each other out too long.

She climbed the stairs slowly, giving herself time to think of something to say to her sister. No magically healing words had popped into her head by the time she stood outside Mindy's door, but she made herself knock anyway.

"Go away!"

Shelly knocked again.

"I said, go away."

Shelly tried the knob. It turned easily in her hand. She pushed open the door. "I'm not going away."

Sunlight through the dormer window revealed Mindy sitting on the side of the bed. She sniffed and scrubbed at one eye with the back of her hand. "I don't want to talk to you," she said.

"I'm not sure I want to talk to you, either, but I think we should." She sat on the bed beside her sister. "Why did you say that down there—about my fame being all you and Mama and Daddy had of me?"

Mindy looked away. "It doesn't matter."

"It does." It mattered more than she'd ever let herself admit.

"Don't you remember anything about our childhood?"

"What do you mean?"

Mindy shifted to face her once more. "You were always different, always apart from the rest of us," she said. "We'd all be in the living room after supper, watching television, laughing together, but you were locked in your room, your head in a book. If we wanted to go out for fried chicken, you whined because you wanted to stay home and have a fancy dinner with candles and stuff. Whatever the rest of us did or wanted, it wasn't good enough for you."

"I didn't like to go out because people stared at me. Sometimes they tried to buy us dinner and stuff."

"And what was wrong with that? If somebody wanted to pay for Baby Shelly and her family's meal, why shouldn't Mom and Dad let them?"

"I thought you all wanted me with you as a meal ticket."

"We wanted you there because you were part of our family. But you never saw it that way."

No, she hadn't seen things that way. Had she really been so wrong?

"You were so wrapped up in yourself, and all your imagined hurts, you couldn't even see the rest of us," Mindy said. "I suppose we shouldn't have been surprised when you finally turned your back on us altogether."

"I didn't think you cared."

"Well, we did. And it hurt." She stood, dashing fresh tears from her eyes. "Did you ever think about how much it hurt?" She grabbed the door handle and wrenched it open again.

"Don't go." Shelly rose and reached for her.

"I have to. I can't stay here with you a minute longer."

Shelly dropped back onto the bed, too weary to chase her sister down the stairs. She felt as if she'd been struck by an avalanche, carried along in a pummeling wave of emotion that bruised and battered her. Scenes from her childhood replayed in her head: evenings spent reading Jane Austen or Georgette Heyer and fantasizing about a close family that sat down together for tea, or went for long walks together in the country. She never heard the laughter from the rest of them, downstairs engrossed in the latest sitcom; or if she did, she blocked it because it didn't fit with her picture of herself as the persecuted princess locked in the tower.

Fresh pain stabbed at her, not the pain of past hurts, but a fresh wound from the realization that at least some of Mindy's accusations were true; she'd been so wrapped up in her fantasies of the life she'd wanted that she'd ignored the good in the life she'd had. If she had never felt close to her family, part of the blame was her own, for keeping such a distance.

The front door opened and she started, hoping Mindy had returned. But the pounding of tennis shoes on the stairs, followed by a slower, heavier tread, told her Charlie and the boys were home. She stood and pressed her fingers beneath her eyes, blotting the last of her tears. Then she hurried to the bathroom, splashed cool water on her face, and combed her hair. She couldn't let them see how upset she was.

She went downstairs to greet them, hugging the boys and kissing Charlie on the cheek. "We're having your favorite," she told Cameron. "Macaroni and cheese."

The boys cheered, and Charlie poured glasses of milk for the children and water for the adults. As Shelly took her place at one end of the table, she glanced at the empty chair beside her, then looked away.

"Where's Aunt Mindy?" Theo asked.

"She had something else she had to do in town," Shelly said. "Now, how much macaroni and cheese do you want?"

"A lot!" he said, grinning.

She served him and herself, then passed the dish to Charlie and Cameron. But instead of eating, she watched them eat, Theo carefully stabbing each noodle with his fork, Cameron preferring to shovel in the food in big bites. She loved them all so much sometimes it hurt, and the things in life that gave her the most joy were the things she did for them. How could Mindy say family wasn't important to her?

She looked up and caught Charlie watching her, twin vertical lines creasing his forehead. She forced a smile to her face and picked up her fork. "Don't eat so fast, Cameron," she said. "Slow down and chew."

At last the meal ended and the boys asked to be excused. "I have to read about Columbus," Cameron said.

"Are there any pictures?" Theo asked. "I want to see."

"You can read to your brother," Shelly said. "It will be good practice for you."

They retreated to the living room and Charlie helped Shelly clear the table. He came up behind her as she ran water in the kitchen sink. "I'm almost afraid to ask what's wrong this time," he said.

"What makes you think anything's wrong?" She scraped plates into the garbage, noticing that Cameron has once again failed to eat all his broccoli.

"Your sister isn't here and you look like you're about to cry. And you hardly ate anything. I thought you two were getting along better."

"We had a horrible fight this afternoon."

"About the book? If she won't take no for an answer, tell her to leave. And take that reporter with her."

"It wasn't about that. She hasn't even mentioned the book in a while."

"What, then?"

She squeezed her eyes shut, struggling to keep it together. "She said it was my fault our family was never close—that they tried to include me and love me, but that I pushed everyone away. I acted like I was too good for them—or they weren't good enough for me."

"She's trying to make you feel guilty." He squeezed her arm. "I've never seen you act that way with anyone."

"But what if she's right? What if I was the one in the wrong?"

"What if you were? You were a kid and kids make mistakes. From what you've told me, the wrong wasn't all on your side."

"I just . . ." She shook her head. "I just wonder if I've been looking at things from the wrong angle all these years." If she'd been so off base about her childhood, what else had she been wrong about?

"I don't know what to tell you," Charlie said. "What do you want to do?"

"I don't know. I was fine with my life the way it was. I thought I didn't need my family, but now . . ."

"It's probably not too late to try to mend fences."

"But what if trying to make things up to them only does more harm than good?"

"My mother always told me that when I was facing a hard or scary decision, to think of the worst thing that can happen in a situation," he said. "Make a plan for dealing with that, and move on. The worst thing hardly ever happens, but knowing you're prepared if it does can be enough to make you push forward."

"That makes sense." She turned to the sink and plunged her hands into the sudsy, warm water, feeling for the dishrag. Maybe washing dishes would help her to sort this out. She wiped the rag across a plate. "The worst thing that could happen would be that my parents would move here to Eureka and my mom would start up the Baby Shelly publicity machine again. Reporters would be calling for interviews or showing up at my workplace to take photographs—or worse, they'd try to talk to the kids. We wouldn't have any privacy."

"Except you're a grown woman now and your mother can't run your life anymore. You can say no and make it stick." He picked up a dish towel and began drying the plates she'd slid into the rinse water. "You get to make the rules and set boundaries, and you've got me to back you up."

She loved him for saying this, but he didn't understand the way things like celebrity took on a life of their own. "Things are already starting to feel out of control," she said. "I can't stop Travis and Mindy from writing their book and saying whatever they want. And Cassie is making everyone think Baby Shelly is going to make a speech or something at the play."

"We can hire a lawyer and threaten to sue the publisher if they publish their book. Or you can decide to ignore it. What they say doesn't have to affect you. And if any reporters come to see Cassie's play, you don't have to talk to them. But I'm still not sure that many people are going to come all the way to Eureka to see you. No offense, but all that happened a long time ago."

"I hope you're right. I just wish I could go back to how things used to be before Mindy showed up."

"But maybe it's good that this happened when it did," he said. "I'm not big on psychobabble, but it sounds like there are a few issues you need to deal with."

"You think?" She managed a smile. "I guess running away hasn't really fixed anything if one conversation with my sister can get me so upset." She gripped a handful of forks underneath the water. "But I'm scared."

He caressed her shoulder and she leaned back against him. "You survived being trapped underground for five days when you were only four," he said. "You can survive this."

"Right." She thought she sounded a lot more confident than she felt. She would probably survive whatever happened, but would she come out on the other side still herself? Or would the things she learned about herself in the process turn her into someone she didn't recognize? Someone she didn't want to be.

"The Chamber of Commerce couldn't have ordered up a better day for this," Rick said, as he and Maggie stood in front of the *Miner* offices Saturday morning, watching traffic flow into town for the Hard Rock Days festivities. Sun bathed the whole scene in a golden glow. Flowers in pots along Main Street spilled over their containers in a riot of colors and the sky was so blue it almost hurt to look at. Many storefronts were decorated with paintings Olivia Gruber had made on the glass windows, depicting more flowers, wildlife, or mining equipment. A large banner spanning the street declared WELCOME TO THE 65TH ANNUAL EUREKA HARD ROCK DAYS.

Distracted by her attempts to arrange Angela's baby sling so the child would stop fussing and Maggie could still juggle her camera and notebook, Maggie only nodded. "What do you want me to cover first?" she asked.

"Visit with some of the vendors, maybe get a few photos," Rick said. "I'll cover the first half of the competition—the mucking and the sledge races. You can cover the double-jacking and single-jacking events. Get plenty of photographs, then we'll select the best shots for the paper and offer up the others to the competitors, for a modest fee, or course."

She glanced down the street, hoping to see Jameso striding toward her. He'd left the B and B early, saying he had something to do, but he'd meet up with her later. She'd been counting on him to watch Angela while she worked, but she hadn't been able to find him, and he wasn't answering his phone.

"You'd better plan on getting some photos at Cassie's pageant later, or I'll never hear the end of it," Rick said. "It might be interesting if she actually gets her big tourist crowd, all anxious to see Baby Shelly."

"For Shelly's sake, I hope not," Maggie said. "She really doesn't want to be in the spotlight."

"I'll bet she secretly misses it," Rick said. "And you still owe me a story on her."

"I told you, Rick. I intend to respect Shelly's privacy."

"She was just making excuses. You can't tell me someone who grew up a celebrity doesn't miss being the center of attention," he said.

"Maybe there's such a thing as too much attention." Maggie shouldered the diaper bag that was doubling as her purse. "I'm going to head on over to the booths. If you see Jameso, tell him to call me."

The front section of Ernestine Wynock Park had been designated for vendors, both arts and crafts booths and food. Maggie was making her way down the first row of stalls when she almost collided with Bob Prescott. "Sorry, Bob, I wasn't looking where I was going," she said.

"At least it was you and not another dang tourist." He scowled at the crowd around them. "You can hardly move for all the people in here."

"Hello, Maggie." Daisy Mott joined them, a pink ruffled blouse making her look more feminine than usual. "Here you go, Bob." She handed him a cookie the size of a saucer. "Danielle says hi." She broke a piece off her own cookie. "The Last Dollar has a booth selling baked goods," she said. "All the money is going to the local food bank. If you want anything, you'd better get over there soon. Everything is selling fast."

"I'm not surprised," Maggie said. "How are the goats?"

"Oh, they're good. The bear hasn't come back."

"I told you," Bob said. "Those rubber bullets are something they remember for a long time."

"How much longer will you be in town?" Maggie asked.

"Actually, I'm thinking of staying in Eureka for a while." Daisy's cheeks were almost as pink as her shirt. "Mr. Alcott says he'll lease me his old home place."

"What brought this on?" Maggie asked, fighting back a smile.

"Oh, I just like it here," Daisy said. "There's something about this place that really grows on a person."

"Come on." Bob tugged Daisy's arm. "I want to get a good seat for the first round of the Hard Rock competition."

Maggie watched them go, amused. She wouldn't have thought Bob was the romantic type, but Daisy apparently saw something attractive in the old curmudgeon. She moved on down the rows of booths, snapping shots of a toddler with an ice cream cone at the Elks Club booth and of two women trying on knit hats made by the Presbyterian women.

"Maggie!"

She turned at the sound of her name and saw Olivia waving to her from the booth Lucille had set up to sell merchandise from her store. Maggie made her way over to the little stall, which was filled with Olivia's hand-painted T-shirts, handmade jewelry, and a few small paintings. "How's business?" she asked.

Lucille turned from the cash box, after making change for a woman who was buying one of the T-shirts. "It's been good," she said. "In fact, this may be the best crowd we've had for Hard Rock Days in a while. More proof that the economy is improving."

"There are certainly lots of tourists in town," Maggie said. "We had to turn quite a few people away from the B and B, and I hear the motel is full, too."

"It's a good thing Duke left when he did," Olivia said. "That freed up a room for more visitors." She was watching her mother as she spoke, and Maggie was surprised when Lucille's cheeks flamed.

"I got the impression he was pretty interested in you." Maggie couldn't resist probing.

"Oh, I don't know about that." Lucille folded and refolded a shirt from the stack in front of her.

"He was very interested," Olivia said. "I don't believe you, Mother. Twenty years of not dating, and suddenly you can't keep the men away."

"Oh, hush." Lucille swatted at her.

"Tell the truth," Maggie said. "What's going on with you and the handsome detective from Texas?"

"Nothing." A slow smile curved her lips. "At least not yet."

Maggie laughed. "Are you playing hard to get?"

"I'm not playing at anything, but I've decided there's nothing wrong with expecting a man to prove himself." She looked past Maggie. "Ma'am, can I help you find a particular size?"

Maggie stepped to the side to allow more room for the customer. Olivia followed. "What do you think?" Maggie asked Olivia, keeping her voice low.

"I think Mom's being cautious, but I hope not *too* cautious," Olivia said. "I like to tease her, but I keep an eye out, too. I don't want her to be hurt again."

A customer claimed Olivia's attention, too, so Maggie moved on. As she photographed customers lined up to purchase roasted corn and barbecue sandwiches from the Elks Club, she thought of what Lucille had said about expecting a man to prove himself. She'd taken that approach with Jameso, too, wary of being hurt after her painful divorce.

But maybe she'd taken that idea too far. How many times did he have to impress her before she believed him? He had skied over a closed mountain pass in a Christmas blizzard to prove he loved her. He took over management of the B and B to prove he could provide for her. Maybe the time had come for her to promise him that he had nothing more to prove.

Travis shouldered his way through the crowd around the beer tent. Half the population of western Colorado must have shown up for this festival. Was reliving the old mining days really such a big draw, or had word about Baby Shelly drawn in fans from far and wide? He hoped it was the latter. When Shelly saw how much her public adored her, she might be more willing to cooperate on the authorized biography he was supposed to be writing. Other than the tapes Mindy had made, he didn't have a lot of material so far. And the quality of those tapes was questionable, the conversation unintelligible for long stretches of time. He'd have to tell Mindy not to shove the recorder so far down in her bra next time. Her abundant cleavage evidently acted like a muffler over the microphone.

"Travis Rowell, is that you!"

The voice startled him, and he turned to stare at a familiar figure from the not-so-distant past. "Greg!" He grasped the hand of a reporter he'd worked with at the *Dallas Morning News*. "What are you doing here?"

"I'm covering Baby Shelly's big debut for the paper." At six feet, seven inches, Greg Albright towered over Travis, and most everyone else in the crowd.

"Which paper is that?" Travis asked. "Are you in Colorado now?"

"No, I'm still with the *Morning News*. They thought the reappearance of a former Texas icon was worth reporting on—Baby Shelly back from the dead all over again, that sort of thing." He looked around them. "So is she really here in this town in the back of beyond?"

"She's here," Travis said.

"She couldn't have chosen a much more out-of-the way place to hide, could she?" Greg said. "I had to take two different flights, then rent a car and drive two hours to get here. Do you see her anywhere around here? Can you point her out to me?"

"No can do." Travis squared his shoulders. "I have an exclusive with Shelly. I'm writing her authorized biography."

Greg eyed him skeptically. "Tell me another one. I heard she doesn't talk to anyone."

"Her sister introduced us. She doesn't normally like reporters, but I managed to charm her. She won't talk to anyone else."

"And I imagine you have that in writing?"

He swallowed, and forced an extra heartiness into his voice. "Of course."

Greg clapped him on the shoulder. "You always were a

terrible liar," he said. "Never mind. I'll get someone else to point her out to me."

Travis fought a sinking feeling. Greg would do it. He could be very charming when he wanted to; men and women found him irresistible. He'd even charmed the management of the paper into letting him keep his job, at a time when they were laying off practically all the other general assignment reporters. The man had a magic touch—a touch that might take away Travis's best chance of paying off his debts and putting together a stake that would allow him and Trish to finally marry.

"Don't do it," he said. "Don't talk to Shelly."

Greg raised one eyebrow. "Or what? You'll let the air out of my tires?" He slapped Travis on the back, almost knocking him over. "Don't think of me as competition. If I do get anything good from her, you can always use it in your book—after it runs in the paper."

He nodded, miserable.

"Say, I saw Trish the other day," Greg said. "Are you two still dating?"

He'd forgotten Greg knew Trish. Had he been trying to charm her, too? "Where did you see her?"

"I was in Zoka's Bar and she was there with some friends. She gave me a big hug and said how happy she was to see me. She was looking great, too. But then, she always was too hot for the likes of you."

"Trish and I are engaged," he said.

"Oh, really. Funny, I don't remember a ring. Then again, I don't always notice that kind of thing."

"We haven't picked out a ring yet."

Greg laughed. "Then you're not very engaged, are you? If it was me, no way would I leave a woman like that alone without at least putting a big fat diamond on her finger to mark her as already claimed. With a woman that beautiful, some other man is always waiting to make a move on her. And who could blame him?"

If Greg hadn't been a foot taller than him and outweighed him by thirty pounds, Travis would have decked him, but punching him now would only end up with Travis in the dirt—or in jail for disturbing the peace. All he really wanted was to get out of here and somewhere he could call Trish. She wouldn't really dump him for some slick-talking jerk, would she?

He spotted a familiar blond head moving through the crowd toward them, and inspiration struck. "Greg, old friend, I'm going to do you a big favor," he said.

"What's that?"

"See that blonde there? The one with the big hair and the bigger boobs?"

"I see her."

"That's Baby Shelly." He clapped him the back. "Have fun interviewing her, and remember—you owe me."

Before Greg could respond, Travis turned and slipped away. Right now he had more important things to worry about than a disaster that had happened a quarter century ago.

After two hours of photographing the vendors and the crowd in the park, plus a break to nurse Angela and grab a hot dog for herself, Maggie still hadn't seen Jameso. She tried calling him again, only to have her call go straight to voice mail. Now, in addition to being angry, she was beginning to get worried. She stood on the edge of the crowd, phone in hand, the other wrapped around the baby, uncertain what to do. If she could find Josh Miller, the sheriff's deputy, maybe she'd ask him what to do. He and Jameso were friends. But there was no sign of Josh, either.

She headed back toward the exit, still scanning the crowd. "Maggie, is everything okay?" Janelle put her hand on Maggie's arm. "You look worried," she said. "Is everything all right?"

"Have you seen Jameso?" Maggie asked. "I've been looking everywhere for him, and he's not answering his phone."

"I'm pretty sure he's over at the Hard Rock Miner competition." Janelle pointed toward the bleachers set up at the far end of the park. "I saw him earlier, with Josh and D. J."

Relief flooded Maggie, quickly overtaken by anger. What was Jameso doing over there with his friends when she needed him here, with her? "Thanks, Janelle," she said, already headed toward the bleachers.

The competition area was packed, the bleachers filled and spectators lined up along the sidelines. "Excuse me, I'm a reporter," she said, ignoring the annoyed looks directed her way by some of the spectators as she pushed her way toward the front. She spotted Rick, who waved her over.

"I was beginning to think you weren't going to show," he said. "They're just getting ready for the double-jacking. Get your camera."

"Have you seen—?"

"Shhhh. They're starting." Rick held his camera up to his eye, ready for the next shot.

"Our first team is the Dark Knight and Badger."

Maggie gasped as Jameso and Josh strode into the center of the cleared-off area. Dressed in tight black T-shirts and faded jeans, the two men elicited whistles and cheers from the crowd—and more than a few sighs from the women present. They smiled and waved to the spectators, then took up the tools of the competition.

Maggie had written about double-jacking for the paper, so she knew a little about what to expect in the event. But the announcer, Reverend Kinkaid, explained things for the crowd, many of whom had probably never seen this kind of competition before. "Miners extracted ore from the mines by drilling holes in the rock, then filling the holes with black powder," he said. "They placed a fuse to light the powder, blew a hole in the rock, and loaded the resulting debris onto ore cars to be processed. That rock is known as 'muck,' and loading it into the ore carts is called 'mucking.'

"Some of you probably saw the mucking competition earlier today. In the days before power tools, the only way to drill holes in rock was by hand, using carbon steel hand drills and hammers. The miners were known as 'Cousin Jacks' and the process of drilling was known as 'jacking.' In double-jacking, the man holding and turning the drill is known as the 'shaker.' The man with the hammer is the 'driller.' They switch places approximately every thirty seconds, and the competition lasts ten minutes. Now, let's begin."

Maggie stuffed her camera back into her bag. "You're going to have to photograph this, Rick," she said. "I'm not even sure I can watch."

"Oh, don't be a wuss," he said. "Jameso's done this before. He and Jake were a team one of the years Jake won his trophy. And I'm sure he and Josh have been practicing."

Jameso knelt beside a shin-high chunk of granite the size of a kitchen table, drill in hand, more chisels at his side, while Josh stood over him with the hammer. D. J. knelt beside them with a water hose to feed water into the hole as they drilled. The water flushed debris from the hole and helped keep the chisels from overheating. Maggie covered her eyes and held her breath.

At the first strike of the hammer on the chisel, another cheer rose from the crowd. Maggie uncovered one eye. Jameso spun the chisel just as Josh struck another blow. Every thirty seconds they switched places, with choreographed precision, changing drills as each became dull. The two men moved so swiftly, like a machine, each blow driving the sharpened chisel deeper into the rock. Maggie uncovered both eyes and watched in awe as her husband rained blows down, muscles bunching, his handsome face a mask of concentration. The sound of metal on rock filled the air, sharp and rhythmic.

At the end of ten minutes, Reverend Kinkaid called "Time," and the men stood back, chests heaving, faces flushed, and watched while the judges—Bob Prescott and Junior Dominick—stepped forward to measure the hole they had drilled.

"Twenty-five point four inches," Bob announced.

"Is that any good?" Maggie asked Rick as around them, the crowd roared.

"Very good," he said. "The record is twenty-six point nine inches in ten minutes."

Jameso spotted Maggie on the sidelines and grinned. Then he and Josh collected their tools and exited the arena. "Where is he going?" Maggie asked, intending to follow.

Rick pulled her back. "He's got to get ready for the single-jacking," he said. "And you've got work to do."

"He's in the single-jacking competition, too?"

"And the mucking and spike driving," Rick said. "He's leading the scoring right now."

"Why didn't he tell me?"

"You'll have to ask him that." She took out her camera again, fighting a dizzying whirl of emotions. She was proud, confused, angry, hurt, and elated. At least Jameso really had been hanging out with Josh and D. J. and not seeing Mindy or some other woman. But why hadn't he told her?

Four more teams competed in double-jacking, including a women's team. Each drilled holes in the rock with varying degrees of speed and agility, but no one was injured and the crowd cheered them on ever more raucously.

"Single-jacking is up next," Rick said when the last team had cleared the arena. "Since Jameso is the points leader, he'll go last."

Which meant Maggie had to wait through three other finalists in order to see her husband again. Two of those finalists turned out to be Josh and D. J., who came out for the first round of competition. In single-jacking, the competitor held and turned a shorter drill with one hand, while striking it with a hammer with the other. For this round, two men competed at a time, each drilling for ten minutes. Whoever drilled the deepest hole at the end of that time was the winner. A second man on each team acted as the waterer.

Maggie had to admit, she was impressed. The men wielded

their hammers with surprising speed and force, never pausing between blows, the metallic ringing providing a steady beat against the crowd's cheers, water and bits of rock flying from the holes with each blow.

"Time!" Reverend Kinkaid called, and both men dropped their hammers and stepped back. The judges moved forward with their measuring sticks, heads together over their clipboards while the crowd murmured, restless.

The judges approached Reverend Kinkaid, who listened a moment, then turned to the crowd. "And the winner of this round is Badger, otherwise known as Josh Miller."

Josh smiled and bowed to the crowd, then he and D. J. shook hands and collected their tools.

Jameso and a man from California who called himself Monterey Jack competed in the next round. When the announcer introduced the Dark Knight, the crowd went wild. Jameso grinned and acknowledged the cheers and applause, then turned toward Maggie and blew her a kiss. She smiled in spite of her determination not to. Whatever Jameso was up to, she'd find out sooner or later.

D. J. served as Jameso's waterer. "Ready, set, go!" came the cry, and they were off, hammers flying, ringing loud on the steel drills. Maggie stood on her toes, trying to get a better view of Jameso, hunched over the chunk of granite, face red, muscles bunching from the strain.

Then his hammer slipped. The crowd gasped, and Maggie cried out. Rick put a steadying hand on her shoulder. "It's all right," he said. "It hit the rock, not his hand."

But that slight fumble slowed him down. Monterey Jack, realizing what had happened, picked up his own pace. Maggie bit her lip, afraid of what would happen next.

Jameso's face was grim with determination as he hefted the hammer again and brought it slamming down on the drill. Sparks flew as he turned and pounded, turned and pounded.

When Reverend Kinkaid called time, Jameso dropped his

hammer and straightened, breathing hard, his expression still grim. The judges made their measurements. Bob said something to Jameso, and his shoulders relaxed a little.

"The winner is Jameso Clark, the Dark Knight," Reverend Kinkaid announced. "He'll compete against Josh Miller in the final round."

In the short intermission between rounds, Maggie went to find Jameso. "Maggie!" he greeted her, face flushed, eyes alight with excitement. "What did you think?"

"You were wonderful." She kissed him. "And awful." She shoved at his shoulder. "Why didn't you tell me what you were up to?"

"I wanted it to be a surprise," he said. "And I didn't want you to worry."

"But I missed half the competition," she said.

His smile faded. "Yeah, that part didn't work out so well. I thought Rick would have you photographing the whole thing. I sent someone to find you, but they couldn't in the crowd."

"What about your phone? I've been trying to call you all morning."

"I left it at the Dirty Sally last night." He looked sheepish. "I was a little distracted."

"Let me see your hands."

He put his hands behind his back. "Why?"

"Let me see them." She held out her own, palm up. Reluctantly, he extended both his hands. She ran her fingers over the bruises and scratches on his knuckles. "That must have hurt," she said.

"Not so mu—" But her lips, pressed gently to the injuries, stopped his words. He closed his eyes, then opened them and reached around to caress the back of her neck. She looked up at him. "I'm sorry if I screwed things up by being secretive," he said. "I wanted you to be proud of me."

"I am proud of you." She straightened. "So proud."

"Okay, men. Time to go." D. J. claimed their attention. "Maggie, better get back to your seat."

Reluctantly, she returned to the sideline. "I can see I'm going to have to do all the work this year," Rick said as he picked up his camera.

"I guess you are." She wrapped both arms around Angela, who blinked at her sleepily. "I've got to cheer on my husband."

"Ladies and gentlemen, Badger and the Dark Knight!"

The roar from the crowd rose to deafening levels as the two men, shirtless this time, stepped into the arena. Maggie had trouble getting her breath as she stared at her husband, his muscular torso gleaming with sweat. From the catcalls and whistles from women in the stands, they appreciated the show as well.

"All right men. Take your places."

Each man stood before a chunk of granite, while the waterers knelt to one side.

"Ready. Get set. Go!"

The hammers beat down *ping, ping, ping, ping, pingping-pingping,* so rapid the sound blended into one long reverberation. Maggie had never known ten minutes could be so long. The men never let up their pace, faces red, muscles straining, hammers ringing on steel.

"They're neck and neck here, folks," Reverend Kinkaid said. "Let's cheer them on to the winner."

The crowd obliged, shouting and whistling. Most of the spectators were on their feet now. Even Rick had put down his camera to clap and cheer.

"Go, Jameso!" Maggie shouted. "You can do it!"

"Time!"

Both men straightened, seemingly at once, their hammers idle in the dirt, though the sound still rang in Maggie's ears. She held her breath as Reverend Kinkaid and the judges approached. The judges measured the depth of the holes, then gave their findings to the reverend, who raised the microphone to his lips.

"And the winner, with a depth of fifteen point eight inches, is Jameso Clark."

Maggie scarcely heard the rest of the announcement. She was already crossing the arena to Jameso, who drew her to him in a rib-crushing hug. "I am definitely proud of you," she said. "But not because you won or lost. Just because you're you—and because you're mine."

She had no time to say more, as they were swept along by a crowd who wanted to congratulate Jameso, patting him on the back and shaking his hand. Angela started fussing, and Maggie unwound the sling and held her, but finally surrendered her to Jameso. He made an incredibly appealing picture, brawny and shirtless, cradling the tiny baby in one muscular arm.

"I hope you know, you are one lucky woman."

Startled, Maggie looked over to see Mindy standing beside her. "Yes, I am," she said. "Sometimes I forget how lucky."

"Just so you know, we never did more than flirt," Mindy said. "It was just a game to pass the time. Anybody could look at you two and know no one else stood a chance."

"I knew that," Maggie said, though she felt her cheeks heat at the lie.

Mindy drifted away and Maggie turned to watch Reverend Kinkaid present Jameso with his trophy—a bronzed miner's lamp. He posed for pictures with Josh and alone, still with Angela in his arms. Then at last the crowd thinned and Maggie was able to claim husband and child again.

"How could you ever think I wouldn't be proud of you?" she whispered, kissing his cheek.

He made a face. "I don't know," he said. "Maybe because your first husband was rich, or because your old man won this competition three years in a row. Jake's been dead a year and people still talk about him as if he was alive."

"You really love me," she said. "That's worth more than anything either one of them ever did."

"Well, I want to do more than that." He looked down at

her, his expression serious. "I'm cutting back my hours at the Dirty Sally."

"You don't have to do that," she said. "I shouldn't have nagged you about it. And if you enjoy the work—"

"It's okay. The new owners have hired another bartender."

"New owners?" How had this information escaped her? "What about that guy in Nebraska who's owned the place for years? Larry somebody."

"Oh, he still owns the building, but he wanted to get out of the management side, so he sold half a share to a local guy."

"What local guy?"

"Me."

She stared at him. "What?"

"I had some money saved, so when I heard Larry might be interested in selling, I called him up and made an offer. We worked out a deal. I probably should have told you before, but I wanted to make sure it was really going to happen. I signed the papers this morning."

She laughed. "I never knew I married such a devious man," she said. "Do you have any other surprises planned? Because I'm not sure how many more I can stand."

"No more, I promise." He squeezed her hand. "So you're okay with this? I won't be bartending as much, but I'll have to spend more time on the management side of things. We may have to hire some help at the B and B."

"We'll work it out." She leaned into him. "That's my new motto: Whatever happens, we'll work it out. There's just one thing."

"What's that?" He looked wary.

"You have to give me the exclusive interview for the paper. After all, new management at the town's only bar is a big deal."

"It's a deal. And I hope you know you always have exclusive access to me."

"I know. I'm sorry I was a jealous shrew."

"Yeah, well, I guess I've proved you're not the only one in

this partnership with some insecurities." He drew her around to face him. "Nobody said this was going to be easy, for either of us," he said. "But we're going to make it work. Just remember how much I love you."

"And I love you." They kissed, a sweet embrace that reminded her of all the good they had created together. She wasn't going to let the past drag at them anymore. She'd remember that what had happened to her before wasn't nearly as important as the future they could build together.

Chapter 18

Backstage at the Eureka Opera House was the typical pre-performance confusion of last-minute adjustments to sets and costumes, actors running over lines, family members hovering, and Cassie issuing instructions to everyone while mostly being ignored. Mindy pushed her way through the crowd around the door. "Where have you been?" Shelly asked. "I was afraid you wouldn't make it. Can you help button up my costume?"

She turned her back to her sister and Mindy began fumbling with the buttons. "I was watching the Hard Rock Miner competition."

"What did you think?" Shelly asked.

"I don't know whether I need a stiff drink or a cold shower. I mean, all those hot, muscular, sweaty guys." She shuddered. "I could hardly stand to leave."

"Who won?" Shelly fussed with the ruffles at the neckline of the 1890s women's traveling costume.

"Jameso Clark. Man, is his wife one lucky woman. Why are all the good men taken?"

"They're not all taken," Shelly said. "You just aren't looking in the right places. Have you seen my script anywhere?"

"Here it is." Mindy handed her the blue folder that contained her copy of the script, with her lines highlighted and, in some cases, rewritten. "But don't worry. You're going to do great."

"I wish I had your confidence." She flipped through the marked-up pages. "Maybe I should run through the scene where—"

"All right, everyone. I need your attention!"

Cassie, dressed in a black silk dress she claimed had belonged to her great-grandmother, and a hat that featured what appeared to be most of a stuffed peacock pinned to the top, had climbed onto a box to address the company. "First, I want to thank you for all of your hard work," she said, when most of the room had fallen silent and turned to face her. "Second, I want to ask you to remember to maintain the dignity and integrity of this presentation. We are not here merely to entertain the audience but to educate and inform them. I want everyone in this theater to leave tonight with a better understanding of and respect for the sacrifices that the founders of this town made on behalf of future generations."

"If people wanted a history class, they'd go back to school," Bob said from the back of the room, where he was overseeing the arrangement of the sets.

"I believe we're going to have the best audience yet," Cassie said, ignoring Bob. "The box office tells me they even had to turn people away."

"Probably half of them are here to see Baby Shelly," Bob said.

Most of the people around them turned to stare at Shelly, who flushed bright red. Mindy almost felt sorry for her sister. All that adulation and fame was wasted on someone who really didn't like to be in the spotlight.

"Some of them may be here to see Shelly," Cassie said. "And they will see her, in her role as Hattie Sanford, which I'm sure she'll carry off wonderfully. And perhaps afterwards, we can allow a little time with her to the press and her fans. But only after the play is over."

Shelly leaned close to whisper in Mindy's ear. "I can't do this," she said.

Mindy frowned at her. "What are you talking about? Of course you can do this. You know all your lines, and even though you're not a trained actress, like me, you do a good enough job for this crowd."

Shelly shook her head. "I can't go out there and put myself on display," she said. "I know you don't understand, but it's just not me." She began untying the strings that held the ruffle to her throat. "Undo my buttons."

"Shelly, no! What about the play?"

Shelly turned and stuffed the ruffle into Mindy's hand. "You do it. You know all the lines and you'll fit into the costume." She grabbed her sister's hand and dragged her back into the mostly deserted dressing room.

"There isn't time," Mindy said, even as Shelly began to shimmy out of the half-unbuttoned dress.

"There's time. It's not as if they'll start the play without you." She handed Mindy the dress and started to work on the corset. "Help me and we'll save time."

Mindy hesitated, torn. "What are you waiting for?" Shelly asked, taking off the corset and thrusting it at Mindy as well. "You know you're a better actor than I am. You'll do a better job and you'll have a lot more fun."

Shelly was right. And obviously, she wasn't going to change her mind. Unless she wanted to let down the whole acting company, not to mention the audience members who had bought tickets to the production, Mindy had to take the role. "All right." She wrapped the corset around her torso. "Go ahead and cinch me up. And give me those combs in your hair."

Twenty minutes later, just as Cassie stepped onto the stage to give her welcoming speech to the crowd, Mindy surveyed the results of her transformation in the mirror. "I wish I had more time to fool with my makeup," she said.

"You're supposed to be a schoolteacher. Plain makeup fits the part."

"You're right." She turned and impulsively hugged Shelly, who had changed back into jeans and a polo shirt. "Are you going to be all right?"

"I'll be fine." Shelly patted her. "Now go on, take your place onstage. And break a leg."

Shelly slipped out of the door leading backstage and let out a sigh of relief. A quick glimpse into the auditorium had shown her she'd made the right decision. Mindy would wow them all with her performance, and Shelly could remain hidden for a little longer.

She made her way down the hall that led to the front lobby, which was almost deserted now, too, as the play began. She'd almost made it to the door when a man stepped up and blocked her path. "Excuse me, but have you seen a pretty blonde, about five-six, big hair, short shorts? I don't know what name she's going by now, but someone pointed her out to me and told me she was Baby Shelly."

"Who wants to know?" Shelly asked, her heart in her throat.

"I'm Greg Albright, with the *Dallas Morning News*. I was hoping to talk to her."

"She . . . she's in the play." She pointed over her shoulder to the auditorium. "She's playing the part of the schoolteacher."

His face lit up. "Really?"

"Really. Just wait in the wings when the performance is finished and I'm sure she'll be glad to talk to you."

"I heard she didn't care much for reporters."

"Shelly? Oh, you definitely heard wrong. I know she'd love to talk to you."

"Thanks." He held out his hand. "I didn't catch your name."

"Oh, I'm nobody important. Go on, now. You don't want to miss the play."

She practically skipped out of the Opera House, and hurried down the street toward the lot where she'd left her car. By the time she'd dug out her keys, she was chuckling to herself. Would Greg Albright ever figure out the switch they'd pulled on him, or would he, like the *Ladies' Home Journal* reporter so long ago, believe he'd spoken with the real Shelly— a vivacious, personable, fun-loving version who made a much better celebrity, after all, than the real thing.

"We ran out of goodies, so I decided to do some shopping," Danielle told Lucille as she stepped into the T-shirt booth. "I've been coveting a pair of earrings from Olivia."

"I'm sorry you missed her," Lucille said. "She's watching D. J. compete for the Hard Rock Miner title."

"And you didn't go?" She held a pair of beaded earrings up to her face and studied her reflection in the little mirror Olivia had hung on the side of the booth.

"I've seen it many times before. It's exciting, but it's more important for Olivia to be there now while I watch the shop." Olivia had said at first she was too nervous to watch, but she'd been so distracted once the competitions started, Lucille had convinced her she'd be better off in the stands, cheering D. J. on.

"I've seen it before, too," Danielle said. "But all those brawny guys showing off their muscles don't have quite the same appeal for me." She laid the earrings on the counter and looked around at the still-robust crowds cruising through the various booths. "It's been a great crowd this year," she said. "More visitors than we've had in a long time."

"Yes, it's good to see. Most of the businesses in town will head into winter in better shape than they were last year."

"Spoken like a good mayor," a man said.

Lucille blinked at the man who had stepped into the booth, then tried to maintain her composure, a surprisingly difficult feat, considering how close he was standing. He smelled good—like fresh laundry and leather. "Hello, Duke. What are you doing here? I thought you'd left town."

"What if I said I'd come back for you?"

"I'd tell you I didn't believe you."

"You're too smart. I had a quick job to do in Texas that, as it happens, brings me back here."

"More to do with Gerald Pershing?" Danielle asked.

"No." He glanced around the booth. "Have you seen Shelly Frazier?"

"She's probably at the theater, getting ready for the Founders' Pageant." Movement over his shoulder caught her attention and she looked up to see a middle-aged couple enter the booth. They clung together, looking lost and uncertain. "May I help you?" she asked, moving around Duke toward them.

"This is Sandy and Danny Payton," Duke said. "Shelly Frazier's parents."

Lucille saw the resemblance now; Sandy was an older version of Mindy, while Danny had Shelly's blue eyes and slightly cleft chin. "It's nice to meet you," she said. She took Duke's arm and pulled him farther into the booth. "What are you up to?" she whispered. "I had the impression that Shelly and her family don't get along."

"Don't worry." He patted her hand in a way that, from anyone else, might have struck her as condescending. "Everything is going to be all right."

"Exactly the words Gerald Pershing used right before he swindled the town out of most of its money."

"It really is going to be fine this time, at least with Shelly and her parents," he said. "She asked me to contact them and bring them here. She's decided it's time to put their past differences to rest."

Lucille relaxed and glanced at the couple, who were talking with Danielle and admiring a T-shirt Olivia had painted with columbines. "That's good, then," she said. "I hope everything works out well for them all."

"You should think about doing the same," he said.

"My parents have been gone a long time now," she said. "And Olivia and I get along fine."

"I meant putting the past behind you," Duke said. "Don't measure every man by Gerald Pershing and whoever else hurt you in the past. Some of us are better than that."

"Yes, I believe that." She met his gaze, steady and direct. "The trick is figuring out which ones. I'm still not sure about you, Duke."

"All I'm asking for is a chance."

She considered this, making him wait while she let the idea sit on the surface of her mind, allowing it to sink in. "Tell me something, then," she said. "And I want the truth. Who sent you here to look for Gerald?"

"His son, Arthur."

His answer didn't make her any more comfortable with her situation. "Does he know about his father's will?"

"He does." Duke shifted his body more toward her, making an intimate angle that shielded them from everyone around them. "That's another reason I came to Eureka. Arthur wanted me to check you out. To see what kind of person you are."

"To find out if I'm a gold-digger, you mean." She could say the words without flinching; it was probably what she would have done in Arthur's shoes. "What did you tell him?"

He leaned closer still, his breath stirring the top of her hair when he spoke. "I told him you're smart and honest and Gerald had used you badly. And that I thought you deserved whatever you could get from the old man."

Her eyes widened a little at this. "What did he say?"

"You'd like Arthur. He grew up with his mother and stepfather and has no illusions about Gerald. And he's a successful businessman in his own right. He doesn't need his father's money. He wanted the matter of Gerald's whereabouts settled, so that he could move on. He's happy for you to have the money."

"Maybe I'd like to meet him. Someday."

"I could arrange that. And it would give me another reason to see you again." He smiled, the lines crinkling around his eyes and deepening alongside his mouth. "So, will you give me another chance?"

"The best answer I can give you is 'maybe.' " Even as she said the words, her heart gave a little leap of anticipation. She was too old for these crazy emotional flights and dips. But was she really ready to spend the rest of her life so safe and so alone? She made a shooing motion with her hands, and caught a glimpse of Shelly's parents over her shoulder. "Now go on over to the Opera House and say hello to Shelly. She's probably been waiting for you."

He took a step back, his eyes still locked to hers. "I'm leaving for now," he said. "But I will be back. That's a promise."

Maggie, Jameso, and Angela watched the Founders' Pageant from two balcony seats to one side of the stage. When Mindy stepped out and delivered her first line, the people in the audience who knew her gasped, realizing that a switch had been made. But most of the rest clapped and cheered, believing they were seeing an adult Baby Shelly, safe and sound at last.

"She's really good," Maggie said as the curtain came down on the first act.

"The play isn't bad, either," Jameso said. "Bob told me Mindy rewrote a lot of the dialogue to make it less stilted."

"I'm amazed Cassie let her get away with it."

"I don't think she asked permission. She just did it."

"That sounds like Mindy. But in this case, it definitely worked."

Act Two was even better, with Mindy even teasing a rare smile from Cassie, and Doug's speech dedicating the new town of Eureka bringing tears to a few eyes. At the end, the audience gave the cast a standing ovation.

"That was good," Jameso said as they waited their turn to file down the stairs to the lobby. "But I miss the fireworks."

"You're the only one. Bob's idea of a big finale last year practically set the building on fire."

"Yeah, there is that." He craned his neck to see ahead of them. "Why is it taking so long to get out of here?'

They discovered the answer when they finally reached the lobby and found Mindy holding court, a trio of reporters and two television cameramen arranged around her. As Maggie and Jameso inched around this roadblock, Mindy laughed, a delicate, rehearsed sound. "She's in heaven in the spotlight," Maggie whispered.

Outside the Opera House, the crowd thinned a little. Jameso shifted Angela to his other arm. "Where are you parked?" he asked.

"I left my car in the lot behind the *Miner*."

"My truck is at the Dirty Sally. I guess we've got a bit of a walk, then."

They hadn't gone far, though, before Shelly hailed them. "Maggie! I've been looking for you." She trotted up to them, cheeks flushed and a little breathless. "I've decided I want to do an interview with you. But just you. You can do whatever you like with the article, but I won't tell my story to anyone else."

"Really?" Maggie studied her face, trying to decipher the mix of both apprehension and elation she saw there. "What changed your mind?"

"I decided hiding from people was only feeding their desire to know more. I'm better off trying to manage the Baby Shelly phenomenon myself, on my own terms. We can talk about that at the interview, if you like, but first, I want you to meet someone."

For the first time, Maggie noticed the couple who had

been waiting a few steps away. Shelly grabbed the woman's hand and pulled her forward. "Mom, this is Maggie Clark. She's a reporter for the local paper and a friend of mine. This is her husband, Jameso, and her daughter, Angela. And this is my mom, Sandy Payton. And my dad, Danny Payton."

"It's so good to meet Shelly's friends." Sandy shook their hands.

"It sure is." Danny shook their hands, too, pumping hard. "This sure is a nice little town y'all have here."

"And a wonderful festival," Sandy said. "All those booths and everything." She looped her arm through Shelly's. "This would be a great place to have the anniversary celebration each year. We could make it a real party, and invite folks to come out and help us commemorate the anniversary of your rescue. And your birthday, or course."

"Mom." Shelly frowned, and Sandy blushed.

"I know, honey. You don't want all that fuss. But I've spent so many years thinking about the best way to honor the day you came back to us—I can't help wanting to celebrate."

"We'll talk about it later." Shelly relaxed a little and patted her arm. "Right now, everyone is coming back to my house for dinner."

"You may have to wait a while for Mindy," Maggie said. "She's holding what looks like a press conference in the lobby of the Opera House."

Shelly laughed. "She's probably having a blast. How was the play?"

"It was really good," Maggie said. "Thanks to Mindy. She really is talented."

"I thought you were supposed to play the schoolteacher," Jameso said.

"I was. But at the last minute I realized Mindy was much better for the part."

"So, do the reporters think she's you?" Maggie asked.

"If they do, it's not my fault. Say, have either of you seen Travis? I was trying to find him to invite him to dinner."

"I saw him this morning," Jameso said. "He said he was headed back to Dallas and a girl he hopes is still waiting for him there."

"Should we go on into the theater and find Mindy?" Danny asked. "We could meet you there."

"Sure, Dad," Shelly said. "I'll be in in just a minute."

"Are you worried about how your life will change now that your secret is out?" Maggie asked Shelly when her parents had walked away.

"A little. I won't like everything that happens because of this, but I realize I've spent too much time worrying about what could happen to enjoy everything that is happening right now. The past shapes us, but it doesn't have to define us."

"Words to live by," Jameso said, and pulled Maggie close.

They said good-bye and made their way to Maggie's car in companionable silence. "We can get my truck later," Jameso said, as he buckled Angela into her car seat.

"Good." Maggie stretched. "I'm ready to get home. It's been a long day."

Jameso handed her the bronzed miner's lamp. "I don't know what to do with this," he said.

"We'll put it in the cabin, with Jake's trophies. He'd be pleased that you're following in his footsteps."

"Except I don't intend to follow too closely."

She smiled, closed her eyes, and rested her head against the back of the seat, more content than she'd been in a long time. After all the pre-wedding and pre-baby jitters, then her troubles settling into married life, she was ready for a calm, even boring routine.

"Uh-oh."

Jameso's voice woke her from a doze as they approached the B and B. "What is it?"

"Looks like we've got company." He nodded to the Cadillac Escalade parked in front of the inn.

"That looks like Barb's." Maggie sat forward. "But she's in Paris."

"Not anymore," he said, as the front door opened and Barb Stanowski, in slim white cropped pants and a sleeveless white blouse that showed off her toned arms, stood on the threshold.

Maggie was out of the car and racing up the walkway as soon as Jameso shut off the truck's engine. "Barb!" She threw her arms around her best friend. "It's so good to see you, but I thought you were still in Europe."

"Jimmy got invited to Scotland, to demonstrate his ball-washing invention to some golf course there, but I was sick to death of traveling. I just wanted to come home."

"Looks like you plan to stay for a while." Jameso, carrying Angela, joined them in the foyer and took in the half-dozen suitcases stacked there.

"Oh, only for a few weeks. Well, maybe a couple of months." She put her arm around Maggie and led her toward the stairs. "I always say my home is in Texas but really, I think my heart is here."

Maggie looked over her shoulder at Jameso and her infant daughter. He winked at her, and she couldn't help but smile. "My heart is here, too," she said. Exactly where she belonged.

Acknowledgments

Special thanks to my editor, Martin Biro, for his encouragement and assistance with this book, and to the whole Kensington team. To Rocky Mountain Fiction Writers, thank you for all your support and writerly fellowship. And especially, hugs and kisses to the Writers of the Hand—you are the best!

ABOVE IT ALL

Cindy Myers

About This Guide

The suggested questions are included
to enhance your group's reading of
Above It All.

DISCUSSION QUESTIONS

1. One of the themes of this book is the ways in which events of the past influence the future. In what ways does our past determine our future? How hard is it to overcome this?

2. Several people in the book have secrets. How do you feel about Shelly's failure to tell her friends about her past? What about the secrets Jameso keeps from Maggie?

3. If you had been in Maggie's shoes, would you have pressed Shelly harder for an interview? Why or why not?

4. Was Shelly right or wrong to cut ties with her family? Can you imagine yourself ever doing something like this?

5. Have you ever been in a situation where you began to believe your perception of the way things happened in the past might have been all wrong? What did you do?

6. Both Lucille and Daisy struggle with their attraction to men they don't think are right for them. Has this ever happened to you? What was the outcome?

7. Shelly finds domestic tasks relaxing. Can you relate, or not?

8. Do you believe in karma? Did Gerald get what he deserved?